ENCHANTMENT'S WARRIORS

once again patrol the many realms of fantasy, sorceresses and swordswomen ever ready to defend those who cannot defend themselves. Join these champions of Law in these twenty-nine original stories as they take up such challenges and adventures as:

"Lorelei"—Would she be the one to evade the siren's call, the first to break free of that most ancient and alluring of spells?

"Falcon's Shadow"—Her people transformed by a powerful curse, would she be forever doomed by her quest to set them free?

"The Proper Balance"—There are laws meant always to be observed but on occasion even the gods might agree that there are some the better for being broken. . . .

SWORD AND SORCERESS X

MARION ZIMMER BRADLEY
in DAW editions:

DARKOVER NOVELS
DARKOVER LANDFALL
STORMQUEEN!
HAWKMISTRESS!
TWO TO CONQUER
THE HEIRS OF HAMMERFELL
THE SHATTERED CHAIN
THENDARA HOUSE
CITY OF SORCERY
REDISCOVERY *(with Mercedes Lackey)*
THE SPELL SWORD
THE FORBIDDEN TOWER
THE HERITAGE OF HASTUR
SHARRA'S EXILE

DARKOVER ANTHOLOGIES
DOMAINS OF DARKOVER
FOUR MOONS OF DARKOVER
FREE AMAZONS OF DARKOVER
THE KEEPER'S PRICE
LERONI OF DARKOVER
THE OTHER SIDE OF THE MIRROR
RED SUN OF DARKOVER
SWORD OF CHAOS
TOWERS OF DARKOVER

OTHER BRADLEY NOVELS
HUNTERS OF THE RED MOON
THE SURVIVORS
WARRIOR WOMAN

NON-DARKOVER ANTHOLOGIES
SWORD AND SORCERESS I
SWORD AND SORCERESS II
SWORD AND SORCERESS III
SWORD AND SORCERESS IV
SWORD AND SORCERESS V
SWORD AND SORCERESS VI
SWORD AND SORCERESS VII
SWORD AND SORCERESS VIII
SWORD AND SORCERESS IX
SWORD AND SORCERESS X

SWORD AND SORCERESS X

AN ANTHOLOGY OF HEROIC FANTASY

Edited by
Marion Zimmer Bradley

DAW BOOKS, INC.
DONALD A. WOLLHEIM, FOUNDER
375 Hudson Street, New York, NY 10014
ELIZABETH R. WOLLHEIM
SHEILA E. GILBERT
PUBLISHERS

Cover art by David Cherry.

DAW Book Collectors No. 917.

First Printing, June 1993

1 2 3 4 5 6 7 8 9

DAW TRADEMARK REGISTERED
U.S. PAT. OFF. AND FOREIGN COUNTRIES
—MARCA REGISTRADA
HECHO EN U.S.A.

PRINTED IN THE U.S.A.

CONTENTS

INTRODUCTION: THE SENSE OF WONDER

The sense of wonder has been a preoccupation of mine since I learned to read, which came very early in my life. It is this persistent and sometimes overbearing sense of wonder that has led me to write science fiction and fantasy stories and novels almost as fast as I can turn them out—so many ideas, so little time! And of course, it must be the sense of wonder that propels me toward each day's pile of manuscripts with eager anticipation; perhaps this will be the day a shining, new, original talent will make itself known to me.

Recently, at some convention or other, a panel of editors and I were discussing the pains and pleasures of editing. Somehow or other, it came up that every editor had to cope with his attitude, positive or negative, toward the huge pile of unsolicited manuscripts (the so-called "slush pile") that must be dealt with on a daily basis.

That was when I discovered, somewhat to my chagrin, that all my fellow editors do not share the unending delight with which I approach the contents of this vast undigested heap of manuscripts; some editors actually look on it with dread. Harlan Ellison thinks, as many of our fellows do, that the slush pile is just one of the drawbacks of the job, to be accepted as a necessary evil. I always thought that getting the *first* look at the slush pile was one of the privileges of being an editor.

I suppose this betrays one of my deadly secrets: that I am—and probably in one sense always will remain—a perpetual amateur. I define "amateur" as one who does what he does, not from professional obligation, but from sheer love of doing it. I'd probably edit for nothing, or even pay for the privilege. In fact, that's what I am doing so far with *Marion Zimmer Bradley's Fantasy Magazine*. This is a temporary condition, of course; I do expect it to pay for itself some day. The point is, I'd rather indulge my sense of wonder in a magazine slush pile than indulge my ego in status symbols like fur coats or Cadillacs.

One of the few negative comments I ever heard my late mentor, Don Wollheim, make about anybody, was when he spoke of a certain editor for a small semi-professional publisher who shall here be nameless. Don's scathing comment was; "Oh. X——. He is, and always will be, just an amateur." I changed the subject immediately, not wanting him to know I secretly shared the amateur's attitude!

Still, one need not let an amateur's sense of wonder interfere with one's professionalism as a writer or editor. One of the first things I heard from my pro desk man at Scott Meredith, when I was a great deal younger than I am now, was that I had a "good commercial attitude." What he meant, I suppose, was that having kids to feed, I was receptive to editorial and other objective input about my work. It's true that even to this day, I have no patience with the would-be professional who has a *prima donna* attitude about the sacredness of every word of his deathless prose.

I also have always had a very strong sense of what I can or cannot do. One ill-advised agent of mine disliked science fiction, and kept trying to tell me, in those very early days, that I really should be writing syrupy romances. I believe my answer was that if I wrote that sort of thing, there wouldn't be enough left of the real me to put in a slot machine. My sense of wonder just doesn't go for romances, I guess. For better or worse, I knew I was a writer of science fiction and fantasy.

When I went to Don Wollheim complaining that my agent didn't want me to write science fiction, he advised me to "fire the bastard." So I wrote to Scott that I was either going to have a new pro desk man or a new agent, and at this point, I didn't much care which. I waited anxiously, wondering if I would be tossed out of the agency. To my great relief, I had a new pro desk man within 24 hours. Soon after that, I had my current desk man at Scott Meredith. The agency obviously believed I had paid my dues; I had written enough salable stuff that Scott considered me valuable. No doubt if I had done anything like this after my first novel, or fifth, I would have found myself without an agent for my pains.

That's one of the things I try to tell young writers; until you have paid your dues, a lot of "artistic temperament" just gets in the way of a budding career. One of the things I am always looking for in young writers is a professional attitude. This consists largely of the willingness to work hard for editorial acceptance, and the persistence to work past those first rejection slips without bitterness—and without losing that sense of wonder that led you to write in the first place. If you can't stand rejection, you're probably in the wrong business, and you really ought to consider knitting as a hobby.

Everybody in the fantasy world has probably heard the story of H.P. Lovecraft. When he submitted his first manuscript, in defiance of all rules of commercial writing, he stipulated that the magazine in question—I think it was WEIRD TALES—must print his story exactly as he wrote it, down to the least comma, or reject it. H.P. Lovecraft died in great poverty; but now those little fanzines for which his contemporaries refused to pay ten cents are changing hands at a hundred dollars a pop. Even some of his noncommercial work is being hunted down and printed.

So if you're in love with your own prose, put those sacrosanct, exquisitely written stories in your desk drawer, and some day editors and readers may be selling every scrap of your work, including your letters, for fantastic sums. But don't count on it, and don't expect editors to hunt you down in the here and now, either!

A true writer must write, because of that nagging, very personal, very individual sense of wonder. A professional writer must also sell, hopefully without selling out. Keep writing what you write, and sending it out for appraisal. You will get better, and you will learn more about writing from your rejections than you could learn almost any other way. The goal is to be true to your own artistic vision and to have commercial success. If you temper your vision with hard work, persistence, and a willingness to cooperate with persnickety editors such as myself, you will probably achieve this goal. The writers in this anthology are well on their way.

LORELEI

by Tina Good

Every year, the first story I pick for this anthology sets the tone of every story that follows.

The first story picked for this year was Tina Good's "Lorelei"; it embodies that fleeting and tenuous thing I try to pin down by the name of a "sense of wonder."

Tina wrote to tell me that my acceptance letter had arrived on her birthday, and that it was "the best birthday present I ever had." She says that it was not only because it was her first accepted story, but because a professor in her writing class at college graded her only a C on it. I had confirmed her faith in her own judgment, something that others have certainly done for me. She added that "in a way I'm thankful for his insistence that it wouldn't work; it cemented my insistence to prove that it would."

The professor may have been right that this story wouldn't work for the *New Yorker;* but then, it wasn't written for the *New Yorker,* was it? Tina tailored the story for me, and I snapped it up. I think you'll like it, too.

As soon as I can see the small boat clearly, I allow my song to falter; just for a note or two, as if I am truly surprised. And yet, in a way, I am.

I knew that the boat would be the same traditional flower-covered dinghy as I had used so many years ago. I knew that my replacement would be much like I had been. But I had not realized it would be so much like looking into a glass and watching myself. Oh, perhaps my hair is a deeper ebony, my eyes jade chips rather than sapphire pools, and my skin a more translucent porcelain, but the *essence* is the same. The youthful confidence and pride unconsciously exhaled with each breath, the air of power shimmering as a bright aura for those to see who can. She is quite sure of herself, clearly believing that the bedecked dinghy is a mark of honor and the glassy calm of *my* seas a sign of her power. It has not occurred to her that the same treatment is accorded to sacrifices. But then, I felt the same way when I was in her position. Undoubtedly, she has a spell prepared for the instant she lands; she will not get the chance to use it.

The bottom of the boat strikes rock and I smile and call out to her. "Greetings sister. I have been expecting you for some time now. I was beginning to think they couldn't find one of us deserving of being sent."

She draws back, startled by my easy assumption of kinship. Her eyes widen, and the spell she meant to cast remains unspoken. In a way I am sorry for her, but Fate cannot be changed by such as I. The game must be played according to the rules.

"Why do you look so startled, sister? Surely you can recognize our kinship?" I soften my expression, allowing just a touch of sympathy in my smile. "No matter, I understand. Once, long ago, I stood in the same place as you do now. Of course, it was not quite so worn then."

She is puzzled. She starts to cast a spell but cannot carry it through. My use of "stood" has completely bewildered her. The slightly unfocused, faraway look in her eyes tells me that she is frantically searching her memories for any hint of what I meant. But she is too young to know the truth.

If she were not so flustered, she could ask the island itself; the very stone at her feet would answer her. Not that she would believe—or appreciate—that answer. She is yet unaware that the instant she stepped foot on the island it became attuned to her, as have all the creatures associated with it. Soon enough she will understand. By then, it will be too late.

"Come, sister, it is far too hot for you to stand there. I have a space here beside me for you to sit and bathe your feet in my pool. I promise you shall find it most relaxing. Perhaps you would like to hear my story? You will find it quite interesting."

She is wary, clearly expecting a trap. She does not realize that the whole situation is a cleverly disguised snare. Her eyes narrow, and her right hand slowly reaches for the amulet at her throat: the focus of her power. She cannot hurt me, but her attempt—or rather its failure—could send her into a panic.

"Sister, please. I merely want you to know my history, so that it should not be forgotten. You need not fear my song, *that* is reserved for those foolish males. Come now, sit and be comfortable." I gently pat the sun-warmed stone beside me.

She is still uneasy, but she does as I suggest. There is still a part of me that can envy her the elegant jade gown, so suitable to our coloring, with its matching slippers over luxurious pure silk stockings. However, the time is long past when I could wear such things. Soon it will be the same with her.

"Comfortable, sister? Very well, I shall begin my tale. My name was Shiara and, like yourself, I was a powerful sorceress. But then, we have to be."

I have startled her again. "Do not worry, you will understand by the time I have finished." I really must be more careful. I do not want to thoroughly upset her. Not that I have much of a choice. But she is waiting for me to continue. "Now, where was I? Oh, yes. I believe I can say in all honesty that I was one of the most beautiful women of my time. Since this was the age of Helen and Cassandra, you can see that mine is no idle claim. Next to sorcery, my greatest talent lay in music. I could play any instrument with the skill of a master, even if I had just laid hands upon it. My skill with the lyre was excelled only by Orpheus, and Apollo himself once praised my song. Only in dance could I be considered less than perfect; but then, for us dance is a superfluous skill."

She begins to understand. Not in the important ways—not yet—but enough to recognize the similarities between us. Still, her eyes repeatedly dart to my sleek tail as it gently flicks back and forth in the pool we share. She cannot yet reconcile it with the story I am telling. She looks up, a question poised on her lips.

"Please, sister. Allow me to finish my tale. It really is not that long, and it will answer all your questions.

"It is the way of our kind to be proud, and I was more so than most. No man was good enough for me. I spurned more suitors in one year than most women see in a lifetime. Even Paris courted me, before he foolishly ran off with Helen. Yet I was not immune to the darts of Eros. One day I found myself captivated by a gentleman just disembarking from one of the ships newly come to our port. He was neither a great hero nor extremely wealthy; he was, however, the most handsome man I had ever seen. Slightly taller than the average male—more like the men of today—he had hair the shade of midnight and eyes like chips of blue ice. Discreet questioning informed me that he had traveled to my city to be wed. In fact, his intended was a close acquaintance: a woman I often named 'friend.' None of that mattered. I determined to have him regardless. I began with my more obvious attractions, trying every wile known to our fair sex.

"To say I failed would be a drastic understatement. He was so completely devoted to his lady that he never even noticed my existence. I suppose that itself added to my desire. Finally I withdrew to a private altar deep in the heart of the marsh, and cast the strongest love spell at my disposal. I had no doubts regarding its effectiveness, nor was I disappointed. The spell began to work almost immediately, and he set out to find me." I pause for a moment, remembering. "It was bitterly cold and the rain had been pouring down for hours, yet he never even thought to take a cloak. He left just as he was: still dressed in the short tunic he always wore while sporting with his betrothed's brother. I watched him in a makeshift scrying pool I had formed out of a bowl of rainwater, but I had no control over his actions. At first this did not concern me; true, his health might be threatened by the weather, but my powers could combat any ills once he reached my side. Then he entered the marsh. . . ." I pause once more; I had not realized it would be this hard.

"Forgive me, sister. Even after these many years it still hurts." I make myself relax, concentrating on the warmth of the sun. I must continue before she begins to question.

"I have said that I could watch his progress, but I could not interfere. Nor could the spell be broken but by death. Thus I was forced to watch in growing horror as he blundered through the marsh which the incessant rain had rendered more deadly than normal. The path, hard enough to follow under the best of conditions, had flooded and was nearly impossible to find. Drawn by the spell, he fought through. He almost reached me . . . then he walked into the deathsand." I stop again, taking a deep breath and struggling to maintain my composure. This, too, after all, is a part of the penance. I can still see it, despite the long years that lie between then and now. Justin had been so handsome, so young and vital. . . .

At my side she stirs, waiting for me to finish. She need not be concerned, I have little choice but to do so.

"I believed no one could trace his death back to me. I was wrong.

"Two weeks later I was offered what I took to be the perfect acknowledgment of my abilities. The city elders requested that I cross the sea and defeat the Siren."

My companion has been lulled into a relaxed state by the heat and the gentle lap of the water against her legs, yet now she starts into total alertness. A sharp intake of breath signals her dawning realization of the full impact of my words.

It is almost time, I need but be patient a short while longer. She must not speak; I can read the question in her eyes. Perhaps I am merely remembering my own reaction so many years ago? No matter, there is more to be said. I smile once more.

"Yes, sister, you did hear me correctly. I see I need not describe my bewilderment when the Siren greeted me with gentle words of kinship and welcome and, after bidding me sit beside her, told a tale much like my own. She then went on to explain the secret of the Siren's immortality, and the reason why men of differing times will give differing descriptions.

"You see, sister, the Siren is not one woman, but many. Each is renowned for beauty, pride, and an extraordinary skill in sorcery and music. Each goes to destroy her predecessor, unaware that she is actually being sent to take her place."

She has gone pale, her eyes dart now not to my tail but to her own legs. Already the change is beginning. The signs are slight, yet they are unmistakably there: a faint tinge of green in skin that suddenly appears scaly, an inability to move either leg separately but for below the ankle.

I am not yet done. "This is our punishment, for misusing the powers granted us in such a way as to cause the death of an innocent—usually a male we desire." I fall silent for a moment, thinking again of poor Justin. Then, giving myself a mental shake, I return my attention to my companion.

"How calm the seas are today, sister. Almost like glass. It is Poseidon's way of marking the succession, as is proper. The original Siren was one of his daughters. Lorelei fell in love with a mortal, but lost him to a sorceress much like you or me. In her sorrow, she withdrew to this island. Swearing that she had no desire to resemble so deceitful a creature as man, she cast a spell that transformed her legs into the tail of a fish. The song we sing is a variation on her lament for the love she had lost. Lorelei soon discovered the mesmerizing effect this song had on mortals, and begged her father to arrange for her lover and her rival to be on the next ship to cross her sea. Her intent was to sing the ship onto the rocks and save only her lover. However, she was young and her new power still unfamiliar. The boat struck the rocks too soon, and *all* were lost. Griefstricken, Lorelei cast herself into the sea crying to her father to take her life as well. Unwilling to completely lose a favorite daughter, Poseidon chose an alternate fate for her: as Lorelei struck the sea she was transformed, becoming the white foam that caps the waves when the sea churns.

"With typical godlike arrogance, Poseidon blamed

mankind for his daughter's 'death,' and demanded of his brother Zeus that a fitting punishment be devised. At the same time he insisted upon a memorial to his daughter. Zeus, in turn, called a council of the gods to discuss the matter. Each one put forth a suggestion until finally only Athena remained silent. After listening to the others argue, Zeus turned to his favorite child and commanded that she add her voice to the council. When her brethren had fallen silent, Athena stood. Stating that it would be unfair to punish *all* mankind, she decreed that only those to repeat such behavior should suffer. Moreover, the punishment itself should serve to honor Lorelei's memory.

"Each woman to use her gifts in such a manner as to cause the death of an innocent must in turn take her place on Lorelei's island. The island shall forever be enchanted so that when the proper woman sets foot upon it she will be instantly connected with it. She, too, will suffer the transformation of her legs into a tail, and will be called Siren; the waves themselves will teach her the song that will call the ships of men to destruction. When her time is up, she will pass her tale on to her successor to ensure that the history is not lost. Then she shall become a part of the sea or, if she so wishes and has truly repented, complete her transformation into one of its denizens. Thus will Poseidon be satisfied, while mankind shall gain a new myth." I pause for a moment to smile kindly upon my companion. "You see, sister, your sentence was passed before you were born. As was my own.

"I have sat here over a century, waiting for you to arrive and release me at last. Each morning I watched eagerly for your boat, and saw only those of the brave men who were lured to their deaths by my song. Only one man has ever escaped my call, but then, Odysseus was blessed by the gods and such are always beyond our reach."

She is paler now. Her hand keeps reaching for her amulet as though it can save her. The tail is almost fully formed; soon it will be time.

"Please do not fear so, sister. You cannot go back. I realize the tail is quite awkward at first, but you'll soon grow used to it. After all, legend does demand that the Siren be a mermaid. It helps to hide the truth.

"You need not tell me your tale. You could not be here were it not similar to my own. Simply remember. You will have to pass it on to your replacement when the time comes. Relax now, listen closely to the sea. You will soon learn the song you must sing."

At last it is time. It is funny, but in a way I shall miss my island. After all, it has been my home for over a hundred years. Still, I have earned my freedom. I have had long years to consider my final fate, now I can only hope the gods will be kind and grant my desire.

I have hesitated long enough. The new Siren sits in my place, listening to the murmur of the waves and humming softly to herself. She looks at me and for one last time I smile. "Farewell, sister. May your term be shorter than mine."

Taking a deep breath, I dive into the sea. Even as I slide under the waves I feel the change begin. In moments it is complete. With a roar of joy I stretch my new body, undulating my glistening coils. A flick of my tail serves as a final farewell to the new Siren.

FALCON'S SHADOW

by Diana L. Paxson

Among the stories which have been presented to *Sword and Sorceress* readers from the beginning, few have met with a better reception than the Shanna stories written by Diana L. Paxson. I had the privilege of printing one of Diana's first professionally published stories in the anthology *Greyhaven* (DAW 1983). Diana showed me that story back when she was still an unpublished writer; I said to her that if I were an editor I'd publish it like a shot. A little while later, I was given my first chance to edit a non-Darkover anthology and, true to my promise, I called Diana that very day and asked her if that story were still unsold. It was, and the rest is history.

Diana lives with her family in Northern California, and recently has added a canine unit to the household. She has several novels in print, including some historical fantasies. She and I are now collaborating on *The Forest House,* an historical novel set in Roman Britain.

And here—so Diana told me—is the conclusion of the Shanna series. I think you'll agree that she's still pretty darned good with falcons. But then, what would you expect of a founder of the medievalist Society for Creative Anachronism and an expert in the history of the British Isles?

The call of the falcon sounded from the darkness above the stage, bitter as memory. Despite her training, Shanna glanced upward, earning a stern look from the guardmistress. She returned to attention, motionless as the rest of the Emperor's Valkyr Guard—a circle of shadow behind him, watching the shadows of life upon the stage. The falcon's cry was not real. It had only been a musician, imitating the bird for the play.

I have been too long in the city—in this city—I should not have been fooled that way. And what was worse, it was not just any falcon. For that moment she could have sworn she was hearing Chai.

Chai had saved her life long ago, in the secret valley where her folk lived in human form. Everywhere else in the world the curse of a long-dead Emperor doomed them to falcon shape, and Shanna had sworn to make his heir set them free. But when the slavers who captured Shanna brought her to Bindir the falcon had disappeared. Chai's loss weighed ever more heavily now that she was free to fulfill her vow.

The rest of the drama was proving as convincing as the falcon's cry. To mesmerize the Emperor, who had seen more entertainments than most folk had heard of, the play must be compelling indeed. Or perhaps it was the theme that fascinated him—the Emperor transformed into a falcon and condemned to wander the earth until his Empress consented to bear him a child, for Elisos Teyn Janufen Baratiren, High Prince of Kateyn, Prince of Galis, Protector of the Misty Isles, Emperor of the North and Monarch of the Middle lands, had no heir.

There were royal cousins aplenty, courted by one faction or another with increasing intensity as the royal wives remained barren and the war in the south went on. There had been plots against his life already—fostered by some of those same great lords who enjoyed the hospitality of the Imperial box today. Shanna herself had foiled one of them, and earned her way out of the Arena and into the Valkyr Guard.

The servants of Saibel whispered that the Goddess had turned Her face against the Emperor. The city was already seething with the reckless gaiety that heralded the Festival of Masks; it would take little to spark that excitement into violence.

Torchbearers emerged from the wings to light the dance of the nixies and tree-mays, and girls in silken draperies twirled and fluttered across the stage. The woman without a shadow darted among them, seeking her beloved. The story had been told in a thousand ways. Sometimes it was the husband, and sometimes the wife who was lost and her lover who searched for her, not knowing that the price was to share her mortality.

Is it ever the brother who is enchanted, in these tales? wondered Shanna. It had been so long since she had set out from Sharteyn to look for Janos, she had almost lost sight of the reason for her wanderings. And like the Empress in the story, Shanna could not bear a child. What else had she given up unknowing? she wondered suddenly.

When next I have throne duty I will speak to the Emperor, she told herself. *He was ruler in all but name, even before old Baratir died. And I found Janos' dagger in the marketplace, so he must have reached Bindir. If something happened to him here, Elisos must know!*

From backstage came a tinny rumbling. Dancers scattered as the evil sorcerer appeared, challenging the Empress to save her husband. Shanna's gaze sharpened as she saw that he was garbed in black and gold—a great deal of gold. If that was by chance, it was all an ill omen indeed. It was the Gold faction—the war faction—that had been loudest in its criticism of the Emperor. Heads turned toward Lord Kandaros, who was the most powerful supporter of the Golds, but he and the Emperor both remained impassive, watching the play.

Once more a thin cry pierced the din, then Shanna blinked as heat lightning tore the sky. In that instant random images imprinted her awareness: the face of the Emperor, frozen in a rictus of alarm; guards caught in the act of reaching for their swords; a dancing girl, her white face turned upward in ecstasy.

Then came the thunder, real thunder this time, borne on a moist gust of wind. A mutter echoed through the amphitheater. Onstage, the Empress looked around her uncertainly. Once more lightning woke the heavens; the draperies of the sorcerer flared gold, and in the wind that followed, Shanna felt the first spatterings of rain. All over the amphitheater people were rising; the actress drew her mantle over her head and fled the stage. Only the figure of the sorcerer remained, a shape of shadow now that the lightning had passed.

It needed no priest to read this omen, thought Shanna as the Guardmistress formed them up to escort the Emperor home. By morning folk all over the city would be saying that the gods had refused, even symbolically, to give the Emperor an heir. *There was an omen for me, as well,* she realized as they marched out behind the bobbing black and silver imperial parasol. *It is time I kept my promises.*

"The dancing girls hear everything that happens in Bindir," the woman who had the bed next to Shanna's had told her. "They go everywhere. People feel safe telling them things because they have no power. There can be a lot of truth in pillow talk." The Valkyra had licked her lips reminiscently. She was a big, honey-colored girl from Menibbe whose eyes slitted like a cat's when she smiled. "But what do you want with a dancing girl? There's plenty inside the Palace walls who would be glad to pleasure you—"

Shanna had nodded, unwilling to pretend she did not understand. In the Valkyr guard, as in the Arena, most of the women found lovers among their own kind. Shanna, delivered from the fear of pregnancy by the Dark Mother's curse, had found it a useful excuse to avoid entanglements with men. Repulsing women was more difficult.

"I am still mourning for the woman I lived with before I entered the Arena. It is information I want from the dancing girls, not love."

Never love—thought Shanna. *Duty is better. I bring disaster to those who care for me.*

The Dancers' Guildhall was located in the old part of town. A bribe to the porter and a few lies got her the name of a dancer who had been active ten years before. She paused before a striped curtain at the end of the corridor, rapped on the doorpost and heard the rhythmic clash of bangles cease within.

"Kilijan? I have a few pieces of silver for a few minutes of your time—" Shanna pushed the curtain aside.

The woman who turned to face her was past the first

flush of beauty that makes the heart stop and the flesh ache, but with the memory of it still showing in the fine bones of her face and the liquid glitter of her eyes.

She wore only a bandeau of cloth to bind her breasts and another around her loins, and a light sheen of perspiration rippled on her taut belly and highlighted long muscles on arms and thighs. Shanna strode like a man, while this woman's every movement was like a butterfly on the breeze, but in both of them, years of hard training had fined every unessential ounce of flesh away. A man might have preferred those muscles to be hidden by a sheathing of softness, but for a moment Shanna found herself wondering what it would be like to feel that limber strength intertwining with her own.

The woman stared, pupils dilating until her eyes seemed wells of shadow, then she shook herself and a little betraying color stained her sallow cheeks.

"Forgive me," she murmured. "I thought you were someone I knew." She pushed back a tendril of hennaed hair.

Shanna felt her hear begin to pound. She had expected to interview a dozen dancers—had the Goddess led her to someone who had known Janos at last?

"Perhaps," she said gently. "I look like someone— No, I have not come to hurt you!" she added as a sudden movement took Kilijan across the room. "I need information, and I will pay. . . ."

Some of the tension went out of the dancer's body. She sighed, swept up a soiled caftan of peach colored silk from a pile of similar garments, and swathed herself in its folds. Brocaded mantles were piled on the low bed, tinseled scarves draped over a sagging screen. But the carpet beneath them was worn and there was dust in the corners. A scent of stale perfume hung heavily in the room.

"I am only a poor dancer," she answered, sinking in a single, unjointed movement to a cushion on the floor. "What could a dancing girl know that would interest a woman warrior like you?"

"Stories. Tell me a story, Kilijan. I am from the outlands, seeking to understand Bindir."

"You do not speak like an outlander—" the dancer

glanced sidelong under her lashes and laughed. "Do you think I do not know you, Red Shanna? You won your freedom from the Arena by foiling a plot against the Emperor and now you are in his guard. Why seek to make game of me?"

"Before the Arena I was a harem guard," Shanna said flatly. "Neither post allowed much scope for seeing the city. But dancing girls go everywhere. How did you come here, butterfly?"

"Ah, you want *ancient* history," once more the dyed lashes fluttered. "Well, I suppose that can do no harm. I have been here for ten years—a long time for a dancer. Some lose their health or their figures; some take to the poppy; but most often it is simply the body that gives way." She rose suddenly at the reminder, stretching her arms above her head so that her body arched against the silk of the robe.

"You will not mind if I continue my exercise?" Still speaking, she folded at the waist until her palms touched the floor, glanced at Shanna upside down and smiled.

Showing off, thought the warrior woman, *for me!*

"Were you raised in the country?" she asked.

"A farmer's daughter. If I had stayed at home, I would have been fat as a cow with six children by now."

Kilijan grimaced, shifted her full weight onto her palms, and tucked her legs up, then lifted them until she was standing on her hands, her body extending like the stamen of a flower whose petals were the folds of pink silk that had rustled to the floor. Then, with the same precise control, she let her feet fall forward, for a moment held the backbend, and brought herself upright once more.

Shanna repressed an impulse to applaud.

"I was very young," said Kilijan, "certain my beauty would conquer all, and it is true that for a time I was the most sought-after dancer in Bindir. I was featured at all the best parties. Men gave me jewels and silk robes and fought for my favor. . . ."

"Exciting times," murmured Shanna. "They always are when one is young. Still, that was when the old Emperor had begun to fail, wasn't it? What an interesting year that must have been."

"Old alliances—" Kilijan grimaced. "The only thing more dead is an old love affair! Who remembers now which nobles schemed to set Elisos Teyn Janufen upon his father's throne without waiting for the old man to die; and which would rather have seen some half-blood country cousin there, the more obscure the better, so long as he was young and healthy and promised to reward them when he came to power."

But old loves did not die, thought Shanna, hearing the bitterness in Kilijan's laughter. They grew or they festered. She wondered what ancient political bedfellows might be fanning the flames of passion anew.

"But you knew them all, didn't you," she said softly. "Who were they, Kilijan?" She paused, feeling her blood chill, suddenly guessing how her brother, innocent and honorable as he was, might have gone astray. "Who would have courted a young prince newly come from the north with a reckless laugh and the blood of Argantir the Conqueror in his veins?"

There was a short silence. Then Kilijan rose with a tinkling laugh and flung off the silk robe.

"How should I know? I did not care who I served so long as they paid me. In those days I could make love all night and and dance the next day like a leaf on the wind. Warrior woman, you have bought all the time I can afford just now." She bounced a few times, loosening the muscles.

Shanna knew when she had been dismissed. "Perhaps we can talk more another time—" Coins clinked softly as she set a leather bag on a little carved wood table, most of whose insets were gone. Kilijan's glance flicked to the bag and then away and she began to twirl.

It was enough for now. Shanna might not yet know how and when her brother had disappeared, but she was beginning to understand why. The dancer was still spinning in dreamlike circles as she left the room.

In the cool of the evening, the Emperor liked to sit in the chamber that looked onto his rooftop garden. By day the place was busy with gardeners, but after sunset no one was allowed into the sanctum at the top of the citadel but the Emperor and those he chose to attend him there.

There was always a breeze at the summit, stirring the gauze that curtained the tall doorways. The air was musical with the sound of falling water and the shimmer of melody from the citarists hidden behind the screens. Wrought iron stems curved from the pillars, bearing many-petaled lanterns of frosted glass. In that room, all was softness, from the black and white rugs layered on the floor to the moon colored robes that swirled around the man who lay upon the divan. Only the woman who guarded him stood like a statue in black armor beside the door.

Silk rustled as the Emperor turned over, staring at the ceiling. He lifted one hand, and abruptly the musicians were still.

"Go, all of you—" Elisos muttered. "You, too—" he said to Shanna. "I need to be alone."

"You are alone," Shanna replied. "My eyes and ears are only for your enemies."

The Emperor gave a bark of laughter and for the first time actually looked at her. "Ah—it is you, my gladiator. Never mind. I know that they would flay you if you left your post, and you have already proven your loyalty."

He sighed. "Talk to me, then. Ask me why I complain? I fought to enter this silken prison, after all!" He glanced up at her, his dark eyes glittering. "You, who have been an Arena slave, are you laughing at me?"

Shanna realized that he really expected an answer.

"There are many kinds of slavery," she said softly. "Yours is simply more comfortable than most."

"And perhaps more dangerous?" Elisos grimaced, ruffling his fingers through his long locks. There was a threading of silver at his temples. Shanna was reminded abruptly of her own father and remembered that they shared a common ancestor.

"I expected assassins when I was fighting the vultures from my father's throat. But now? Last week it was a man with a knife who sprang out of the crowd. Yesterday it was poison in the Menibbe melons. How can I preserve the Empire when I must fight for my life at every turn?" He shifted restlessly on the black cushions.

"The Greens yammer for peace, and the Golds press me to pursue the war. I am deluged with prophecies from every Temple in Bindir, and threatened with the wrath of their deities. I would abdicate if I thought anyone they might put upon my throne could do better than I!"

He reached for the wine flask and splashed the last of the pale liquid into his cup.

"Show that you mean to go your own road, since you cannot please everyone," Shanna said quietly.

The empty cup clicked loudly as Elisos set it down. "True, true. I was bred to this burden—shouldn't need you to remind me! You're strong," he murmured. "Perhaps it's your strength I need. . . ."

"It is here to serve you, lord," she replied as he lay back against the cushions, eyeing her.

"An' your beauty . . . you'd make strong sons, Shanna. Take off th' armor . . . let me touch you. . . ."

"I am barren, my lord," Shanna replied stiffly. "I will make no children for you or any man—" As always, she was surprised by the pain.

"Is so? Pity." His voice was growing more slurred. "Then guard . . . a few hours . . . safe sleep. . . ." His head sank back, and after a few moments the wine cup rolled from a nerveless hand.

When the Emperor was asleep, Shanna summoned his attendants to bear him to his bed and began her patrol of the garden, fighting for calm. Moonlight glittered on polished leaves and glowed through pale petals. As wind stirred the branches, cooling air released the perfumes of a hundred different flowers. But the beauty brought no peace.

Above the chirring of the frogs in the fountains, Shanna thought she heard a sound like the falcon's call in the play. No ordinary falcon flew by night, and yet she had once known one that would do it if there was need.

"Is that you, wind-daughter?" Shanna called into the darkness. Foolishness, surely, but who was there to hear?

"Chai, are you there? I have not forgotten the promise I made you in the Temple of the Winds. It was not my fault I lost you, little one—have you found your way here on your own? Call out if you can hear me, and I will beg Elisos to set you free!"

She stilled, listening, and it seemed that all the small sounds of the night had ceased as well. Once, she had been able to mind-speak the bird. She allowed her awareness to wing outward, seeking her friend's fierce courage, and touched a core of wildness that startled her so that she broke the contact. Had she touched some wild bird, or had Chai lived in falcon form for so long that she had forgotten her human soul?

And then, once more, she heard the bitter cry. "Chai—" she called, "come to me!"

There was a stirring in the branches. A dark shape lifted and she saw the shadow of the falcon stark against the moon. Then it disappeared. For a long time Shanna stood looking after it, and then, when the tears that pricked beneath her eyelids had dried, resumed her patrol of the scented trees.

It was the first evening of the Festival of Masks, when folk make offerings to the spirits of their ancestors. The Emperor would spend that night in the Temple of Hiera, burning incense before the images of his predecessors, and the Valkyr guard were free. Shanna made her way past torchlit houses towards the Dancers' Guildhall, Kilijan's ambiguous message folded in her hand.

It was only when she pushed through the curtain that she began to understand.

The tawdry disarray of the dancer's chambers had been transformed. Lamps cast a forgiving light across the worn furnishings, and there were flowers everywhere. Kilijan herself stood clad in red silk, wreathed in roses, her cheeks a little flushed, as if she had already been at the wine.

"I give my honored guest good welcome." She laughed suddenly and crowned Shanna with a garland of fragrant herbs. "Come, share the feast!" With a single fluid movement she draped herself across the cushions beside a low table where there were beancakes and honey and wine.

The food of the dead—thought Shanna. *But who is she honoring?* Carefully she seated herself on one of the cushions.

"Drink, Janna—Shanna—" said Kilijan, giggling, and Shanna shivered, realizing that "Janos" was the name the woman had meant to say. *She knew my brother.* Suddenly it was a certainty. *He is dead, or she thinks he is, and she is offering this food to him through me.*

"I drink," she said gravely, "to those who are gone but not forgotten." As she sipped at the wine she saw the laughter in Kilijan's eyes replaced by tears. "Who do you remember?" she asked as they continued their strange meal. "To whom to you make your offerings, Kilijan?"

"Who does a dancing girl have to honor? My own family disowned me years ago!" Abruptly her mood changed. Goblet still in her hand, she rose and began to dance about the room.

"Your lovers, Kilijan?" asked Shanna. "You must have had many, for you are very beautiful." In the lamplight it was almost true. Silk rustled softly as the dancer whirled.

"Many . . ." she nodded. "All the handsome young men who died in battle and—" she paused, drank again, and fluttered over to Shanna. "But you cannot sit comfortably laced into a brigandine! Let me help you remove it—you need no armor here!"

Shanna wondered, but the protection she needed was not physical. "And?" she echoed, allowing the other woman to undo the clasps. "How did the others die?" She felt the dancer's fingers brush her shoulders as the leather casing fell away. Then Kilijan was up again, her limber body arching as if to embrace an invisible lover.

"So strong . . . so handsome . . ." she murmured, twirling coquettishly. Shanna could almost see the invisible presence with whom she flirted. "He laughed with me. He said he would make me his queen. . . ." Bells tinkled on wrists and ankles as she danced that courtship.

"Who was he, Kilijan?" Shanna whispered. The

dancer stilled, then her eyes focused on her guest once more.

"Let me pull your boots off, Janna—" she said, caressing Shanna's feet and calves as the hard leather slid away.

Shanna could smell the other woman's perfume. Her head was throbbing, and she was not entirely sure it was from the wine. This was all wrong, but if she stopped it now she would never know what the dancer was trying to say.

"He gave me things—" whispered Kilijan. "He gave me that dagger you wear. I had to sell it for food. Take it off—you do not need a defense against me—"

But I do, thought Shanna, as the other woman loosened her belt and tossed it aside. Soft arms stole around her neck, and when Kilijan kissed her she did not pull away.

"Janos—touch me! I am cold, I am lonely . . . make me warm!"

I am not Janos, Shanna tried to say, but the other woman's need was too great, and she could no longer deny her own. The flames that Kilijan had lit to honor the dead trembled to their gusty breathing as they sank down.

"I am Janos' sister . . ." Shanna whispered when all at last was still. "For years I have looked for him. Tell me, Kilijan. What happened when he came to Bindir?"

The dancer sighed. "He was rich and well-born and very young—I know that now. When he arrived, the Emperor was too sick to see him. While he waited, all the great families courted him, and he accepted all their invitations. How could he know the dangers? How could I? He saw me when I danced for lord Kandaros and loved me. I lived with him in his chambers in the lower Palace for a year—"

Shanna could feel the dancer's thin shoulders shaking and tightened her embrace. Lord Kandaros was said to favor the pretensions of the Emperor's second cousin. Whom had he supported ten years before?

"What dangers?" she whispered. The flickering lamps sent shadows chasing around the room.

"They wanted to use him or destroy him—all those powerful men. He had the blood of Argantir."

"Who?"

"Kandaros ban Chosiren . . ." the words came slowly, wrenched from memory. "Irenos Aberaisi . . . Tallen of Gallis . . . the Prince of Menibbe."

Shanna sucked in her breath. Except for Aberaisi, who had been implicated in his wife's plotting and lived now in semi-captivity in the countryside, the others were still alive and powerful. She had seen most of them in the Imperial box at the play, draped in the silken robes of their clans. Some of them had candidates of their own for the diadem, connected by marriage or opportunity. Which of them would have found Janos a threat, and which might have tried to make him a puppet for their ambitions all those years ago?

"Janos would not have let himself be used . . ." Shanna said slowly. She felt Kilijan tense as she went on. "It might take him a while to understand, but he was loyal. He would not have known how to disguise his disgust when he realized. Is that what happened? Did he refuse to help and turn a friend to an enemy?"

Abruptly the dancer pulled free. Most of the lamps had gone out and her face was shadowed; Shanna could read nothing there.

"I know nothing," she said in a dull voice. "He sent me away, and when I returned to Bindir, he was gone!"

"But you must have known who was trying to use him—" Shanna reached, but the dancer's silken draperies flowed through her hands. "I will protect you, Kilijan. Don't be afraid!"

"I can tell you nothing . . ." Kilijan was weeping now. "Go away. You are not Janos. Janos is gone. . . ."

On the third night of the Festival, men dressed as gods and demons fought a great mock-battle in the great square of Bindir. Their weapons were eggs filled with confetti and flowers, but sometimes more dangerous missiles got mixed in with the others, and blood flowed. As Shanna made her way through the streets of Bindir she felt a cold prickle of apprehension. Far too many of the men with the god-masks were wearing green ribbons for it to be chance, and far too many of the demons wore gold.

It is to be tonight, then, thought Shanna, as she hurried toward the Dancers' Guildhouse. She snarled beneath her raven mask, fending off a drunken bravo with a jab of her elbow. Guilt stabbed her for having left the Palace. It was not her duty night, but if the Valkyr Guard were mustered she would be missed, for she had come out without leave. When she returned she would tell the officer of the Black Boars who guarded the outer precinct of the palace. If they needed telling. The Emperor had spies, and this attempt was surely expected. No doubt those who mattered already knew.

"Green or Gold, warrior?" Shanna whirled as someone pawed at her arm. A gap-toothed man waved a yellow steamer in her face and laughed. A half dozen more crowded up behind him, their faces painted into demon-masks, heads bound with yellow bands.

"My color is Black," she answered, letting her hand drift to the pommel of her sword.

"Black is no color . . ." he said very seriously, leaning toward her.

"It is the color of the Lady of Ravens," she said, feeling the blood lust of the battle-goddess begin to beat in her veins, "and it is mine."

The man seemed to sense it, for he drew back and let her pass. But as she continued, Shanna's face was grim beneath the mask. It was no night for anyone to be out uncompanioned, even armed. She would not get home again without blooding her sword.

But in her pouch lay another message in Kilijan's unschooled hand. *"I am alone and afraid. I will tell you about your brother. Come to me!"*

In the old quarter near the Guildhouse it was quieter. Shanna knocked once at the gate and then went in, wondering where the porter had gone. No doubt most of the girls were at parties tonight. But Kilijan's career was almost over, and it was no surprise that the dancer should be without employment even on this night of festival.

She will be anxious, thought Shanna, and quickened her step down the hall.

A single lamp burned in Kilijan's quarters. Its flicker showed her the shape of the dancer lying against her cushions. Shanna thought she must have fallen asleep waiting until she saw that the scarlet upon Kilijan's breast was not a flower, and understood that though the other woman might still be waiting, she would never be anxious any more.

"What was your message? What did you want to say to me?" she bent over her. This could not be Kilijan—it must be some doll they had put here to mock her. Even after making love, the dancer had never lain so still. The open eyes glittered in the lamplight. Gently Shanna closed them, and crossed the dancer's arms upon her breast. The body was still limber. If she had come more quickly, she might have been in time.

Kilijan still had something clutched in her left hand. Even now the clenched fingers were reluctant to yield their treasure, but suddenly it seemed important to take something of this woman with her. "At next year's festival," she whispered, "I will burn incense for you."

It was only a silver amulet in the Galian style. As Shanna picked it up, she heard a footstep. She looped the chain over her head with one hand while with the other she drew her sword.

They had been waiting in the corridor. There were six of them, but they had not reckoned on meeting a survivor of the Arena in a killing rage. Shanna's first thrust took the leader in the chest. A step to one side put the weight of her body behind her blade in a whirling stroke that took out the next two. One hung back and tripped over his fellow. An upstroke gutted him and continued on through the throat of the man behind him. The last man turned and ran.

Shanna chased him all the way to the Avenue of the Kings before she lost him in the crowd. By then, her instinctive fury had become a black sorrow that made her even more dangerous. *My fault—my fault*—it was a litany— *Kilijan died because of me!*

* * *

The crowds in the Avenue were better dressed than those in the Old Quarter and perhaps more drunken, but the air throbbed with the same dangerous gaiety. But Shanna was more dangerous still. She stalked through the crowd like a beast of prey, and those who crossed her path made way.

But there was no fighting the current, like a gathering floodtide, that carried her toward the great square. More and more people were crowding into the open space before the Palace where the Greens and Golds swirled back and forward, battling for power. It was the custom for the Emperor to observe the fighting from a balcony while the priests took omens for the coming year, but the space behind the balustrade was dark. If Elisos were watching, it was from some safer spyhole.

"Down the Greens, up the Gold! Down the weak, up the bold!" the fighters cried, and *"No war, no more!"* came the reply.

The best of the costumes were displayed in the square. Shanna blinked as a man swathed in the draperies of Ytarra traded blows with a Menibbe sand demon, and a demon-mask of Saibel attacked a masked Toyur. They were all here—all the gods who had aided or tormented her, and all the devils as well. Her own guise began to seem less and less a costume as she fought her way around the edge of the square. Grinning demon-faces yawned and yammered before her. It took all Shanna's control to keep from drawing her bloody sword. As she neared the side-gate, the chant changed.

"Down the Greens, up the Gold,
Up the new, down the old!"

Stones thudded against the carven fretwork that faced the Palace sending stinging chips of marble everywhere. Someone screamed; there was a deeper cry as a man fell. From the Palace a horn blew, and a tremor of anticipation ran through the crowd. Shanna, fighting to keep her feet, saw the top of the great gate swing open, heard metal clash and the tramp of boots as the Black Boars moved out to face the crowd.

"Come out, coward!" someone yelled. "Don't hide behind your pigs!"

"See, the tyrant sends his bullies to cut us down!" another replied.

"Death to Elisos! Death to the Emperor!" Now many voices were taking up the cry.

Shanna took advantage of the crowd's distraction to slip along the side wall. Breathless, she banged on the kitchen gate, where there was a porter who knew her. Astonishingly, it swung open. At that moment she became aware that the person behind it was not the porter, and that men were coming after her. She stabbed the traitor and tried to close the door, but the weight of men pressing in behind her knocked her against the wall. A roar from outside told her that fighting had broken out in the square.

Gasping, Shanna tried to think. There was a dreadful familiarity about this, as if she had experienced it, or envisioned it, before. Had she been picking up Elisos' nightmares? Her head swam with a distorted vision of the Emperor's garden. Of course—that was where he would go. In the year she had lived in the Palace she had taken care to learn its warren of passageways. Heart pounding, she forced herself up the winding stairs.

"Get back—how dare you—ah, it is you!" The Emperor's voice cracked with relief as Shanna pulled off her mask. "You, at least have come to defend me!"

Have I? she wondered, as he moved out from the shadow of the fig tree at the edge of the garden. This time Elisos was the quarry of the ravening monster that roared outside, but ten years ago he had been foremost among the beasts of prey. And who would have been more likely to note Shanna's interest in a worn-out dancing girl who knew too much than one of the Emperor's spies?

Someone had blown out all the lamps, but the sky was red with the light of something burning. She could see the twitch of muscles in Elisos' cheek as he looked at her. Suddenly she felt his fear as if it were her own. It had *been* her own, as she relived the terror of their common ancestor in the vision in the Temple of the Winds that she had shared with Chai. Her gaze searched the treetops for the dark falcon-shape she knew must be there.

"Elisos Teyn Janufen," she said slowly, "I have come to ask you some questions. . . ."

"Janos of Sharteyn?" he said when she had finished. At least this Emperor had a little courage. He was trembling, but he had stripped down to his underrobe so that he could move freely, and he had a sword. "That was ten years ago. What does he matter now?"

"He was my brother," she said quietly, "and someone killed him because they thought he might claim the throne. Was it you?"

There was a long silence.

"Shanna . . . of Sharteyn!" the Emperor stared at her. "I will answer when you tell me if you mean to keep your oath to me?"

Shanna crossed to the marble balustrade where she could keep an eye on the courtyard below and leaned against it. All her running about the city was beginning to take its toll, or perhaps it was the maze of unresolved conflicts that was her life.

"I have sworn so many oaths—" she said tiredly, "to find my brother or avenge him, to reconcile you and a girl whose only language is a falcon's cry. I cannot keep them all."

"Tell me about the falcon and I will tell you about your brother," said Elisos desperately. It seemed to Shanna that the noise of the battle was getting louder. The guards were still fighting, but they seemed to be outnumbered. If the attackers reached them first, both she and the Emperor would die.

"Long ago the Emperors were served by were-falcons. Did you ever hear the tale? But the last of them flew away when his master fled here to hide from just such a mob as will soon be coming up those stairs, and the Emperor cursed him to stay in bird form until an heir of his blood should forgive the were-kin."

"A fairy-tale—" said Elisos. Another building caught flame. She could see him more clearly now.

"Do you think so? Chai—come here to me—surely this

has awakened your memories! If you are out there, come to me now!" She stood and lifted her arm, waiting. For a moment she thought she had been wrong. Then a fragment detached itself from the darkness, and the shadow-shape of the falcon swooped toward her hand.

Despite her grief, Shanna felt a lifting of the heart as the warm weight of the bird settled upon her arm. *Sister, I have missed you!* her spirit called.

I was lost . . . lost . . . came the reply, *but now I remember. I am Chai!*

"So," she laughed a little as wonder momentarily replaced the Emperor's fear. "Will you forgive her now?"

Light spilled across the lower courtyard as someone opened a door below. Men clattered across the flagstones and stood pointing upward, muttering. Elisos heard them, too, and Shanna saw then that the blood of Argantir was in him after all, for he straightened, though he was still trembling.

"They will not kill me like a rabbit in a hole." He looked back at Shanna and Chai. "Nor will I ask her to stay and die with me. I see now that no one can evade the fate his nature earns. That is how your brother died," he said then, "fighting the men I sent to hold him until I should be safe on my throne. If you can forgive me that, I will forgive your bird, and let her, and you, go where you will!"

Chai's talons dug into Shanna's arm, but her cry was lost in the shouts of the men who were coming through the antechamber.

"Fly away, my sister!" she said softly. "At least I have saved you!" She swung her arm and the falcon burst upward in a flutter of drumming wings as the first of the attackers came through the door.

For a moment they paused, confused by the two figures before them. And Shanna, facing them, felt at last the clear blaze of certainty she had first known when she took oath to Yraine's holy fire.

"Make me your blade, goddess," she murmured then, "to spare or to slay!"

As the men moved forward, Shanna's sword hissed from its sheath and she settled to guard, wondering how many of them she could take before they brought her down. But as the first man attacked, a blur of motion filled the air. He screamed as talons raked his eyes, then Chai was sideslipping toward the next, splitting the air with her cry.

"Demons!" cried one of the men, "demons of the air defend him!"

By the time the others began to move, Shanna had downed two of them. The others surged toward her, glad to have a foe they could understand. She felt her point pierce someone's chest and whipped it free. There were more cries and light and a confusion of new faces.

It is over, then, she thought, lifting her sword.

But instead, her attackers were retreating as the newcomers fell upon them. Shanna became aware that she, too, was bleeding, and that the fighters who had rescued her were the Valkyr Guard. She swayed, and felt small hands on her elbow.

She blinked at the brown-haired girl who was supporting her. She had forgotten what Chai looked like in human form.

"You're free," she muttered as the girl helped her to sit down. *And so am I,* she thought as she watched the Emperor pull himself together and start giving orders to the guards, *so am I. . . .*

THE PROPER BALANCE

by Robyn McGrew

Robyn McGrew is one of my success stories. Like Lynne Armstrong-Jones, she resolved to sell to me; but her first effort was not quite salable. So I sent back a rejection slip, and—as I always hope will happen, she obeyed my advice to "Keep trying," and sent me several other stories before writing one I could use. She says, "If my barrage of submissions hasn't convinced you, I more-or-less live and breathe for writing."

She was born in August 1956 and started writing at the age of six. She has supported her writing habit by housecleaning, waiting tables, and working as a "temp"; currently, she is a receptionist for an offset printing company, and teaches martial arts. (Writers have to do the darnedest things to make a living; I worked in a carnival as target for a knife thrower, sold fashion frocks door to door, and wrote "confession" stories, to name but a few.)

Robyn is female—married and with two cats. She lives near Las Vegas and tries to write at least one short story a week.

She requests that "The Proper Balance," her first published story, be dedicated to the memory of her mother, Fern Jordan, who died on May 7, 1992. Robyn says, "She . . . was a good friend and the first person who truly believed that someday I would find success as a writer. I only wish she could have been alive to see my work in print. . . ."

"You may admit the next supplicant," the priest told the acolyte who served at the door.

The girl responded and a tall, strong-looking

woman walked into the audience chamber. The priest recognized her as a junior officer in the Temple Guard. "You are out of uniform, Centurion Vala."

"Yes, your Eminence," Vala knelt before the priest. The muscles in her neck rippled, as she bowed her head in submission. "I have broken my trust," she confessed.

The priest's face dropped and the smile faded into a frown. "Speak," he commanded her.

"I fell asleep at my duty last night." Vala explained without looking up.

"Were there extenuating circumstances?"

"Does it matter? I have broken my oath to my Lord Teir, and deserve to be punished."

"Do not add impudence to the charge against you; remember where you are," the priest warned. He felt sorry for the temple guard. Vala had always worked hard to please their Master, and the priest knew she would not have failed without good reason.

"I beg patience, I meant no disrespect."

"Confess your trespass before the Lord and know His hand is just."

"I had finished my duty yesterday afternoon when the Watch Commander approached and asked me to cover the night shift. I knew at the time that I was too tired to accept. I had pulled a double watch the day before." Vala paused, the next words coming more difficult for her. "I also knew accepting would look good on my record and in the eyes of my superiors, so I agreed. About mid-watch, I fell asleep, waking just before the relief came."

"Was any harm done?"

"No, Eminence."

"Did anyone come upon you while you slept?"

"Not to my knowledge, sir."

The priest hated to ask the next question, he could see the woman was torturing herself enough already. "Why do you come to confess? Are you seeking leniency?"

"No, sir."

"Then, why?"

"I know there is nothing we can hide from our Master. I would rather come to Him now, of my own will, than to be brought before Him as a prisoner, adding deception to my sin." Vala's shoulders sagged and the priest dreaded what he knew must come next. Lord Teir had been in a harsh mood of late.

Resigned to his duty, the priest knelt at the altar and sought the will of the God. Words which were not his flooded into his mind and out of his mouth. "Vala, you have made grievous offense against the Lord Teir. You set your pride and ambition above service to your God, therefore you shall live the 'life of shame,' for the period of one year." With the last pronouncement, the words stopped and the priest was left to finish on his own. "Take this one to the city gates to be prepared and expelled."

Two temple guards moved to stand behind Vala. She knew them both, they had served in her command only a month before.

Unseen by His followers, Teir, the God of Duty and Loyalty, smiled, satisfied by the outcome. He'd been aware of the woman's trespass and had planned on making her an example to her fellow guards. It was her first mistake, but that couldn't be helped.

"Teir," the voice sounded in His head. It had been several centuries since He last heard it, but Tier knew it instantly.

"Yes, Master?"

"You will come to Me at once."

"Yes, Master." A moment of concentration and Teir was kneeling before the throne of His Master, the Lord of the Gods.

"Your punishment was too harsh for the offense."

"An example had to be made, Lord," Teir protested, in defense of His judgment.

"You have made too many examples of late, Teir," the Master scolded.

"But Lord, they must be kept to strict discipline, if We are to keep order as You have commanded Us to."

"You have lost Your balance. When I first created You and gave You dominion over a portion of this world, You thought out Your decrees and were a good, impartial judge. Now, You use threats and examples to enforce

Your will. You have lost touch with those I gave You care of. This would not have happened, if You would walk among them as the Others do and as I have commanded."

"I had not the time, Lord," It was a poor excuse; Teir could have made the time, if He'd wanted.

"Then I will make the time for You."

The world swirled around Teir. In the chaos He heard, "Now You shall learn what it is to be mortal."

An undetermined amount of time later Teir woke up. At least, that's what he thought he was experiencing. He felt weak, as if something were wrong with him. Then, he realized the source—he was mortal. His Master had stripped him of all his godly attributes. "Master, no. I beg You. Anything but this."

"Easy, friend, you shouldn't try to get up so fast." The voice was familiar. Opening his eyes, Teir found himself staring into the face of Vala.

He tried to pull back and away from the woman, but her strong hands easily held him to the ground. "I said 'easy.' After a fall like that, you shouldn't get up right away."

"Fall?" he asked cautiously.

"I assumed you fell; there's a fresh slide near here and you were at the bottom of it. You didn't fall?"

"I guess you could say I did." It was more of a push, Teir thought to himself.

"I moved you into the shade and waited; you were unconscious for several hours."

"What?" Teir was having a difficult time believing he'd actually been unconscious.

"I don't know how long you'd been there when I found you, but it's almost two hours past sunset and time for evening meal. Do you feel up to eating?"

"I'm not sure," Teir couldn't decide what was causing the noise and burning in his stomach and wasn't sure he should risk aggravating it further.

"The way your stomach's growling, I know you must be hungry. I've made some broth for dinner. It's not much, but it will help you keep your strength up."

"Very well, I'll have some." Tier acquiesced, hoping

it would make the all too attentive woman go away, at least for a moment.

It was night. He surmised this from the lack of light and Vala's comments. His audience with the Master had been in the early morning; had he been unconscious all that time?

Vala turned from the fire, holding a wooden bowl in both hands. "It's hot, so drink it slowly."

He noted she didn't serve herself and there weren't any other bowls available for her to drink from. Sipping the broth, which was surprisingly quite good, he asked, "Will you not share some of this with me?"

The expression on her face changed from compassion, to one of profound sadness. "I am condemned to a 'year of shame.' I may not eat with you or anyone else." She pulled back her hood, revealing her hair, which had been cut close to the scalp with a dull knife. The hair was varying lengths and many cuts were clotted with blood, where the knife had come too close.

"Oh, Master, what have I done?" Teir whispered to his Lord. He hadn't realized the punishment he'd decreed was this severe. He'd thought she'd be ostracized but not like this.

Feigning ignorance, Teir said, "You don't seem to be the kind of person the gods would punish so severely. What happened?"

Both the statement and the question brought obvious pain to the former guard and Teir regretted having said anything.

"The Gods punish the guilty, as is right. It has little to do with how one looks or acts after the fact. My crime was one of pride and infidelity. Were I allowed the privilege of prayer, I would thank the Lord Teir for His mercy toward me."

At this, the fallen God turned away, hiding the shame he felt for wronging one with such faith in him. He may have been the God of Loyalty, but she could teach him a great deal on the subject. "Do you have a name?" he asked, wanting something to say.

"You must be new to this area. You're not supposed to ask me, but since you did, my name is Vala."

Reaching into her pack, she pulled out a moth-eaten blanket and offered it to him. "What are you called?"

"Teir, that is, Teirin."

At the mention of the God's name, the woman paled. Concerned, he moved toward her, "Are you all right?"

"Yes, it was just, at first, I thought you had called the name of the God I have wronged. Your name is very similar to His."

"I'm sorry."

"Don't be, I brought this onto myself."

Tier couldn't stand it any longer. He made up his mind that he had to put a stop to this.

"Vala, is there some place I might have some privacy, the broth . . ." He let his voice trail off, intentionally giving her the wrong idea.

"Just on the other side of the ridge."

"Thanks."

"Don't mention it."

Teir moved as quickly out of sight as he could. Arriving at his destination he knelt and cried out, "Master, I know You can hear me, I want to make a deal."

"I am listening," the voice sounded in his head.

"I didn't know, I swear, Lord, I didn't know."

"That is why I sent you here, to learn."

"And I have, Master."

"You have begun to," his Master corrected, then added, *"you have much more to learn."*

"Yes, Lord, but I," the word was foreign and came hard for Tier, "beg You, not at her expense."

"She will suffer regardless, this is the punishment you meted out to her."

"She doesn't have to. Please, You have the power, Lord. Let me finish her year and let Vala have my place in Your court."

"You would have a mortal reign in your stead? An interesting concept, she would not be able to return afterward."

"I would replace her memories. Please, Lord, I can not bear to see what I have done. Punish me for my selfishness and shortsightedness, but don't make another pay for my mistake."

"So be it."

The world spun around Teir again, only this time he could see Vala was also in the void and both of them were changing. He became weaker and his head hurt from the many gashes and cuts on it. She became radiant as Her body changed to accept the power. When it was finished, they stood face-to-face, Goddess and man.

"Forgive me, Vala, for the wrong I have done You. It is I who deserve the chastening, not You. I ask You, Goddess of Duty and Loyalty, as Your first supplicant, grant me one prayer before ostracizing me as the law requires."

"Granted."

Kneeling, the former God bowed his head. "You have a year. I pray You, undo the damage my foolishness has caused. You know the people, their ways and which judgments are too harsh. Save the sentence I serve, reverse the unjust ones."

"I will do as much as I can, Teir, but a year isn't much time. You must leave here. This is sacred ground now and you may not remain." Vala didn't want to send him away. She had too many things she wanted to talk to him about. She had learned so much in the transference and even more in the brief communion with the great Lord of the Gods, but this was all new to Her and She could use some help.

"I will guide You, little one," the voice sounded in Her head startling Vala. *"Teir will come back to a new world, but he shall not take Your memory from You, rather he shall be assigned a new fief, as God of Repentants."*

The Master of the Gods was pleased with Himself. He had rebalanced this world and taught an irresponsible child a lesson in the bargain. Not a bad day's work at all.

THE GIFT OF MINERVA

by Dorothy J. Heydt

Dorothy Heydt is another writer whose work has appeared in many of the Darkover and *Sword and Sorceress* anthologies, and in *Marion Zimmer Bradley's FANTASY Magazine.* She has now written—and sold—a novel, but it is under a pen name. Dorothy has a gift for writing about intellectual and esoteric themes, and has an annoying habit of making me violate my own guidelines, her writing and storytelling are so skillful. Dorothy has two teenagers, both of whom have now sold stories to me; indeed, we may have a dynasty in the making.

She shares her Northern California home with her husband, children, cats, and computers, and she has one of the loveliest soprano voices I've encountered in some time.

This is a very compact detective story involving Cynthia, a character Dorothy has been developing in these anthologies for a number of years, and a boatful of Romans. . . .

Even when one is in love—even when one is drowned and deep in love as Atlantis in the sea—even then there comes the time when a person has to relieve herself. Cynthia approached the gilt-handled chamber pot with distaste, for neither of them had gone abovedecks during the mistral, and it had been blowing three days. But—yes, the howl of the wind, muffled as it had been by the thick planking of the deck above them, had fallen silent. She could hear the tiny sounds of Komi's breathing; he was too lean and fit a man to snore. Cynthia carefully picked up the pot and crept up the ladder, pushing up the trapdoor with her shoulder.

The morning was cool and bright; sun, sky and sea all looked fresh-polished. Their boat, on the other hand, had had most of its paint stripped off it by windborne sand and looked much less like stolen goods than it had before. The boat had drifted away from the shore, and the island Phaneraia was no more than a sullen mountain-shape fringed by smoking beaches. The northernmost bits of Sicily and the southwesternmost bits of Italy were blue smudges on the horizon, and toward the east—

"Oh, curse it," Cynthia said aloud, and emptied the chamber pot overboard.

"What's the matter?" Komi said, coming up the ladder.

"Ship on the horizon. No, it's not the Mamertine hulk, that's still beached on the island. Over there."

Komi gripped the mast with hands and feet and climbed it almost to the top. He squinted into the east, where the rising sun turned the sky golden and blackened the approaching ship. "Greek ship," he said after a moment, and slithered down again. "That's a stroke of luck; they're not likely to meddle with such small fry as us. What's left of the food?"

"Not much."

"Then I'll catch us some breakfast." With one of Cynthia's hairpins bent into a hook, and a few fathoms of light line, he had three little fish gutted on the deck by the time Cynthia had the brazier lit to cook them. Then he looked up and said, "Ah. Our luck just ran out." The ship that had pulled alongside them had been made by Greeks, no doubt of it. But the stern-eyed nobleman at her prow, and the dozen or so armed men lined up behind the siderail, and maybe even the fellow with one foot up on the railing and the grappling hook in his hand, were just as certainly not Greeks but Romans.

"How's your Latin?"

"I have none."

"Then I'll have to do the talking—and that stuffy-looking Roman won't care for that. Ah, well. Keep an eye on the charcoal." She went to the railing nearest the Roman ship, and the nobleman stepped between two of his soldiers to face her. "Hail, my lord."

"Hail, woman. What brings you into these waters?"

"The mistral that blew three days ago drove us through the straits of Messana and on northward to here. It was only by the favor of the gods that we weren't drowned." All that was true enough, except for the parts she had left out.

"The favor of the gods! O happy people, if you have that." And descending suddenly from the high style, "I wish some of it could rub off on us." He shook his head. "Forgive me. I am Caius Duilius Nepos."

"I'm Cynthia, daughter of Euelpides; my man's name is Komi son of—" (an instant's horrified blankness, and a snatch at the first letter of the alphabet) "—of Akhilleus. Formerly of Alexandria, lately of Syracuse."

"And cannot your husband speak Latin? No? Oh, well," Duilius said predictably. One of the soldiers—a decurion, if Cynthia read him right—stepped up to Duilius and murmured in his ear. "Really," Duilius said, and to Cynthia, "the decurion asks if you are that Cynthia, called the witch of Syracuse, who put down both a plague and a slave uprising, all in one year. And he says that if you are she, then truly you have the gods' ears, and you may be able to help us. But that if not, you are probably spies and we should hold you for questioning."

At the thought of "questioning" Cynthia's heart turned over—and they had to get to Panormus, and that soon, but she couldn't tell the Roman that. "O Duilius, the tongues of men have made my deeds much greater than they were. Yet I have spoken with Arethousa, patroness of Syracuse, and had her help in the past."

"Come aboard, then," Duilius said. "You, there, lay a plank between the ships and help our guests aboard. You, Lucius, go and bank their coals for them. Come, we can at least offer you a better breakfast than grilled sprats."

And he did so, offering them wine and sausage rolls and honeycakes. Duilius ate one bite of each, as if to reassure them that nothing was poisoned, and drank a few sips of wine. Seen up close, he was a younger man than they had thought, thirty perhaps, with the face of an eagle and hair as black as a raven's wings. He stared out over the sea and said nothing until they had finished eating. Then he poured more wine and began.

"I own not inconsiderable lands in Italy, south of Rome and around Neapolis. They are fertile, and well-farmed by good, honest people. We gathered surpluses enough, even with the demands of the Army for the Tarentum campaign, that I thought of trading with other nations for such goods as we don't produce in Rome. I sent out messages, and presently the trader Hamilcar of Carthage came to Rome to discuss this trade with me."

The Roman's jaw tightened. "He stayed in my house. He was my guest. This was while there was peace between Rome and Carthage—" he broke off. "Ah. Join us, Hanno; this concerns you."

The young Carthaginian glanced uneasily at Cynthia and Komi, and at the Romans, and slowly approached. There were deep shadows under his eyes, and he looked sick. "Hanno was the companion of Hamilcar," Duilius explained, "his nephew and secretary. While we were still in negotiation, as I said, the affair of the Mamertines in Messana came to a head.

"For reasons I still cannot comprehend, the Senate resolved to drive the outlaws out of the city they had taken—though they had allowed others just as base to remain in other places, on the soil of Italy itself. To no one's surprise, the Carthaginians moved in to garrison Messana and protect it. It seemed almost certain there would be war—and that I could not guarantee Hamilcar's safety, even in my own house. So I hired this ship to convey him safely back to Carthage.

"We left Ostia two days ago, though that same mistral was blowing and we could make little headway against it. But I felt no anxiety, for I assumed that Hamilcar was safe on the ship, now that we were out of Italy. But last night, as we think, someone put a drug in the wine served to our Carthaginian guests. This morning we found Hanno sick near to death from the drug, and Hamilcar dead—from a dagger's stroke.

"I have questioned everyone on the ship, both my own Romans and the Greek sailors. No one knows anything—rather, no one will admit to knowing anything." He sighed. "We are honest men in Rome. We tell the truth, honor the gods, and keep our word. How am I to tell, out of all the people on this ship, which one is lying to me?"

"Just a moment," Cynthia said, and translated a summary for Komi. "What do you think? Is there anything we can do to help this careful, upright Roman?" (She said this rather than "damned fool," which was in her thoughts, lest Duilius know more Greek than she hoped he did.)

Komi scratched his chin and said, "Hmmmm."

"Because if I cannot find the guilty man," Duilius went on, "then I must go on to Carthage, to return Hamilcar's body and his nephew to their people, and offer myself in place of the killer. That is the only honorable thing I can do."

Cynthia translated. "If we go to Carthage," Komi said, "I'm a dead man. And so, I think, is Duilius."

There was the sound of a throat being cleared, from one of the sailors at the railing, a pleasant-looking fellow with blue eyes and a straggly beard. "Forgive the intrusion," he said. "Your man's right, you know, mistress witch. The Carthaginians will kill master Duilius if they get hands on him. Speaking for the men of this ship, to whom Duilius has been a very fair and honest master, we'd rather it didn't happen."

"So what am I to do?"

The sailor shrugged. "Find the killer. Easier for you than for the master; he's not a stupid man, but he said it himself: he doesn't know a liar or a rogue when he sees one."

"And if he goes to Carthage, we all go with him?" The sailor nodded. Cynthia got to her feet, feeling she could sit still no longer, and went on to the railing. Go to Carthage, and that stubborn, honest fool Duilius would die, and Komi with him, as a thief and runaway slave—and Cynthia, too, because she could not conceive of any life without him.

She stared at the dancing waves as though the answer might be written on them. What god—if the gods had not all fallen asleep, as she had cause to know—what god might have helped her now? Wise Athena? Better yet, Autolykos prince of thieves, son of Hermes and grandfather of resourceful Odysseus. What would Odysseus have done in her place? Sneak away clinging to the belly of a dolphin instead of a sheep? She closed her eyes and tried to empty her mind, so that a divine voice could speak to her if it chose to. But there was nothing, only the little slaps of the wave against the ships' sides, and the scream of gulls.

She opened her eyes. Komi's abandoned fishline had caught something bigger than sprats, a young tuna maybe, and the gulls were swooping overhead watching it. And a thought slipped into her mind, easy as a foot into an old shoe. "Whose birds are those?" she said, in a voice that did not seem to be her own.

"What's that?" Duilius said, but she answered herself, "Those are Athene's birds, whom you call Minerva. She has sent us aid." (Never mind that Athene's bird was properly the owl of the Acropolis. The Roman didn't have to know that.)

"Look—" the gulls had found the gutted sprats, and had descended onto the deck of Komi's ship to squabble over them. "They have accepted our offering."

"With enthusiasm," Duilius said, looking hopeful for the first time since they had met him. "A good omen."

(Of course, Cynthia commented silently. *A hungry gull gobbles dead fish and he takes it as a message from the gods. These Romans are so superstitious.* The plan was branching out in her mind, taking on leaves and flowers of divine beauty. *Thank you, Athene, Autolykos, Odysseus. If in truth you sleep, this is a fine dream you've sent me.)* "Now I know what to do," Cynthia said to the waiting Romans. "I need to go back to my ship for a moment. Steady the plank, my good man. Thank you." She crossed over before Duilius could say anything. "Thank you, good birds," she cried, and the gulls rose up in a clatter of wings. "Give her my thanks," she shouted after them as they flapped away toward Phaneraia. Cynthia took a moment to pull up the tuna on Komi's line and drop it into a bucket. If they survived

all this, they might still want to eat it. Then she went below.

Before Duilius had a chance to get anxious again, Cynthia came up the ladder carrying a bundle wrapped in purple silk. (A tunic found aboard the stolen ship, too big for Komi and too small for Cynthia, but the Roman was not to know that either.) "I shall need a dark room," she said as she came on board. "What I have here may not be seen by the eyes of any man. It is the veil of Minerva, given to me in the Temple of Isis in Alexandria." (Lies, lies; she'd never even set foot in the place. Surely Odysseus was on her side.)

"My cabin," Duilius said promptly, and made a sign of reverence. (Cynthia did the same, and so did all the men within earshot—including Komi, who still had not understood a word, but knew a cue when he saw one.) "We can cover the window with blankets."

They blanketed the window and shoved Duilius' Spartan furnishings aside; they hung another pair of blankets inside the door, and they took the lamp away. While Cynthia was inside making arrangements of which she would not speak, Duilius set up a jar of water and a basin outside the door, as she had commanded.

"Now let my words be heard by every man," Cynthia said when she came out again. "Inside that room, safe from the profanation of your eyes, hangs the veil of Minerva, all-wise daughter of Jupiter. Each of you will wash his hands, then go inside. Stretch out your hands till you touch the sacred veil; then, holding it between your hands, swear to her that you are innocent of the blood of the Carthaginian Hamilcar. Then come out again, and stand there by the railing.

"One of you, of course, will have sworn falsely. One or more, perhaps. The goddess will tell me. Or perhaps she'll simply strike the guilty man down—it doesn't matter; she has promised me there'll be no mistake. Caius Duilius, you shall go first, as a sign that the innocent man has nothing to fear." (*Because if Duilius is the murderer himself, then he is such a great actor that he deserves life, or else I am such a fool as deserves to perish.*)

Duilius did not speak, but nodded in the Roman fashion. He carefully washed and dried his hands, as pale as though it were his young bride in the room, instead of what was actually inside—well, for a pious Roman, maybe it was understandable. He went in, closing the door behind him; he came out again; he went to the railing, clasped his hands in front of him, and did not speak.

The next man followed, and the next. Cynthia did not try to impose any sort of order on them, other than making sure that those who had come out did not go in again. One or two of the Romans looked so distressed that Cynthia said, "You know, you are only swearing that you are innocent of the blood of Hamilcar. Anything else you might have done is between you and your own priests." The gods knew, and Cynthia did not care, what small imperfections these stiff-necked Romans might have on their burnished consciences.

Every man had gone in, from Hanno and the decurion to the grimiest of the sailors (his clean hands looked startlingly pink compared to the rest of him). "Now," Cynthia said.

Beginning at the near end of the line, she went to every man and lifted his hands between her own, raising them to her face; quietly she drew in breath and let it out again, while looking the man directly in the eyes. Some of the men trembled with fear; some blushed and could not meet her gaze; the blue-eyed sailor caught her eye and winked; the Roman soldiers stood as if on parade, their faces grim. Hanno still looked sick. Last of all she came to Duilius, who gave her his hands with a look of perfect trust. His hazel eyes were steady and clear, confident in what they did not understand. He made Cynthia herself feel unclean, not quite as grubby as a sailor's unwashed backside, but close enough. She made an effort and smiled.

She turned to look at the long line of men, and raised her voice. "The wise goddess has spoken," she said. "One man is stained with the blood of Hamilcar; the others are innocent. That man—" she paused for a moment, but no one crumpled at the knees to save her the trouble; they had no sense of the dramatic. "I'm sorry,

Caius Duilius, I don't know whether this will please you or grieve you. The murderer is the nephew, Hanno."

Now the Carthaginian did crumple, and fell retching to the deck, fouling himself with the sickness he could no longer keep at bay. Sailors dumped a bucket of water over him; soldiers hauled him away. The rest of the men went back to their stations.

Duilius remained where he had stood, shock in his eyes. "Why?" he said. "Why would Hanno murder his uncle? His own flesh and blood?"

"I don't know," Cynthia said gently. "Though you ought to be able to get him to answer a few questions between here and Carthage, once he finishes puking. Maybe he planned to inherit his share of the family business. Maybe he just didn't like him. There is a lot of evil in the world, O virtuous Roman, and no one has ever found a way to make it go away. I need to take away the things in your cabin. And then, may my husband and I have leave to go?"

"Readily," the Roman said, and walked her to the door with respect. When she came out again with her purple bundle, she saw the sailors loading bundles onto her deck: Komi was already back on board, shaking out the square sail and tying it to the yard.

"A small gift," Duilius said. "Far less than what I owe you; you have saved both our lives and our honor."

"Your lives, maybe," Cynthia said. "I can hardly save what is imperishable. Go with the gods, Caius Duilius. Komi, we need to catch the wind." She almost ran across the plank bridge and saw it withdrawn. "Get away from here," she muttered under her breath. "Just in case."

"I'm working on it, I'm working on it," he said, and let out the sail and let the wind fill it. They moved away to the west, the Roman ship tacking to the south. When it was no bigger than a peapod floating on the water, and their own ship running lightly before a good east wind, Cynthia let out the breath she had been holding and sat down on the deck.

"So," Komi said. "I perceive you found the man his murderer and got us turned loose; but what did you *do*?"

She told him what she had said and done, and he

laughed. "Apart from the question of what the veil of Minerva would be doing in the Temple of Isis—"

"Oh, pious Romans don't ask questions like that. They've already decided their gods are the same as the gods of Hellas, never mind how many differences in their stories and their habits. It's no strain for them to believe in a few more."

"So what was the thing really?"

"One of those big table napkins, the fine linen ones. I hung it up from the rafter and sprinkled it with that bottle of mint essence I'd just bought at the market the day you snatched me out of Syracuse."

"And only the guilty man didn't dare to touch the veil, and only his hands didn't smell of mint. Well done, love. So the Wise Goddess didn't speak to you at all?"

"I don't say that," Cynthia said. "*Somebody* put the idea in my head." Among the Roman's gifts was a pile of wine-jars; she picked up a small one, broke the seal, and poured the wine overboard. "Thank you, Athene, Autolykos, Odysseus. Whoever. To the God Unknown whose altar stands in Athens. Komi, is there anything left of those coals, or do I need to light more? If the gulls didn't get that tuna after all, we can eat him for dinner."

FRIENDLY FIRE

by Mercedes Lackey

I had the honor of publishing "Misty" Lackey's first story, back when she was known to science fiction/fantasy fandom only as a filk singer. Her first Darkover story was so good that I knew as soon as I read it I'd have to redo my whole anthology line-up, which had been tentatively completed just that day. When I told Misty about the "trouble" she was causing me, the poor kid thought I was cross; but it was quite the reverse. An editor is always glad to get something that good, no matter how inconvenient it is.

Misty has become a prolific writer of novels and short stories for which she is justly famous, and has just finished writing the first of the Darkover collaborations, *Rediscovery,* with me. *Return to Darkover* will be our next project.

Since discovering really good writers and seeing them prosper is one of the few real delights of an editor's life, I couldn't be happier if I had written her books myself. This is a kind of memorial to my mentor at DAW Books, the late Don Wollheim, who was himself the greatest discoverer of talent in the past fifty years.

This is a Tarma and Kethry story, and even I have to admit that it's funny. Writers have been driven to despair trying to make me laugh; but here's proof it can be done.

Misty lives in Oklahoma and is married to a professional fantasy/science fiction artist Larry Dixon. She keeps falcons, some of which had been turned loose in the wild. And yes, she still writes filk songs.

Tarma shena Tale'sedrin, Swordsworn Shin'a'in, was up to her earlobes in a different kind of battle than she usually fought.

A battle with current finances.

Where does it all go? I could swear we just got paid. . . .

Huh. Down the throats of the mares, us, and that eating-machine that calls itself a kyree, *that's where.*

She and her partner, the White Winds sorceress Kethry, had taken to the marketplace armed with slender pouches of copper coins; no silver there. With luck, they would be able to stretch those pouches of coin enough to cover provisions for the two humans, the two Shin'a'in battlemares, and Warrl, the wolflike *kyree*. Those provisions had to last for at least three weeks, the time it would take them to get to their next job.

There was a certain amount of self-provisioning they could do. Warrl could hunt some for himself, and so could Tarma and Kethry if they were careful. Warrl was quite intelligent enough to confine his hunting to nondomestic beasts, and there were always rabbits living in hedgerows that could be snared. But this was farm country, and there was very little for the warhorses to forage on along the roadside—and if those rabbits proved elusive, any fresh meat would have to go first to Warrl.

It was at times like this that Tarma wished her partner had been a little less generous to her ex-"husband"—or rather, to his other victims. A spot of judicious blackmail or a decision to claim some of the bastard's blood-money for herself would have left them with a nice cushion to get them over lean spots like this one. Granted, once they arrived at Kata'shin'a'in, they should have no trouble picking up a caravan job—and with luck, it might be a very lucrative one. Their friends, Ikan and Justin, had promised to put in a good word for them with the gem merchants whose caravans they habitually guarded, and a good word from them would mean a great deal. *They* did so well over the course of a year that they never had to scramble for work during the lean season; they were able to find a friendly inn and take a rest over the winter, if they chose.

But first, she and Kethry had to get to Kata'shin'a'in, and the start of the caravan routes.

And to get to Kata'shin'a'in, they needed provisions.

They were so short on money that they were not even staying in an inn; despite the bitter, early spring weather, despite the very real threat of sleet and foul weather, they were camped outside the city walls. Their tent cost nothing, and the walls were overgrown with weeds—dried now, but sufficient fodder for a couple of days, so long as Tarma supplemented their gleanings with a grain ration.

Tarma would be bargaining for the horses' grain; Kethry, with the remainder of their slim resources, was to buy the humans' rations, and Warrl's. The *kyree* himself remained at the camp—between the presence of Warrl and the warhorses, the camp was safer than if there had been two armed guards there. In a way, Tarma pitied anyone who was stupid enough to try to rob it.

There were at least a dozen folk in the market selling grain and hay, and Tarma intended to check them all before making a purchase. She made her way down the stone-paved street of the beast-market, with the cobbles wet and slippery under her boots, and the calls, squalls, and bellows of everything from huge oxen to cages full of pigeons on all sides. The stalls for the feed-sellers themselves were simple canvas awnings fronting stables, corrals and warehouses, none of which had anything to do with what was being sold under the awnings. There was a scattering of grain on the cobbles, and a great deal of straw underfoot. The air was damp, chilly, and smelled strongly of too many animals crowded too closely together.

Eleven of the twelve were unremarkable; farmers, and all within a hair of each other so far as price went. Tarma was not in a position to buy so much that any of them were likely to make a special price for her. The twelfth, however. . . .

The twelfth was some kind of priest, or so it seemed. He wore some kind of rough brown cassock with an unbleached linen surcoat and a rope belt; with him were two young men in similar robes, but no surcoat.

Tarma had always gotten along fairly well with other clergy, and these folk looked friendly, but harried. The elder of the trio had a frown of worry, and the two younger looked rather harassed. She watched them as she made desultory attempts to bargain with the last of the farmers, a stolid, square fellow, and began to feel sorry for them. It seemed that if it weren't for ill-luck, the three clergymen would have no luck. Their straw bales would not stay stacked, toppling anytime anyone brushed against them. The canvas roof of their stall drooped, threatening to fall at any moment. One of their carthorses had gone lame and wore a poultice on its off-hind foot, and the canvas they had used to cover the hay on the way in had leaked, spoiling half the hay, which had burst its bales and now covered the street and the floor of their stall.

Another customer, more eager to buy than Tarma, engaged the farmer's attention. She made no attempt to regain it; instead, she drifted over to the sagging stall of the clerics.

"Greetings," she said, carefully, for although she got along well with other clergy, sometimes the reverse was not true. This time, however the chiefest of the clerics greeted her with something like harried enthusiasm.

"And to you, Shin'a'in," he replied in the common Trade-tongue. "I hope your fortune this day has been better than ours."

"I cannot see how it could have been worse," she replied, just as the sagging canvas gave way, and the chief cleric dodged out of the way. The two assistants scrambled to prop it back up again, one of them swearing with a most unpriestly set of oaths and tone to his voice. His superior gave him a reproachful look, and the offender flushed with embarrassment, bending quickly to his work. The elder cleric simply sighed.

Tarma shook her head. "Its' hard for the young to adjust," she offered. "Especially under provocation."

The priest only smiled wearily. Very wearily. "We have been experiencing somewhat extreme provocation lately."

As the canvas gave way a second time, this time swatting the poor young men in the side of the head, Tarma bit her lip, torn between sympathy and laughter. "So I see," she replied tactfully. "Ah—have you any grain?"

* * *

Kethry sighed, and told herself to be patient; Tarma never shirked, and if she was late, there was a reason for it. The lot of partnership was to pick up when your partner wasn't there to deal with her share. Tarma had done that in the past for Kethry, and while the sorceress was muscle-sore, hot, and tired, she kept her temper carefully reined in. She simply did the work, and when Tarma finally put in her appearance, the Shin'a'in looked as if she had been through just as much as Kethry. Beads of sweat ran down her temples, bits of hair had escaped from her neat braids and straggled into her eyes. Her shoulders sagged under bags of grain, and she was breathing heavily. "How did you do?" Kethry asked her partner. "I hope your booty was worth the wait."

She had already packed up the tent and both sets of gear; the horses were saddled and bridled and standing ready. Even Warrl was pacing back and forth under the walls, impatient, ready to go. They had planned to get their provisions quickly and be on their way before noon; it was nearly that now, and Kethry could not imagine what had kept Tarma for so long.

"Yes and no," Tamra replied, frowning a little. "I got the grain at a pretty good price, but—Keth, I swear there's a plague of bad luck going around this town! I'd no sooner gotten the grain and my change, than some damn fool upended a cartload of stable-leavings across my path. And from there, things got worse. Everywhere I went, it seemed like there was something blocking the street. I got involved in street brawls, I got trampled by a runaway cart horse—I wound up going halfway to the other side of town to before I could get back to the gate. I caught the bags before they were about to split and managed to save most of the grain, but that meant I had to get new bags. I can't wait to get out of here."

"Well, that makes two of us," Kethry replied, with an eye to the gathering clouds. "With any luck, we can beat this storm."

Tarma stowed the grain bags carefully in their packs. Too carefully, it seemed to Kethry, as if she didn't quite trust the sacks to hold. That seemed odd, but maybe Tarma had gotten spooked by all the misfortune in town. *She* was ready to be out of there; the sooner they got to Kata'shin'a'in, the better.

But it seemed that the plague of bad luck that had struck the town had decided to follow them. Already they were half a day late on their schedule; and when they were too far down the road to turn back, the sky opened up, even though it looked as if it was about to clear.

There was no warning at all; one moment the road was dry, the sun peeked through the clouds—the next, a cold, sleet-laden downpour soaked them to the skin.

There was nowhere to go, no place to shelter from the torrent. There was nothing on either side of the road but fields; fields of cattle that had wisely huddled together, fields of sheep who also huddled in woolly mounds, or empty fields awaiting the farmer's plow. No trees, just hedgerows; no houses, no sheds, not even a single haystack that they might burrow into to escape the rain.

So they rode onward under the lowering sky, onward into the gathering dark.

Kethry was chilled to the bone in the first candlemark, so cold that she couldn't even shiver. She simply bent her head to the rain, which penetrated her clothing and plastered it to her skin. The cape she wore, which had been perfectly waterproof until that day, was not proof against this rain.

Warrl paced at the heel of Tarma's horse, head and tail down, fur plastered against his skin and looking just as miserable as Kethry felt. At least she was riding—poor Warrl splashed along the road, ankle-deep in mud.

And even as she thought that, Hellsbane slipped and slid in the mud—and a moment later, so did Ironheart. Kethry clung to the saddle, dropping the reins to let Ironheart find her own footing; for a heart-stopping moment, she thought that her mount was going to go over, falling on her—

Her heart clenched, her throat closed, and her hands

clutched the saddle-bow. Ironheart scrambled to get her feet under her again; went to her knees—

And rose. Kethry caught her breath again, as her heart fluttered and slowed. Then her heart dropped into her stomach, as the mare staggered and limped.

She dismounted quickly and felt blindly for the mare's rear hock. Sure enough, her probing fingers encountered an ankle already hot and swelling. She looked up from under a dripping curtain of hair to see Tarma doing the same, and shaking her head.

"Lame," her partner said, flatly, when she caught Kethry's eye. "Yours?"

Kethry could only nod glumly.

Just before nightfall, they finally found shelter of a sort. They took refuge in a ruined barn, with just enough of its roof intact to give a place for all five of them to escape the rain. By then, Kethry had more bad news. She was not normally prey to female troubles, but the twisting in her guts and a deep ache just behind her navel told her that this session of moon-days was going to be one of the bad ones. . . .

While Tarma struggled to light a fire, she rummaged in the saddlebags for herbs to ease her cramps. And came up with a sodden mess of paper packets. The seam on the top of the bag had parted, letting water trickle in all during their ride.

Behind her, she heard her partner sneeze.

Sneeze? Tarma? She never—

"Sheka," the Shin'an'in swore, her already harsh voice with a decidedly raspy edge to it. Kethry whirled, alarmed.

A tiny fire smoked and struggled to burn already wet wood, and the face Tarma turned up to her partner was red-eyed and red-nosed. The Shin'a'in sneezed again, convulsively, and sniffed moistly.

"Oh, *hell,*" Kethry swore. "Oh, bloody *hell.*"

Tarma nodded, and coughed.

There was nothing for it; wet and sodden as the herbs were, they were all she and her partner had to take care of their ills and the sprained hocks of their horses. She emptied out the saddlebag, carefully; separated the packets of herbs while Tarma tried to find them something dry to change into and started two pots of water boiling on the fire. Herbs for the poultices went right into the wet bandage; for this, at least, it wouldn't matter that they were soaked. As Tarma bandaged the warsteeds' sprains, she made two sets of tea, blessing her teachers for forcing her to learn how to distinguish herbs by taste.

And, given that everything else had been going wrong, Kethry made very certain that the metal pots were no closer to the flames than they had to be—and that they were quite dissimilar.

Eventually, Tarma found an odd assortment of dry clothing, most of which was ill-suited to the chill of the air. Still, it was dry, and with enough clothing layered on, they might pass the rest of the night a little warmer, if not in comfort.

The tea, as might have been expected, was lukewarm and weak, but it was better than nothing. And meanwhile, Tarma's sneezes and coughs grew more frequent, and Kethry's guts twisted.

They sipped their tea, nibbled the soaked remains of one packet of their travel bread. Neither of them had the heart to check further to see if the rest of their rations had suffered from the leak.

"Cand you casd some kind ob sbell?" Tarma asked miserably. "Healig, or somedig?"

"Not while I've got—cramps," Kethry replied, pausing for the pain to ease. "Anything I do will backfire. I can't hold the concentration."

"Ad I sbose Need wond do anydig, since ids nod life-threadenig?" Tarma sneezed convulsively, and wiped her nose with a leftover bandage-rag.

"That's right. I can't believe this," Kethry said, teeth clenched against a spasm of her stomach. "It's like everything that *could* go wrong *has* gone wrong! It's like we've been cursed—but who would have bothered? And why?"

"Damn ib I doe, Greeneyes," Tarma said thickly. She turned out her purse on the blanket they shared, and a few small copper pieces chinked together. "Ib we ebber get to a town, is this going to be edough to ged more herbs?"

Kethry reached for the coins, and froze, her hand outstretched. There was something there that was not a coin.

"Where did this come from?" she asked, stirring the coins with her fingernail, and turning up something that *looked* like a coin, but wasn't.

It was about the size of a copper-piece, but was bronze, not copper, and inscribed with odd symbols. Tarma looked at it, her expression puzzled.

"Dond know," she replied. "Wid da change, maybe. Wad is id?"

Kethry decided that there was nothing more to lose by picking the thing up, and her jaw clenched. "You *must* have gotten this in with your change," she said, angrily. "From those priests. *This* is why we've been having all this bad luck, dammit! It's a cursed coin; there's a sect of Lurchan that makes these blasted things."

Tarma shook her head, baffled. "I dod unnerstad. Lurchan's a luck-god. Ad those priests were'd ob Lurchan—"

"They make them for Lurchan's followers to distribute to enemies," Kethry replied, realizing that she was adding a headache to her aching guts. "They're—a counterluck talisman. They make anything that can possibly go wrong, do so." She forced down tears; crying wasn't going to help right now, much as she'd like to indulge herself. "Don't think we can just leave it here, either," she continued bitterly. "It'll just show right back up in your pouch. You can't leave it or force it on someone; they have to *take* it from you. Like you did, taking it with the change."

Tarma nodded glumly. "Dow I doe why de priests were habing such trouble," she said. "Hodestly, I dond think they eben dew they had this. Or whad id was, anyway."

"Maybe not," Kethry replied with a sigh. "Probably not. They'd have tried to conceal it, or they'd have gotten it back to the Lurchan-priests. They probably didn't recognize it any more than you did. I guess it was probably just a case of 'friendly fire' getting us."

"Fredly fire idn't. Wad can we do?" Tarma asked plaintively, her eyes watering, blowing her nose on her rag.

"We'll have to get rid of it somehow." Kethry sat back against her packs—but not without first checking, carefully, to make certain that the packs were steady. "It's not going to be easy. Whoever takes it has to want it—and I won't pass this thing off on someone innocent, I just *won't.*"

:Admirable,: Warrl said dryly. *:Stupid, but admirable.:*

Kethry turned on him. "Don't *you* start!" she snarled. "If you want to do something useful, we should reach Ponjee tomorrow morning, help me find someone who deserves this damned thing, then help me think of a way to make him take it!"

Warrl recoiled, his ears flattened, and he blinked at her vehemence. Tarma made a choking sound.

It sounded like a suppressed laugh and Kethry raised an eyebrow. "What's so funny?" she asked.

"You wond like id," Tarma said, still chuckling between blowing her nose and coughing.

"If it's enough to make you laugh—"

"He said, 'Mages be glad I'b a neuder.' "

Kethry blinked slowly, then smiled slowly. No point in getting angry—and besides, she had just thought of something useful.

"Well, Warrl," she said sweetly, "It just occurred to me that these things have a range of about ten furlongs. And we need meat. Now obviously, anything *we* do is doomed to failure—but *you* can go out there and catch us all something outside that range. *Can't* you."

Warrl's ears drooped, and he sighed, but he obediently got up and padded out into the wet and dark.

Tarma held her laughter until he was out of range, then chuckled. "Revenge id sweed," she observed.

"And even a neuter should know better than to annoy a female with an aching gut," Kethry agreed. "Now—let's figure out how to subvert this stupid talisman as much as we can. . . ."

* * *

The rain stopped before dawn; Warrl brought back two rabbits and only dropped them in the mud once. They had decided that the way to deal with the talisman was to make very certain that there were as few opportunities for something to go wrong as possible. Which meant *nothing* could be taken for granted. Everything must be checked and double-checked. They were to check each other and remind each other of things that needed to be done, no matter how annoying it got.

And it got annoying very shortly, yet somehow they both managed to keep their tempers, mostly by reining them in.

The village of Ponjee was not terribly prepossessing. A huddle of mud-and-daub huts around a center square, straddling the road. No inn, but careful inquiries brought the name of someone who sold herbs. Tarma kept the talisman in her pouch and waited outside the village until Kethry was outside of the damn thing's range; the mage bought the herbs they needed without incident, and stowed them in the still-waterproof saddlebag before Tarma brought the thing close again.

As if their attempt to get around its powers angered it, before they had a chance to leave the place, Kethry's blade Need "woke" with a vengeance.

Immediately she had a splitting headache—and as if to make certain that there was no mistake about a female in trouble, the sounds of shrieking and a woman being beaten sounded from the last house in the village.

Kethry had no choice; given the way the sword was reacting—and the pain it was putting her through—she wouldn't even be able to get past that hut without blacking out. If then. Need could be very persistent in seeing that her bearer dealt with the troubles of those women unable to help themselves.

The door was open; right up until the moment they reached it. Then it slammed shut in Tarma's face, and Tarma hit it at a dead run, like a comic in a farce. She bounced off it and landed on her rump in the mud of the street; Kethry, several steps behind, prepared to hit it with her shoulder and ram it open—

But it opened again, just as she reached it, and she staggered across the threshold and into a table laden with dirty pots and pans. The table collapsed, of course, and the pots and pans fell all around her.

By then Tarma was up and through the door. The man who had been—quite clearly—beating his woman, stared at her in amazement as she blundered inside.

And slipped on the mess spilled from the dirty pots. And fell again.

Need had, by now, taken over Kethry; she couldn't stop herself. She was on her feet, sword out—

Overreaction, of course, but that was the talisman's doing; it couldn't stop the sword, so it was making whatever it did be the worst possible response to the situation. And as Kethry realized that, she also realized that it had made certain Need was entirely inflamed, so that it took her over completely.

The man was unarmed and unarmored; it didn't matter. Need struck to kill.

At the last moment, Kethry managed to get enough control back to turn the flat of the blade on the man rather than the edge, and to hold back the blow a little.

It hit him in the head like a club, and he went down without a sound. But, thank the gods, not dead.

The moment her man went down, the woman screamed with outrage.

Kethry couldn't quite make out what she was shrieking; the woman's dialect was so accented and so thick that she didn't get more than one word in five. But the meaning was clear enough— "How dare you bitches hit my man!" She grabbed crockery and anything else she could reach, hurling it and invective at the two of them. Tarma seized a pot-lid to use as a shield; Kethry wasn't so lucky.

That was when the rest of the village decided to get involved.

"Now I know how Leslac feels," Tarma said wearily.

"Leslac doesn't have two battlemares and a *kyree* to hold off the enraged populace while he makes his escape," Kethry replied, blotting at a bruise on her forehead. "*She'enedra,* we have got to get rid of that damned thing. Either that, or we'd better take up living in a cave for a while."

:Your troubles are not yet over,: Warrl cautioned them. *:There is a band of robbers on the road ahead. If you wish to avoid them, we will have to go back to the last crossroads and detour three or four days out of our way.:*

Tarma cursed in three languages—then stopped, as something occurred to her. "Keth—how helpless can you look?"

"Pretty damned—" understanding dawned on the sorceress' face, and she nodded. "Right. *Don't say anything.* I don't know how the curse works except that it doesn't seem to read thoughts. Here—" She unburdened herself of everything except Need and the money pouch, and handed it all to Tarma. "Furface, you follow me on the other side of the hedgerow and call Tarma when the time is right."

Warrl nodded, and wormed his way through a gap in the hedge to the field on the other side. Kethry left her mare with Tarma and trudged on ahead, trying to look as much like a victim as possible.

The road twisted and turned here, and rose and fell as it went over gently rolling hills. Shortly Tarma was out of sight. Kethry might have been worried—except that she was feeling too cold, sore, and generally miserable to bother with something as simple as "worry." Of course, given the way the talisman worked, the robbers would appear at the worst—

Her foot hit a rock, and her ankle turned under her. She yelped with pain—she couldn't help it—and she hit the ground hard enough to add yet more bruises to her already considerable collection.

Her ankle screamed at her. Without a doubt, she'd sprained it, but she felt it gingerly to be sure.

It was already swelling. And she looked up to find herself the focus of five pairs of amused and variously hostile eyes.

" 'Tain't every day a cony drops right inta the snare!" one of them said with a nasty chuckle. "Wot a nice little bunny it is, too!"

The half-formed plan she had made was now in pieces; obviously she wasn't going to be able to run—or even draw the sword. There was only one thing she could do.

She snatched the purse off her belt and flung it at them.

Two or three coins spun out of the open mouth; three of the men scrabbled after them and retrieved them, shoving them into the front of their shirts, while the man who had spoken snatched the purse out of the mud. Kethry heard a warning howl and ducked, hiding her head in her arms.

Warrl vaulted over the hedge and over her; a breath later Tarma and the mares charged up the road and leapt her as well.

The bandits scattered, too taken by surprise to make any kind of a stand. Tarma and Warrl pursued them just long enough to make certain that they weren't going to come back any too quickly.

By then, Kethry had levered herself up out of the muddy road using Need as a crutch, and stood there waiting for them.

Tarma pulled her mare up as Kethry's mount came close enough for the sorceress to pull herself into the saddle. Which she did, with no mishap. Proof enough that the curse was following someone else now.

"That was the last of our money," Tarma said, as Kethry ignored her throbbing ankle in favor of putting as much distance between them and the robbers as she could. "We're going to be spending the rest of the trip sleeping in haystacks and eating half-raw rabbit."

Kethry noticed that her ankle hurt less with every moment—as did her bruises. Need was making up for her misbehavior earlier, it seemed.

And Tarma's nose wasn't red anymore, either.

"Getting the curse to stick on someone else depends on how much you're willing to sacrifice to get rid of it," Kethry pointed out. "I just threw away all our money. The curse is *not* going to come back. And—" she continued "—have you noticed that your cold is gone?"

Tarma blinked in surprise, and sniffed experimentally.

"I think," the Shin'a'in said carefully, "that this is a

wonderful time of the year for camping out. And rabbit is excellent when rare."

Kethry laughed. And after a moment, Tarma joined her. The mares ignored them, continuing down the road at a brisk walk—

With no signs of lameness.

But behind them, Kethry thought perhaps she heard, faintly, the sound of someone cursing.

HEART IN A BOX

by Lynne Armstrong-Jones

Lynne Armstrong-Jones, who by now is well-known to readers of my anthologies, is another of my success stories. She has the kind of persistence that so often is rewarded with success; she met every rejection with a new, and better, manuscript, and now has sold to *Weird Tales* and *Marion Zimmer Bradley's FANTASY Magazine,* among others. I think I had seven of her stories from which to choose for this anthology; and this year instead of wondering if any would be good enough to use, I had to make a final painful decision about which ones I could bear to reject.

She says, "I actually enjoy writing novels, and have finished several, including fantasy, dark fantasy, science fiction, as well as more mundane topics." There will some day, I predict, be happy editors out there; because if there's one thing an editor always wants, it's a writer who can keep up a steady high level of writing . . . somebody on whose work he or she can generally rely to be good, and invariably readable, even if he or she can't use that piece right now. Oh, would that I could be the happy editor to read your first novel! (Hint.)

Lynne calls this story "something a bit lighter"; I found it also to be compellingly suspenseful. Anyway, it's the one I couldn't bear to let go.

Lynne teaches adult education (English) in Ontario, Canada. She comments, "I only hope that the criticisms I give my students will inspire them the way Marion's did me." She and her husband have a six-year-old son and a six-month-old daughter. They also have the "requisite two cats, both now nearly fourteen years old."

"Well, old woman, what *is* it?" demanded the rather large villager, arms folded across his chest.

I was just a girl, a servant; it was not up to me. If it *had* been, the scowl upon the face of the rather large man would have prompted *me* to tell all!

But my mistress only whispered her reply: "It is a box." She motioned to the simple, crude wooden thing upon the small cart.

"I can *see* that!" thundered the large man. "What is *in* the box, old woman?"

I glanced from one to the other, my heart pounding. The villager was a strong man, a rough man, by the look of his crooked nose and callused hands. And my mistress? Small, thin, her unkempt hair nearly white in most places.

Many took her to be a sorceress. She did not bother to either confirm or deny this. And yet I knew that she had been made to suffer, had been made unwelcome in the village because of fears about her "magical powers." Powers which even I had never seen her put to use.

And so it was that I was nervous, hating to see this little, elderly gentlewoman face-to-face with an irate hulk.

"Come now," boomed the villager again, "tell us what it is! The children are frightened. They say you've told them it's something terrible—"

My mistress looked up at the man, searching his brown eyes. "It *is* something terrible. And something wonderful."

The villager's eyes widened, then narrowed. "What trick is this, woman? How could it be both?"

"Yamir! She—she told my boy she has a—a *heart* in there," came a somewhat higher-pitched voice from somewhere behind. It was a trembling voice, its owner clutching her small son to her bosom, as though to protect him. "Drive her out, Yamir! She can't come here with something like *that!*"

"Is this true?" demanded Yamir in a somewhat softer voice; the woman's son was known for telling fancies.

Yet my mistress sought not to deny this accusation. "Do you think it true?" she asked of Yamir.

"A heart?" Yamir hesitated, glancing around him at the crowd. "A *heart?*"

He was quiet a moment, and when he spoke once more, his voice was very soft, indeed. "Tell me, then, old woman, where did you come by this heart? To whom did it belong?"

My mistress replied, equally softly: "It is that of a scourge, a beast—"

"A beast!" Yamir spoke triumphantly, nodding to the crowd. "You see? There is nothing to be alarmed about! Simply the heart of a beast!"

"Yes, yes, a beast," came the murmurs. And the crowd began to thin, some hurrying away while others lingered, almost as though unable to move.

"A beast, a beast," they said, although many still clung to their children as though fearful *they* could somehow end up inside the box.

"A beast," they murmured, almost as though to reassure themselves that this could truly be.

I swallowed—or at least, I tried to, but the lump still made my throat feel thick.

"M–mistress?" I whispered, almost afraid to disturb the sudden quiet.

"Shh," she whispered. "It will not be long, now."

That was what I was afraid of!

And of course, she was right. As she always seemed to be. Perhaps she *was* a sorceress. . . .

The guards found us quickly. It was as my mistress had said it would be; we were to be taken before Lord Pendrake. The Great Lord Pendrake, as he liked to call himself, Ruler of the Three Hills and Beyond.

The citizens, though, had other names for this vile man who'd plundered the area, and taken so much for his own comfort. 'Twas said that he feared only one thing—sorcery. And, as we were led to his great palace, I found myself wondering yet again if my mistress just might be only an ordinary woman. Perhaps an ordinary woman who was just a bit not right in her head.

At any rate, we were led inside the grand palace. The

room in which the Lord awaited us was larger than my mistress' entire abode! That lump seemed to have taken over my entire throat. . . .

There he awaited us, the Great Lord himself. He was reclining on huge, soft pillows, a young and beautiful "companion" on either side of him. At first I thought that he must be a patient man, for he seemed willing to wait forever while one beauty peeled a grape for him. But, oh, how wrong could I be! There was a loud *smack* as he struck her across the mouth; apparently she *had* taken too long.

She shrank back, fingertips trying to stop the bleeding from the corner of her lip. She opened her mouth to speak, tried to apologize, but the Lord dismissed her from the room, and with a wave of his hand, summoned the guard to take her. She screamed as he did so; apparently she was *not* heading toward a pleasant place.

"And so," he began, at last turning toward my mistress and me, where we knelt before him. "And so this is the nameless sorceress. It is said that you have a heart in that box. Tell me; why is it that you would burden yourself with such a strange load?"

His voice certainly *sounded* reasonable, yet still I trembled, his brutality with the woman, and the rumours of other atrocities filling my mind.

How I longed to speak, to tell him that we were sorry for so disturbing him, to beg forgiveness and leave. Yet I would not. For all my concerns and questions about my mistress, I knew her to be intelligent and well-intentioned. I did, despite my uncertainties, trust the woman. And I would hold my peace.

"I burden myself, my lord, for the same reason that anyone would do so. It is for the betterment of our land," replied my mistress humbly.

The lord snorted, raising himself to a sitting position. He shoved aside the remaining woman's fingers as she sought to soothe him. "Tell me, nameless sorceress. I am your Great Lord. What heart is this that you would seek to carry it with you? Is it of man or beast—"

But he stopped himself, sudden understanding lighting

his eyes. "It is a *man's,* then. For no beast's heart would warrant such. Yes?"

"It is both," said my mistress quietly.

"Both!" The Great Lord's voice was no longer so patient. Indeed, it sounded more like distant thunder now. "And how could it be both, bold magician? It could not be so, unless the beast was part-man, or the man a beast—"

He rose now to his feet, advancing toward us where we knelt before his throne. He placed a hand upon the top of the box. "I know what they say of me," he said softly. "Tell me, sorceress. Tell me the truth."

He was so close now. Just in front of the mistress, off to my left. I could smell his perfumed body, the stink of wine upon his breath. I could almost feel the softness of the silks in which they'd dressed him.

I could almost feel the coldness of our deaths as he lost patience with us. And so I closed my eyes and bit my lip. I would do nothing to ruin my mistress' plan . . . whatever it was. . . .

"It belongs to someone horrible, ruthless, who has refused to listen to the needs of his people," whispered my mistress.

There was silence for a moment. I expected to feel a guard's spear in my back. Yet there was nothing . . . nothing save the sighs of the lord.

"You are saying, then, sorceress, that it is *my* heart inside that box." Silence again, then suddenly the Great Lord laughed. "Yet that could not be so, sorceress," he proclaimed loudly, "for my heart is right here."

Both my mistress and I gazed upward to see him strike himself mightily upon the chest.

"*Is* it?" asked my mistress quietly.

"What do you mean, sorceress."

"Is it there, Great Lord? Or did it die when you had Hassim killed for being too slow in carrying out your orders? Did your heart wither and die when you took Riann's daughter and had your way with her, only to cast her aside when you tired of her? Is it still there, Great Lord? Or did it somehow flee your body when you had thirty townspeople whipped and killed for no good reason at all?"

The Great Lord was becoming very angry; this was quite plain. Our moments were numbered for certain! For the tall man was grasping at his silky shirt, as though wanting to feel his heart with his very hand. He was breathing very quickly, and when I stole a glance I could see how very red his face had become.

"You wish to see what is inside the box, Great Lord? Well, I am but your subject, and I will obey your command." My mistress reached her fingers to the handle of the box. "Look inside, Great Lord! Yes, look inside! And see *your own heart!*"

"No!" cried the Great Lord. "No, no, please!"

But the lid was open, and bidden to do so or not, his eyes sought the awesome sight. He screamed once, his hands grasping at his chest. The guards closed in, spears lowered in our direction, but the Great Lord ordered them away. He cast one more look upon my mistress, and tears filled his eyes. He began to babble nonsense, then he fled.

His guards followed him. I was certain that we'd be executed. Yet we were left alone.

"M–mistress," I managed to stammer, my own heart feeling as though it wished to depart, "what—"

"Look for yourself," replied my mistress, a wry grin twisting a corner of her lips.

My hand on my own chest, I peered inside. I struggled for breath; the sight and the foul, rotten stench of the blackened, greenish, moist thing was almost more than I could bear.

"B–but w–what . . . ?"

My mistress chuckled, very softly. "It is the remains of that awful rabbit stew we had for our supper a tenday ago."

She laid a hand upon my shoulder as we stepped to the door. "There are few things in life which are totally without usefulness, my friend."

We stepped outside, into the sunlight, and began to make our way homeward. And, as we walked, I wondered for the hundredth time whether my mistress was truly a sorceress or not. I guess it all depends on what one considers "magic" to be.

DANCE OF DEATH

by Donna Bocian Currie

Donna Bocian (rhymes with "ocean") Currie is a professional writer whose list of fiction and nonfiction sales is impressive, but who is new to *Sword and Sorceress.* "Dance of Death," she says, "is my first acceptance of a fantasy story for publication in an anthology."

I liked this story primarily because Donna has developed the character of a true sorceress in a very small number of words. Every year I reject dozens of what I call "generic sorceresses," about whom I say repetitively in rejection letters, "It's not enough to call a character a sorceress; we must also see her doing something magical or she might as well have stayed home doing the dishes."

Donna, like so many of my writers, says, "I've wanted to be a writer since I realized there was a real person on the other end of all the books I loved to read." She has sold to various "small press publications"—which is not only a good but a terrific place to start. It gets the writer accustomed to actually sitting down, applying the seat of the pants to the chair, and writing. It is interesting to note that one of Donna's credits is a column called "Smashing Writer's Block," which first appeared in *New Writer's Magazine* and is soon to be reprinted in *Gila Queen's Guide to Markets.* If her list of publications is any indication, she has taken her own advice!

Donna says she lives in Chicago with her mutt, Shadow ("I am not a cat person. Cats make me sneeze."), will acquire a husband in August 1992, and, unlike most other writers, doesn't have a novel in progress. But, she adds, "I already have a plot that just might work better as a novel than as the short story it was originally meant to be." Well, Donna, that's how it all starts. . . .

She lies dying, her area of influence shrinking with each passing breath. Now she controls little more than this small stone room, while I can feel my own strength growing. I reach out to the village, to the foot of the mountains, I come back to squeeze the stone room, feel her gasp, watch her eyes widen in recognition, then fade. Her barriers are still strong, I cannot get within, but neither can she move without.

Her frail hands cannot make the signs, her lips cannot croak out the words; only her mind can control, yet that is still strong. She will not let me in.

I have grown up with this woman, born not of her flesh, but of her control. I was given as a child to this old woman, even then beyond childbearing years, to be her student, her slave, and sometimes her tormenter. And now I must seem the crone of death, awaiting her final breath; yet bound to her service, feeding her, tending her fire, caring for her bodily needs as though a mere maidservant. I will not be free of her until she is truly gone from this earth, and I struggle with myself to hasten that end.

A strong brew, a hand at her throat, or a small knife would surely end her mortal life, but before she goes, I want to break that last barrier, get within, and steal all she has not yet given to me.

Yes, she trained me to be a sorceress, after the years of being no more than a maidservant and the years of being an apprentice. I saw those of my age grow up and marry and bear their broods of children while I struggled with the old woman. And now I am old, beyond childbearing years, beyond dreaming of another life, and so I wait.

There were times I wished she had never chosen me, when I rebelled against her teaching. Those years faded, and I began questing for more and more knowledge, even to setting traps for her, hoping to hasten her end and win my freedom from her bondage. She was ever too strong, and even now she struggles.

She looks the old crone now, not wasting her power on the illusion of youth, or even that of graceful old age.

She is bent, sallow, and stinking of death, yet she keeps me out. Her shell is shrinking, she can control little more than a handsbreadth about herself, but her shell is strong.

Weeks ago, she asked for herbs that I refused to collect. She tried to influence others to bring them to her, but I kept them away. She would have stilled her own heartbeat in an instant, and thus eluded my grasp. So now I hold her even as she holds me. I cannot leave her side, I tend to her physical self, all the while attacking her mental barriers.

As much as her physical death would free me from her bondage, her mental defeat would win for me all of her powers, her sorceries, her hidden knowledge. I do not know which I crave more, freedom or power, but as the moments tick away, I know my choice is near. I stroke her throat, knowing that she would not struggle as I cut off her breath. She would go quietly, taking the rest of her secrets with her.

Which would be the better, to know freedom at last, to leave this place without bonds, or to know utter control, complete mastery over this countryside and all of its inhabitants? The struggle within me is almost as great as the lifelong battle for power between us. I wait for her death, knowing that everything I am she gave to me. I should be grateful for what I have, yet I hate her for not giving it all to me.

In the last few years, she devoted herself to teaching me the spells, the herbs, the signs, and the ancient runes that would decipher the many books she owned. She forced the knowledge upon me: days of fasting, sleepless nights, countless hours of intense concentration. Because of her, I have the skills of a sorceress, but even though she is weak and dying, I cannot defeat her.

I watch yet another sunrise as I watch the old woman's power dwindle. It is a thing I can see, an orb of influence that glows around her head, and reaches out to surround her throbbing heart. Cautiously I venture out with my mind to test the orb. It is soft and warm, like a living thing. I squeeze it here and there, looking for a soft spot, testing for even a tiny hole where I might enter before she takes her last gasp.

I feel her probing back, little gnarled fingers pushing back against my thoughts. I feel a tear, and the gnarled hand reaches out. I grasp for the hand, and our fingers entwine a moment just as her eyes dim and her power fades. I feel a moment of dizziness, a double vision, then a strength I never imagined. A voice, not mine, echoes in my head, "You did not learn, we must dance once more."

In the village, a newborn child takes its last breath, its soul flees, the body goes limp. The midwife sets the child down, then starts as the child shudders, takes a breath, and cries. The sign of three stars appears on the child's cheek as she reddens from crying.

I struggle, feeling myself not one, but two. "Bring the child to me," I say, although I know not why. The midwife obeys the distant, unheard command, bundles the child, covering the newborn's head and face with a scarf to avoid seeing the dull gray eyes that stare unseeing. "Without a soul," the midwife tells the mother, and hurriedly delivers the child to my keeping.

I gently touch the three stars, and the child's eyes shift from gray to blue to violet. Again, the double vision. I see the sorceress and I see the child, her eyes suddenly widening in recognition. The sorceress calls for a maidservant to take the child, another to remove the body of the ancient one, now nothing more than ashes and scraps of cloth.

I test my strength, feeling beyond myself, to the one closest to me. The maidservant gasps as I fumble with her thoughts, almost dropping me. She brings warm milk and blankets, and I smile. Yes, this time I might win. Let the dance begin.

EARTH, AIR, FIRE, AND WATER

by Kirsten M. Corby

I am always pleased when a writer tells me I am the first to publish his or her work. This is Kirsten Corby's first published story; I just had to buy it because she grabbed my attention with her very first paragraph and didn't let go of it until the final sentence. A lot happens in a few pages, all of it compelling and interesting. That really is the key—keep the reader so engaged in the story that he or she doesn't come up for air until it's over.

Kirsten Corby is twenty-six and lives in New Orleans with "my boyfriend Sam, black cat Curton, and black-and-white Spike, who is surely the dumbest cat in the world, although one of the cutest. I have worked as a housepainter, a security guard, a tour guide in a museum, a clerk in a medical library and a salesgirl in a gourmet shop although I hate to cook."

Kirsten says, "I am female, just in case there is any doubt." (I know the problem; I still get letters addressed to Mr. Marion Bradley.) "Right now I work in a rock shop." (See? Another writer doing really odd jobs to make ends meet!) "I have a B.A. in history from Louisiana State University." (Well, when I earned my B.A. degree, it was not so important then as it is now; these days, you need some kind of degree to qualify for anything more than fast food service.)

I presume from the quality of her story that Kirsten aspires to professional writing, although she doesn't say so in her letter. If that's true, it's a pleasure to give her her first break; and I hope you enjoy "Earth, Air, Fire, and Water" as much as I did.

It was the dark of the Moon of Gathering-In. The city lay dark and silent as the people barred their doors and quenched their hearthfires to protect themselves from the horrors of this night. Every house, even the meanest hovel, was so sealed, save that one which most had need of it. Here the torches still burned in the sconces and the velvet drapes were open to the night. This was none other than the great House of the royal family, the castle on the high northern hill.

In the castle a tall man stood at a window, studying the empty streets. "Disbelieve all you like," he said, "but She will come at midnight tonight, as She always has."

"Come She may," answered the angry woman who stood behind him, "but I need not entertain Her."

The man made a gusty sound which was part sigh, part tragic laugh. "It is your doom. For every Queen of this city, the demoness Sulkris comes in the seventh year of her reign and takes that which she most loves. It is the bargain the Witch-Queen Aelfret made; the demoness gave you your crown, and you give her your heart's dearest blood."

"No, Tarrin," said Elanor, who was the Queen.

Tarrin moved away from the window. "It is the price all your ancestors paid for their throne. And you shall pay it, too, like the Queen you are."

Elanor paced away from him and twisted her hands in her skirts. "I am not completely defenseless. Let Her challenge me, and I will fight."

Tarrin shook his head. "It would do no good, Majesty. Your magic comes from Sulkris, part of the Witch-Queen's bargain. You cannot defeat the demon with a gift of Her own making. All your spells will avail you nothing."

The Queen clenched her fists. "Then let Her take my gold and jewels. The woolen rugs, and the silk hangings here in my chambers. These are what I love best."

Tarrin laughed sadly. "No, my Queen. You cannot fool the demon with the words of your mouth. Sulkris will take no earthly things from you. She knows what in all the world you love the most, and She will have it."

There was a long silence. "Although it is a secret to all but us, we are pledged, Elanor," Tarrin said at last. "She will have me."

"No, do not speak of it, Tarrin!" Elanor cried. "Be silent!"

"You need not speak of it, for Sulkris to know."

The Queen pressed her hands to cheeks suddenly wet with tears. "I never said I loved you, Tarrin," she whispered.

He gave a melancholy smile. "Nevertheless."

"I tried to send you away, but you would not go!"

"You could send me to the Forgotten Islands, and She would find me yet."

Elanor did not answer. Tarrin looked at the stump of the hour-candle burning itself out on the table. "Behold," he breathed. "Midnight is nearly come."

Elanor stared wildly at the candle. Then, with a strangled sob, she threw herself into her lover's arms. He caught her and held her close. Elanor buried her face in his fine linen shirt. Great sobs racked her.

After a moment, Tarrin released her and held her at arm's length. "Come, Majesty, enough. We have already said our good-byes."

"How can you meet death so calmly?" Elanor cried.

Tarrin gave a wry little smile, but deep inside his eyes were haunted. "Believe me, Elanor, I tried not to love you, but I could not. So be it. When I was knighted I gave my oath, my Queen, to die in your service if need be. It is my honor to fulfill it."

Elanor's heart broke within her at his valor. She barely deserved his love; in no way did she deserve his death. She clenched her hands in her betrothed's shirt, pulling him close.

"I won't let her take you, I won't!" she wept. "I swear it on the Witch-Queen's name!"

Tarrin took her in his arms for a last embrace. "Don't swear oaths you cannot keep," he whispered. "Just swear that you love me."

But Elanor could not swear it, she could not say it aloud, for to do so would be his life. Instead, she left him alone in the splendid room, for the hour of midnight was approaching.

Elanor moved quickly through the corridors of the castle. She was alone; the servants and the courtiers alike hid in darkened rooms, in fear of the demon's coming. She walked toward the castle's Great Hall, with its thick tapestries and ancient coats of arms. The demoness was coming to take her due, but Elanor would meet her in her own hall, on her ancestral throne, and robed as a Queen.

But she was too late. As she went, the bell in the highest tower began to toll the first stroke of midnight. Before the next note could follow, a terrible wind tore down the corridor, whipping the torches to a leaping frenzy, and the very stones of the castle quivered and boomed underfoot like a great brass gong.

The demoness Sulkris had come.

Elanor ran.

She ran to the Great Hall, but whether she was running to her doom or away from it she did not know; she only ran.

The oaken gates to the hall hung askew in their frame, their polished wood scorched and blasted, and the gray stones of the walls were burned and cracked. Beyond, the hall was swollen with light as if it were all afire.

Elanor stepped to the doors and looked in.

At the far end, the ebonwood throne had been knocked full off the dais and lay smashed against the wall. The dais was occupied by two figures, one standing and terrible, the other lying deathlike at its feet.

"Queen Elanor," the first one said. "And so we meet."

The demoness Sulkris had the form of a woman, a woman nine feet tall, with the claws of a bird on hands and feet. Her body burned with orange flame as if she had been drenched in oil. But the burning left her unconsumed, though her skin was blackened and crazed, and her long hair danced in the heat.

"What do you want?" Elanor said.

The demoness laughed, a sound to wake the dead.

"The bargain sealed, Queen. Your heart's desire." She pointed at what lay at her feet. "That."

Elanor moaned. It was Tarrin, plucked from her own chamber, lying stretched out and silent as if on a bier. Whether he was living or dead, Elanor could not tell.

"He lives," the demon said, as if she had snatched the question from Elanor's mind. "No use to take him from you already dead. Who loves a corpse?"

Elanor raised a hand to shield herself from the awful sight of the demon's burning visage. "He means nothing to you, save that through him you can torture me. Let him go!"

The demoness laughed again, and the flames crawled into her mouth. "The bargain, Queen."

"I made no bargain with you!" Elanor shouted.

Sulkris sneered. "Three times seven generations ago did your foremother Aelfret strike a pact with me. She offered up her bloodline for my pleasure, and I made her Queen in this land. So I take from you what you need the most, because it pleases me, and because it is my due. Now, say farewell, O Queen—you shall see neither of us again!"

The flames swelled and rose up from the demon's form. They swirled and licked out, surrounding Tarrin's body. The demon raised her arms.

"No!" Elanor screamed from the depths of her being. She ran forward, into the flames, reaching for Tarrin. The balefires surrounded her, wrapping like snakes around her skin; they seemed to fill her lungs, choking her, burning in her nose and mouth. The demoness shrieked in surprise, while the floor tilted and spun under Elanor's feet.

Then the flames were gone, and the ground firmed again underfoot. Elanor jerked her head up, to stare about her.

They were no longer in the Hall.

The three of them were on a flat and featureless plain. It stretched unchanged and unhindered to an indeterminate horizon. Puffs of gray, dead soil arose and tumbled in a fitful wind. A watery, indeterminate light came from nowhere, yet was all around. There were no plants, no trees, no sun in the sky. There was no sound but the forlorn whistling of the wind.

Elanor put a hand to her mouth, not believing what she had done.

She had come to the demon's place.

She looked down. Tarrin lay at her feet, silent as a stone in the enchanted sleep which lay upon him. Beyond him Sulkris stood, burning still, and laughing.

"A brave deed, Queen," the demoness called, "to throw yourself into my spell. You could have killed yourself, as well as him."

Elanor sank to the ground, aghast that she had put herself so at the demon's mercy. "I have no life without Tarrin," she said wearily. "No matter where you take him, I'll follow. Not earth, air, fire, or water will stop me."

The demoness howled with wicked glee. "A mighty oath, O Queen!" she taunted.

"On Aelfret's name, I swear it!" Elanor said grimly.

"Then prove it!" roared the demoness.

Elanor flinched in surprise. She raised a hand. "What do you mean?" she asked wonderingly.

"I bargained with Aelfret, now I bargain with you. Fulfill your oath, Queen Elanor; cross earth, air, fire, and water for your love, and you may have him back. But fail, and I shall keep him, and Aelfret's Curse shall descend upon your House for three times seven more generations. Choose, woman! Do you deal with me, or no?"

Elanor hesitated. She knew that demons dearly loved to wager, but only when they were quite sure of winning. And how could she cross air for Tarrin—she could not fly. How could she cross fire?

But how could she not?

"I accept your wager, Sulkris," she said.

The demoness crowed with delight. Out of nowhere, a great structure suddenly appeared—a many-spired palace which gleamed even in the dim light as if made of glass: the demon's abode. It seemed to drift in and out of view, first near, then hovering on the ghostly horizon, then close again.

The demon and Tarrin appeared on its steps. The palace slid away into the hazy distance.

"Your first test will be Air," the demon called from very far away. "We will be waiting."

At once a mighty wind blew up from nowhere, whipping wildly across the empty plain, battering Elanor where she stood. The thin gray soil rose up in choking clouds. So stiff was the gale that Elanor could barely stand against it. The wind and the dust half-blinded her, as the wind tore at her hair and clothes, and the gritty dirt clogged her mouth. She crouched down, huddling against the wind, covering her face in the folds of her skirt.

For a moment she cowered there, helpless. But Elanor was not the Witch-Queen's child for nothing. She knew spells, part of her tainted birthright, spells to calm the elements when they threatened the kingdom, or to whip them up to rout the armies of her enemies. Whether they would work in this hell-place she did not know.

But with a whisper and a twist of her hands, she tried. And the magic held. Slowly, spreading her arms out and speaking the spell past the grit in her mouth, she was able to forge a globe of calm air around herself. The dust storm boiled around the edges of it.

Still chanting, Elanor moved forward and the spell moved with her, so that she walked unhindered through the maelstrom. Doggedly, she set out for the demon's palace on the far horizon.

Without warning, she was abruptly at the foot of the steps, as if her spell had also erased the intervening distance. Sulkris, with Tarrin's body, stood above her. Unhesitatingly, Elanor mounted the steps and reached for Tarrin. "Through Air I have come," she told him. But just as her hands touched his chest, he was suddenly not there; Elanor found herself thrust back a vast distance on the empty plain.

The castle was tiny and very far away.

"Well done, Queen." The demon's voice reverberated in the empty air. "But now, face Water!"

The wind stilled. There was a fearful rumbling, and water came boiling up in a hundred places from the dry earth. The separate streams surged together in one great wave which poured across the flat landscape, becoming an instant flash-flood in this terrible desert. Before she could move, the crest hit Elanor and smashed her off her feet. She was carried along by the force of it, as more water continued to gush from the sterile earth.

Elanor let herself be tumbled along by the current, resisting the urge to scramble uselessly for a handhold. With her magic she reached out to the water, searching for its angry spirit. "Ssh," she said, "hush now. No need to be so angry." With her heart and mind she touched the waters.

The flood calmed a little. She felt the ground scrape under her feet. She spread out her hands over the water, gesturing for calmness as if it were a naughty child. And slowly, slowly, the waters calmed and sank as she whispered over them, first standing, then kneeling in the shallows, until at last the water was stilled and bubbled back into the earth.

The test completed, she found herself back at the demon's hall. She stood, and slogged up the steps. She dropped to her knees beside Tarrin. "Through Water I have come," she gasped, and stretched out her hands to her lover. Sulkris gave a fearsome hiss of annoyance, and even as Elanor clutched Tarrin's shirt, she felt it dissolve beneath her hands. She was alone again on the plain.

She gave a scream of pure frustration. Sulkris laughed as if it were a fine jest, and brought forth the third summoning—"Fire!"

Elanor was encircled with a solid wall of flame, burning blue and orange and stinking hellishly of sulphur and blackwater oil. The heat singed her hair and tightened the skin of her face. She could barely look at it, so close it was and so fierce was its light.

She stretched her hands out to it, hoping to calm and dampen it as she had the water. "Lie down," she told the fire.

But Fire was the demoness' element, her special power. And this was no earthly flame, fueled by wood or coal, but a devil-fire burning the power of magic itself. Try as she might, Elanor could not bend it to her will.

Instead, it only burned bluer and hotter under the touch of her power.

For a moment Elanor let weakness overcome her, and she slid to the ground, weeping with fear and hopelessness. As she cowered there, the fire began to move, creeping toward her over the dusty ground.

She turned. Behind her the wall of flame was also advancing. The circle was closing, tightening in on her. If she did not fight it, she would be consumed.

For a moment she still huddled there, terrified. But she could sense that the fire burned only in a thin circle around her, and did not cover the plain. And her clothing was still soaking from her journey through Water.

Elanor stood. Touching her lips and belly in the Earthmother's blessing, she ran forward and jumped through the fiery wall.

She hit and rolled on the other side, screaming and beating at her smoking clothes. The heat of the enchanted fire had dried her sodden garments instantly. The eyebrows were nearly burned off her face.

She was shocked to find herself fetched up against the steps of the wandering palace. She crouched on the cold stones a moment, her eyes dazzled and more than half-blinded by the passage. At last she rose and crept up the stairs.

This time she did not attempt to touch Tarrin. She stood on the top step and croaked, "Through Fire."

And the demon thrust her back down the steps for the final challenge.

When she saw what it was she sat on the ground and whimpered like a lost soul, for she knew she was beaten.

The palace had not moved. It stood before her still, beautiful and unholy. Its front wall was a single pane of unbroken clear glass from end to end. High-arched gates lay open within it.

But the gates were clogged from floor to ceiling with a mountain of dirt. A hundred tons of the dead gray soil lay piled in the doorway in a massive heap, the edges spilling out and down the steps. Not a crack, not an inch of the entrance was left unplugged.

Elanor wept like one of the damned. Earth, she had

thought, would be the easiest passage, but there was no way she could cross this. She could not leap through a mound of solid earth. She knew no spells to move such a quantity of earth, the most inert of all Elements. Removed from contact with the living body of the earth, it would not respond to her coaxing or her commands. And if she dug for nine days and nights, or what passed for days and nights in this place, she would never break through.

The demon's crooked plan was now apparent. Muffled from behind the dirt but still frightfully clear, Sulkris laughed inside her castle. Elanor hid her face in shame at her failure.

"So, Queen, the wager is settled," Sulkris called from within the clotted gates. "You have broken your vow, Majesty. Earth remains uncrossed. I have won."

Elanor raised her head and faced the scene of her defeat; the mountain of earth, surrounded by the clear wall of glass.

And she jumped to her feet.

"Wait!" she cried desperately. "Wait!"

She ran up the steps to the smooth expanse of the glass wall. Taking a deep breath, she ducked her head and threw herself against it.

The glass shattered, and she pitched through and fell heavily on the shards, cutting herself in twenty places. She stood, gingerly brushing glass splinters from her hair.

"Through Earth I have come," she announced.

Sulkris bawled with indignation. "What trickery is this?"

Elanor stooped and picked up a shard. "I came through glass, which is made from sand." She held the shard up. "From Earth."

"No!" bellowed the demon. The flames leapt from her body.

Elanor spoke a Word of Minor Unbinding, and the shard in her hand crumbled into a pile of fine white sand. She let it trickle through her fingers to the floor, to mix with the dirt scattered there.

"Earth," she said.

And the demoness shrieked in absolute fury, for it was plain that the wager was won.

Elanor raised her empty hand and clenched it into a fist. "I have passed through Earth, Air, Fire, and Water. I have won here tonight." She took a step toward the demon, then another. "And by right of victory I claim my prize, and more: I banish you from my keep and my kingdom, on this night and every night, for three times seven generations. Come back in four hundred years," she shouted, "and see who will wager with you then!"

The demoness howled as the binding was laid upon her. The flames from her body flew up in a whirling torrent. They exploded outward, filling the glass hall. They engulfed Elanor.

Elanor blinked. She was back in her own Hall. Sulkris was nowhere to be seen. Before her, Tarrin lay alone on the dais.

Elanor ran to him. This time as she touched him he did not disappear. He roused from his spellbound sleep under her hands.

"Tarrin," she breathed, and the tears made tracks in the dirt on her face.

He blinked once in confusion, then remembrance filled his eyes.

"The demon!" he cried. "The Night of Gathering-In!"

The Queen put her fingers to his lips. "Hush," she said. "Sulkris is gone from this place. I have beaten her, as I swore to you I would."

She waited while he struggled to understand. "And Tarrin . . . ?" she finished.

"What?" he asked wildly. "What, Elanor?"

"I love you," she answered. "I love you, Tarrin, my betrothed."

And she bent to kiss him as he wept to hear those long unspoken words.

FEALTY

by Kati Dougherty

Kati Dougherty begins her biography with a list of vital statistics: she's female; will be 23 in October, 1992; and lives in Bremerton, Washington which is, according to *Money* magazine, America's most livable city in the 1990s. (I don't quite know what *Money*'s standards are—or why anyone would accept them—but it seems believable enough.) This is her first fiction sale, though she has had poetry published, and six of her plays have been performed by a Western Washington University theater group. In her search for permanent employment she has been a receptionist, a newspaper folder, a day-camp counselor, a public relations counselor, and the Easter bunny. (Better that than the Playboy variety, I should think.)

She adds that she bought her first copy of *S&S* in Vienna and her second one in London. (Well, there you are; I didn't get to London until I had nineteen books in print.) It seems that Kati is a travel writer for a local paper, so it all makes sense.

I bought this story because of the skill in the telling: don't make up your mind too soon who's the sorceress.

Crack! The fire popped wickedly, sending shadows dancing madly about the small stone building. Orange-red light glinted off dozens of vials crammed onto narrow shelves. Some, cut of heavy crystal, refracted tiny rainbows onto the high ceiling.

Caytin ignored the colorful dance above her head. A steady drip of sweat ran down her nose; it was the only sign of strain she exhibited. Her hands, encased in thick leather gloves, gripped the tongs firmly. Almost there . . . the blade brightened as the flames of the forge engulfed it. Then, in the space of a breath, it reached the perfect color, a cherry red that glowed from the very core. Murmuring a quiet prayer of thanksgiving, Caytin removed the blade from the fire and lowered it into a wooden barrel of briny water. It would hold.

"I hope I'm not interrupting." Dylas stood hesitantly at the threshold.

"Don't be ridiculous." Caytin rubbed the sweat from her brow and pulled off the heavy gloves. "Come in."

Dylas stepped into the room, seating herself on the wooden stool Caytin pulled forward. "Such hard work and dedication."

Caytin shrugged. "It's what I do."

"Don't be so modest. You do it well. But I still don't understand why you refuse to use your magic. I think it should make your life easier."

"Not necessarily. 'Magic when necessary, hard work always.' "

"Quoting your mother again?"

Caytin smiled. "She was a wise woman."

"Yes, she was." Dylas pondered what Caytin had said. "When *is* magic necessary?"

"When . . . when it's necessary, that's all." She pushed a grimy hand through her short black hair and changed the subject. "Two weeks to Fealty, isn't it? I'm afraid I'm having a hard time adjusting to your new position."

Dylas looked down. "Not half as much as I."

Caytin sobered then, looking at Dylas out of the corner of her eye. The last month had been a hard one for the young princess. Still in mourning for her father, she had been rushed through lesson after lesson after tedious, endless lesson, preparing for the rigors of leading a country. It should have been the work of several years, not several weeks. Caytin knew the strain Dylas was under. It was to her that Dylas escaped, in the evening after High Supper, to complain and gossip and laugh and cry, as she had since childhood.

She looked at Dylas again. The young heir was moving restlessly through the small building. She picked up crystal-cut vials and set them down again, running delicate fingers over the faceted edges. Tendrils of red hair escaped her waist-length braid. Her slight, fragile body belied a bright and solid spirit. Few people took her seriously, even as heir to the throne.

"What are you thinking?" Dylas asked, turning from the overburdened shelves. "You've been very quiet, heartsister."

Caytin smiled. "I could say the same, my twin." The two laughed at the old endearments. At the age of ten, they had sworn the oath of heartsisters, clasping hands solemnly in a dark corner of the smithy. And Caytin's mother had called them the twins since their birth, for as different as the two girls were, they had been born on the same night. A cool, crisp autumn midnight, when the two moons hung low and the wind groaned in sympathy, when two girl-children had first squalled angrily at the world, one from silk sheets, one from a bed of straw.

And the twins they remained, no matter how loudly the court women clucked in disapproval. Caytin looked down her nose at Dylas and grumbled, "Well! Who would have believed it—a smith's daughter, a dirty commoner, calling herself the twin of the princess! That's what comes of women smiths, you know, evil children. Leading the sweet young thing astray! Humph!"

Dylas shook with laughter at Caytin's imitation. "Leading me astray, indeed! I believe I was the one who thought up all those crazy schemes that got us into trouble."

"Oh, fine. Take all the credit."

"Thanks, Caytin." Dylas took Caytin's strong, callused hand between her palms. "You always make me feel better." They sat quietly, holding hands.

It's time, Caytin thought. She turned Dylas' hand over and studied the palm. "Hmm . . ."

"What? What is it?" Dylas snatched her hand away, laughing nervously. "Don't tell me you know palmistry, too?"

"I am a woman of many talents, twin. Swordcraft, metalmagic, Mother taught me much." She eyed Dylas surreptitiously. *Please, oh, please . . .*

Dylas thrust her hand forward imperiously. "Then read my fortune, wise one." She grinned, but sobered at Caytin's solemn look.

"I see much love, here where this line curves. You see?"

"Yes, yes, a tall and handsome stranger, I know. Come now, Caytin, be serious!"

"I am serious. And I don't mean a love that warms your bed or increases your kingdom."

Dylas glanced quizzically at the dark head bent over her hand. "Then what do you mean?"

"Hush. Prophecy is never easily understood. Just listen, and remember what I say." Dylas nodded, and Caytin continued. "I see weights added and lifted, tears shed and laughter shared, danger and safety. And," she shifted imperceptibly, "I see pain."

"Pain? Where?"

A rough finger traced the life line. "Dylas, I'm sorry . . ." Caytin's grip tightened and held the hand imprisoned. With a small, sharp knife she pricked the fleshy part of the palm until blood welled up. Dropping the knife, she picked up a vial from the shelf and squeezed the droplets into it. Then she released Dylas' hand and stoppered the vial.

Dylas clutched her wounded hand to her chest. "Caytin, why?" Her eyes grew wide and she stood so abruptly the stool crashed to the ground. "Oh, Goddess Bright, bloodmagic. You're practicing bloodmagic within the castle keep. That's prohibited! It's evil!" Caytin reached out a hand in supplication, but Dylas slapped it away, shaking with rage and fear. "No! You have betrayed me, heartsister. Don't touch me again." She whirled and escaped the confining smithy.

Caytin squared her shoulders, biting her cheek until she tasted the sweet-salt of blood. "Forgive me," she whispered. "Please, forgive me."

No visitors stopped by the smithy for many days, leaving the small building oddly quiet except for the chink of hammer on metal, late into the night. Dylas was uncommonly silent, but her advisors took it as a sign of nervousness, due to the swiftly approaching Fealty Ceremony.

The line of Oathswearers stretched across the length of the banquet hall and looped back again. Dylas squirmed uncomfortably on the Royal Seat, wincing slightly at the pain in her shoulders. No one could find the aches and tight muscles as well as Caytin; no soft lady-in-waiting could match her strong hands. She straightened and dismissed Caytin from her mind. It did no good to brood over the past.

"M'lady?" The young girl looked frightened; she had the air of a puppy that had been beaten too often and praised too little.

"Yes, dear?" she answered, smiling brightly and making a mental note to speak to the Lord Chamberlain about the treatment of castle servants. As Queen, she definitely had to keep a closer eye on matters at home as well as Outland.

"M'lady, there's another gift fer ya, we seem to 'ave fergotten to give it to ya earlier wi' the rest of 'em." She thrust the small package at Dylas.

"Don't fret. Who could remember everything on Fealty Day?" She smiled again and opened the package. In a bed of cotton nestled a piece of jewelry. Dylas lifted it out, brushing aside clinging strands of cotton.

Thin gold metal was twisted into the shape of an eye. At the pupil lay a deep violet stone, unlike any other precious jewel Dylas had ever seen. It glimmered and cast sparks of light across the royal dais. She looked the package over again. There was no note, nothing to indicate who the gift was from.

"Oh!" gasped the serving girl. "Please put it on."

"How can I resist?" Dylas opened the clasp at the back and fastened it to her ceremonial robes. The surprisingly strong gold held the thick fabric securely. Dylas threw back her shoulders. "Tell the Lord Chamberlain I am ready for the Fealty Ceremony to begin."

The line had dwindled considerably, and the crowds around the feast tables continued to swell. Dylas wished fervently that she could join her subjects in a mug of ale and some roast fowl, but duty called. She sighed and turned her attention to the person standing in front of her. What was his name, Lorci something or other, another one of those hangers-on who had a place in court only due to family title. He stepped forward and bent one knee, crossing his wrists, hands palm-upward, in the ancient gesture of Fealty.

Dylas leaned forward and stretched her hands above his, ready to clasp them in acceptance. Suddenly, the air filled with an angry humming, as if a horde of maddened bees had invaded. Dylas jerked backward as if burned. Lorci stood, glancing around fearfully. A moment later, his eyes rolled upward and he slumped to the floor. A stiletto blade quivered from his chest, both wrists caught in the wicked knife.

A crowd gathered around the dead man. Someone pointed to his fingertips. The force of the blow had driven the pointed fingernails into his chest, and a green ooze now trickled from the points of impact.

Dylas leaned on the Royal Seat, breathing heavily. For the moment, she was forgotten. A shadowy figure peeled away from the wall and approached her side. "Deathwort," it said in a low voice.

"Yes."

"He would have killed you."

"How did you know?" Dylas asked, looking dully at the crowd before her.

"How did you?"

"Caytin, don't play with me. You knew I was in danger, so you killed him." She glanced down. "It was the clasp, wasn't it? Your Fealty gift."

"Yes. The stone is truth-seer. It can sense danger, when placed in a proper setting." Caytin looked away, then took a deep breath. "A setting that is tuned to the wearer with two drops of her blood."

Dylas shivered and plucked at the clasp. "Take it back. I cannot wear bloodmagic. This evil is an abomination."

"No!" Caytin's voice stilled conversation around the body. She glanced up self-consciously, then continued. "No, Dylas, *that* evil was an abomination. That person who tried to poison you on Fealty Day. Without a warning like the clasp, he would have killed you. Look, I wanted to tell you about the clasp, but I knew how you felt about bloodmagic. As I said, Mother taught me many things. Bloodmagic is powerful, but not good or evil. It can be used for both purposes. You know that I would not do magic of evil intent. Dark magic visits upon the one who practices it." She looked at Dylas with a silent plea in her eyes.

"Caytin, I know that you want me to wear the clasp. It is a hard gift for me to accept, no matter the good intentions. But you saved my life today, and for that I will wear it."

"Thank you."

The dead man had been wrapped in black cloth and the Lord Chamberlain was overseeing his removal. Still muttering, the remnants of the Oathswearers line regrouped. Caytin found herself at the head of the line. She knelt at the foot of the Royal Seat and crossed her wrists. Dylas grasped her hands.

"Fealty I swear to you, my Queen and my friend."

"Fealty I accept from you, my subject and my friend."

Their eyes met over the connected hands, and Queen Dylas and Smith Caytin smiled.

HUNT FOR THE QUEEN'S BEAST

by J. M. Cressy

J.M. Cressy replied to my query about other writing sales with "none whatsoever," so I am pleased to present another new discovery. She says, "I never planned on being a writer; I always thought I'd just be an artist." (She's in distinguished company; George Barr, Diana Paxson, and Tanith Lee did the same thing.) "I started writing histories and stories of a fantasy roleplaying campaign I created . . . and got a flood of inspiration for my efforts. The results are: four short stories, an evolving mythic tradition, a system of writing, and a developing language." Yep, I know how that goes.

Her interests include Poekoelan Tjimindie Tulen (an Indonesian form of kung fu—there's a nice exotic interest), the Society for Creative Anachronism, and D & D, to which she adds that she is one of the few female dungeon masters. Ms. Cressy lives in wonderful, rainy Portland, Oregon.

"Hunt for the Queen's Beast" is about the quest of a chieftain's daughter in the Bronze Age of an alternate Britain. J.M. Cressy says, "You are familiar with the word 'sidhe,' I am sure. I use it in the story in place of the almost overused 'elf.' Besides, the story's base is Celtic, not Scandinavian." If you've read my guidelines, you know I never buy stories about elves. Well, almost never; I think you'll see why I liked this one well enough to change my mind.

Broneudwen huddled close to the newly made fire, shivering in the predawn chill. After singing in the sun, she would have to be off, continuing her hunt across these strange, forbidding lands. Far behind lay the lands of her people, the moors of the Traegleoch; what lay ahead, only the Gods knew. Still, her resolve had not weakened, even after a fortnight of travels through these northern wilds. This was good, for the omens of the earth showed still much to come.

Broneudwen broke her fast with traveling cake and garlic. When the halo of dawn appeared on the clear horizon, she set her food aside and rose. She held her arms out, palms facing east, and started the Sunsong, as her people had done in her mother's time, in her greatmother's time, and as they did now far to the south. It was by singing that the sun was given the strength to break free of the Night Sea and travel the blue vault of heaven. And as the first ray of light broke the horizon, Broneudwen's voice rose to a keen, then stopped. The sun was free.

High above a raven croaked; as the bird flew over, Broneudwen saw it made its path east and north. Each morning of her journey Raven had come after the Sunsong to scribe the path for the day. She doubted not the Raven's wisdom. North, then, to the dawn country; so be it.

"Sing you well, for a human," said a cheery voice at Broneudwen's back. Spinning on the turf, hand on the hilt of her bronze sword, she faced the large gray stone that had shadowed her sleep. On it sat a child of no more than seven summers—flaxen haired, pale, and bright eyed. He wore nothing but a short white shift; what was a child doing so far from clan?

"I thank ye for thy courtesy," Broneudwen said. "But are ye not a bit young to be roving the wilds?"

"Hardly," said the child with a gay glint in his eye. "Truly, in years, I am as old as those who bore you."

A breeze ruffled Broneudwen's hair, whipping dark tresses across her face. Brushing them away with impatient fingers, she took note of the child's fine features and deep, bottomless eyes. A nervous hand steadied the metal clip that held most of her chestnut hair as Broneudwen realized this boy was not human.

"Are ye a sprite?" she queried.

"Nay," said the child. "I am Obue of the Sidhe, girl."

"Woman, ye'll find," Broneudwen corrected. "I be a woman at seventeen summers, nary a girl."

"Is that a long time in the reckoning of your people?" Obue asked, his voice light with merriment.

"Do thy people forever live as babes?" Broneudwen retorted indignantly.

"Certainly not," he said. "Else there would be no more babes. But when you are gray and battle scarred, your withered tets hanging low, I shall still be in my youth."

Broneudwen's face burned in dismay. "I have no time for faerie vulgarity," she said, gathering her supplies as she prepared to travel. "As ye are in no need, I'd thank ye to leave my presence."

"Leave?" exclaimed Obue, sliding off the stone. "But I would not think of it. You may need my assistance."

"This be not a festive romp," Broneudwen said, fastening her square plaid cloak about her shoulders. "Besides, I need not the help of a child, especially a rude child."

Broneudwen looked over the grass covered hills before her. In the distance rose a haze, the rising morning mist, she supposed. A light wind from the south billowed the kilt around her knees, urging her forward. She set off, north and east, giving no mind to the sidhe child.

Obue's voice drifted on the wind to Broneudwen's ears. "Not even to find the Queen's Beast?" he said.

Broneudwen stopped in her tracks, turning sharply. "How do ye know of what I seek?" she asked.

"How is it that you seek it?" Obue countered.

"Ye know of it?" she pressed. "Tell me!"

"Perhaps," Obue said, dancing ahead of her. "But why should I share what I know?"

"Ye must desire me to know!" Broneudwen said. "Why else offer me assistance?"

"It is not my desire that is relevant, but the seeker's," Obue replied. "I may help one with the Queen's Beast, but that one must give me good cause."

"Aye, very well. Follow and listen, and I'll tell ye," Broneudwen said. "My sire was chieftain of the clan

Traegleoch, as his mother before him. Two moons past he lay on his deathbed, uncertain whom of my three brothers and I, to name as successor. Then one night Raven came to him in a dream, and, on waking, he decreed that the one of his seed to win the High Queen's Beast would be chieftain after. On his deathbed he spoke thus, and so shall it be."

They walked a way in silence. The haze over the horizon deepened.

"Truly?" asked Obue.

"Aye, truly," Broneudwen replied, fingering the heavy collar of twisted wire around her neck. "See this neckring of gold? It is worn only by those of the chieftain's family."

Now the ground rose sharply into a high slope, beyond which came the calls of strange birds.

"Now would ye tell me the whole of this queen and her beast?" asked Broneudwen.

"Why should I not go to one of your brothers?" Obue queried.

"Pah! One is a glutton, the other a fool."

"And the third?"

"Aye, he gives one pause. He'd take the clan far, but for his own reasons, sparing none. Ice, not blood, runs in that one's veins, and he has a stone for a heart."

They crested the slope and now looked out over a dense fen, covered with a murky haze of rot the sun could never burn off. The marsh lay dead center in the Raven's path, as if this were the chosen task of the day. Now the sun rode high, a good time to start such a venture. Would the child follow? Not that it mattered. Broneudwen's path was clear, and she must keep to it. She started down the slope to the wetlands below.

"Hai!" Obue called after her. "You will traverse the fen?"

"Aye," she replied.

Obue ran up, catching hold of Broneudwen's kilt to stop her. "Be aware, there are many dangers within," he said. "Ages ago, when the Rift shattered the Summer World, many souls were trapped in mortal forms, some fair and others not, according to their natures. Most dwell in wild places, such as this."

"I be a chieftain's daughter," Broneudwen said. "I've no fear of the wilds. What name has this place?"

"No name is known for it," the sidhe answered.

Broneudwen peered into the mists, past matted reeds swaying under dark, gnarled trees. "Be there a path?" she asked.

"None save the one you choose."

"Above, in the branches of a moss hung willow, a raven croaked. Then it took to the air, its flight taking it over the fen and a bit east.

"The path is chosen," she said, setting foot into the marshy lands.

"Then we must tread carefully," said Obue.

With every step, Broneudwen's feet sank into the soft muddy ground, water seeping through her leather shoes. The sun was high, shedding a thin, watery light, but drying nothing; the air was hot and damp. Soon, what few locks had escaped the hair clip were plastered to the sides of Broneudwen's face with moisture. She minded them not, using her hands to push aside reeds and branches. The sidhe seemed to defy the dank mood of the marsh, leaping from tussock to tussock or running on root and branch, jumping from tree to tree. Even his shift had kept most of its whiteness, while Broneudwen's kilt was stained with muck.

"Ye have not yet told me of this queen," she called.

"In due time," Obue said, crouching on a tree limb by her shoulder. They had come to a shallow, murky lake, choked with bracken.

"Come, lad, I've told ye why . . ."

"Shhh," said Obue, a finger on his lips. He swung down from the branch, landing lightly beside her and pointed to the waters.

"Take care," he whispered. "This is the home of a spined eel, a bastard spawn of the water wyrms. They have intelligence but are also cruel."

Broneudwen could not see much in the murky water, but for a moment there might have been a long dark shadow. From somewhere came a soft splash. "Well, it has no cause to trouble me. Neither my clan nor I've any quarrel with it."

"It may need no cause, save that you walk on two legs," said Obue.

"Pah!" exclaimed Broneudwen. "Ye'd have me balk at the mist, if ye had thy way."

The foul pool would be a trial, but that was where the path lay. As Broneudwen stepped into the water, it rose to her knees and her shoes filled with mud. Then something large swam by, brushing the backs of her legs. Startled, she staggered forward deeper into the brown water. A moment later, a sharp finned back arced through the water's surface, passing at least three lengths of a stallion before sinking again. Its wake lapped around Broneudwen's thighs.

"That be an eel?" she yelled, her voice strained with excitement.

"Truly," Obue said. "The spined eel. Have a care; 'tis said the spines are poison." Obue then darted ahead, and, so fast and light of foot or by some faerie trick, he ran on the water's surface until he reached the far side of the lake. There he squatted by the water's edge, cocking his head and listening.

"It is angry," he said. "You must move quickly or do it battle."

Broneudwen drew her sword and started wading through the water, wide eyes alert for any movement in the depths.

"There!" shouted Obue. "Behind you!"

Broneudwen whirled around, splashing in the muddy water. "Where?" she called, seeing nothing but the eel's wake.

Obue's second shout was lost as the creature erupted through the water's surface behind Broneudwen. The force of its rising had blown her cloak over her head so that she staggered blindly in the muddy lake, frantically trying to clear her sight with one hand and flailing futilely with the sword in the other. The force of the creature's body came from the right, almost unbalancing her; she felt her shirt catch and tear on its spines as the eel passed. There was a dull splash, then nothing.

Gasping, Broneudwen finally freed her head of the cloak, in time to catch a glimpse of the eel's form, gray-green and about as thick as her waist. She could see the ragged tear in her shirt; fortune had spared her flesh. The water-logged kilt hung heavy on her hips as she stepped forward; the creature circled her. Again it broke through the water, but now Broneudwen was ready for it. As it arced over her, she thrust her sword into its side, letting it wound itself with the force of its passage. The worm trumpeted in pain, thrashing away, the dark, steaming ichor of its blood foating to the water's surface. There was a sharp pain in her sword hand and she let the blade fall. It did not sink but spun and sputtered on the water like pig fat on a griddle. The creature's blood had the strength to burn sword bronze; after a few heart-beats, the blade had vaporized, its hilt sinking to the lake bottom. Broneudwen cradled her blistered hand, wading to the far bank where Obue stood.

"There be a loss," she said once across. " 'Twas a good blade."

"Only if it were a silver sword could it have withstood the demon's blood," said Obue. He examined her hand, but there was nothing that time would not heal.

"Aye," agreed Broneudwen, "a silver blade would be a boon. My greatfather carried one, a sidhe gift to our clan long ago, but it went with him the last time he traveled north. Neither he nor it was seen again."

Broneudwen then saw the eel's blood had sprayed and scorched her leather shirt; with that, and the ragged tear, it was ruined. "Come," she said, ripping off the useless garment and casting it to the reeds. "I would find comfort if we be free of this place ere dusk."

After several hours, they reached the fen's edge, bordered by a stony hilled ridge. A spring bubbled down a gully, creating a narrow stream that fed the swamp. Before the ridge's foot, straddling the stream, a dead tree stood, barkless and windblasted. On a high branch sat a raven; spying Broneudwen, it cocked its head, croaked, and flew over the ridge.

"It bids us follow," Broneudwen said.

"Then so we must," Obue concurred.

They began climbing the rocky hill. The mud-slimed soles of Broneudwen's shoes slipped on the stones; she had to use both hands and feet to make any progress. There was no break in the ridge, no water cut defile for passage; they would have to hike to the top to see what lay beyond. At last, scraped and weary, Broneudwen crested the ridge. A few grasses grew out of crevasses of windborne soil. Sitting to rest, Broneudwen took a look around.

Back over the fen, the sun was sinking to the horizon, preparing for its nightly dark journey. A heron's cry rose from the lowland mists; above, ragged clouds caught the fire of the setting sun. The ridge ran a great way both north and south, a rock wall cutting off the advance of the fens from the eastern lands. That country was now shadowed in deep blue dusk; directly below was a stony valley opening onto a dim, barren plain. On the valley floor stood an assembly of giants, or so it appeared in the fading light. Broneudwen began her descent into the valley.

After a while, she could pick out an uneven stair of stones, of no design or craft of tribe, but as if the land itself was guiding her to a place of its choosing. In a short time she stood near the valley floor where she found another mystery. Six feet above the valley floor the path ended in a wide shelf of stone set into the hill-side. In its center stood a ring of glass, as tall and broad as a house and open to the sky. It was as smooth and perfect as the rim of a chariot wheel; Broneudwen could not see how it had been fashioned, save by magic. Walking over, she peered within but saw nothing except the stone beneath.

Out over the vale, Broneudwen saw the assembled giants she had fancied were rings of great standing stones, concentric in plan and seven in all, with a small circular field of rocky earth in the center. There a post of wood or iron had been set, and a man-sized object was bound to it, but from where she stood it was hard to tell what it was. Broneudwen's eyes sought the sidhe child in the darkening gloom; finding him perched on a boulder above the glass ring, she asked, "What place be this?"

"It has many names," Obue replied. "Vale of the Ancestors to some, the Queen's Court, to others."

Broneudwen wrinkled her brow. "I do not understand," she said. "I see no barrow and what queen would hold court here?"

"Why, the High Queen, of course," said Obue. "The Queen of Heaven. See how she favors us with her eye?"

Following Obue's gaze, Broneudwen saw, over the far open plain, the pale rim of the rising moon. Obue's voice sounded mocking as he asked her, "You were not, I hope, expecting a mortal queen?"

"I can no more tell what to expect," Broneudwen answered in pique. "Ye might have told me."

"To what end?"

"My mind's peace."

"That, you can't yet afford," Obue cautioned. "The night lies ahead of us. Come, you must go within the circle." Obue then leapt down the rocks, jumped off the stone shelf, and started wending his way through the stones.

"But what of the Queen's Beast?" an exasperated Broneudwen called after him. Getting no reply, she jumped down from the stone and followed the sidhe the best she could.

The stones were twice the height of a man, old and weathered; some had fallen. By the time Broneudwen reached the center field, the first handful of stars dotted the heavens. The earth had been trampled repeatedly by the hooves of a large beast, especially the ground around the post, where Obue now stood. He beckoned her over.

The thick wooden pole was covered with tree runes, carvings of scores and gashes along an inscribed line. Lashed to it, with a wide strip of mantle cloth, was the withered figure of a dead man. He leaned to one side, naked but for the collar of gold around his neck, the shriveled flesh above his hip torn as if by a spear. He had died on his feet, at least. The full moonlight drew

Broneudwen's eyes down. There, in the sandy earth, lay something long and shimmering. Brushing the soil away, Broneudwen saw a sword she had not seen since she was very young. It was like liquid moonlight and perfect in form; as she grasped it, her spirits soared. A wordless song struck her soul and she felt herself merging with all those who had held the sword before her, becoming part of a chapter in a story forgotten to history.

Broneudwen rose suddenly to her feet, and, holding the sword high, saluted the stones and sky. The words she spoke came unbidden: "I, Broneudwen of the Traegleoch, as my greatfather before me, claim this blade for the honor of land and tribe. How answers the earth?"

And a shout rose from the stones as the earth responded: "Hail!"

Broneudwen started, blinking as if waking from a dream. The earth shout still echoed throughout the vale, but now came another sound, a low steady beat as if from a great distant drum.

"It is starting," said Obue. "You must remove your shoes; we are on sacred ground."

"What is starting?" Broneudwen asked sharply, as she unshod her feet. "And what beating is this?"

"The land's heart," Obue replied. "It has been waiting. So has she."

"She? Who?"

Then Broneudwen caught sight of the shelf against the ridge. The moonlight poured through the glass enclosure, and, by stages, revealed a white form within. Quadruped and hooved, she was akin to a horse, but possessing the graceful lines of a deer. Her coat was white as the first snow, hooves the hue of opal, and the mane that flowed from crown to tail was a cascade of sea foam. Two large eyes of indigo reflected the blue twilight; between them a white light shone, as if a star had been set on her brow. She cocked her ears forward, facing the vale expectantly.

"Hai!" Broneudwen crowed, striding forward. "My hunt is over and my dotard brothers beaten. She be mine!"

A small hand grabbed her arm, restraining her with unexpected strength.

"No!" said Obue. "That is not the way. Do you not see? You cannot hold or capture the Queen's Beast; she must be won."

"Won? How?" asked Broneudwen.

"Have you not read the tree runes on the post?"

"I be a warrior, no druid," Broneudwen retorted.

"It says 'by making the Black Bull sacred,' " said Obue. "She is in need. The spell that protects her from His advances also imprisons her in the crystal cage. When the Bull is redeemed, it will be broken." Obue ran to one of the great stones, and with amazing skill and nimbleness, climbed to its top. From there he called, "Stand ready, Broneudwen of Traegleoch; He comes soon!"

Broneudwen felt the drumming of the earth through her feet; its tempo rose. She feels it, too, Broneudwen thought, seeing the Queen's Beast pace agitatedly within her enclosure. The earth beat drummed louder, amplified by the standing stones, echoing in her memory the rites she had witnessed that were part of the life she knew. It was a power dance, calling the Old Ones to join in celebration. Her feet began to move of their own volition, her step matching the earth beat, and she began to See. It was not only the Queen's Beast that suffered, now drumming the ground wildly with her hooves. The land itself had been blasted barren by some force, its vitality sapped and trapped.

An ominous presence, yet unseen, approached.

The earth beat rose again, pushing Broneudwen's body to its limit. But she did not dance alone. As she whirled, circling the post, sword spinning in her hands like quicksilver, all those who had held the blade before her danced with her. The horse beast's hooves struck the stone in her bucking frenzy, matching the pace of Broneudwen's feet in time with the earth's beat. Broneudwen was heedless of the sharp stones, her labored breath, or the sweat that stung her eyes. Her cloak had fallen aside somewhere; it did not matter. To make the Black Bull sacred. . . .

Then the tempo dropped to a faint pulse; Broneudwen stood breathless and trembling. The Beast had also stopped, facing east, her foamed flanks shivering. Turning east herself, Broneudwen saw Him standing at the field's edge.

A bull of great mass, he was as black as night. He had no eyes, only sockets rimmed with fire. Pawing the ground with a hoof, he turned his attention to Broneudwen, who stood between him and his desire. But his desire had twisted, born of a need to possess that which he was not. To make the Black Bull sacred. . . .

The earth beat rose again, and the bull charged. It thundered across the field toward Broneudwen; she stood steady, sword in both hands, blade low and feet braced wide. The bull bore down on her, hoof and heart beating in time, His red gaze meeting her eyes. To make the Black Bull sacred. . . .

As it came on, the sword came up in Broneudwen's hands, flashing in the moonlight. She stepped aside, drawing the blade hard across the throat as it passed. Hot blood sprayed over her as the beast's bellow almost shattered her ears. It crashed into the ground. The flame had gone from its eyes, now mortal and staring white-rimmed as it lay, its life blood flowing to nourish the earth.

Sacrifice.

Broneudwen stood, alone, heady with triumph, thinking of the glory she would achieve when she returned home. Tasting sweet victory, she kicked the dying beast with contempt. Then came a movement faster than the eye and Broneudwen screamed as pain erupted in her belly.

The bull had not been completely spent, and with its last strength it had thrust its head in defiance, goring Broneudwen above her left hip with one horn. Then the bull fell, breathing its last.

Holding her wound, Broneudwen sank to her knees beside the bull.

Blood spilled through her fingers as as her strength ebbed, she fell on her back, gasping in agony. And laying there, staring into the night sky, she understood; it was a blow against pride, not for revenge. The stars wheeled above, circling the moon, the cold light soothing her fading spirit as the darkness of passing closed in. They spun faster, merging with the moonlight, keeping the dark at bay. After an eternity, the pain faded, but the light remained.

Broneudwen blinked. Above, the sky was pale blue and her left side was warm with the rays of the rising sun. But the white light still shone upon her; raising her head, she saw the Queen's Beast standing at her feet. Her brow, too, still shone, but it was dimmed in the sunlight. Patient blue eyes watched her.

Broneudwen sat up, looking at the injury she had thought surely was mortal. A white crescent arc marked the flesh above her hip; she would carry the scar for the rest of her life. To her right lay a great mound of dark earth; the clever eye could even find the form of an ox in its lines. The earth around it was ochre-red, and between the loose stones green shoots had already risen, heralding the first spring in this land for ages.

"She has healed you," a voice behind her said. Looking over, Broneudwen saw the sidhe child, his hair a halo of gold in the dawn light. In his hands he held her cloak, but its colors were changed, the brown now black, still with white threads, but with the edges stained red. He offered it to her, saying, "A chieftain's mantle, stained with the blood of the bull."

She rose and accepted it, wrapping it around her shoulders. Then she picked up the sword, sheathing it. The fate of her shoes she did not know, but it seemed she would not be walking in any case. Broneudwen approached the Queen's Beast.

She was larger than a stallion. Broneudwen held out her hand, not to entice, but in offering of friendship. The Queen's Beast nuzzled her hand in acceptance.

"You have done well," said Obue with a grin.

"Aye," Broneudwen answered. "But not as well as I might have. Now, tell me truly your story, sidhe."

"I was her caretaker before her imprisonment," he said. "Knowing the terms of her freedom, I set myself to ensure only the worthy candidate achieved her. I will miss her, but as she goes with the one of her choosing, I cannot argue. She is called Rhionae."

Rhionae neighed at her name and tossed her head, impatient to leave. In a leap Broneudwen mounted her. From her seat she saw the shattered remains of Rhionae's prison, shards scattered on the stone. Perhaps there, too, lay the remains of her false pride.

" 'Twas a day for learning," Broneudwen said.

"Indeed. And what did you learn?" Obue asked.

"As a chieftain I be able enough, but the Good Chieftain finds strength in compassion, not contempt."

"A lesson your brothers would miss?"

"Perhaps. Will ye ride with me?" Broneudwen asked. "You will be honored greatly for thy comradship."

"I thank you, but my path lies elsewhere at this time," Obue replied. "But be assured, we will meet again."

"Then I thank ye, and, for now, bid ye farewell, Obue of the Sidhe," Broneudwen said.

Above, faithful Raven croaked, flying from the sunrise to the south and home. Carrying Broneudwen, Rhionae cantered to the vale's mouth and onto the plain. Then, turning south, she broke into a gallop that outpaced the wind.

Obue ran a short way with them, stopping on an outcrop that overlooked their passage. He called joyfully after them, saying, "Keep her well, Broneudwen of the Traegleoch, and she will bring you fortune for the rest of the days of your life!"

ROBES

by Patricia Duffy Novak

Patricia Duffy Novak is well known to readers of both the Darkover and *Sword and Sorceress* anthologies, and her work has also appeared in *Marion Zimmer Bradley's FANTASY Magazine.* She is an Associate Professor of Agricultural Economics at Auburn University, and her husband is an Assistant Professor in the same Department. They make their home in Opelika, Alabama with their "charming two-year-old daughter"; indeed, I never met a two-year-old who wasn't charming—it comes with the territory. They also have the statistically mandatory three cats and two dogs.

"Robes," says Patricia, was written "just for the fun of it." And the story, as promised, is a lot of fun to read. Her skillful use of dialogue to bring the characters to life was the selling point for me. But then, Patricia Duffy Novak has never sent me a poor story. (Please note that a poor story is qualitatively different from a good story that I can't use!) Writing fantasy must be a welcome change from the daily rigors of Agricultural Economics. Long may she need the diversion!

Alvyn came down the hill at a run, skittering to a stop inches from Kaitlyn. For a moment, she'd been afraid he was going to plow into her, landing them both in the stream.

"Have you heard?" Alvyn asked. "Morl survived the challenge. He's a wizard now." His dark eyes flashed in excitement, and he was breathing hard from exertion. Sometimes Kaitlyn thought he acted more like a child of ten than the young man of eighteen she knew him to be.

"Come on," he said, gesturing impatiently. "Leave your chores till later. Let's go see him choose his robe."

Kaitlyn set her bucket on the ground. "What color do you think he'll take?"

"Who cares? He survived. That's what matters. He'll be a wizard. Think of it."

Kaitlyn tossed her head and felt her long braid thump against her back. Of course it mattered what color he chose. Only the White robes were worth wearing. If Alvyn weren't such a child at heart he'd know that, too. "I will wear a White robe," she said.

Alvyn shot her a skeptical glance. "Master Fen says no one knows what color robe they will choose until *after* they've survived the test. Now come on or we'll miss the ceremony."

Without further argument, she followed Alvyn up the hill and into the old stone castle everyone called Wizards' Keep. But silently she told herself that Master Fen was wrong. She'd known from the day she'd been accepted into the Keep that she would become a White Wizard, one who fed on power from the forces of Good. Not for her the Red of Passion or the Blue of Dark Illusion. And never, no never, the Gray robes. The Gray of the neutral forces, a power that was neither Good nor Evil, but simply power.

When she and Alvyn reached the audience hall of the castle, the room was already nearly full. Masters in their wonderful billowing robes of shiny silk—White, Gray, Red, and Blue—occupied the places nearest the hearth. Next came the younger wizards in more modest cotton robes of the same colors. Finally, apprentices in their green tunics and brown breeches crowded behind. Alvyn and Kaitlyn took their places among these last.

"Look," Alvyn whispered. "There's Morl." He pointed to the dais in front of the room, where a young man stood. "Do you think he looks any different?"

Kaitlyn craned her neck, trying to see Morl's face. "He looks tired and kind of sad."

"Don't be silly, Kaitlyn. He's a wizard now. Why should he be sad?"

She shrugged. Odd that she and Alvyn should be such

friends. They never agreed on anything. But they'd come to the Keep on the same day, two frightened children, and a bond had been forged between them, in spite of their differences.

"Look," Alvyn said, his voice rising in excitement. "It's Master Fen with the robes!"

And indeed the White-robed old mage had appeared on the dais, holding in his arms a colorful stack of neatly folded cotton robes. Kaitlyn saw Morl look up and nod silently. But if words were exchanged between the old Master and his former pupil, they were spoken too softly to carry to the back of the room.

As Master Fen extended his arms, a random ray of light from one of the room's narrow windows fell upon the top robe, the White one, and it seemed to gleam with power. Surely, Kaitlyn thought, this was a sign. Morl could not help but choose the White path. And she saw, with a feeling of satisfaction, that his hand did indeed come to rest on the White robe.

Came to rest, and passed on. He chose the Red, pulling the scarlet robe gently from the pile, slipping it about his shoulders, fastening it around his neck as if he'd been born to wear that color.

"No." Kaitlyn must have spoken aloud because Alvyn gave her a sharp poke in the ribs with his elbow.

"Hush," he said.

"But the Red—" Kaitlyn shuddered. "Drawing power from lust and greed, all the nasty vices and passions." She shook her head vigorously, then sighed. "But I suppose it's better than the Blue, or—" She shuddered again. "—the Gray."

Alvyn frowned. "What's with you lately, Kaitlyn? Acting so weird about those White robes. Power is power, and Morl's a wizard now. There'll be ginger beer and cake in the dining hall. Fix that long face of yours into a smile, and let's go celebrate."

"No." She shook her head. "You go without me."

He rolled his eyes. "Suit yourself, Miss Better than Everyone. I'll have your share."

With that, he turned his back on Kaitlyn and wound his way through the crowd. She could just make out the back of his head as he bobbed around a corner, his compact form nearly hidden in a crowd of fellow apprentices. Fine. Let him go and swill beer and stuff himself with cake. She didn't feel like celebrating. Morl had been a friend; she felt his selection of the Red path as a personal betrayal.

She left the hall and went outside, back to the stream and her abandoned bucket. But she didn't feel like hauling water, either. Instead she seated herself on a protruding tree root and slumped forward, staring blindly into the water, head cupped in her hands.

"Missing the party?"

She looked up, startled, her heart thudding hard against her ribs. She'd thought she was alone. "Master Fen," she gasped. Then, recovering herself, "Excuse me, Sir. I wasn't expecting anyone."

"So I see." His kind old face creased into a smile. "But why aren't you inside with the others? This is a joyous time. Today a new wizard has been initiated. And I thought Morl was your friend."

"He is. Or he was." She turned her face away and locked her arms across her breast.

"Is something the matter, child?"

She glanced obliquely at Master Fen, at the tall old man in the flowing robe of purest White. Surely, such a one as Master Fen, advanced in wisdom, deep into the White way, could not rejoice in Morl's selection of the Red robe. And yet the old man had seemed genuinely pleased for Morl.

"I don't understand," she said. "The Red robe. Passion's way." She swallowed. Master Fen was her favorite of the Masters, but she was questioning one of the fundamental premises upon which the Order of Wizards was founded: that each way to power was different, but all were equal. No way was preferred to another.

"The White robes," she finally managed to say. "I wanted him to choose White." She hung her head.

"Ah," said Master Fen. "You think the White way is better than the Red?"

His words were gentle, and his face, when she dared to look at him, was full of warm concern. She nodded.

Master Fen shook his head slightly. "You are mistaken, child. Each way has its own dangers, its own rewards. In the test, each candidate learns his own strengths—and failings. If you choose a path you are not able to walk, your destruction will be quick and merciless."

He was telling her nothing she had not already heard. But the White wizards must surely be the best, the truest, the purest mages. The others—the Reds, Blues, and Grays—they were the ones with flaws, with failings that kept them on the lesser roads. The Masters could say whatever they liked about the other colors, Kaitlyn could divine the truth for herself.

"Yes, Master Fen." Her words sounded hollow, even to her own ears.

"Ah, child," Master Fen said softly. "Things are not as simple as you believe. But you will learn. In time you will learn." He nodded and turned away, walking up the path toward the castle. Kaitlyn watched him, her eyes riveted on the flowing White robe that fluttered softly in the breeze. The robe that spoke to Kaitlyn of the Good powers, of the clear conscience and the kind heart.

She would have a robe that color or she would not be a wizard at all.

On the third day after his initiation, Morl left the Keep to take his place in the world. Kaitlyn and Alvyn stood on one of the castle's long balconies, watching, as the young wizard set off down the road alone. They'd been sent up there to sweep away the acorns that had fallen from the branches of an enormous oak, but they'd dropped their brooms to watch in fascination as Morl emerged from the castle's main door. They'd known he was leaving; he'd made the official farewells the night before.

Alvyn leaned over the wall, an envious expression on his face. "The world," he said. "The wide, wide world. And Morl a wizard in it!"

"So," Kaitlyn said. "Is that what you're planning to do? To leave the Keep as an initiate instead of staying here and continuing your studies?"

He turned to face her, resting his elbows on the wall.

"Maybe. I mean, there's plenty of time to come back for more study later. Why not have some adventure? Some excitement?"

"Hmmph." She didn't try to mask her disapproval.

"Look, Kaitlyn," Alvyn said. "There's more than one way to become a Master. You act as if you know it all. And you don't. Master Fen says we cannot know our own hearts until we survive the test."

She felt her shoulders stiffen, but there was no point in arguing with Alvyn. He refused to listen.

"Look at Morl," Alvyn said, with a mischievous gleam in his eyes, "off to seek adventure, to apply what he knows in the world beyond this Keep. And the Red way is an interesting one. Feeding on passion, on the strongest human emotions."

"And I suppose that's what you want," Kaitlyn said, goaded into arguing, even though she knew that's what Alvyn wanted. "Red robes, indeed."

"I don't know," Alvyn said, becoming more serious. "The Blue is interesting, too. The Dark way. The power of night and illusion. I might like that."

"Oh, you would, would you? Maybe you'll be a Gray wizard. That would suit you, since you don't have any moral convictions of your own!"

He was laughing; she could sense it, although he had covered his mouth with his hand. "Oh, Kaitlyn. It's so easy to get you angry. With that temper, I don't doubt you'll end up in Red robes, just like Morl."

She picked up a small acorn and lobbed it at him. The acorn hit his chest with a satisfying "plink," but he only laughed harder. She picked up her broom and started to sweep.

The summons came when they were at lessons with Master Davida—both Alvyn and Kaitlyn to report to Master Fen at once. The two apprentices exchanged nervous glances, wondering if they had done something wrong. But Davida's voice was gentle and reassuring as she bade them go.

As she and Alvyn left the room, Kaitlyn was acutely aware of the glances of the half-dozen apprentices who remained behind, their interest in Fire Magic momentarily overshadowed by this unusual development. Two students summoned to Master Fen.

If Kaitlyn had been summoned alone—or if the order had come for Alvyn instead—she would have guessed the purpose. The great test.

It had happened that way with Morl. One moment he had been seated at the long table, one apprentice among many in the Earth Magic class, and the next time she'd seen him he was in the audience hall, selecting his robe.

But she and Alvyn together? Her stomach tightened. Was something wrong? She could think of nothing, no mischief they had caused. Unless there was something Alvyn had done alone that she was being blamed for, too. She couldn't rule out the possibility of Alvyn pulling some idiotic prank—as he'd done many times before. She shuddered inwardly as she recalled that awful incident with the frogs.

As they stood in the hallway outside Master Fen's suite of rooms, Kaitlyn shot Alvyn a heated glance. "So help me, Alvyn," she said. "I'll kill you if you've done something to get us thrown out of school."

"What are you complaining about now? I haven't done anything. And you don't find me accusing you of getting us in trouble, do you?"

She shook her head, feeling mild chagrin. Whatever was coming, Alvyn was her friend, and she shouldn't turn on him. He was right about that. "Sorry," she said.

"Forgiven." He flashed a grin.

A door swung open. "Come in. Come in, children," said Master Fen, his expression warm and welcoming. At the sight of him, the cramp in Kaitlyn's belly eased. He was clearly not angry.

He ushered them into his private study, got them seated comfortably on a small couch, and then took his own place in the large chair in the corner of the room. "Well," he said. "It's time. Your apprenticeships are over. Time to take the tests."

"Together?" Alvyn's face had a comically quizzical look.

Master Fen smiled. "You will take the test at the same

time, yes, because I judge you both ready. Not so very unusual, given that you started your studies on the same day and have both been excellent pupils. Odd perhaps, but not unheard of."

Master Fen's face became more serious. "But you will each be alone. That is the nature of the test. Even sitting in a room full of other students, an apprentice taking the test would still be all alone."

He tapped his forehead. "The test is here. Inside."

Kaitlyn listened eagerly. The nature of the test itself had always been a secret. She knew that it was dangerous, that she could die or go mad in the process. And she knew that the test would reveal the true source of her own gifts. But she knew nothing of the process.

"Now," Master Fen said. "The first part of the test is easy. We will learn what powers you can summon. One or two of the ways will probably be closed to each of you. To summon a particular power, you must have an affinity, a special talent, a bond. Most of our students are able to summon three of the powers. Almost no one is able to call all four."

He reached into a pocket of his robe and pulled forth a handful of stones—White, Red, Blue, and Gray—dull, lifeless things that seemed to lie sullenly on his open palm.

"You first, Kaitlyn," Master Fen said. "Look at the stones and use the magic Davida taught you to make them glow with inner fire."

"All right." Kaitlyn closed her eyes, holding the image of the stones in her mind. White, Red, and Gray she lighted, but the forth stone, the Blue, stayed stubbornly cold.

"Very good," Master Fen said. "The Blue way is closed to you, Kaitlyn." He smiled gently. "But I had expected as much. You have never shown much respect for the Dark powers."

He spoke kindly, but she heard the reproach in his words. She felt a momentary surge of regret—perhaps she should have tried to be more open minded—but overall she felt a great relief. The White way had not been barred. If she could summon the power of Good, nothing, she thought, could keep her from her goal of wearing a White robe.

"Now you, Alvyn." Master Fen turned his attention away from Kaitlyn, who watched with curiosity as Alvyn lighted the stones—White, Blue, and Gray. This time, the Red remained dark.

A vague look of disappointment crossed Alvyn's face. He hadn't been kidding then about the Red robes, Kaitlyn thought with disgust. Well, he'd be more than welcome to her power in that area, but she knew of no way to give it to him.

Master Fen was nodding. "Good. Good. But now the hard part of the test begins. You must learn how to know yourselves. To understand what you are and what you might become. Three paths lie before each of you, but only one will bring you wisdom. The other paths will bring you doom."

Master Fen folded his hand across his chest and leaned back in his chair. "In the old days, before the test was developed, wizards chose their paths at will, using whichever of the Powers they believed themselves to prefer. That way lay madness and destruction. Wizards set themselves up as gods wielding power without control. The world would not long have survived had not the High Council intervened, developing the test, demanding it of every apprentice who would wear the robes of initiate."

He paused, studying them for a moment before continuing. "You, Kaitlyn, and you, Alvyn, have sworn to obey the Council's laws and have signed your oaths in your own blood. You will die if you willingly break your oath. But that is not enough. The power is not a tool, to be wielded at will. The power flows through a wizard, channeled, directed, but never held, never fully contained. Choose the wrong way, and the power will eventually control you, stripping you of your will. This we cannot allow. The test reveals the weaknesses of your souls, showing you the one true path. Your oath then prevents you from treading any others."

He shook his head gently as he studied them. "So young," he said. "And the test is not without risks. There are those who cannot endure to see their true souls revealed. Madness and death have resulted. Those risks are known."

Alvyn and Kaitlyn nodded. Most of the initiates survived the ordeal, but once, five years ago, shortly after Kaitlyn and Alvyn had come to the Keep, a young woman had died during the test. The apprentices still talked about it.

"Now, go," Master Fen said. "And rest yourselves. Tonight you are excused from all duties. In the morning, report to me." He rose, smiling again, as he ushered them from the room.

But in the morning, Kaitlyn did not feel rested at all, having spent the greater part of the night lying awake in bed. Even Alvyn looked grim, his customary good humor notably absent.

"Kaitlyn," he said as they once again waited in the corridor outside Master Fen's suite. "I just want you to know you've been a good friend. In case anything happens, I want you to know how much you've meant to me."

More than anything else, Alvyn's sudden seriousness made Kaitlyn acutely aware of the risks they were about to take. She took his hand and squeezed it. "We'll be all right," she said. "I know it. And tonight we will be wizards." *In White robes*, she added silently. Or at least her own would be White. Alvyn would no doubt pick another color just to spite her.

Once again the door opened to reveal Master Fen, who led them to his private study. This time, he gave them goblets full of clear liquid. When Kaitlyn held it to her lips, she nearly gagged from the smell of it—like corn liquor, only stronger, and with a pungent undertone. "Drink up," said Master Fen. "It tastes better than it smells."

Kaitlyn would have disputed that claim, but the liquid took effect too quickly. She had barely time to grimace and say "ugh," before she felt a horrible sensation in the pit of her stomach. At the same time, her vision faded so that all she could see was a dull gray mist. She felt as if she were spinning drunkenly in a void, her body bobbing and floating on a cold wind.

Kaitlyn. A voice in the darkness. Whose voice? Not her own. Not Alvyn's. Not Master Fen's.

Kaitlyn, take the path.

Her vision seemed to clear; at her feet she saw it: the White road. The path led cleanly through the darkness. She took one step and then another and more and more, until she was almost running. At the horizon, a tower appeared, an enormous building of gleaming white marble. But the sun that shone upon the tower was hard and cold, blindingly bright, but not warm. And the grass around the tower's base was brown and dead. No birds sang in the branches of the bare trees.

Kaitlyn approached the tower and, finding the main door wide open, let herself in.

There was a woman inside. The woman's face was vaguely familiar, but Kaitlyn could put no name to her. The woman was tall and slender, built much like Kaitlyn herself, but this other woman was regal and haughty, her face a mask of cold arrogance.

"I am Kaitlyn," said the woman. "All this is mine."

The last of the three visions faded into mists. Kaitlyn blinked, becoming aware of the world around her. She was alive. That much was clear. And if she was mad, she was not yet aware of it. The room was as she remembered it. Master Fen in his chair. Alvyn beside her on the couch. Alvyn's fingers were still clutched about the stem of his empty goblet and his eyes were fixed in a vacant stare.

"You have returned," Master Fen said to Kaitlyn. "I am pleased. Have you chosen your way?"

She said nothing. Her heart felt heavy, like lead.

"All roads are honorable," Master Fen said softly.

"I failed."

"No, child. You would have failed. Now you will not. Your robes will not be White, but you will be honored as one of the greatest wizards who ever lived. That much I, too, have seen."

She felt a hot fullness across her eyes and then the

coolness of tears on her cheeks. "Proud," she said. "I was so proud and terrible. A monster."

"That wasn't you, child. Only what could have been."

She wiped her face against her arm and blinked back the rest of her tears. "But I swore I would wear the White robes or none."

"That was your pride speaking, not your heart. And you have seen where your pride would take you."

She lowered her head. "I will wear the Gray." Each word stabbed like a knife in her heart. Even the Red way was barred to her, although that vision had not been as dreadful as what she had encountered along the White path.

She looked at Alvyn, still lost in the world of his mind. His face was drawn and haggard, and beads of sweat were erupting on his brow. Kaitlyn felt a rush of concern that took her mind off her own problems. "Will he be all right?"

Master Fen nodded. "He's coming to himself now. We shall see."

Alvyn let out a long shuddering breath. "Gods," he said. "Gods." An abrupt movement of his hand sent the goblet tumbling to the floor. Kaitlyn winced at the sound, but Master Fen smiled tolerantly.

"Welcome back among us, little brother," Master Fen said. "You have chosen your way?"

Alvyn nodded. "I have." His face was set in grim lines.

Master Fen smiled. "Then we will call the others to the audience hall. A most joyous occasion! Two new wizards at once."

As they followed the old Master down the long corridor, Kaitlyn and Alvyn were careful to avoid each other's eyes. Kaitlyn found herself wondering what visions Alvyn had seen. Try as she might, she could not imagine him having a vision anything like her own. She could not picture Alvyn as a self-righteous and power-mad monster, invoking the ideals of Goodness and Purity as justification for destroying everyone and everything in his path. But whatever vision he had seen, it had obviously upset him deeply. He was still breathing hard and his hands were shaking.

When the crowd was assembled, she and Alvyn stood with Master Fen on the dais. When he gave the signal, Kaitlyn took the Gray robe from the pile in his arms and tossed it about her shoulders. She felt her face flame as she did this, imagining the others would know her disgrace, but she heard nothing but a mild murmur of approval from the crowd.

Then it was Alvyn's turn. He bowed his head and stood silent for a moment, as if conquering some remaining doubts. Then, with a quick motion, he plucked one robe from the stack. The White robe. The way of Good.

Kaitlyn felt her jaw drop. Alvyn, the irreverent and carefree Alvyn, to be a White wizard. She would have cried if she weren't the object of public interest. Instead, she forced herself to smile at the well-wishers who were now flooding towards her.

Somehow, she got herself through the next hour, walking to the dining hall, drinking a glass of ginger beer, enduring the congratulations of wizards and apprentices alike. Alvyn was kept busy in his own corner of the room, surrounded by a crowd of young men who were laughing and toasting him vigorously. But Kaitlyn thought the smile on Alvyn's face looked as forced as her own.

When she could break away, she went outside, down to her favorite spot beside the stream. As she seated herself on the bank, the Gray robe wound around her legs, an unfamiliar but not uncomfortable presence. She supposed she would get used to it in time.

"Can I join you?"

She looked up, not really startled. She'd been half-expecting Alvyn to seek her sometime, if only to tell her good-bye. And the thought of saying good-bye to Alvyn made her heart ache all the more. As much as he annoyed her sometimes, she had difficulty imagining not having him around.

He sat without waiting for an answer and stared into the water. "Awful, wasn't it?" he finally said.

She had no need to ask him what he meant. "Yes."

"Want to talk about it?"

"No."

"Well, I do." He shifted forward, leaning his arms on his knees and letting his White robe pool on the ground. "The Blue way," he said. "That was the worst vision. I was drunk on the Darkness, dissipated, a bloated spider of a man." He shuddered. "The worst of it was, left to my own devices, that's the way I would have chosen. I mean, I didn't really care all that much what path I took, but I thought the Blue would be most interesting." He shuddered again. "It was interesting, all right. So interesting, I can hardly bear to think about it."

"And I was drunk on pride," she said softly. "Self-righteous. Cruel." She stopped. "I really don't want to talk about it."

He picked up a small stone and tossed it in the water. "But we're all right now. The test saved us, didn't it?"

"I guess."

"I mean, look at me. I'm a wizard." He sat up and grinned, his customary humor flashing in his eyes. "And a White wizard at that! Who'd have dreamed it? People expect the White wizards to be so holy and sanctimonious. If they only knew."

"But in the test, didn't you find out that you really *are* holy and good. Why else would you get the White robe?"

He started to laugh. "Oh, come on, Kaitlyn. Haven't you figured it out yet? The power of Good is the only power I'm not attracted to strongly enough to be corrupted by! Even the Gray power had enough wickedness in it to get me in trouble. Now, you—" He leveled a finger at her. "You can't have a White robe because you wanted one so badly."

She stared at him for a moment, finally understanding what Master Fen had tried to tell her all along. "Oh."

He poked her lightly in the ribs. "See? I told you you didn't know everything."

In spite of herself, she smiled. Alvyn in a White robe. Her in the Gray. The whole situation was funny, really, now that she could think about it clearly. "So what now?" she asked. "Are you off to seek adventure?"

"I guess. I suppose you'll stay here and study?"

She shook her head.

Alvyn raised a brow. "What? I thought you'd made up your mind."

"Well—" She sighed. "I used to think that was the best way. But I was wrong about the robes. And I was probably wrong about other things, too."

Alvyn's face lit up with a broad smile. "Kaitlyn wrong? Signs and wonders! That I would live to see the day!" His smile flattened to a grin. "But I'm glad you've decided to venture out in the world. I've gotten used to you. I hate to admit it, but I would have missed you. I'd almost decided to stay here myself, if you wouldn't come with me."

"What makes you think I'm going with you?"

"But of course you are." The last trace of his smile disappeared. "Aren't you?"

Now it was her turn to smile. The look of distress on Alvyn's face was so uncustomary, it was almost comic. "Oh, why not," she said. "Someone has to keep you in line."

His smile returned, broad and bright. "The world," he said, flinging his arms wide as if to embrace it. "The wide world. And me a wizard in it. Can you imagine?"

"Only too well," said Kaitlyn, remembering those frogs. A plague of them in the girls' dormitory. "Only too well."

BONDS OF LIGHT

by Vera Nazarian

Vera Nazarian submitted this story to me last year, but I thought it was too long and over-written. So she tightened it up, and this year I bought it. I usually don't encourage resubmissions; but I really wanted a story by Vera for this tenth *Sword and Sorceress* anthology. When I bought her first story in 1984, Vera was still in high school, and she's been getting better ever since. She's one of my success stories; and no, I never get tired of saying that!

She works for a major computer printer company in Santa Monica, California, being paid to "do technical writing, program and operate a Voice Automated system, program a LAN-based hypertext infobase, open up computers and printers and swap hardware, and do a whole lot of other crazy stuff." She also does customer support, which tries her patience on the best of days. She writes whenever she's not at her computer job, complaining that, "Basically I have no life."

She adds, "I still have all those cats (7) and a BIG dog named Marta. And I'll be turning 26 on this Memorial Day, May 25, 1992. Time flies, doesn't it?" Indeed, Vera; don't remind me!

What I noticed about "Bonds of Light," was that the colorful, strong writing style that Vera has worked on for years has come to full fruition—it doesn't get in the way of the story. And the story itself is beautiful.

This is a tale of myth and madness, of prophecies fulfilled and unfulfilled, and of hands white and fine like silver. The hands belong to the seventh son of the West Emperor, the one given the name Erester which in that tongue means "light," while some say it also means "destruction," and a curse of uncontainable power upon the imperial line. With those white hands he was known to harness light, to hold it and wield it, like one who would mold a thing of the earth. And because of these hands, these hands cursed with light, some said, Erester the seventh son—who was really half mad—would speak prophecy.

The West Emperor lay dying, having himself long ago prophesied his death moment—for such knowledge was in the blood of this imperial line. And he called his seven sons to him, to declare his successor.

Long he held each of his sons' two hands in his wrinkled own—once also pale and silver—and at last his hands came to clasp those of Erester. The other six sons looked on, some with haughty wounded hearts, others with knowing humility, and one, the oldest, with righteous anger. Many had been hoping to the last. Yet it was no surprise to any as to the final outcome.

"Things have come full circle . . ." breathed the old Emperor, his breath and voice issuing as though out of the deep faults of the earth, the final crypt. With trembling fingers he removed a seal-ring from his hand and placed it in the hands of his seventh son. "Take this, and let this help you know the truth that will emerge from madness. There must be no conflict between the seven of you. . . . You, Erester, you will be the one. My child of light. You, with the doe-eyes of the innocent. And yet, it is not all complete. Promise me . . . one thing. There is a woman, who even now comes to you, from the solar plexus of the East. She comes to you in state, for I had called upon her thus. . . . She comes to wed you. You must now consent to have her. Speak!"

The seventh son lifted his onyx eyes, filled with *otherness,* wildness, and yet gentle wisdom. "Why, Father? Why must I take this—queen of queens—this woman? I cannot consent until you tell me why."

"And I cannot tell you why. Only that . . . things must come full circle. Trust my wisdom and agree to this thing. Quickly now, for I have very little strength left. . . ."

A slowly blooming star of defiance came to the unearthly eyes of Erester, but he was wise indeed. Averting his gaze he spoke: "This wedding, Father. It must not be. And yet, only because I respect Thy Wisdom, Lord, I . . . consent."

Those words were the last the old West Emperor heard on this earthly plane.

Arirante rode a stallion hued like silver. Its trappings were precious leather and gold, and pearl-drops of opal and topaz hung from the beast's neck. The woman herself wore no adornment, only black and gray warrior's garments. A single ring of metal was on her right hand, and that only to bear the seal of state. Her hair was bound tight in a circlet of pale silk, and braided into three strands that swung to her waist: one strand for the South, one for the North, and one for the East. The Western strand she could not add yet.

Behind Arirante came her warrior escort-train. Ten thousand were in that train, and they filled the road far to the eastern horizon.

At the gate of the great West City, they were welcomed with strewn rose-petals and scattered amber. The young West Emperor himself stood waiting, and as Arirante leaned down from the great height of her stallion to grasp his pale exquisite hand, her living gaze met the remote twilight of his. But then, as she came to stand before him, tall and straight like himself, Erester lifted his hands—finer than the purest ivory she had seen—and simply placed a garland of white flowers around her neck. Light appeared to spring forth from that garland, to dance for an instant with sublime madness, and a shiver went through her at its touch. From that moment on, Arirante, who had never loved before, loved, without knowing why, this twilight-eyed man who could not be and yet had to be her husband.

Three days hence, in a monolithic temple of gold and granite, three Archpriests married the queen Arirante and the young West Emperor. And on the night of the third day, after their secluded fasting and cleansing rites,

Erester and Arirante were led to a single room in the deep vaults of the Palace, and left alone.

Twilight shone dimly in the chamber, throwing long eerie shadows on the bare walls and the great ancestral bed that was in the center. Arirante stood before him in a white shift, half-faint with hunger, and with resigned haunting eyes that for the moment lacked the usual energy. Her hair, unbound, was like a sunset. And her hands, Erester noted, were pale and elegant, and very much like his own.

And although something acute and warm stirred in him then, at the sight of her, and he yearned for this woman, Erester stood coldly, and watched her with unyielding eyes. "My lovely queen," he said. "How well my Father chose for me. And yet, I must decline this pleasure. I'm afraid, Lady, that we cannot be joined now as they expect us to be. You see, 'things must first come full circle.' "

Arirante's surprise lasted only for a second. How well she had anticipated that this one, the seventh son, would be *different*. She looked into his unreadable eyes, her gaze also focused now, and said: "I see. . . . Then this wedding was not of your design. Well, then." She straightened her back. "To tell you the truth, Lord, these woman's clothes do not really suit me at all. Nor my hair, hanging wanton and loose like an army harlot's. Indeed, it is highly regretful that the irrevocable ceremony has been completed and you have not explained yourself to me earlier. Which, by the way, is the only thing about this matter that I don't understand."

"Then it appears we both regret the misunderstanding." He smiled, like a razor. "But—let me explain. My father, before he made me his successor, asked me to agree to this marriage, as a condition. I have done so, although he would not explain his reasons. I am now the West Emperor."

He paused, his eyes searching hers for the impact of his words and also for some other thing. And then his expression focused, intensified. "However," he said. "To marry you was the *only thing* I promised to a dying man.

It was his choice made *for* me. And I always keep my word, Lady. Only—in all things I choose for *myself.*"

"And you would not have chosen me. I see now." Arirante was pale as the shift she wore. "Then, my Lord, I can only despise you," she said. "For, unless you're as innocent as a caged songbird, you have misled me as well as yourself, in this game. You have sold yourself for the throne, not even knowing what the future of the throne was to be. And now, let *me* in turn explain your old Emperor's reasoning to you: Only some time from now, your old ailing father was secretly faced with an imminent war—not with my own Eastern Empire, but with the barbaric nomads from the far south, those peoples without a name that the Empires must fight, from the dawn of our history. Knowing his own weakness and the weakness of his army, and knowing the power that lay in the East, the West Emperor made a deal with me, Erester. He gave me his son, yourself, his fair successor, as he had long known he would through his gift of prophecy. And together with you, Lord, he *gave* me the West Empire.

"Only—my fair Erester—I have never asked for you, you who welcomed me with white blossoms. I agreed to this marriage, my husband, because this was the most peaceful and simple way to unite our two Empires. There was no need for any marriage. Indeed, the old West Emperor's heir and his six brothers would have been welcomed as honored generals in my army. Or—" and Arirante's eyes flamed with power, "—they just as easily would have graced the cells of my dungeons, for disloyalty to their new Empress!"

As she spoke thus, Erester's manner grew frozen and even more remote. "Stand away from me, woman . . ." he whispered then, wildly, with unnatural affect. And again she saw the telltale signs of pecularity in him, the oddness that the old Emperor himself warned her about.

"You sicken me! I welcomed you then on an impulse of madness. In that madness I thought I recognized in you something, a light. But, oh, how we have both been deceived! Locked in an accursed marriage that stands before us both as a fact, to encircle and strangle us! And I am to be your obedient slave! Oh, Gods!" And the young man sat down on the bed, putting his pale ivory hands on his head, vulnerably, desolately.

"So, I sicken you?" whispered Arirante, angry that he drew so much response from her, and thus more harshly than she meant. "Well, then, words I have not to express what I feel at the sight of *you!* Especially since I came to you with an open soul. . . . In the East there is honor and sanctity that is expected of the union of a man and woman. I see now, there is none of that left here. . . ."

With a sigh, the woman gathered her long radiant hair, and with fingers that also seemed to send forth light, she began to braid it into one long rich strand. No matter, then," she said coldly, in a voice of power. "Know, then, that Arirante needs no more reluctant slaves. You are free to go and be as you wish. Our marriage vows, meaning nothing, I now declare broken—just like my deal with your father. Also, Lord West Emperor, I throw back in your face your West Empire. It might be madness and pride on my part, but I have no need of it, Lord, since I already have *three* Empires. I leave this City tomorrow, and wish you all the luck . . ." She laughed then, proud, herself confused, wild-eyed. "And you will need it, seventh son and wielder of light, when tomorrow or the next day all the hordes of nameless rabble come knocking on your Empire's door!"

Erester looked up, his twilight gaze also focused with all the blackness of night, and not a trace of gentleness. "When they do come, I shall not need *you* to help me keep them out," he said rationally. And then, with a stab of sarcasm: "And by the way, my Lady, thank you for graciously giving me back my Empire."

And then he paused, stricken, like a child, as he looked at her pale fine hands, pale and white, as they moved pleating the hair. In that moment a sense of certain things came to him, and he knew true prophecy.

He continued, in a different tone, looking at her with puzzled eyes. "However, I see, it is easier said than done. My thoughts wander. I have always had too much honor for my own good. Also, I admit that—my mind is not always my own. And now I'm afraid we cannot nullify our marriage, no matter how much we both wish it, simply because I have given *my word* to my Father. I *see* now that the game he has been playing is not yet complete, and I know also that, like my own half-glimpses of truth, he was always guided by a greater knowledge. 'Things must come full circle,' he said. Gods only know what he meant, but I do know one thing—all of the prophecies are converging upon us now. This has indeed been prophecied as a time of madness. A time when East and West, North and South, shall be one, like the strand of your silken hair, Lady. When seven make eight, which in turn make one. . . ."

Arirante, who only an instant ago had been ready to storm out of the chamber, watched him weary and blank-faced. "And what manner of madness do you speak now? I thought I married a weak-minded coward, but now I see I married a blathering idiot! What prophecies? What mean you by all this?" She spoke meanly thus, because there was an inkling of truth to what he said. A truth she had long feared.

And then she sat down with her back toward him, on the other side of the great bed, and surprising even herself started to laugh bitterly, shaking off that fear in one blow. "We are, both of us, blathering idiots," she concluded. "Throwing an Empire back and forth between us, in a childish game of pride. She looked back over her shoulder then, again poised and serious, almost gentle. "This night has been full of surprises, my Lord. Fasting has made me light-headed. And it put me off-balance. It seems fated then, that we keep this bargain made with a dead old man. Let us start anew. If you wish—I ask forgiveness for my rash stupid words. Words not worthy of myself. You need ask no forgiveness, having been made a victim of my and his scheming."

She got up then, and neared him. As he stared upward, curious, into her pale strong eyes, Arirante leaned and placed a cool sealing kiss on his forehead. "No bargains will be broken, thus. And yet, *husband,* I, too, have honor. We will be bound in name only. This kiss is my word to you that you are *free of me as a man.*" And turning away, she quickly left the chamber.

Erester sat, stricken for the second time that night,

because where her lips had been, his forehead burned as though branded, and he knew no words for the feeling that filled him at that touch.

The enemy, when it did come, attacked from all sides. East, West, North, and South, the barbarians seethed—their number like grains of sand on the seashore—and they lay siege to the West Empire. The Emperor and Empress rode at the head of an army of many thousand. Pennants of fire and silver flew high in the wind.

Arirante, grim in her stark steel armor, atop a war-stallion, carried a razor-tipped lance. A broadsword of black metal hung at her side, but was not half as sharp as the look of her pale relentless eyes. Sorrow she hid in them, deep where none would see—for none could face her acute gaze long enough to know her.

Erester, the seventh son, wore armor of light. Whiteness seemed to gleam from his polished steel, and congealed about him in a manner almost material. Cold-eyed and feral, with none of his former gentle manner, he never once turned to look at Arirante. His habit now was to pretend she was not there. And occasionally his fingers wandered to tighten reassuringly over the ring given to him, the one with the seal of state.

His broadsword, like a dark beast, was in his pale elegant hands—white and fine like silver.

One of the six sons, the eldest, neared the West Emperor. "Our armies stand ready to fight for you, Brother." He spoke tonelessly, and Erester thought how this one, too, had never learned how to speak to this brother of his, to the seventh son. Blank and remote he seemed to Erester, like the other five of his brothers.

"It is not for me that you will fight," replied Erester, looking him in the eyes, with a glimmer of the old softness. "It is for *her*. To her you now answer." And he moved one pale white hand, newly gloved, in the Empress' direction, and whispered oddly: "She has usurped me . . . I no longer have a sense of self."

From the corner of her eyes, sharper than a hawk, Arirante saw the gesture, and she heard the words. "It is not for you *or* for me that these soldiers fight," she said loudly. "It is for this land that we will all shed blood." And she thought. *For a land to which I somehow bind myself, as I bind myself to this mad one.*

Erester's lips curved in a bitter smile. "Truly you speak now, Lady. For indeed, blood will be shed today. I have seen one of us, children of this imperial line, lie bloodied and lifeless, as the others look on and weep. . . ."

"Much good your prophecy does us now, fool!" exclaimed Arirante, inflamed. "Indeed, tell all of us how we all lie dead and cold, and that right before the battle! Hah! I have had enough of this, all of this, I spit upon any and all prophecies!"

And with that, she spurred her stallion ahead, while trumpets rang to announce the battle.

Erester looked in her wake gravely, and uttered quiet words to his eldest brother, before they also followed: "She might scorn the prophecy, but she does not know that the dead man I speak of will be *myself*. . . ."

Arirante fought like one possessed. White light and silver rang in her mind—as always during battle. She did not know the limbs she severed, never heard the cries of agony as her broadsword struck, again and again. She fought for this land—only remotely her own—and for the man with the gentle eyes that had put a garland of flowers about her neck. And it was the gods that now acted in her stead. The barbarians fell back, clearing the way before her and the imperial army.

On the other side of the battlefield, Erester burned like a beacon of wild light, and the slaughter wrought by him was also superhuman. Long had he ceased to wield the battlesword, but instead grasped the source of Whiteness itself, the sun, in his hands, and he struck them down with raw energy. Dark beastly faces of the enemy, barbaric shadow forms—no longer even remotely human—came flickering by his eyes, and the battle was now only a whirling dream.

I do not need you, woman! he cried within his own mind. Echoes of chaos answered him. And it seemed to Erester that not only must he die today, but he must take her with him, this woman who was bound to him unspeakably, unto death, he now knew, by an empty promise. Yet, how could that be? He hated her like he hated the madness imposed on him, and he hungered for her, like he hungered for the other side of his self that had also been imposed on him—prophecy and truth.

And through the raging battle—that was long since concluded in their favor, and yet which went on continuously now in his mind—Erester came through the field of slaughter, searching for her that held him in more ways than one.

Arirante, helmet unlaced, stood in deadly silence to wipe the sweat from her face. She was unarmed when he came from the back upon her, to strike. And yet, the white light still sang warning in her head, and the last traces of battle gave her a sixth sense. Just enough to know *him* coming.

She whirled, grabbing the sword at her feet, and parried a deadly blow.

"Die!" he cried, "Die with me now, and let things come full circle, at last!"

"You don't know what you speak, Erester!" she cried in turn, striking back at him.

"I know only that I *make my own choices,* woman! Oh, how he tortures me, the old one in his grave. Oh, how he stifles me now, with a promise that presses upon me like a curse! He gave me the ring and told me to look at it and to find truth. There! I look now! And where is the truth to be found?"

"Is it your pride that wounds you now, or your madness? Can you not bear that a single Choice has once been made for you?"

"I am the seventh son, woman! The seventh is always said to be blessed by the gods—or damned and bound, as in my case! And you are my curse!"

"I'm no such thing, you dramatic fool! Listen to me! I am—"

Their broadswords shattered as one. Only hilts remained in their hands. The man and the woman crouched, facing one another, both mad-eyed. But the woman knew her own madness, while the man did not.

Instead, he began to ply the thin air about him, with

his hands, pale and fine like silver, until a blade of light appeared, solidified. And he raised it, to strike.

But the woman raised her own hands up, in a timeless gesture of defense, and where her hands had been—pale and fine like silver—grew a shield of light. When the two sources of light met, there was only *sun*. It blazed behind their closed eyelids. And then, in their minds, thunder.

And afterward, there was nothing. Erester stood with pale lifeless hands, staring in silence at Arirante who also stood before him, drained of light.

"You are now no longer the seventh son . . ." she whispered then. "And you are therefore free, of both the blessings and the curses." She stretched out a trembling hand with her seal ring on it, and took his own ringed hand, so that he could see that the two rings were identical, like their hands were.

"There had never been a seventh son, Erester. Instead, the seventh labor of your mother resulted in twins. We are not really alike, you and I. Indeed, if our Father had not decided it was *time,* and told me, and showed me my own truth, I would never have believed this yet another tale of madness, in which I had to lie and lie. . . .

"They had to separate us, Erester. Two children like us, together, bore too much light and destruction for one land to contain. And yet, things had to be resolved ultimately, to come full circle."

"A sister . . ." Erester looked at her with thrice-stricken eyes. "And I wed you!"

"And yet you have not. . . . You had known, always, deep inside. It held you back. Only—your madness developed instead, as a result of our separation. The power that ran through us was hungering for the other, was never complete. . . ."

Erester was looking somewhere into the distance. "I feel it no longer . . ." he whispered. "The sense of prophecy. It is gone now, like the wildness in my soul. . . ."

He exclaimed, "Why, then, did I not die? I saw it clearly, my bloodied corpse."

"Because, my beloved-hated brother, half-prophecies

never tell more than half-truths. What I saw before the battle was yourself, *reborn.* And that was my side of it. Our Father 'wedded' us symbolically, I now see—for that was the only thing I did not understand even then. I, too, had been made insane by the power. It clouded my reason and hid half-truths from me, while I hungered for Empires. . . . I had lied so much to you, attempting to disguise my self—forgive me!—and yet *you knew me,* even back then, the only one who knew me ever."

Erester, with onyx eyes of the doe, looked into her eyes. "I am no longer sure if I even know myself, or am capable of Choices. Only one thing shows me what I am now, one place—the reflection of myself in your eyes."

Then the six brothers of the West Emperor approached them, through the empty battlefield, and the eldest one reached out, welcoming, with his own fair and silver-white hands. His expression as he spoke, was more clear at last to Erester than it had ever seemed before: "Welcome back, Sister, Brother. We have waited so long for madness to recede, and for things to come, at last, full circle."

NIGHT, WHO CREEPS THROUGH KEYHOLES

by Francesca Myman

After selecting this story for this *Sword and Sorceress,* I was astonished to find out that Francesca Myman is only fifteen years old. This, her first published story, to me has a flavor of the early work of Tanith Lee; it's a grim little story, with a shocking ending, like many of Tanith's works. When I first met Tanith Lee in London, she looked to me very much like a twelve-year-old, but when I saw her 'tarted up' for an autograph party, she looked at least thirty—which, I think was nearer to her real age.

Francesca is also an actress and a "vocal feminist," she says she has acted all her life as well as singing at concerts. It's too early to tell at fifteen what she will do with her life—at present she is writing a book (so was I when I was fifteen). At fifteen, my own daughter was an actress, and not a bad one. She's now in her twenties and is a harpist and singer of folk songs. Music is perhaps the one profession harder to get a start in than writing, but my daughter has done it—and so has Francesca in both writing and acting. Only time will tell what so young a writer stays with, but she's made a good start.

Francesca wishes to dedicate this story to Foof, Prime Shredder and Book-Pal.

"Who are you?" the young king asked, his exquisite features clenched in a tight knot. The horse beneath him had long since gone, and his mind, blurred with battle-lust, could not recall where or when, or if it was dead. His king's regalia had disappeared somewhere in the midst of the roiling men, and what was left of it was slicked with dirt and blood. Only the gold of the king's insignia glittered, subdued, under the filth on his breastplate. His sword seemed to have somehow vanished, and the other's lithe blade forced him to his knees. The unfamiliarity of his pose drew breath sharply through his lips. "Who *are* you?"

"I am sometimes called the Night," the figure said, its voice scarcely a voice at all, but only a breath, and in a reluctant brush of moonlight the mouth of its hooded face parted and gleamed in a feral smile. "And who are you?" it politely asked. He did not reply.

The glossy richness of his eyes gleamed under the hesitant moon. The Night leaned forward with the fascination the dark has for closed doors, with the tentative interest with which shadow creeps through the keyhole, turning the air eerily gray and motionless under its exploratory eye.

The Night drew the sword's fine edge twice across his shoulders and once, thinly, along his breastbone, and left him fainting, as silently as it had come.

And yet it was the troops of the king that won against Syldad that night, their hands trained to a rare and flawless precision, dealing out calm pain until the quickly assembled army of the invaded land broke, not to run, but to die.

It was as it always had been. An invaded land will snap as easily as a poorly made sword if pressure is applied in the proper places. This king was a master of pressure. He learned it on the spines of small rodents, just where to press, and how quickly, to make a bone like butter. Countries were like animals to him, with backbones of flesh and places that could be twisted to produce pain. A hundred lands had squealed like rats in his fine, beautiful, dispassionate hands.

Those hands had been the death of thousands, but his blood had not once been spilled in return, until Syldad. He had believed himself impenetrable, and his personal myth was now scarred with his skin. There was a vague uneasiness in him that dampened his feverish excitement at the capture of Syldad, an excitement almost innocent in its purity and freedom from guilt. Syldad was a rich land, the spires of its capital city lavished with gleaming gold, its people pale and frightened and subdued with fear for him and what he might do.

His uneasiness faded with the healing of his wounds, and by the time he reached the heart of Syldad, they were almost gone. He mounted the broad steps to Syldad's palace, and, devouring the sight of the city about him, ordered that the rulers of Syldad be brought forth.

Her hair was flat and paled to a chalky gray with the white dust of the road where she had been thrown, speckled with red from the blow they had dealt her on the back of her head. "It is the queen!" announced a guard triumphantly from the milling group of soldiers, at least two or three deep all around her, and they flung her cruelly from their excited midst to the foot of the throne. She did not flinch.

"No longer so," commented the man's voice, filled with strange joy. The room about her was pale and golden, sparkling with tasteful treasure, a room that she had known for years of her life, but the man, who sat upon the throne whose shape was molded to her body, was unfamiliar. She tried to see his face from her position on the floor, and cursed the throne for its height.

"Where did you find her?" asked the voice.

"Outside the palace, in a marketplace, with her people about her."

"Fleeing," said the voice flatly, contemptuously.

"Never," hissed the queen.

"Then what?" asked the voice, with detached derision.

"Rallying my people," she said willingly, and a soldier kicked her for her insolence. Brief fire leapt to her eyes, but she said nothing. Instead she attempted to rise, determined to see the face of the man who had killed so many of her people. The same soldier trod quickly on her hand and stood there, throwing all his weight upon the one leg. Her face became red with pain, but she made no other indication that he was hurting her.

The king frowned curiously. He could not see her face, and her silence made him wish to.

"Stop," he said suddenly, and the man took his foot off with an automatic haste of obedience. Before the king could order her to stand, she had risen, her hand held rigid and limp to her side, the skin broken. Her lower lip she held gently under her teeth. There was a strange glint of humor in her eyes as if she were laughing privately to herself.

Her face was thin and sharp and young. Her eyebrows swept thickly across her high dark forehead, and her straight nose jutted defiantly into the air. Her whole face seemed to be sharp—her chin, the edges of her lips, held so tight that they sliced into her skin, her cheekbones, her eyes, snapping and liquid and dark. Her body was small and slender, rounded in a few places, and so tensed that it, too, seemed to be an instrument that could be used for harm, sharp enough to hurt.

She looked at the man who sat in her throne, taking his measure with eyes as hard as his own. Some of the humor went out of her as she saw how beautiful he was, sitting there. He fit more into this room than she ever had. His skin was golden, his features kingly, and his eyes more beautiful than eyes should be, large and amber and green, fringed with golden lashes too long for a man, and inexplicably fascinating in their locked, veiled splendor. His fine eyebrows drew together as he looked at her. For a moment, he had the strange feeling that she was looking upon him purely as an object, judging his worth, how much she would pay for him if he were for sale.

The strange silence was broken into by the harsh voice of one of the soldiers, blind to the quiet.

"The king will find a suitable death for you," he said with habitual enjoyment. "He always does."

It was a tradition. It was what he always said to the cowering monarchs of great countries, and it pleased his small mind to say it.

"Silence," said the king in a quiet, intense voice. The man's mouth gaped in surprise, and he stepped back suddenly, cowering. The king wondered at his own tone. It was nothing but the truth, after all. He always found "suitable deaths," and inventive and original besides. He had had one in mind for her. But there was something in the look she had given him that interested him.

"I hope you *will* find a suitable death for me," she said suddenly, ignoring the interchange between the soldier and the king, and the sharp mocking had returned to her eyes, along with something new that he could not place. "If you do not, I will either be forced to find my own death, or I will capture my kingdom back from you." She paused, as if she were choosing her words with care. "Slime that you are, I cannot imagine that it will be too difficult."

There was a brief shocked pause, and then the back of an open-mouthed soldier's hand cracked across her face.

"I presume that the legends are true and you are demon-spawn, for only demon-spawn could willingly do the harm that you have done to my people these past days," she continued, and the laughter was gone from her face. Her eyes were, briefly, deep with sorrow, and the anger in them fought to keep their pain at bay. The soldier's hand hit the back of her head viciously where the blood from an earlier blow was still wet, sending her lurching to her knees, and this time she could not keep from making a faint, harsh noise. Stubbornly she went on, her eyes fixed on the king's face.

He stared at her in fascination, certain that she was deliberately baiting him. But he was unable to feel anger at her insolence. He was not sure what he did feel. He remembered women who had groveled at his feet, men who had wept and pleaded, people he had delighted to see reduced to mere hunks of flesh, and he tried to feel the same contempt for this woman that he had felt for them. But there was some strange quality in her voice that knit his brows together, something compelling that made it hard to hear her words separately. The sense of her words was lost in their cadence, and the offensiveness of them could not reach him through their beauty.

"Indeed, I hope that you are demon-spawn, so that I might at least feel sympathy for your cruelty, you dirty . . ."

Before she had finished, several soldiers rushed on her as one. They would have killed her then.

But the king stood, his eyes alive, and he did not need to say anything. Scarcely understanding, the warriors backed away from her, looking questions at each other.

"Leave us," said the king, his mouth twisting around the unfamiliarity of his own words. They paused in complete confusion, almost willing to risk their lives with objections, and then left before his stare, unable to do it.

"Go on with what you were saying," he said, and settled back into his throne.

"No," she said perversely, and he started.

"Why not?" he demanded harshly after a moment, trying to sound frightening. He felt odd, confused with the novelty of her words.

"I want a bath," she said, testing, "and healing liniment." She dragged herself painfully to her elbows and stared up at him. He could tell that having to angle her chin back to see him was agony to her.

He breathed out suddenly, and smiled, almost painfully, his face stretching in unfamiliar directions.

"All right," he said slowly, wandering why he acted as he did. "It will be so."

"I do not think that you were born a queen," he said suddenly.

She looked at him shrewdly where he sat across from her, two glasses of sweet diluted wine between them, and leaned back into her heaped cushions, hoping that she did not betray to him the pain that the liniment had not eradicated. Her hair, still a little damp, felt blessedly cool on her battered skin, and clean, washed free of matting blood and white dust until it became almost black again, and as straight as her shoulders. She held her shoulders so straight because she was made uncomfortable by her comfort. This was too easy.

She knew of this young king. People called him a demon, for he was too perfect in his beauty and too cruel to be human. He was cruel not with malicious intent, but with a strange indifference, and a distanced fascination for death and for blood. The only time he would dirty himself was upon the battlefield, the only ugliness he could stand to have about his beauty was the ugliness of war's death. The single-minded force of his purpose swept thousands of men along with him, leaving ravaged countries lying in his wake under the careful eyes of unswervingly loyal regents. The fear the king's troops held for death had become their fear for him, and with this security they fought with ruthless uncaring. Death mattered nothing to them, whether they gave it or got it. It was only the endless fascination their king exuded that mattered.

He would spend only a month at the most in each newly conquered country, exhilarated with the change he had caused in its peaceful aspect. And then he would begin to plan. And his plans would find fruition, for he was brilliant, and charismatic. Too brilliant to be a member of the royal families, so long inbred, who lost their hold on their land as easily as on their sanity.

"No," she answered finally, "I was not born royal. And I doubt that you were either."

He paused, and smiled that painful smile again. "No, I suppose not," he said. "But I was not born of demons either."

"Then what is it that makes you so ill?" she asked of him.

Her candor startled him.

"I cannot say that I am sorry for asking that," she told him in quick response. "My death will come sooner rather than later. It does not matter what I say, and so I might as well say it."

He looked as though he wanted to protest, but she did not give him time. "How is it that you can be as you are and still be human?" Her sharp liquid eyes accused him, mockery hidden in their depths. He was not sure that he wanted her to hate him.

"I *am* human," he assured her wanly, uncertainly, and rushed on. "If you were not born a queen, then who were you born to?"

She saw him without quite completely looking at him, and once again he had the uneasy feeling that she was coolly calculating his value.

"I am a prostitute's daughter," she said, and then

paused for a moment as if she surprised herself by saying what she said. For a moment, in the absence of the persuasiveness of her voice, he wondered if there was not something hidden behind that artless hesitation. "I can't imagine who my father is, but my mother was a hard woman, with ambition that she died for, and passed on to me. I refused her profession, and became a thief for lack of a better occupation. Then I grew to love it." She looked at him oddly.

"Yes?" he prompted, the sound of her voice endlessly intriguing to him, her eyes holding his gaze captive, carving away artfully at his composure.

"I made so many mistakes that I *had* to learn from them, and I became the cleverest thief this country has ever known." There was pride in this admission. "I stole so softly and so cleverly that no one could catch me. No lock kept me away, nothing could hold me outside.

"And one day I stole the kingdom, softly, cleverly, so carefully that no one quite knew what had happened. The old ruler was a decaying man more concerned with his drink than with Syldad, and so I was seen as a liberator, rather than a usurper. Yet at first people had some difficulty accepting me, for I was very young." She paused and looked at the king, who sat tautly across from her. "Why am I telling you this?" she asked him.

"It is the drink," he offered.

"I have had none," she reminded him, troubled.

"You were very young," he reminded her.

"I was very young," she repeated, "And even if I was a liberator, I had killed the old king in cold blood."

"So you see," he said eagerly, "You, too, can kill in cold blood."

She looked at him without contempt, and did not answer. He was incredibly beautiful where he sat, more beautiful than anything she had ever seen or owned or acquired. Emotion passed unwillingly across his cruel beauty, as if it should not trouble such perfection with the semblance of life. "I was young, but I had a brilliance like no ruler this place has ever had." There was no pride in her voice at what she said. It was bare truth, and nothing more. "The old king had so few supporters that after the shock died down, they were more loyal to me than they had ever been to him. Oh, I am not saying that there was no uproar. Of course there was. But I and my supporters were ruthless, small in numbers though we were, and far more willing to die than the old king's soft followers, and so we held off with great ease those that would have killed me immediately for my deed."

She looked at him, rapt as he sat, and smiled privately, tasting her triumph again as if it were the sweet wine she had not touched. There was a thrilling excitement in her words that transmitted itself to him. "I allowed one of the men to go free to spread the word, and by the end of the day the entire populace of the city of Syldad had gathered about the castle, or as close to it as they could get. And I spoke to them all. I spoke to them with words of a thief, and I cleverly and silently crept my way into their imagination, until they were afire with excitement for the idea of me. I stole them, and my passion for them was greater than my passion for anything I had yet stolen."

He looked at her with hungry eyes, unsure what it was about her that made him lean forward. Her voice was round and beautiful, and compelling, like the clear ringing of steel. Her sharp young face was softened, and the edges of her lips no longer cut into her skin. They were relaxed, full and voluptuous, and sensitive, their movement smooth and even a little sweet, with a poignant sort of sweetness. The humor in her eyes was not mockery, but it made him uncertain, and unbalanced him entirely. Her body, that had before seemed sharp, and so like a knife, did not seem so any longer. Instead it seemed exquisite in its precision, in the perfection of its smallness. He became aware that she smelled like some rare forbidden spice, became aware of the curve of her small breasts.

"You see," she told him softly. "That is the difference between you and me. I have a passion for the things that I steal. I can love, while you cannot."

"Is that so?" he breathed, "Is that so?"

He reached for her hand, knocking over a slender goblet of wine. He trembled, and he hesitated before touching her. He brushed his lips across the palm of her hand, surprised at himself, and then he ran his hand down her cheek, and his thumb over her lips. She did not protest. Her eyes were as fever-bright as his own, and her quick smile was one of exultation, even of triumph. She had stolen his heart, deliberately, stealthily, and she responded to him with the passion that she responded to all things that she stole. He was beautiful, his body like the knotted ripples of rushing water, and she had stolen him with enormous mastery. The cruelty that he kept like a screen over his heart was unlocked like any other lock, and he was as careful of her bruises as he would have been careful with strategy for overcoming a country, as certain of winning her as he was of winning war, and as fascinated with her body and her dark sharp eyes as he was with death.

He lay beside her, watching her with the peculiar focus of a man who believes that he is lovesick. Her fingertips traced his barely healed wounds with an odd intensity, over his shoulders and his breastbone, and she looked into his eyes for the first time with truth, without looking through him. He smiled at her, his face glorious and his eyes unlocked, and he looked down at her fine hands on his chest, feeling a searing twinge of pain. A knife's handle sprouted from his breastbone as if it were a part of him, and he raised his eyes to hers.

She drew on her clothing and prepared to collect her followers. She would steal first the respect and then the hearts of his warriors. They would forget him. He was only a small part of what she could have. To her it was the act of stealing that was sensuous, and not always what was stolen. But she had stolen Syldad, and she loved it still. It was uncomplicated. It did not require things of her which she could not give. It required nothing of her that it did not deserve.

"I am sometimes called the Night," she said to his dead body, her voice scarcely a voice at all, but only a breath, and the moon flinched and hid from her smile. "And who are you?"

OATHS

by Leslie Ann Miller

I always think of Leslie Ann Miller as "one of ours," since when I bought her first story for *Marion Zimmer Bradley's FANTASY Magazine* she was actually working for us as a typist. There's nothing like working in an editor's office; it saves on postage for return envelopes, for one thing.

Since then, she's moved back home to Stillwater, Oklahoma, and I've bought two more of her stories, the first for *Sword and Sorceress IX* and the second for this anthology. She says there is only one word to describe how she feels about acceptance: "addicting." (It's nice to have an addiction that pays you, isn't it?)

Leslie works as a Fire Safety inspector for Oklahoma State University, doing everything any fire marshal or firefighter does, but for the University. (Me, I collect descriptions of strange jobs for writers.) She says she read Tolkien in the sixth grade, started her first novel in the seventh, finished it in the ninth and has been writing ever since. She adds that getting a degree in English almost turned her off writing forever—which, I think says more about the way English is taught than about Leslie.

She has a border collie named Gwen, and a Manx cat named "T.W. Cat," short for "Tail-less Wonder." (It would be even more wonderful if she had a Manx cat that *wasn't* tail-less!) She fights in the SCA (fires just aren't enough), tends roses, and—you guessed it—is writing a novel.

"Oaths" is a remarkable story—full of blood, thunder, guts, and adventure, but told with remarkable sensitivity and attention to detail. This one held me from beginning to end, with strong characters that novice adventure writers would do well to study.

I saw the scene as if it happened yesterday.

Blood stained the hillside red, and the vultures circled thick and dark overhead. My father lay dead at my feet, a spear through his throat; my mother was hacked to pieces somewhere down below. The bodies of my friends were scattered across the plain. Only my brother stood with me, father's banner held high in one hand, his sword dripping blood in the other. We faced the remains of Gallard's army, a mass of red and black and cold, gray steel.

Gallard's herald called a halt. The masses circled the hill, then parted as the Wizard himself came forth. He rode a black steed which might once have been a horse, and his robes were scarlet red. He stopped at the base of the hill and stared up at us, smiling.

"Hail, Ronar's children!" he greeted us, and his voice was grating though he tried to smooth it with sweetness.

"Damn you, Gallard!" my brother shouted. "Come fight us one to one!"

The wizard laughed. "I think not. I have an army to do that." He leaned forward in his saddle, and held out his black-gloved hand. "I come to offer you a choice. You have fought well today. I admire skill at arms. Join my cause and I will let you live!"

I spat blood to one side. "And become one of your mindless slaves? Never!!" Despite the sword cut on my arm, I grabbed the spear stuck through Father's neck and threw it at him.

The aim was true, but with a flick of his wrist the wizard knocked it aside with a spell. It struck a black-clad shieldman in the front rank, and he fell back with a scream, clutching the shaft protruding from his chest.

My brother swore.

Gallard laughed. "I like your spirit, girl. You've a strong arm. I need warriors for my army, true warriors, not scum like that. Join me as captains—I'll give you a hundred men to command. Together we can conquer Librinia and invade the wealth of Artoa! I promise you power and riches beyond your wildest dreams!"

A longing filled my heart. The sight of Gallard was washed away by a vision of Artoa's tall spires adorned with my father's coat of arms; and me, leading a victorious army under young King Normar's castle gate. The cheering crowds on either side of the cobbled street chanted my name, "Raelynn, Raelynn, Raelynn! Duke Ronar's daughter! Raelynn!"

"Yeeessss . . ." Gallard's soothing voice drew me back to the battlefield. "A vision!" he said, and I saw my brother shake his head as if to clear it.

"I've sworn fealty to King Carner of Librinia," my brother said. "I'll not have it said that the new Duke of Locwood betrayed him."

Gallard smiled. "Yet he has betrayed you! Where now is the army he promised your father? He left you to fight with but a handful of warriors. While your friends and family fought here for their lives and his lands, he sat in his castle chambers drinking wine and laughing with the women! Such a man does not deserve your fealty! No! But I will not betray you, Duke Rolan. I will treat you with the honor due your station." He dismounted, and took a step up the hill, black gauntleted hand still held out toward us.

His words seemed fair, and I wondered how I could have thought his voice harsh at first. I took a step toward him, but my brother grabbed my arm and pulled me back.

"Wait Raelynn," Rolan said. "He ensorcels us! Can you not feel the power?"

I shook my head, and blood dripped into my eyes. I tried to wipe it away, but my arm was now nearly useless.

Rolan planted Father's standard in the dirt and took the end of his tabard to wipe my face for me. He held my eyes for a long, long moment; and I fought the urge to cry. My brother, the Duke of Locwood.

"Duke Rolan," Gallard called. "Join me, and I'll let your sister go free."

Rolan's head jerked up.

"No, Rolan!" I said. "We die together with Father and Mother!"

"My word of honor," Gallard continued. "Upon my soul, with gods as my witness, I will let her go unharmed."

I watched in horror as Rolan slowly wiped his sword on the grass and sheathed it. He put his hands on my shoulders, and his face was grim. "Raelynn," he whispered, and I knew he was whispering to keep his voice from cracking, "last night Father asked me to protect you today. And Mother, she told me this morning: 'Save your sister,' she said. 'She was born with a special destiny. Save her if you can!' And I swore that I would."

I shook my head in denial, and the tears ran freely down my face. "No Rolan, don't do it! He will enslave you like the others! It's better to die! *It's better to die!*"

He closed his eyes in anguish. "On your thirteenth birthday the Seer of Locwood pronounced that you would 'save all Librinia.' We laughed, then, I know. He was mad, we said. But, Raelynn, listen to me. You must live. You must go far from here and heal your wounds. And then you must find some way of stopping Gallard. Do you understand? You must find a way to stop Gallard."

I nodded dumbly, and Rolan smiled grimly. "He won't find me an obedient slave, little sister." He turned to Gallard. "Your word, then, Wizard. Let her go!"

"My word, Duke Rolan. I will!" He gestured at two of his captains, and they cleared an aisle through the ranks for me to pass.

Rolan left his standard flapping in the breeze and helped me down the hillside. I could hardly see for blood and tears, and I was shaking badly—confused, frightened, and feeling sick to my stomach. I had not noticed the pain while I was fighting.

Rolan stopped when we reached the bottom and kissed me on the forehead. His lips came away bloody. "I love you, sister," was all he said.

"I'll free you Rolan," I swore to him. "By my honor and my soul, I'll come back and free you."

He smiled, trusting, and turned again to Gallard.

I did not watch him as he took Gallard's hand, and kissed the ring on the wizard's middle finger. I staggered down the aisle between the ranks of soldiers and stumbled into the woods surrounding the plain.

I headed south, away from the castle that had been my birthplace and which I could no longer call home. It didn't take me long to figure out I was being followed. The part of my mind which was still semilucid chided me for believing, even for an instant, that Gallard might keep his word. The wizard had no soul to lose, and what had he to fear from the gods when his own evil deity protected him? I stumbled on, determined not to let Rolan's sacrifice be for naught.

"General." A voice at my side interrupted my memories.

Suddenly, I was back in the present, standing on the same hilltop eighteen years later. The trees were gone now, I realized with a shock. Locwood had gone to feed the fires of Gallard's spells. The bodies of my friends and family had long since disappeared beneath the grass and soil, and the castle that had been my home stood dark and abandoned in the distance.

But the army which faced me across the plain was the same black and red and cold, gray steel. Only the banner had changed. It was the same that I had seen flying from the towers of Artoa in my vision; the same that Rolan had left flapping on the hillside when he helped me down the hill; my father's banner—my brother's now, the former Duke of Locwood, named for a forest which was no more.

"General," Prince Carner repeated. "The army is ready. King Normar awaits your command."

One moment," I said, taking a deep breath. The memories gripped my mind like a mailed fist. I would have to deal with them before I could lead my troops to battle. Normar had learned patience. He would wait.

But Carner was eager for victory and shifted restlessly. "Should we not attack while Locwood hesitates, General?"

"He will not move," I said with certainty. Rolan had chosen his ground—the open field where his cavalry and spears would be most efficient together. "He waits for us." For me, I thought. By now he knows who I am.

The Prince nodded reluctantly, accepting my judgement. He did not know who I was, nor why I was so adept at predicting our enemy's movements. But seven years of constant warfare had taught him that I was almost always right. He wanted his father's crown back badly, but he would obey me, the so-called Liberator of Librinia.

I returned to my memories.

The underbrush was thick and green and hid me from pursuers. I had known Locwood well, back then, better than any of Gallard's henchmen. Even wounded, leaving a trail of blood, they could not catch me. Perhaps the gods helped me more than I ever knew, but somehow I escaped. A farmer fleeing south on Riner's Road hid me in his wagon. He drove the horses near to death, but his tender care, I'm certain, was all that saved my life.

The next day we passed a troop of Carner's men traveling north—too little, too late. I was too weak to tell them much, just that Father was dead and my brother captured. I begged them to save him, but they escorted us to Rinewood instead. They did not wish to fight Gallard by themselves. I understood the rationale, but despised them nonetheless.

My anger and despair dissolved quickly into fever. The farmer left me with Rinewood's healer, and it was during my delirium that I first felt my brother's pain. Through the bond that families sometimes share, I felt Gallard's whips tear the flesh from his back, and heard honey sweet words twist the darkness in his mind. His agony added to my own, and at times I was not sure whose pain it was I felt, his or mine. The healer could not stop the visions, nor heal the agony in my mind.

Later, when the fever passed, the link remained. I felt my brother's loving heart, by degrees, fill with hate, and I cursed my weakness as his hope of rescue dwindled slowly to despair. He could not hear me calling his name, nor could he see that the visions of my betrayal which filled his mind were products more of Gallard's sorcery than truth. He saw me as an honored guest at Carner's court, heralded as a hero, my oath to him forgotten—his pain ignored; his sacrifice for nothing; his king betrayed through my betrayal.

In truth, I was lying on a dirty straw mat in the healer's hut, trying to clench my fist and raise my head. I was far too weak to sit up, much less stand, and the healer feared that I would lose my arm. It did not come to be, thankfully, but I suffered doubly for the pain. My brother! I had to save my brother!

During the weeks that I grew stronger I learned what Gallard taught his slaves: hatred, fear, and arrogance. Their hatred made them powerful, their fear made them obedient, and their arrogance made them slaves to what they perceived as his greatness and wisdom.

The day I finally raised my sword arm, empty, above my head, I felt Rolan curse my father's name and mine. He'd held out long, two seasons full, but finally the pain became too much. The link through which I'd felt his torture severed, and I knew then that he was lost. I wept. The healer did not understand. I should be glad, he said, that I would recover fully in time. I wronged him greatly, then, by leaving, bitter and ungrateful for his efforts.

I moved south, town by town, still trying to regain my strength. Come spring, Gallard's army advanced behind me. King Carner's forces could not hold him back. Gallard had a new weapon more deadly than his spells—a daring general, clad in black and red—young Duke Rolan Locwood whose eyes, it was said, could paralyze the common man. Carner's troops fled before him like sparrows from a hawk, and Librinia fell in two years.

The old king died a valiant death defending his throne. Gallard had the remaining heirs beheaded; all but one, that is, who escaped his net and landed in Artoa. Gallard crowned himself King of Librinia on midsummer's eve, and declared war on his neighbor the following day.

I fled the kingdom before the troops began to march that fall. Artoa's border was crowded with King Normar's armies; Normar was no fool. I left my name behind when I joined an Artoan army training camp as Raena, a poor Librinian refugee. Locwood, in two kingdoms, was a greatly hated name.

My sword arm was still weak, but my aim with a spear

was true as ever. Gradually, with use, my sword work improved, and my spear became a legend. My officers could not deny my skill, and slowly I rose through the ranks.

The war with Gallard lasted nine long years. Land was lost and land regained. Castle Bromshire changed hands four times in as many years, and the graveyards in the farmer's fields grew wider by the year like the orchards standing next to them. Many times I fought on the same field as the wizard and my brother, but never did I face them. Never, that is, until the battle of Longford, the battle to decide the war.

Longford and its fine stone keep were all that stood between Artoa's heart and Gallard's spells and slavery. Normar's entire army was camped at the keep on the river's southern bank. If we failed to hold there, nothing would stop Gallard from marching south. Nothing, and we knew it.

I was but a captain then, in black leather armor and a dented steel helm. I was commanding the rank of spears guarding the ford's east edge. It was a misty morning and steam rose from the water. The first wave of cavalry thundered out of the fog just after daybreak.

The horses came at us through waist-high water. They clanked and jingled with sturdy steel plates. Their riders dressed in heavy mail. Though our spear points blunted against their heavy metal armor, the shafts worked nicely to dismount them. The river did the rest. They found it hard to swim with fifty pounds of metal on.

At first we let the horses through unharmed, but soon their hooves churned the grassy banks to mud. Our footing became slick and treacherous, and our task more difficult as we had to fight the beasts as well. The ford became choked with bodies and the water flowed thick like blood.

We held the ford through two attacks. But Gallard would not give up. He sent two spells to fill the air with smoke and fumes. As we coughed and choked and our eyes watered mercilessly, the third wave struck. We could not see them till too late, and the fumes made it hard to fight. Several horses made it to the southern bank, and as I stepped forward to make a thrust at one, I was hammered by another. I toppled, stunned, face first into the bloody water.

I lost my spear but did not sink. The water shocked me fast awake, and I struggled to my feet amidst the churning current. Horses charged to either side, and drowned and fallen bodies shifted under foot. An armored knee lashed out to hit me in the face as it passed; I lunged in desperation and latched on tight. I grabbed the chainmailed thigh and threw myself backward. The rider followed with a splash and gurgle. I stepped on the drowning body and launched myself at the horse as it floundered, confused at the sudden lack of weight and guidance. I struggled into the saddle as much to escape being trampled as to avoid being drowned.

"Forward, you fool!" a familiar voice shouted beside me.

I looked through the smoke and saw Gallard there, urging his beast forward to join his cavalry at the besieged keep's walls while his infantry began to cross the ford.

I nodded and spurred my horse with my heels. Covered with mud and blood and shielded by the smoke, Gallard mistook me for one of his own. Who else, he thought, would be riding through the ford? I followed him up the muddy shores and grabbed a spear standing from the bank. This time, I thought, I would not miss.

I did not.

I shouted challenge, and threw. The spear struck his chest as he turned in the saddle, and I saw the tip come out his back. He toppled with a hiss and sputter, smoking, and sparks flew from the soft ground where he landed. My horse reared in sudden fright, and I did not remember hitting the ground.

I awoke a knight by Normar's hand, and was promoted again—to general. I'd hoped the war was over since we held the ford and Gallard was dead. I'd thought that his evil would die with his body, but I was wrong. The remains of Gallard's troops regrouped to the north, and winter gave them time to heal. Duke Locwood, The Terror, crowned himself King of Librinia on midwinter's eve, and took his master's place.

Come spring, I had such success against The Terror that I was made Commander of the Army. Prince Carner II became my second in command, and together we drove my brother back. In three years Artoa was freed. Three more and south Librinia was as well. It took only one to drive them to the hill where I now stood, waiting and watching, hoping to spot my brother on his black-maned steed which might once have been a horse.

"I suppose I can't blame you for savoring the moment," Carner commented. "We've fought long and hard for this day. Finally, we've got the bastard where we want him."

I smiled bitterly. How long had I endured the cursing of my family name? How long had I kept silent, knowing I could not defend it for fear they would ask why. I knew they could never trust me if they discovered I was sister to The Terror.

"I have waited long for this moment, yes," I said quietly. "But I do not savor it. No."

"Something is wrong," he said, always perceptive. "What is it, Raena?"

I shook my head. "Memories. It all started here, you know."

He looked concerned, and puzzled.

I smiled and raised my hand before he could respond, and blew my horn. Other horns sounded down the ranks, and the first wave of cavalry swept past below.

They charged around the base of the hill and headed for the enemy's left flank. Spears bristled in the morning sun from Rolan's shield wall, and arrows fell like rain. A mass of black stirred behind the lines, and Rolan's cavalry charged forth to meet my own.

I blew another blast on the horn and the second wave galloped forth. The timing was important. The second wave would hit as the first was falling. They would charge through the chaos and break or turn the wall. My infantry followed the cavalry with banners waving and horns blowing. A cloud of arrows preceded them.

The left flank crumbled quickly. I knew it would. Soon my second cavalry would crash through the ranks behind the main shield wall. Rolan's men were spent and desperate. They would not hold against us. They could not.

"It goes well," Carner commented with satisfaction as we watched the battle rage. "Shall we join the fray?"

I nodded and turned to my squire who stood behind holding our horses.

She stepped forward. "My lady?" she asked eagerly. She wanted badly to ride in the final battle of the war.

"I will hunt alone today, Katrina," I said. "You may do as you will."

She bowed her head to hide her disappointment but held the reins while I mounted. She handed up my shield, and I slid my arm through the straps.

Carner grabbed my horse's bridle. "You're in a foul mood today, Raena. Perhaps you should not go. I fear for your safety."

I looked out across the field and saw my brother's standard where he waited with his Elite. The shield wall in front of him was disintegrating rapidly. I would have to hurry.

I drew forth my sword and smiled wryly at my future king. "I have an oath to keep," I said, and spurred my war horse down the hill.

His swearing passed me on the wind as he scrambled to mount his own.

I followed King Normar and his Blue Guard into battle. They cleared a path ahead of me as they, too, made for Rolan's banner. My eyes were focused on that one thing, and I hardly saw the milling fight around me. My sword arm swung, struck, and parried without attention. I did not notice when a stray arrow pierced the armor on my leg, nor did I notice when Normar fell and his Guards swerved to help him.

I charged straight through the lines and did not stop till I faced my brother and his guard. They sat on their steeds quietly—watching, waiting—with Rolan in their center. I was not afraid that I was alone. The Elite did not matter. Finally, I was facing my brother.

His beast stepped forward, and he held up his blackmailed hand. "Hail, Ronar's daughter!" he cried, and his voice was harsh though he tried to smooth it with sweetness.

"Hail, Ronar's son," I replied with equal sweetness. "This is our battle, Rolan," I said. "Let us fight it one to one."

He laughed. "Nay, Raelynn, I have a Guard to do that. I have stayed to offer you a choice!"

"A choice?" I asked, unprepared for this approach.

Rolan rode closer, and took off his helm. I saw my brother's face, and it was young and handsome still. His hair was golden and his eyes sky blue. They held me.

"Raelynn," he said softly. "You betrayed me once, but I forgive you, now. Join me, and let us die together on this day!"

My voice caught in my throat, and I could not move.

Rolan dismounted and walked forward, still holding out his hand. "I love you, Sister. Join me, and all will be right!"

"Rolan," I whispered, and slid from my horse's back. My wounded leg collapsed when I hit the ground, and I staggered to my knees.

Rolan's eyes seemed to glow. How could anyone call him "Terror," I wondered, looking up at him? I saw my brother as he had been . . . as we played together under the green leaves of Locwood building castles out of sticks . . . as he smuggled me cake from Father's table when I was too young to sit with guests . . . as his hair flashed in the sunlight while he taught me how to wield a spear . . . as we laughed when the seer said I would save Librinia . . . as he stood, so fair and proud on the hilltop holding Father's banner with all of Gallard's army before us. "Oh, Rolan," I repeated, and my eyes filled with tears.

He stood above me, smiling. "Raelynn," he said, and held out his right hand. There was a ring on it, with the Royal Arms of Librinia. "Kiss my ring—and the hand of your king," he said.

The spell broke, then, for I heard not my brother's voice that spoke, but rather Gallard's arrogance. I looked again into Rolan's eyes, but instead of love, I saw only triumph.

Somewhere behind me I heard Carner call my name, and the horses of the Elite thundered past. I kissed Rolan's ring. "I love you," I said, and thrust my sword between his ribs.

He fell forward into my arms, gasping, and I held him while his blood ran between his fingers and the life flowed from his eyes. "Raelynn?" he asked, recognizing me, and I felt our link return. I felt his pain, his confusion . . . his love.

"By my honor, my soul," I whispered as he died, "I've set you free, big brother!"

DOUBLE VISION

by Lucas K. Law

Lucas Law says that his parents Leonard and Florence, with whom he still happily lives, are responsible for his writing career; in fact, he wishes to dedicate this story to them. It all began when eleven-year-old Lucas asked his long-suffering Dad to read his collection of fairy tales. (We parents are responsible for a lot, aren't we?)

He says he is "a Gemini sign sent to Borneo Island (Land of the Headhunters) twenty-six years ago." Now, he resides in the more sedate environs of Calgary, Alberta, living the life of "a petroleum engineer for North Canadian Oils Limited by day and a creative writer in the basement by night."

He keeps the creative juices flowing in a number of interesting ways. He "has traveled extensively from Europe to Southeast Asia to Costa Rica to Western Canada. He swims long distances to test his endurance, plays tennis to vent his frustration, and goes whitewater rafting to heighten his "perception of life and death." Then there are his favorite places—science fiction and occult bookstores, the cardstore, "the place for feeling in the heart," and the bakery store, with its "lifestream of chocolate and pies." He is a graduate student of Writer's Digest School under the guidance of Ardath Mayhar, but he obviously had the requisite talent and determination beforehand.

"Double Vision" is a darn good story. Lucas takes a difficult premise, develops it skillfully, and carries the story line through to a clear and satisfying ending. This story would be very easy to do badly, and much longer; in writing as in everything else, sometimes less is more.

From the tower platform, Ashanti gazed at the dark silent valleys. A very unusual night in Rosnin, she thought, just like the night her father passed on, dead silent except for a lantern carrier struggling up the damp cobblestone steps toward her. As soon as Ashanti recognized the familiar shadow, she called out, "Greetings, Sasha."

"Any answer yet?" asked the newcomer.

"Not this night," Ashanti said, trying desperately to hide her quivering voice. "Seven sunsets past and not a single sign of Mother Superior. No message. Nothing. The coastline shifts in the next full moon."

Sasha sighed. "Two more sunsets."

"We need her for the stringing of the beads."

"Maybe she hasn't found the masked man."

Sasha gave her a consoling hug. Feeling better, Ashanti gathered her cloak and walked down the frost-covered passages to her bedroom. Once inside her comfortable little space, she slipped out of her weathered gray tunic and deerhide sandals and washed her face. She took a quick glance at her reflection in the basin of minted water, hoping that it had changed.

For a moment, a sharp pain struck her. The bitter memory of the curse came back. Her thighs cramped. Her hand reached for her stomach, feeling a churn of nausea, a slight touch of numbness. It couldn't be too late, not now. What would she do if Mother Superior never came back? She was too young to die. Dying at the hands of the Balkains was far better than staying in the monastery for the rest of her days. She wanted to explore the shifting coastline of Rosnin. She wanted to be loved by a man, wanted to lie beside him, to feel the warmth of his arms and to have his child. Why shouldn't she be like any other Malkai woman? Alas, an impossible quest! She knew as soon as she stepped outside the fortress walls that others would recognize her imperfection—a woman's body having a man's face.

Everyone in the monastery told her she had the loveliest green eyes, greener than all the emerald mines in

Rosnin. All she ever saw was a reflection of a boy who grew up to a man, wearing the same wicked grin that taunted her, reminding her of the spell that could be only broken in death. It was her father's fault. Why did he refuse to invite the Colored Tempest to the Council?

She lay on her back, staring at the saber hanging in the dark corner above her chestbox. It was a sore reminder of a war lost in history; a lost cause as far as she could recount, the cause of her sufferings.

Twisting and turning, she dreamed of dying and being reborn. The winds beyond the dunes called her name, for her to come and play to their restless beat. The dreaming subsided when she heard the faint call of the rooster. Then came seven horn blasts.

Ashanti rushed out of bed, put on a violet wool gown, and tied a chain of heart-shaped emeralds around her forehead, holding in place a veil across her face.

She hurried outside to the platform. In the distance a caravan trampled across the brown marram meadow: tiny horses, two guides with a dozen followers. Then they disappeared into an underground tunnel.

Ashanti felt it was going to be a good day. Even the sparrows agreed by leaving their nests and circling high above her. The morning dew tickled down the scented leaves of nearby jasmine plants, and her ears caught the sweet mandolin sound of waters streaming down the fountain in the central courtyard, surrounded by seven ivy-grown stones and tendril-clasped pillars. Seven. What a good number, Ashanti concluded.

The main gate lowered to the outside world. The sound of horses galloping was even bearable for Ashanti today. Mother Superior was finally home.

Like everyone else, Ashanti bowed. Although life had changed in Rosnin in the last fifty years, tradition continued to reign within these walls, giving her strength to go on for another day. Too much freedom caused revolution, she recalled hearing from the merchants who came with their food supplies every spring.

The drum beat thrice before they rose to welcome their leader. Ashanti looked up and all the nerves in her body froze. The Balkains! They were tricked. Her sisters shrieked and cried. Her own feet stood still, refusing to move. Then a man clad in light silvered mesh-mail rode to the front and drew his sword. At that instant, all noises stopped.

"Good sisters, we mean no harm as long as our requests are met. Where is your spiritual healer?"

Without giving a second thought, Ashanti stepped forward. "I'm the one you are looking for."

He steered his black stallion toward her. "That's what I like to see. A quick friendly response."

"We are taught by the oaths to be civil; we need not be friends to our enemies," replied Ashanti in a firm, cold voice.

"How could you call us enemies? We have never attacked any of your monasteries."

"Then why are you here?"

"We need you to heal our leader, Rax."

"What's the problem?"

"The Kalaharis poisoned him. There isn't any antidote, so we hanged them. Oh! What a pleasure it was." His laughter sounded like the purr of a sword sliding from a silken sheath.

"No such talk around here," Sasha growled, her chin jutting truculently.

"Who are you?" The warrior raised his double-edged sword towards her face.

Sasha stood firm. "I am the chief priestess for the Waters of Malkai. Where is our Mother Superior?"

"It's our honour to meet you, Lady Malkai. My name is Chezmar, the army superintendent, second-in-command. Your leader came down with hot sores. She is sleeping comfortably in her carriage."

"I want to see her," Ashanti demanded.

"Hot sores are contagious; you should know," Chezmar warned Ashanti.

"As long as I do not touch her."

"No! My soldiers have a long journey ahead. I warn you. No further or your sisters' deaths are yours to bear."

What woman would want such an arrogant man with

a high nose? Not just big, but ugly and sharp-pointed, Ashanti noted.

"Who are you? The chief priestess is always the healer."

Sasha, not ready for him to bully her prime scholar, snapped back. "Ashanti is the best healer in the whole of Rosnin. She's an herbalist, knows the art of the blind, has the skill of the deaf."

"Pleased to hear that," Chezmar replied. "Show us where to put our leader."

Ashanti motioned them to follow her through the oval door of the monastery, leading them into a narrow passage enveloped with the smell of roses. A strong breeze rushed through, sending shivers up Ashanti's spine. Her heart sensed that their leader was not an ordinary man. Unlike the others, his vibrations were affecting her spiritual balance, giving a mixed emotion of love and comfort, hate and helplessness. She was pleased to reach the center of the monastery, the source of birth and death.

"Lay him on the altar with his head toward the seven-pointed tiara," Ashanti instructed.

"Hurry! We have little time to spare," Chezmar ordered.

"Within these walls, time is the master. You must leave us now."

"How can I trust you with him?"

"I was sworn to the oath of Healing. If there is any harm, he did it to himself already," Ashanti said, moving toward the motionless body on the altar.

A sudden weakness seized her as she saw a leather mask over the stranger's face. Before she could touch it, Chezmar grabbed her wrist. "Stop!"

"What?"

"Leave his mask on. Never take it off or your life . . ."

"Don't threaten me. It wouldn't work," Ashanti shot back, wriggling her wrist free.

Realizing his mistake, Chezmar quickly bowed to Ashanti and left. An invisible force prevented her from peeping at the stranger's face. Maybe it was his sorrowful moaning, the sound of rejection. Maybe it was his enticing lips. All she could hear was her heart telling her to trust him. Why?

After filling a bronze chalice with red olive sticks, date leaves, lotus buds, candle bar, and plum vinegar oil, she set the candle bar aflame. A smoky indigo fume rose from the chalice, dancing, drifting, aiming for Rax's body. Ashanti unbuttoned his shirt, placing her hands on his chest, gently massaging his swollen breasts, slowly moving down to his underside. She felt her blood racing through her veins and arteries, sending pulses of attraction. She enjoyed the feel of his soft matted silver hairs and of his hard abdomen, developed through the years of persistent training. Then her hands came to rest. She channeled her energy into his skin, into his cells to release the pain from within. Ashanti closed her eyes and meditated. Her palms got warmer and warmer until a greenish fume seeped through her fingers from beneath his skin.

The chirping of cicadas called for another nightfall. The healing drained her energy, sending her to the chamber floor.

"Lady, are you all right?" A sweet voice rang in her ears, followed by strong slender finger brushing her cheeks.

Ashanti lay still, hurting all over and enjoying the warm touch. Breathing was becoming an effort. Their eyes met and she realized her sudden weakness. She quickly drew back.

"Don't be afraid. I won't hurt my savior," Rax whispered.

"You had better leave now."

"May I know your name?" Rax asked.

"Ashanti from the House of Nardial."

"So it's not a myth. The lost art of herbal healing."

As Rax stood up from his kneeling position, his body went limp. Ashanti caught him in time. Her mind told her to let go; he was not worth the trouble. Her instinct told her to stay; he was her only chance of salvation.

"What are you thinking?" Rax asked.

"I should leave you to die," Ashanti declared.

"Absolutely."

Taken by surprise, Ashanti did not respond. Rax continued, "Ashanti, why did you heal me?"

"So I can demand an answer as to why you kill my people."

"We have to."

"You change my world and my life. We are peaceful people. Why don't you just leave us alone?"

"See that?" Rax pointed to his weapon. "That's the Heavenly Sword given to me at birth, a curse, for I shall remain restless until I find the other half, which is among your people."

"Why kill my people? Just ask for it."

"My own race is dying because of my sword, the Sword of Death. For us to live, we sacrifice your people to the gods."

"Why my people?" Ashanti asked, becoming impatient.

"Its sisterly sword is the Giver of Life. They work hand in hand."

"Exchanging death with life. Why don't you throw your sword away?"

"It always finds its way home. Each time my bones ache even more."

Ashanti recognized the multicolored moonbeam insignia, the mark of the Colored Tempest, on its handle. The same sign was on her saber. Who was this blond leader, she wondered, promising to bring peace? How could she refuse such an offer?

"I can help you," Ashanti said reluctantly.

Rax's face lit up with his deep blue eyes gleaming with pleasure. He sat up straight. "Tell me."

"First promise me a peace treaty. Five years have passed and Rosnin still cries for her sons."

"I swear by my sword." He showed her the inscriptions on the blade.

"Don't take those too lightly, Rax. You are in the chamber where life and death begin," Ashanti warned.

"Tell me the name of the sword."

"Are you looking for the Dragon Saber?"

"Yes, yes . . . yes . . . where can I find it?"

"I have it."

"Let's get it now."

"At midnight."

Ashanti urged him to rest and then went through a secret underground passage into the courtyard. The lanterns cast irregular shadows, a painful reminder that she should not be there. She sneaked into the caravan, hoping to surprise her Guardian and to tell her the good news. There were her ceremonial dress, her beads, her prayer book, her staff, but no Mother Superior.

Her heart sank the instant she saw blood stains on a white veil. She wanted to scream, to cry, or both. The tears would not come. The voice was lost, so was her protector and the last chance before her disease attacked her mind. Just imagine handing him the saber, she thought. She must avenge her teacher's death; that was the Malkai warrior code.

Taking the saber from her room, she headed for the chamber and crept toward the sleeping figure on the altar. Before she could strike, Rax sprang up. The fright caused her to stumble. She quickly got up, leaning her back against the wall.

"Ashanti, why?"

She could not let his soft voice stop her mission. "You killed my mother. How could you?"

"Mother Superior was your mother?"

"She brought me in from the storm and taught me to love, to care what is good. And you destroyed everything I have ever loved. Chezmar told us you never touched a Malkai sister."

"I didn't know. Ashanti, listen to me."

"No. You shall die tonight."

"Please . . . there will be regrets."

"Why didn't you tell me about Mother Superior?"

"Would you have listened?" Rax asked in a weary voice. "After I was poisoned, Chezmar took her life to prolong mine so we could make this journey. I did not have the strength to stop him."

Although it didn't make sense, she believed him. She couldn't deny her feelings. It was not his fault that Chezmar made that dreadful decision, but it didn't change the fact that Rax was in charge. "Liar! Why didn't you tell me earlier? You never care for anyone but yourself."

His face changed to a darker color. "Give me your saber. I leave Rosnin alone."

"I'm not a fool."

Ashanti charged forward. In an instant, the blades flamed and licked, seeming barely to touch each other and leap apart; then, with a sudden twist, he caught her saber, forcing it back on her shoulder. Ashanti cried out at the fury of that stroke.

Rax reeled back suddenly, blood spurting over his own shoulder; his sword slipping from his numb fingers. "Ashanti, I never meant to hurt you. Forgive me," he whispered before giving in to the hands of darkness.

As a healer, her heart reached out for him. Her trembling fingers ran across his cheek. As her tears dropped to his lips, she removed his mask and saw the familiar look; the face she had been wearing all these years.

Remembering her dream, she turned aside. "Mother kept her promise. She died for me so I could live."

Ashanti aligned her dragon saber with the heavenly sword beside the lifeless body. Both inscriptions on the weapons combined to read, "One begins, one ends. It happens every day."

The shiny blades reflected her own image, setting her troubled spirit free to smile at last. What a lovely smile, she thought.

THE PHOENIX MEDALLION

by Diann Partridge

Both here and in the Darkover anthologies, Diann Partridge is one of ours; as she reminded me in updating her autobiography, this is the eighth story of hers I've bought.

She says, "I am currently 38, and still living in this little town (Lovell, Wyoming) where gossip seems to be the main form of recreation, if you don't include religious procreation." She has two teenage girls, a pre-teenage boy and has been married to the same husband for more than 18 years. The household includes two cats and a copper-colored mouse that bites.

Diann quit her job in a pizza parlor and underwent carpal tunnel surgery on her wrist. Now she is planning to pay off a vet's bill by fashioning some stained glass for him. (And people credit me with enough imagination to make up something half as good as that? I'd never have dared to invent that copper colored mouse!)

This dark and savage story starts slowly, gathers suspenseful momentum, builds to a wonderful dramatic climax, then ends with almost a sigh of relief, which the reader shares. I like the pacing here, and the sure hand that supplies the reader with enough information to fully appreciate the story's outcome.

"Girl, where'd you get this?"

Zarz jerked back, preventing the soldier from touching the pendant. Amid the din and clatter of the marketplace shutting down for midday, she hadn't realized he was talking to her. Neek's chuckle rippled through her mind as she cursed herself silently.

The pendant had slipped out of her chest band to dangle against her stomach. Covering it with her hand, she glared.

"Legal find. Law marked. None a yore business."

"Would this help make it my business?" He pulled a ring of coins from beneath his sword belt and removed two copper tils.

Neek agreed silently. Pocketing the two tils, Zarz opened her hand. He looked without touching. Neek approved. Then he motioned for Zarz to turn the medallion over. He nodded at what he saw. Oval egg on one side, a flame on the other. There was a tax mark near the edge. Lawful find.

"Where'd you find it?"

"Two tillets."

He didn't even bargain. Just took off two silver coins and handed them over.

"Found it down south. Neek 'n me, hunt the Ruins for a livin."

"You're brave. Anyone else ever hunt down there?"

Zarz shook her head. She continued packing up the little trinket stand. It was almost noon and the wise had retired inside to wait out the heat. She glanced at the soldier's uniform and wondered how he stood it.

"How would you and your partner feel about guiding me and some friends back to where you found this?"

Neek pushed back the flap that covered their stall and stepped out. To the soldier's credit his eyes only widened at the sight of her. Not too many Tammers came this far north. She was shorter than Zarz by two fingers, shorter than the man by a whole hand. She smiled a toothy grin with her lipless mouth.

"Too hot. Come back later."

With that, Zarz gathered up their wares, ducked into the little shack, and tied down the flap. Both shook with silent laughter. The man was left standing in the rapidly emptying market under the cruel noonday sun. He took off the wide brimmed hat and wiped the sweat off his face.

Inside, they stepped carefully down the earth cut steps,

into the cool damp darkness of the hole they were paying a whole tillet a moon to rent.

"He saw the pendant."

"Legal find. Law marked. No worry. He'll be back. Now sleep."

They curled up on woven mats and dozed. Zarz comforted herself with dreams of the fresh water bath one of the tillets would buy.

Kilean was sweating profusely by the time he made it back to the inn. He descended to his room and drank two glasses of water. No matter how much he drank it didn't quench his thirst. It was just too damned hot and humid. The encroaching sea permeated everything with its salty dampness. He wiped his gritty face with a wet towel and put on a dry shirt.

Light coming from the room at the end of the hallway was tinged with the blue of magic. Kilean knocked softly on the door, waiting for permission. There was a quiet "enter" and he went in quickly.

High Lord Vanceret Dosard sat at a desk with his back to the door, bright blond head bent over a map. His sister, Silini, lay on the bed; her long hair trailing over the side to make a silken puddle of light on the floor. The thin diaphanous gown she wore hid nothing. Kilean swallowed hard against her attraction and averted his eyes. Silini's lips smiled.

"Did you find anything, Kilean?" Vanceret asked softly. The sweat that had plastered the clean shirt to Kilean's back turned cold in the magically cooled room.

"Yes, my Lord, I found Lord Vinceray's phoenix medallion."

Silini pushed herself up on one arm. The gown molded itself over her taut breasts.

"Did you get it? Do they know where he is?" she asked sharply.

Kilean shook his head to both questions. "No, my lady. It was claimed as a lawful find from the Ruins by a female scavenger."

"Did she see anyone else there?" The High Lord did not bother to look up from his map.

"No, my lord. It was noon and all the shops were

closing up. If I want more information, I am to go back later. They said they would talk."

"They, Kilean?"

He hesitated briefly. "There's a Tammer with the woman, my lord."

Vanceret raised his head. Only Silini saw him smile.

"A full blood, Kilean?"

"No, my Lord. A crossbreed. Mature female, as I judge it."

Vanceret's smile widened and Silini shivered.

"Very good, Kilean. If Vincerey went south, then that must be where the Leak is. Go back this evening and talk to them. Pay them what they want, but make sure they will guide us to where they found the medallion. Do not fail me in this, Kilean."

Kilean swallowed hard, shivering involuntarily at the soft, menacing tone. "No, my lord."

Vanceret dismissed him with a languid wave of his hand. He backed out the door, suddenly grateful for the humid heat that engulfed him.

Silini lay back on the bed. "How will we be able to stop the Leak, Brother? We are only two among so few left. And our Magic grows weaker the farther south we go."

"Humans don't realize that, my love. They are still afraid of us, even down here." The High Lord rose and directed his gaze toward Silini.

"A Tammer."

She met his eyes and smiled. With a flick of his finger the sapphire robe he wore was gone, as was the gown that covered his sister. He crossed to the bed, his desire evident and she welcomed him into her arms.

The oppressive heat lifted a little at twilight. The marketplace reopened. Servants and slaves, along with poor housewives, bargained for fresh fish, the least moldy bread, but most important of all—fresh water. The noise made talking impossible. Kilean invited Zarz and Neek to a nearby tavern. Zarz left their wares inside the shack and tipped a neighboring vendor a til to watch the place.

The remains of the damp-rotted tavern creaked and

groaned over their heads when they descended into the large room underneath. Metal poles braced the ceiling every few lengths. Kilean wrinkled his nose at the smell of mildew and the stink of unwashed bodies. At a wink from Zarz the barkeep led them to a table, then brought them a dark bottle of wine. She pulled out the medallion.

"We will require you to lead us to where you found that. Buy whatever supplies we will need and you will be paid five gold lettles when we get there."

Zarz was careful not to let her surprise show. In her mind she could hear Neek crowing with delight. It was a fortune.

Instead she bargained. "Six apiece."

"You're crazy. For that amount I could hire the whole city."

"All right. Do it." She tapped the medallion on the table.

"Four apiece. No more. And you buy the supplies out of it."

Neek shook her head and took another pull on the bottle.

"Five. Apiece. You buy the supplies."

Kilean reached for the bottle and looked directly at Neek. She grinned back. Little pointy teeth glinted in the candlelight. He had never been this close to a crossbred Tammer before. She smelled of exotic lust and his mouth was suddenly dry. If she had this effect on him, he would well understand a Tammer's legendary attraction to the High Lords. A membrane flickered across Neek's slanted vermilion eyes and Kilean jerked, toppling the bottle. Neek's narrow little hand flashed out and caught it.

"All right, five apiece. But we split the cost of supplies. Half now and a lettle apiece when we start. The rest at journey's end."

"Pay now," insisted Neek.

"I don't carry gold lettles around with me, girl. The High Lord will pay you when we start out."

Neek stiffened instantly. "High Lord?" she hissed. "You said nothing about High Lords. The Tammer'ehler have nothing to do with damned High Lords. The deal is off!" She hammered a sharp-nailed fist down on the table. Ignoring Kilean's protests, she hissed again and spat, then jumped up and stormed out. Everyone moved quickly out of her way. Tammer skill with the sharp-bladed knives she wore in crossed bands over her chest was legendary too.

"You agreed, both of you, to this deal," snarled Kilean, desperation chewing at him at the thought of displeasure on Vanceret's face. High Lords had no morals and no loyalty except to themselves.

"Sit down," whispered Zarz in a snarl. "Shut up. Everyone is looking."

Kilean sat back down. Zarz took the last drink from the bottle.

"You shouldn't have mentioned High Lords. Everyone knows Tammers won't work for them. After what they did to the Ancestors, would you?"

"It's not my problem," answered Kilean. "*I* do work for a High Lord. You and your friend will work for me, if you like that arrangement better."

"Still," Zarz braced both elbows on the table and rested her chin on her clasped fists, "you know how High Lords are about Tammers. Can't leave 'em alone. He'll have to promise to leave her be." Suddenly she felt quite mellow towards this soldier. It must be the wine.

"He'll promise nothing. She will have to take her chances." Kilean took a long drink to hide his nervousness. "What are you doing working with a Tammer anyway? How do I know I can trust either of you?"

"Ya don't. Take yore chances. Neek's family. See," she turned to the light so he could make out the ridged scars on her shoulder. Clan marks. "Her people claimed me when my own were kilt in the last war. I don't remember anything before them 'cept screams and flames and the sound a soldiers' feet marchin in the street. Tammers always take in the leftovers."

Kilean wished she'd shut up. "Can you convince her to come along?"

"I'll work on it. Maybe she'll feel differently in the mornin. Here, finish this up." She pushed the bottle toward him. The wine was rough, but it left a warm glow.

They finished off two more bottles. Kilean was beyond

discretion by then, totally desperate. Zarz kept stringing him along, never promising completely. By the fourth bottle she knew he would agree to anything. Her lewd suggestion startled him almost sober. Looking across the table, he considered her. Vanceret had said to pay them what he must. Kilean wondered if the High Lord would consider this payment? He'd bedded worse looking women in his life, but never one who shaved her head or notched her ears.

"Where?" he asked drunkenly.

"I know a place."

She led him out of the tavern and up the hill. The building was above ground, dark and windowless except for a dimly lit sign over the door showing a pattern of rain drops. Zarz knocked and they went in. He paid what was asked to a large black man with a steel hook in place of one hand and she pulled him down the hallway to a room.

Inside the room, with the door barred and one small candle lit, she was all over him. The chest band and clout she wore were gone in an instant and he was hard put to get his own clothes off before she ripped them from him. Her hands and lips were everywhere. Kilean felt her desire flash over him like a hot wind. Rational thought became impossible and he let himself be swept away. They coupled like mindless animals upon the thin pallet on the floor.

Sometime during the night she woke him and they went underground to a bathing room. He paid for fresh water, watching in drunken amazement as the attendant shaved Zarz' head. It seemed like hours later that he realized that she was moving once again on top of him, then he passed out completely.

Something prodded him painfully in the side and he woke up. Zarz was standing over him, grinning.

"Get up," she prodded him again with her bare foot. "Neek agrees. Gimme the money. Dock side, night tide."

Groggily, Kilean sat up, holding his head with both hands. He peered up at Zarz through gummy eyes.

"Hurry up. Money."

He rummaged around on the floor until he found the ring. Sliding a handful off, he gave them to Zarz. She grinned wider and gave him a mock salute, saying as she left, "Pay the man. I took another bath."

Kilean groaned.

True to her word, Zarz and Neek were waiting at the dock after dark. Neek hissed savagely at the sight of the High Lord and his sister. She ducked behind Zarz. The rest of the people bowed and scraped as they passed, then quickly forked a warding off sign. Even in the darkness it was too warm for anyone human to be bundled up in heavy hooded cloaks. Come too close and the sharp crackle of magic shocked you away.

Kilean stowed the packs in the boat. The High Lord's lingering gaze caused the crest on the little yellow Tammer's neck to flare in irritation.

Zarz tossed a tillet to one of the free rowers and they tied on to the boat and rowed them out to where they could catch the sluggish current. Once they were caught in it, Neek stood in the stern and sculled just enough to keep them on course. Light from the two moons gave the water a greenish cast. The water here wasn't deep, but every year the sea rose a bit more. Some said it was caused by the war that the High Lords had fought among themselves. Others claimed it was because the Tammer'ehler had withdrawn from the world rather than be used to satisfy the High Lords' lust. Whatever the reason, the sea rose.

Three days they traveled the current, Zarz and Neek taking turns with the sculling. Traffic thinned out the further south they went and they saw no one after the third day. During the oppressive heat of noon they holed up under the thick branches of the giant swamp willows. Always, the High Lord and his sister reclined behind a magically cooled partition.

When the second moon rose on the fourth night, Neek beached the boat on a small island. There were trees on the knoll, surrounded by a broken stone wall. Kilean realized that they were coming closer to the drowned cities of the south.

Vanceret conjured a huge tent. His power made Zarz

uneasy. Her hand crept to the belt knife she wore. He watched Neek, stalking her with his eyes. His kind were responsible for creatures like Neek, magically breeding with the pure-blooded Tammer'ehler. Zarz knew all the clan stories of how the High Lords hungered to lie with their creations. Neek had sharpened all the knives in her bands earlier that day.

Kilean built a small fire away from the glowing tent. Neek went fishing, returning with several catfish and a thick black eel. He gutted the fish, spitting them on green willow sticks over the smoky fire. Neek whacked the eel's head with a rock and ate it raw.

High Lord Vanceret emerged from the tent. Lines of blue Power swirled around him as he beckoned with a long slim finger and Neek jerked upright. Zarz felt herself held in place by the same force. Struggling did no good. Neek silently put one foot in front of the other and followed the High Lord inside.

When the flap dropped, Zarz was released. Kilean tackled her in the same instant, pinning her to the ground.

"It'll do you no good to try and help her."

"Let me up," she snarled, squirming beneath him. "I'll kill him. He has no right. Done enough to her. And mine. Git off me!"

She broke free just for an instant, but he was on her again.

"Let it go, Zarz. He'll kill you both if you interfere. He's a High Lord, don't you understand that? He can do what he wants."

He caught her arms before she could claw his face. Sweat dripped off his face and he panted in the heat. Quick as a striking snake, she arched up and bit his chin. He jerked away and slapped her hard. From the tent came a low moaning shriek. The High Lord and his sister made no effort to shield their lust and it rolled over Zarz and Kilean. They were immediately caught up in its compulsion. There was no rational thought beyond personal satisfaction. The moaning went on and on throughout the night.

Toward dawn Neek staggered from the tent. Together

she and Zarz swam away to another small island and disappeared into the brush. They collapsed on the ground.

"Did he hurt you?" Zarz whispered as soon as she could talk.

"No imagination," answered Neek. "The sister is more interesting but has no will. Their Power will be drained very low after last night." She hissed this last with a bit of pride. "The soldier?"

"Adequate. Thinks he must protect me."

They stifled their laughter.

"He may have planted a seed. Won't know for days. You?"

"Drained him. Our clan will increase."

"We must go back."

Kilean was pacing the shore when they returned. Zarz shook off his helping hand. They ignored everyone. Vanceret supported Silini into the boat.

"We'll be there by nightfall," stated Zarz as she sculled back into the current. It was stronger here. Vanceret collapsed next to his sister. Neek winked at Zarz, then curled up to sleep. Kilean glanced around nervously, then took up a guard position between the High Lord and the Tammer.

It grew hotter and more humid as the day wore on. They were now in among the drowned remains of city, crumbling chimneys and rooftops provided roosts for aquatic birds and small animals. The water was thick and murky, covered with an oily sheen. Kilean fought to stay awake. Occasionally he heard a large splash. Zarz sought no shelter from the noon sun. She guided the boat deeper into the maze toward the only land in sight. Kilean shook himself hard and saw in horrified amazement more than a dozen Tammers swimming behind the boat.

Zarz ran the boat aground and more Tammers and a few humans helped pull it out of the water.

"Wake them up," she snapped at Kilean, motioning toward the High Lord and his sister.

He drew his sword. Dozens of hands automatically went to knives in crossed chest bands. Kilean stepped toward the High Lord, noticing how dull and shrunken he looked. He dared to touch Vanceret's shoulder.

"My Lord? Wake up. We're here."

High Lord Vanceret pushed himself up. Silini slept on. He looked around slowly, taking in the Tammers and human females who awaited him.

"This is where you found my brother's medallion?"

Neek nodded. "He made it this far. He found the Leak that was draining your magic away. But he couldn't close it. We wouldn't let him. We used him, as you used the Ancestors—as we will use you before you are gone. You destroyed the Ancestors in creating us, now we will destroy you in increasing our Tribe."

"Kilean, protect me!" Vanceret demanded. The soldier moved beside the High Lord, sword drawn.

"You will be protected, High Lord," spoke up one of the Tammers, green with age, a half-smile pulling her thin mouth away from sharp teeth. "We have a great need for you. Would you like to see?"

Without waiting for his answer, the group moved as one toward the High Lord and Kilean, herding them farther away from the shore. High atop the island stood a well-like structure. It hurt Kilean's eyes to look directly at it. The shiny surface reflected the harsh sunlight in brillant streaks. The air around the structure pulsed slowly.

"It's one of your toys, High Lord. Left over from long ago. Do you remember how it works? There are no shields on it now. In your battles with your own kind you would place the vanquished Lord inside and drain off his magic. Do you know what we do with it now, High Lord?"

This last question brought screams of laughter from the rest of the Tammers. The noise woke Silini, who was being dragged along by several women. She struggled weakly and began to moan.

"You have no power over me," snarled Vanceret. He pulled himself up to his full height and glared.

"You have no power now, High Lord. Our sister Neek took most of it into herself last night. What is left is being drained by this construction of your kind. Use your

Power and you will be gone that much quicker. Soon you will be nothing, as the First Mothers were nothing when you finished with them. But we will protect you, High Lord. For a time."

This brought more laughter and the Tammers moved in. Kilean raised his sword and instantly dozens of sharp bladed knives thudded into him. He looked down in surprise before he toppled to the ground. High Lord Vanceret raised his arms and muttered a spell, but the syphoning from the well caught his Power and sucked it in. He staggered and fell toward Silini who was lying on the ground. Her hand caught his. He turned desperate eyes on her and she shrieked one last time as he drained what Power she had left.

"Good, High Lord, good. Make yourself strong. Just remember, if you use your Power here, the Well will suck it in. Here, you are no High Lord. Just another male who will provide an increase for many Clans."

"Take him away. Gently, sisters, gently."

His hands tied, they guided him back to the boat and rowed away. Several of the Tammers gathered up Silini and carried her to the Well. Her long hair stirred in the current and swirled up and over the edge. With a bright flash her body was sucked in. Kilean's body was disposed of in the same manner.

"It's too bad about the man," said one Tammer to Zarz. "We could have used him, too."

"He was adequate," she answered. "We can always find more. Here," she pulled the phoenix medallion from around her neck and handed it over. "It's your turn now. Neek and I have finished our Trial. We can go home now."

Neek just grinned.

A RUN IN THE FOREST

by David A. Pillard

David Pillard works for an environmental consulting firm in Fort Collins, Colorado; he enclosed his business card giving his occupation as Aquatic Ecologist/Toxicologist. David adds that, in addition to writing, he spends time working in the garden, cross country skiing, and woodworking in his shop.

He has some scientific papers to his credit, but this is his first fiction sale. David says he's enjoyed science fiction and fantasy for years, much to the dismay of his English teachers. I think we've all had that experience; many literature and writing teachers seem to think fantasy is un-English or something. I prefer to think they're just jealous, or worse, have pedestrian imaginations.

David thanks his wife, Wendy, and her brother, Drew, for "their comments and criticisms of my stories." He claims his black Labrador retriever, Tarma (named after Misty Lackey's character, of course), prefers dog biscuits to sword play, but does "occasionally display telepathic abilities."

The idea of the sorceress bereft of magic is often used; but this cleverly crafted story gives a new twist to an old theme. And throughout, it is hard for the sorceress, and for us, to tell what is real and what is magical . . .

Rhelan had been running for several hours when she felt the tingling sensation began to trickle through her limbs. Even though she was in wolf form and her mind was bent only on the thought of escape, she recognized the feeling as it came over her.

Not now, she thought, please not now.

But she knew pleading with herself or the gods would do no good. She stopped running and lay down on a bed of soft leaves, panting heavily to rid her body of the excess heat that had built up over several miles. Slowly her body began to shimmer, her rich gray fur changing into pale skin; her paws transforming into hands and feet. Within a few moments the sleek wolf was gone; replaced by a young woman shivering on the ground, naked except for a crude amulet hanging from a leather thong around her neck.

Rhelan knew she had to keep moving. She had been running very fast, using every trick she knew to hide her tracks. But while Lord Jextan's hunting hounds might lose her trail, she suspected the spell hounds would not; as a wolf she was a creature of magic. In human form she no longer had her magic, but nor did she have the stamina of the wolf or the protection of her fur. Even as a wolf, sharp stones and sticks had done their work on her paws and muzzle. She looked at her hands and feet which had several small cuts and scrapes on them; she could imagine what her face looked like. She had fled in such a hurry she had not taken the time to put her clothes into a bundle that she could carry as a wolf. In any case, if the spell hounds lost her trail, the hunting hounds would take over.

"Catiz!" she swore out loud, "If I ever get my hands on Hulif, I'll turn him into a frog and put him into a marsh full of hungry herons!" As she lay on the forest floor catching her breath and gazing up at the half moon, she remembered with distaste the events of nearly a year ago when Hulif, a relatively unskilled minor adept, cast a spell which took away her magic. Rhelan suspected that he did it by accident rather than design, since it was a quite powerful spell. Even though she finally regained her powers they would occasionally disappear for short periods of time, often at the most inopportune moments, as they had tonight. And now Lord Jextan's soldiers were closing in on her and if she didn't keep moving they would surely catch her; after that, well, she didn't like to think about it.

Rhelan pulled herself up from the ground and, brushing her short, black hair from her face, began pushing her way through the thinning trees, the moon casting just enough light to help her avoid the most serious branches. Only hours before she had been sitting comfortably by the fire in the Blue Boar Inn at Forintbury, enjoying a mug of ale. She had been in a good mood when she left the inn to return to her own lodgings, but as she passed under the shadow of the Temple of Zirkan her good mood was swept away. On the east side of the tall, black building lay the last pile of stones that were to be set in place in the tower. Soon the temple would be completed and Rhelan shuddered to think of what would happen then. She remembered when she was young and her family had fled the southern city of Oyt. The atrocities of the Temple of Zirkan had become unbearable. Children and young men and women had disappeared; odd sounds and smells emanated from the temple and local vegetation began to shrivel and die. Her family, along with several other worshippers of Mithal, fled the city and came to Forintbury and the surrounding countryside. She had nearly forgotten Zirkan when the first priests came to Forintbury. When old Lord Wesslen died and Jextan seized control, no one doubted that Zirkan's priests were involved.

So whether it was her harsh memories of Oyt, or the excessive amount of ale she had consumed that night, as Rhelan stood outside the Blue Boar gazing at the cold, evil building, a great hatred rose up inside of her. Grasping the amulet of Mithal which hung around her neck she called magic to her and, in an impressive surge of great power caused the dark temple to collapse on itself, leaving nothing but a pile of rubble. Almost instantly she regretted her actions; not because she didn't hate the worship of Zirkan, but because she suddenly realized that the retribution she would suffer would be tremendous. How foolish she had been. She could easily have left Forintbury; others could have as well. She did not have to stay around to witness the horrors of Zirkan. But it was too late. The temple was down and soldiers would be there soon. She was too drained of magic to put up a defense, so she ran.

Rhelan had made her way through the trees to the bank of a large stream. The stream, she reasoned, probably drained the Yellow Dunes farther to the north, for the river banks consisted of wide stretches of deposited sand. Thankfully she began running on the cool smooth sand which was much easier on her battered feet. Her amulet began to swing back and forth as she moved and she grasped it with her left hand to hold it still. Although it now hung loosely about her neck, in wolf form her thick neck and fur held it securely in place. The amulet, given to her by her father, was a hexagon inside of which a circle represented the shining sun of Mithal. Inside the sun an intricate design represented the interaction of all living and nonliving things. As she ran along the sand, occasionally splashing through small pools of water, Rhelan considered that perhaps she should have gone to more worship services, even though she distinctly disliked the arrogant, fat priests of Mithal. They were not evil like those of Zirkan, but they still took advantage of the worshipers. Even so, maybe Mithal would help her now if she had been a little more attentive. Rhelan shrugged and muttered a prayer anyway.

The sandy stream bank began to disappear and up ahead Rhelan could see that the stream narrowed and disappeared into a small canyon where she could not go. Rhelan paused to catch her breath. She tried to call her magic, but it still refused to answer her summons. It was then that she saw the path on the other side of the stream leading into the forest. It was old and unused; shrubs and small trees had nearly taken over the road, but Rhelan could still tell it was a path of some kind. Rhelan clenched her teeth and waded into the cold water. As she left the stream and entered the forest a chorus of unearthly howls pierced the night air. The trembling that Rhelan felt was not due only to her wet skin.

Despite the overgrown vegetation the trail was easier to follow than Rhelan would have thought. It went on for quite a distance into the thick forest, turning this way and that as it cut through the trees. Exhaustion was beginning to engulf Rhelan when the trail ended rather abruptly. She stubbed her toe on a large rectangular stone before she saw the building materialize in front of her. It wasn't much of a building. The walls were once composed of gray stones similar to the one she had just tripped over. Now, however, most of the walls were only two or three rows high and the layout of the structure had largely disappeared under the rubble of the fallen stone. Curiously, toward the rear of the structure, which was set against a natural stone face leading up to a cliff 100 feet above her head, some of the building was still standing. She entered the structure through a crumbling doorway, trying not to cut her feet on any sharp stone shards. Overhead, moonlight showed through holes in the vaulted roof, casting a dim, pearly light on the building's interior. Rhelan sat down on a block of stone and stared forlornly at the forest through the door. She knew she should keep on running, but she was exhausted and battered. She resigned herself to resting here until her pursuers caught up with her, and hoped her powers would return by then.

It was after a few moments and her eyes had grown accustomed to the dim light that she noticed the glow out of the corner of her left eye. At first she wasn't sure it was real, but as she walked toward the glow it grew brighter. The light lay in the rear of the structure and she realized as she continued walking that the carefully-carved stone blocks had given way to natural stone. Apparently a cave led from the building into the rock wall itself. As the red light became brighter she realized it was a bed of glowing coals; the remnants of a fire. Beside the coals an old man sat, wrapped in a large blanket. Rhelan supposed she should have run; she was naked without a weapon of any sort and her magic still refused to return. But she did not run. She simply stood in the cave staring at the figure, who watched her from the confines of the blanket. She stood there for several minutes and was startled when the figure finally spoke.

"Do you always wander uninvited into other people's camps without any clothes on, or are the rules of courtesy different in this part of the country?"

"I . . . I fell off my horse while riding through the forest and lost my way," Rhelan said, hesitantly, "I've been wandering for hours. I did not mean to intrude on your sleep."

The old man smiled at Rhelan, "I don't sleep much and you're welcome to rest here." Reaching into a bundle that lay at his feet, the figure pulled out a rough wool blanket and tossed it over to Rhelan who quickly draped it around her cold body. "Tell me, milady, did your horse also take all of your clothes? I would suggest you invest in a new mount if it did."

Rhelan realized her story had several flaws, but she was uncertain as to whether she should tell this stranger the real reason for her current predicament. She watched as he added wood to the fire and stoked it into life. With the increased illumination Rhelan saw something that lifted her heart and gave her comfort. Around the neck of the stranger, peeking out from under the blanket, was an amulet of Mithal, very similar to her own, although more carefully crafted. Taking a deep breath she quickly told him the whole story, from her destruction of the temple to the loss of her powers earlier in the night and her trek to this collapsed structure. The stranger said nothing but simply sat and listened. When she finished, the figure quietly stirred the fire with a stick before resuming the conversation.

"And now that you've done what you've done," he asked, "do you regret your actions?"

Rhelan sighed and looked into the fire.

"If I hadn't destroyed the temple I wouldn't be sitting here without any clothes, about to be ripped apart by Lord Jextan's hounds. I could have left the city; others did. It really wasn't my responsibility to rid the city of that atrocity."

"No, it wasn't your responsibility. But if the temple had been completed, what would have happened?"

"I suppose the same thing that happened in Oyt and all of the other cities dominated by Zirkan's worshipers. Innocent people would have died; the land would have been poisoned."

"So by risking your own life you may have saved many others."

"They'll only build another temple." Rhelan replied

disconsolately, "Destroying a temple does not destroy a religion."

"No. But it might provide enough time for those opposed to Jextan to organize and force him and those hell-spawned priests out of power."

Rhelan had not thought about that before. It was true that there were many nobles who, although they had no strong feelings about Zirkan, were at least unhappy with Jextan and his thugs who overtaxed them. Already rebellious groups had organized and were making periodic raids on Jextan's tax soldiers and properties. She looked at the figure across the fire with renewed interest and began to wonder if maybe this was one such rebel.

She was about to inquire about the loyalties of the stranger when she heard a distant howl permeate the cave. She quickly rose and made her way out to the doorway of the building. To the east the early sun was shedding its light over the horizon. Again she heard the howling, this time a little closer. Looking outside in the growing sunlight she could see that there was nowhere else to run. She would have to make her stand here. Rhelan turned back to the fire to make one last attempt to call her powers. However, in the expanding radiance of dawn she saw something she had not seen before. Lying on top of some of the collapsed blocks was a large, flat rectangular stone, worn smooth around the edges. On top of the stone was a pattern carved into the rock. Rhelan kneeled and blew the accumulated dust and dirt away from the pattern; her eyes grew wide in amazement. The pattern, though faint, was an exact duplicate of the amulet which hung from her neck and the neck of the stranger.

"This was a temple!" she called to the man. "A temple of Mithal!"

There was no reply from the figure in the cave and when she returned to the fire no one was there. The blanket the man had worn was gone along with his bundle. The fire remained, and beside it shimmered the amulet of Mithal which the stranger had worn. Rhelan could now see that it was indeed a finely-crafted piece. The intricate inner pattern was inlaid with gold and mother-of-pearl, and several jewels adorned the thick, gold chain. Without thinking she picked up the chain and, with little hesitation, placed it around her neck alongside her own crude decoration. It was then that she felt the power returning; growing inside her. This time, however, it felt different, stronger, and she knew it would not leave her again tonight. As she pulled the woolen blanket around her, she was not surprised to find it was no longer a rough blanket but a long blue and green cape with silver stitching and a hood which she pulled up over her tangled hair. She smiled, kicked dirt over the fire, and returned to the front of the structure. In the forest she could hear the horses and dogs beating their way through the underbrush of the old road. She was no longer afraid. The magic that gathered around her was so thick it felt almost solid; Rhelan knew she could make it solid if need be. She touched the amulet again and, casting a glance over her shoulder at the ancient stone altar, considered that after she returned to the city she ought to attend more worship services. In response to her unspoken musings she thought she heard a faint voice rise from the back of the temple, inside the cave.

"No, Rhelan, why bother?"

OLD AGE AND TREACHERY . . .

by Nancy L. Pine

Nancy Pine writes to us that "Now that classes and concerts are over, at least temporarily, I can write out that biography you wanted. I live in Kingston, New York and work at the Kingston Area Library. My spare time, outside of writing, is taken up with my choral group and college classes. I am working on a novel, and since this one hasn't bored me silly by chapter ten, there seems to be a good chance that I will finish it."

She sounds like a girl after my own heart; libraries and choral singing are two of "the fondest things I am of." I don't have too much religion, but I do believe in J.S. Bach; my favorite piece of choral music is the Brahms *Requiem,* which I want played at my funeral. (Not right away, though.)

Nancy loves "all bookstores, but the ones that sell used books are the ones that make my eyes light up. I also love animals, Maine, and pastrami sandwiches. You can make of that what you will."

I liked "Old Age and Treachery" because so little, and so much, happens. The protagonist is an old woman who can barely move, and whose stated motive for repelling an invasion is that it will interrupt her meal schedule. Still, by the end of the story, you realize what she must have been. . . .

It was good, very good, to sit here in the sun and warm her old bones. Della stretched her shoulder muscles, stopping when one of her joints complained. Across the compound she could see the youngsters warming up, swinging their practice blades in the stylized moves that she had learned when she was that age. It seemed hard, now, to believe that she had ever been that young, but she must have been.

And now, here, at the West Borderhold in the country of Melliya, she had come to rest, after being a mercenary for twenty-five years, and after spending another twenty training raw youngsters like the ones across the compound. After years of getting up every morning and exercising muscles, after years of not being sure where her next meal was coming from, she was here, resting her bones, with someone to look after her and bring her meals and make sure that all was well.

The trainer, Kylora, snarled at the trainees, and one of the girls dropped her wooden practice blade with a nervous gesture. Della shook her head. It seemed that every year the students became dumber, and more feckless. She may, possibly, have been that young. But she had never been that silly, of that she was sure.

She eyed the girls from her porch chair. They had started training with practice blades a week ago, and she didn't think they were making much progress. Why, that tall one over there, she was still holding her sword more with her fingertips than with her hand. Try using a fingertip grip when setting out to slay a dragon. See how far it will get you then.

The trainer shook her head in exasperation, and Della sympathized. She had done her fair share of training back when she was younger, and had first come across this country where all women were welcome, and most of the men died at birth. Nearly ten women to one man, those were how the odds ran in Melliya, and any woman from any country who was in need of sanctuary was welcome. It was a country that would welcome a merc in her middle years who was beginning to wonder what would become of her when she was old, provided the merc was willing to work for as long as she could. Work had never frightened Della. Not much ever had, except the thought of loneliness and need in her old age. So she had come here, and trained recruits, and sworn at them as Kylora was doing with the current batch of recruits, and then her bones had begun to shrivel up, and she started turning into an old crone, and now she was allowed to sit in the sun and rest her bones, and watch the current batch of recruits drop their weapons. It was a standing joke that she kept her eating dagger as brightly polished and as sharply honed as she had ever kept her sword.

She winced as another weapon fell to the ground, then winced again as Kylora slapped the offender across the knuckles with the wooden blade. Then she closed her eyes against the direct glare of the sun as it began to drop. A nap would be pleasant now, and before long the young apprentice who was assigned to her would bring her dinner tray, and she could eat.

She could sense a batch of apprentice mages going by, with the scorched aromas from failed spells still on them. And from the workrooms nearby she could hear someone hammering at the forge, and there was the sound of women talking as they worked their looms, or tended the gardens, or did any of the thousand and one chores that were connected with running an establishment of this size so close to the border. From the kitchens came wonderful smells that made her stomach rumble, and she smiled.

Another, older, batch of recruits went by, and she heard someone murmur something about, "useless old crone," before she could be shushed by the others. Useless old crone indeed. Wait until that girl had faced a band of brigands by herself, or had ridden up to a dragon's lair, or had to plot the moves that would save the throne for a king. By the time she had been through all that, and then had spent twenty years training recruits, she, too, would be glad to relax in the sun, and would learn to resent youngsters who made stupid remarks.

Her brief flame of indignation flickered out, and she fell asleep in the porch chair.

It was the growing silence that brought her back to awareness. The clack of the wooden blades had stopped, and the steady clanging from the forge ended abruptly. The chattering stopped, and Della opened her eyes to see a group of men standing across from her, actual *men* in the compound.

And not men of Melliya, who tended to be self-effacing, and who mostly stayed home and tended the children. These were men from other parts, and they were watching the man in the center of the compound, who was wearing the white robes of an Adept Sorcerer.

Invasion, thought Della in astonishment. Melliya has been invaded. She started to rise, to deal with this threat as she would have in her younger days, when her bones protested and she remembered that she was no longer a fighter, but an old, rheumatic crone. She watched as Kylora started forward, forgetting that she carried only a wooden practice blade, only to be frozen as her eyes met those of the sorcerer.

The man in the center was speaking, glancing about him as he spoke, and every time any of the women moved he stared at her, and brought her to frozen silence. His words seemed to wash away in the fear that was growing throughout the compound.

Della sat still. She knew what this was. This was the Eye-Holding, and she had seen it bring a whole town to silence. The sorcerer had picked his position carefully, where no one could come up in back of him. The sun was at his back, and in the eyes of those who might try to attack him. Now he could silence each person who seemed likely to cause him problems, and when all opposition had been stilled he would take whatever it was that had caused him to risk this attack. What it might be ranged from an apprentice mage with remarkable potential to three spell-swords that were being created in the forge. Della didn't know, and she didn't particularly care.

The important thing was to stop this nonsense in its tracks, before other men got the idea that they could enter Melliya with impunity. Otherwise they would be having an invasion every week, and it would raise havoc with the meal schedule.

Della waited until the sorcerer had turned to stare the women from the forge into statues before she dared stand up. The bones in her back caught her, and she grimaced, but she was standing, and beginning to move away, before the sorcerer had turned away from the smiths. She had no sword, here in this quiet place, and her throwing knives had long since been passed on to one of her trainees. All she had was the little eating dagger at her side, and that was not balanced for throwing. She began to scuttle along the walkway, heading away from the mage.

The sorcerer had just frozen the weavers when he glanced up and saw her, and laughed.

"Old woman," he sneered. "Old woman, your bones will rot in the sun." He raised his head to stare at her, and she raised her little dagger, holding it sideways and glancing at the sun to make sure she had the angle right.

This had better work, she thought grimly. She kept her eyes on a post next to her, rather than risk staring at the sorcerer and getting caught. A moment passed, and she peeked around, to see the sorcerer standing shock-still. The sun had caught the dagger at the right angle, and reflected his glance back into his own eyes. There had been much arguing among mercs as to whether a sorcerer or magician could be caught by his own spells. It looked as though they could.

The little apprentice who showed such promise emerged from under the porch where she had taken shelter, and approached the sorcerer carefully. She touched one shoulder, then nodded and turned her attention to the soldiers before they could realize what had happened.

It was good, very good, to sit here in the sun and warm her old bones. Della stretched her leg muscles, ignoring the creaks in her joints, and looked across the compound. The frozen statue in the center of the compound was being examined by several apprentice mages, and the trainees were beyond the garden, digging holes for the remains of the soldiers. Now and then someone glanced at her with wide eyes, then looked away again. Della closed her eyes and decided to take a nap before supper.

IN SHEEP'S CLOTHING

by Lawrence Schimel

Since Lawrence Schimel was in our area for a time, he's one of the young writers I think of definitely as "one of ours." I had the pleasure of publishing his very first story "way back when"—at which time I believe he was not out of his teens. He's now twenty and has story credits in five different anthologies, *Isaac Asimov's Science Fiction Magazine, Modern Short Stories, The Writer,* and others. He is, or was at this writing, a junior at Yale University and plans to spend the summer of 1992 traveling in Europe, dancing flamenco in Spain and practicing Calo (the language of the gypsies in Andalusia).

"In Sheep's Clothing" is a story done as a series of short dialogues and vignettes, woven together to make a compelling whole. This story, in the hands of a less skillful writer, would have been much longer and a lot less interesting.

The rumor was handed to her at market, included free with her purchase: a wolf had been heard on the moor last night.

Balía thanked the fruitseller, tucking the rumor in the bottom of her basket among the cabbages and potatoes, to tell to Morfelao later. The more delicate foods were placed on top, and pulling the cloth to keep them shielded from the sun, she continued on her way.

The wolf is not a solitary creature. Had a pack been heard Balía would have worried less. But a lone wolf was odd. A lone wolf meant shapechanger, human in borrowed form.

Balía had been given other rumors before. When she first came to Minagra, the townsfolk informed her that Morfelao was a sorceress, and her tongue cut out as a consequence, to still her evil incantations. The women who worked in Morfelao's household said she had been a heretic since her husband's death, and moreover, a persuasive one, thereby garnering the Inquisition's wrath.

To the townsfolk's dismay—for "she seemed such a nice girl"—Balía had accepted the post. What other work was there for a literate woman? Because she could not speak, Morfelao issued her commands by pen. No scriptorium would allow a woman to enter the grounds, let alone entrust one with a book. Yet, sometimes Morfelao would have Balía or one of the other girls read to her, just to have voices in her life. Furthermore, they were at liberty to peruse the library when the chores were done and they so chose. But the townsfolk did not understand. All they saw was superstition.

Should a single sheep be absent, or worse, a man attacked, the townsfolk would blame Morfelao the wolf. They would find her written notes and say, "Look! She has been writing curses. *This* is why my crop was lean. *This* is why there was no rain. *This* is why your horse dropped her foal early. We should have known. Burn her! At night she takes the form of a wolf! Burn them all! They have trafficked with devils." They would come with torches and knives, rope, and cords of wood.

Balía shivered and left her basket on the counter in the kitchen for Fariel to deal with, hurrying upstairs to find Morfelao. She found her at her desk in the study, pen still in hand as she stared blankly at the wall, absorbed in thought.

She had written: There is a wolf.

"How had she known?" Balía asked Fariel as she helped to mash the potatoes smooth enough for Morfelao to eat.

"A ewe was attacked last night. Korka found it, near dead, this morning after you'd left. Not sure why the wolf didn't kill. He tore a hind leg and left it."

"Does she live?"

"Keep mashing, she'll live. Though I can't say for how long. A lame sheep is easier pickings for a wolf, and she didn't give him much trouble the first time."

The moonlight seemed to find her eyes no matter what she tried, keeping her awake. Although frustrated, Balía lay still, so as not to wake Korka with whom she shared a room. She had tried everything she knew to put herself to sleep, but the most common—counting sheep—merely increased her worry. She wanted to dash outside to the barn and count that they were all still there, especially the now-lame ewe. Even though they had locked them in for the night, Balía mistrusted that they were safe. She even began to slip from bed once, if only to stand at the window and look across at the barn, but Korka had rolled over, disturbed by her wakefulness.

Best not to go outside, anyway, Balía reflected as she stared up at the dark ceiling, realizing she should fear for herself as much as them should she leave the safe confines of the house.

"Stocking up?" the fruitseller asked the next morning.

Balía blushed. "I forgot these yesterday."

"Well, at least you don't have to worry about the wolf when you make that long walk. Against a lone girl . . ."

"Was it—was it killed?"

"Yup. Shapechanger it was, too. Young thing, not more than ten or eleven. Just goes to show you can't trust anything in this world. They'll be burning the body this evening if you want to watch."

Balía did not want to watch. Her stomach folded in on itself. "A child," she whispered. "How could they?"

The fruitseller shrugged. "Three copper," she said, holding out her hand.

Most importantly, Balía and the others served as Morfelao's voice in the outside world. Balía had remained calm at the news of the boy's slaughter, and even as they paraded the body through the marketplace towards the temple. As soon as she had returned to the house, however, Balía broke down.

"A child," she cried to Morfelao, "a mere child. Innocent, too. He couldn't even kill our sheep, but resisted the impulses of his form." The bitterness in Morfelao's eyes was mute testimony that she could never underestimate human cruelty.

Balía fled from the house, and its human inhabitants, running outside to the barn, where she collapsed in the hay to cry. She was roused by a nuzzling at her back, and turned to find a sheep nibbling at her shirt. They had returned for the evening, still fearing a wolf in the woods, perhaps.

"The wolf is gone," Balía told them. "It is the human you must beware." They watched each other in silence as dusk advanced. To her surprise, Balía found that the ewe who had been attacked was nearly healed. In fact, it seemed to heal further as she watched. She stood. What was occurring here? Balía moved closer, to inspect the ewe in what moonlight entered from the open barn doors.

Her wool was grayish, as if tinged with ash from the fireplace. Or was it burning? Balía felt an intense heat radiating from the ewe. Her vision shimmered, like when she stared over the plains on a hot summer day, and the rising heat wavered over the grass, almost visible.

Staring down at the molten gray form below her, Balía knew what was happening. She, as human, must finish what the boy, as wolf, had been unable to. To let it live would be too dangerous. The ewe would not know what she did, when the lupine instincts took over, and she attacked her own family and flock in the moonlight. And the townsfolk, they would be riled from the first wolf, the shape changer, and would love nothing more than to find that Morfelao harbored another.

But this is all that remains of that child, Balía thought. Could she really kill it? Especially when he could not. Must she so soon prove the truth behind her statement to the sheep to beware the human, not the wolf.

There was a compromise she could make, a compromise that would keep alive one small part of the child the townsfolk had killed. Without any hesitation Balía made it, reaching out for the wolf, one hand around its neck, the other stretching towards its muzzle. She would avenge the child.

And now on those days when she goes into town and the fruitseller tells her a wolf had again been heard on the moor, Balía merely nods her head and smiles.

HER MOTHER'S SWORD

by Stephanie Shaver

Stephanie Shaver is no longer the youngest of the writers I've published—that dubious honor probably belongs to Margaret Heydt—but is probably the youngest writer to have become a full Active Member of SFWA. And she is certainly the youngest writer to be so prolific. She came up to Berkeley a few days this summer for a signing at a local bookstore, and far from being a 'nerd' which seems to be teenage slang for the bookish kid who really thinks she is in school to learn something instead of honing her social skills, she is a very pretty young girl, considerably younger than my own younger daughter, with dark brown hair and blue—I think—eyes. Not that there seems to be anything wrong with her social skills—at seventeen she possesses more of them than I did before I was fifty. Girls do, these days. She's looking forward to her first Nebula banquet next year. She's now in the business of seriously collecting rejection slips, and learning guitar, with the Renaissance Faire "in the middle to keep my brain from collapse." She adds that she "still can't sing. My dog enjoys howling with me. My cat enjoys hiding under the bed." She wound up saying she had to go get a refill on ginger ale, and throw the cat out of her room—sneeze, cough!

I faithfully promised my roommate when my last kids left home and took the last of the cats, that I'd respect her allergies and acquire no more livestock; so all we now have is the wolf-malamute, Signy. When my previous editor gave me a very realistic stuffed Siamese cat, (toy, not taxidermist's sample) I thought she would burst into tears . . . it was very realistic and probably fooled her into thinking it alive.

"The First Legion?"

"Dead."

Commander-General Leondyr vega Ysanne bit her lip, hard, until the blood welled.

"The Second?" she whispered, long fingers whisper-fine on her cup of kafa.

The scout swallowed, wiped blood from his face with a ragged bit of cloth Leondyr handed him. "Gone," he said at last. "Half dead . . . the other half ran back to camp."

Now the Commander-General swore, ripping out an oath that made the scout blanch.

"And the Third . . . ?"

"Never went into battle, majesty."

Leondyr, Commander-General of Amack and Queen of the Umbra Throne, settled back in her cot and closed her eyes, silently damning the leg wound that kept her from the field.

"Leave me."

The scout did. Quickly.

She turned tired eyes on Arolyn vega Heryhy, her war advisor, who was kneeling beside the Commander-General's cot.

"What," she said slowly, "is making my army turn tail and run like this?"

Arolyn lifted one elegant, wing-swept brow. "Why," she replied, "the pirates' leader, Yashan Rogian, majesty."

"One man? How?"

Arolyn's face went into a study of concentration. "I couldn't tell you, Majesty. My spies believe that it's his visage that causes the terror in the men and women."

"How?"

"Well, majesty, he seems to be *everywhere* when you meet the pirates in battle—left, right, in front or behind you, breathing down your neck or screaming in your ear. It's some magic of his, or so my informants have told me. And it's unnerving for the troops, lady. The fact he's not human isn't helping the situation, either."

"What do you mean, 'not human'?"

The woman blinked, a comma of graying blonde hair touching her faded blue eyes. "I mean precisely what I said. Yashan is only called a 'man' because to call him an 'it' would make him all the more terrifying. Whether Yashan was *ever* human is still being debated, but whatever he is now . . . let's just say he doesn't walk on two legs, majesty."

"Hmm." Leondyr stared at the top of the canvas tent, watching the animal-skin covering lighten with the rising of the sun outside, letting her thoughts scatter. After three minutes of uneasy silence, she spoke.

"What about getting a Healer in here?" she asked, patting her left leg where an enemy sword had sliced through her greaves two days ago. Then, the scores had been even. Then, it hadn't mattered that the focal point of the Amackian morale—Leondyr—had been put out of the field for a while. She had fought like a hero, and had received a hero's welcome as she rode back to camp (with the help of Arolyn).

But that was before Yashan—and whatever magics he was using to scare the hell out of her troops—and before the First Legion had been slaughtered.

"The Healers are—uh—preoccupied, majesty," Arolyn replied. "And it's rather selfish to demand their attentions when you're in no danger of dying. They . . . have a lot of wounded to tend, after all."

Leondyr raised her head a bit, noticing the falter in her counselor's voice.

"Really?" she said in a light tone. "Well, as soon as one is free, send him over."

"Yes, majesty."

"Now go get some rest."

"Gladly, majesty." The seventy-year-old veteran of two wars left, her steps only slightly stiff.

Silence again, and Leondyr waited for a moment before she spoke to the only other person left in the tent. Chacar, her court wizard.

"He's using magic."

"I know, majesty."

"Can you negate it?"

"I've already tried, majesty. In fact, all of the wizards

have tried. It doesn't work. Whatever spell he's using, it's nothing we can touch."

The woman swore again, tearing the words from her lips and hurling them at Yashan and his future generations.

"Lee, it's not as bad as it sounds—" Chacar started.

"Oh, *those* are hollow words if ever I did hear them! My army is falling apart, I have *something* waltzing toward the capital acting like my soldiers were gnats, and here I am, lounging in a cot!" Leondyr exclaimed, sitting up and rubbing her leg. "Where're the damned priests when you need them?" she muttered.

"Now, Lee," Chacar said, using her nickname again, "you're not getting up, are you?"

"Damned right I'm getting up!" She swung her legs—stiffly—over the cot and groaned a little. Glaring at Chacar defiantly through a shock of black hair, she tossed her head, pushed up with cord-muscle arms, and wobbled to her feet.

Chacar sat, face composed, with a look in his gray eyes that said, *Any moment, you're going to collapse.*

Leondyr not only didn't collapse, she also belted on her mother's sword as she left the pavilion.

"Lee!" he shouted, bustling out of the royal tent.

She paused, leaning against a post that was meant for tying horses to. She crossed her arms in a casual fashion and looked at him with a sober expression as he scowled at her, looking very much as her governess used to when she found Leondyr doing something that wasn't "proper." Or, for that matter, her mother Ysanne, when Leondyr didn't fall into sword-stance correctly.

Mother.

Leondyr shoved her memories of Ysanne vega Kalyra aside for a moment, instead concentrating on the *here* and *now*.

"I'm going to go raise morale," she said softly, pushing away from the post and limping toward the small city of tents that composed the sleeping quarters of the army.

"Lee! You're not supposed to *walk*, much less rally ten thousand people!" Chacar argued, marching after her.

"That was yesterday!" she said over her shoulder. "I'm feeling *much* better today!"

Leondyr slowly wound her way down to the men and women that composed the army. Most of the soldiers were either waking up to a hot cup of kafa, or repairing gear. Some were missing, faces she remembered but didn't dare think about now. The First Legion, and half of the Second.

Leondyr did what only she could do. She slapped people on the back, shared about twenty cups of kafa with the men and women, and talked about things *other* than war. She raised their hopes with her banter and idle chat while Chacar stood behind, a sour nursemaid. But after an hour of bending and walking, Leondyr was ready to collapse, and already she knew what little hope she had instilled was probably fading.

Some queen I am, she thought. *Not a queen at all, really. I don't even know what the hell I'm doing here. Maybe I should just give up and go back to the capital and let Yashan conquer. Either way, without me in the battle, the chances of us winning are nil. If it was only me and the army like it's always been in the past when they've attacked, and if the pirates didn't have Yashan and his magic, we'd sweep them. If only this damned leg wound could get healed—*

"Can we go back now?" Chacar asked, interrupting her caravan of thought as they got closer to the end of the pseudo-city of tents and, subsequently, closer to the tent of the Healer-priests.

Leondyr shot him a look; there was an ugly note in his voice that she didn't like, but that still started her thinking. . . .

"No," she said coldly, and limped toward the Healers, new resolve in her soul.

"Leondyr," and she noticed a note of panic in his voice, "you're not going *in* there, are you?"

Leondyr didn't answer, hobbling onward instead.

She parted the tent flap slowly, willing herself not to see the horribly mutilated bodies that lay on the pallets within. What she was about to do might be against Arolyn's wishes, but it had to be done. Besides, if what she had heard in her advisor and Chacar's voices this morning was correct, then this wasn't going to be selfish at all. . . .

The Commander-General moved to the back of the massive tent, where the sickroom was separated from the Healers' quarters by a curtain of canvas. Quickly, before Chacar could stop her, she untied the flap, pulled it back, and stepped inside.

Twenty Healers looked up in surprise at her from where they nursed cups of kafa.

A split second later, they were kneeling.

Leondyr ran her eyes over them, and then caught the eyes of Arolyn, who was sitting in the back with the Master Healer, Shayrn.

"At ease," she said softly, knowing the words *should* have been: *you may rise.* But this was a state of war, and the Healers damn well knew it. *At ease,* by the ancient laws, was the only order she could give to subjects who knelt before her now.

"What," said Shayrn calmly, "does your majesty desire?"

Leondyr smiled, and limped over to him. "Oh," she replied, "just something small. Something simple."

"Such as?"

"I want you to Heal me, by the Lady, and I want you to do it *now.*"

Shayrn's mild expression didn't change, but Arolyn's turned to one of a peasant child whose hand had been caught in the fruit basket on a royal feast table. Leondyr crossed her arms, sat down heavily, and accepted her twenty-second cup of kafa in that day.

"Well . . . majesty, I'm afraid I can't do that."

"Yes, you can."

He looked at her with mild surprise.

"Why do you want me to do this?" he said at last.

She leaned forward. "Because I am your sovereign leader, and I order it of you."

She saw the flat look in his eyes, and knew that in a moment he was going to tell her *exactly* what she could do with her orders, royal or not.

She cut him off before he could speak. "And," she said, "because I have a plan to take down Yashan."

"Majesty—" Arolyn began.

"You!" Leondyr scowled at the old woman, who scowled back. "I don't know what game you're playing but I'm not a child to be led around blindly! Besides," she added in a softer tone, "you've never been much of a liar, Arolyn."

The elder woman sighed, and let her shoulders slump.

"I know you were trying to protect me," the Commander-General continued. "You were keeping me from being Healed deliberately, correct?" The advisor nodded. "Why?"

Arolyn frowned. "You're young, majesty," she said. "I didn't want you getting killed out of foolishness. The only heir is your uncle and his children, and to tell you the truth, your uncle wouldn't make a very good ruler."

"Well, I thank you for worrying about me, but even if I live, I doubt there'll be anything to *rule* if Yashan hits the capital. Frankly, we can't win this battle if I'm being spirited off to another realm, and I have no desire to win back the Throne through a long rebellion like Kalyra did."

Arolyn bit her lip. Obviously, *that* had been exactly what she planned on doing. Leondyr chuckled inside.

"Majesty," Arolyn said slowly, "I hate to tell you this, but even with you *in* the battle, I don't think we'll be able to win."

"We didn't expect Yashan," Shayrn explained.

"And we didn't expect you to have a brain," Chacar added.

"Well, we have both now, don't we?" Leondyr said sweetly. "And if that's what you think, Arolyn—and I'm afraid I have to agree—then I have a plan."

"Which is?" inquired Arolyn, eyes shrewd.

"First," Leondyr said, raising a finger imperiously, "*I* get Healed. Then I tell you my plan."

Shayrn sighed, rolled up his sleeves, and unwound the bandages from around her leg as Leondyr eased herself onto a nearby pallet.

"I have a feeling that we're not going to like this 'plan,' " Chacar muttered.

"Oh, I guarantee Arolyn won't," Leondyr replied with a clenched grin.

Then she ground her teeth down as the painful process of Healing began.

Leondyr listened to the storm of disapproval flurrying around her, and ignored the voices with trained royal calm.

"No! Absolutely *not*!" Arolyn's face was drawn furiously, her washed-blue eyes glaring at the Commander-General.

"You're insane!" Chacar said.

Shayrn groaned, "I Heal you just so you can go out and challenge some Nether-spawned creature to a duel. Wonderful."

Leondyr sat, hand on her mother's sword, as the clamor died. The general Healers had long since left to tend to other patients, and it was only the four of them in the tent now.

The pain in her leg had faded to nothing, much to Leondyr's delight. There would always be a little pink thread of scar on her leg, but besides that, it was flexing and bending fine.

Which was good, because she'd need all her agility if she managed to pull off this little duel with Yashan.

"It's the *only* way," Leondyr said softly. "Look, if I don't challenge Yashan to a duel, he'll just slaughter the rest of the troops and move on to the capital. Even if I lose—" and she caught their eyes, letting them know that she understood *exactly* what losing would mean, "—the outcome will be the same as if I didn't challenge him. But if I kill him—even if *I* die—we have a good chance of winning. If I *don't* do this, we lose. The only thing left is to gamble and maybe gain.

"Will you let me do it?" She didn't implore, she just asked.

The three sat, silent. Leondyr waited. Finally, Shayrn said, "Majesty, you don't *need* our permission. Do what you will. But if it's my blessing you want, my blessing you'll get. I'll Heal you if—*when* you come out of it."

"Thank you, Shayrn. Chacar?"

"I'll set up the ring magically so that even Yashan can't use his spells to cheat."

"I'd appreciate it. Arolyn?"

The old woman caught the younger woman's eyes. "You remind me of your mother, Leondyr vega Ysanne."

Leondyr swallowed hard, remembering the day Ysanne died suddenly of lungrot, not two months before. For a moment, she relived the hasty coronation that had followed, and the long speech Arolyn had given her about the duties of being a monarch.

She tightened her fingers around her mother's sword. "Thank you, Aro, but will you let me do it?"

Arolyn laughed without humor. "Sure. I'll go issue the challenge. When do you want it?"

"Tomorrow at sunzenith."

The advisor nodded, bowed, and left.

Chacar and Shayrn followed her.

Alone in the tent, Leondyr drew her mother's sword slowly. The steel hissed, singing softly. The sword of the House of Mestrus had the hilt of a two-handed weapon and the blade of a long sword, the only weapon she had ever seen made so. It was surprisingly light, thick in the forte and then closing to a narrow point. The hilt was made for hands long and strong, like hers, and a set of runes spelling *Shaselingas* on it told her the blade's name. It was said that Kalyra vega Imadrail made the sword the night before she died and gave it to Ysanne as a gift the next morning. How even the legendary Kalyra could have done this in one evening still puzzled Leondyr, but that was the legend, handed down straight from her own mother. Perhaps the gods had helped Kalyra, and if they had, Leondyr hoped they would be watching *her* tomorrow.

Shaselingas, *forged by my grandmother, but my mother's sword. If the gods ever blessed you, sword of Mestrus, lend your blessing to* me.

Leondyr closed her eyes, kissed the blade, and began to resheathe it in her hip-scabbard.

She stopped in startlement, blade half in, her ears straining.

Was it her imagination, or had she heard a gentle humming sound as she placed the sword to the sheath?

Leondyr waited, holding her breathing, listening for bells, lighting, *anything*. But when all she heard was the moans of the dying in the other tent, she shook her head and gave up the sound as a wishful fancy.

The Commander-General quickly slammed the sword home and exited the Healers' quarters, heading for her tent.

Sunzenith arrived with startling speed. Leondyr had spent the morning of the duel and the day before in sleep and practice. Yashan had accepted the challenge less than half an hour after it was issued by Arolyn. As Leondyr had expected, he had sent his reply in a very extravagant form; a raven to be exact. The Nethers-spawned thing had screamed obscenities over the army and answered her challenge with a harsh, death-rattle laugh.

Two hundred arrows had brought the bird down, fired straight from her archers.

She had eaten breakfast, but the food had tasted like ash on her tongue, and the only thought that ran through her mind as she took in each mouthful was, *Is this the last meal I shall ever taste?*

Since the challenge and the place—on the beach—had been her choice, Yashan had chosen weapons and the duel terms. The weapons were, luckily, swords (which allowed the use of her mother's sword, even if she was better with the dagger) and the terms were—again, as she had suspected—to the death. And, of course, that the winner be allowed to walk away untouched.

The troops were lined up proudly to watch their Commander-General go, and many cheered her as she rode down to the makeshift fighting grounds that Chacar and the mages had created. The magic-twisting, shining battlecircle, inscribed with silver and mercury, made her eyes itch.

As her horse's hooves touched the black sand of Amack, Leondyr examined the looming horizon. A line of ships cut off the sky, huge galleons with four masts each. The pirates of the Southern Isles had made a "bridge" connecting each ship to the other, and she watched the bustling activity on it. Other "bridges" connected each ship to the water, and allowed the pirates a vast "gangplank" to run across and up the beaches to the grassy stretch of flatland that bordered the Tamatian Wood. Leondyr had tried earlier on to burn the "bridges" with pitch arrows, but they seemed magicked against mortal fire. When Chacar had attempted his arcane flames, they had fizzled and died. The "bridges" stayed, no matter what subterfuge the Commander-General tried.

Leondyr dismounted from her mare's back, and watched as a steward led the horse away. She hadn't had time to grow attached to the steed, and in a way was glad of it. The mare was one less thing to lose.

Then Leondyr took a long breath, looked over at Arolyn and Shayrn—who edged the phalanx-formation of her troops—nodded once, and stepped into the circle.

A bright flash of light, and the circle glowed gold now. Leondyr drew *Shaselingas,* and waited.

She did not have to wait long.

Yashan came like a swarm of locusts; buzzing fitfully on massive batlike wings. His eyes were that of an insect's, dwarfing the human skull into which they were inset. The skin was thick and bloated in some places, hard as seashells in others, and leather-shiney on his appendages. He had four legs that twisted out of his armored torso like molding growths. His arms, long and spindly, sprang as agile as a scorpion's tail from his corded shoulders. A claw on one arm gleamed razor-sharp in the revealing light of day, snapping and clicking at her in anticipation.

The other—a distorted but unnervingly human hand—held a sword.

Leondyr swallowed down her breakfast as the stench carrying from him on the seabreeze hit her. Bile ate at her throat and tears stung her eyes, but she did not loose her grip on her mother's sword as Yashan Rogian landed.

His voice was brassy, cold. His smile—like a serpent's—was permanent.

"Woman!" he hissed.

She didn't answer, waiting instead.

"Whore!"

Leondyr closed her eyes, feeling her body tense with the thrill of fear/anticipation/fear that coiled deep within.

"I shall make you my wife if you live!" he laughed, and Leondyr's stomach flipflopped.

"And I," she said in turn, her voice surprisingly strong, "shall make you a trophy on my wall when you die."

Yashan leapt through the circle in a flash of light, roaring incoherently as his blade swung down.

Leondyr parried, bringing her mother's sword up in a shower of sparks, and glad now that the weapon was sword, not dagger. No matter how good she might be with a knife, the slashes that Yashan was throwing in her face were too powerful for a small weapon, and she doubted she was quick enough to avoid half of them. The creature screamed, and a claw clicked in her face. The Commander-General jumped back, slashed out with *Shaselingas,* and side-kicked viciously. Her foot connected with air, but her sword nicked through one dough-soft cheek, and something black began to seep out of Yashan's face.

First blood . . . or at least I think *that's blood,* she thought as the creature shrieked like a disobeyed child, and lashed out with his claw. She slammed the sword back, meeting the claw with steel, and ducked as his sword flashed toward her eyes. A wisp of fine black hair floated off her head, and disappeared into the sand.

Balanced on the balls of her feet, Leondyr felt warmth and bloodlust sustain her as they exchanged blows. Really, he wasn't all *that* much of a challenge; he had a body that was naturally armored, but those wings often bore him down and made him slow. The claw was powerful, but it was clumsy, and the legs were a waste of flesh—

That was what she thought, until Yashan did something she hadn't thought possible, and probably wasn't with a normal body. One spiked leg lifted, rotated like a wheel, and struck at her chest with the wicked, spear-like point that served as a "foot." Air whooshed out of

Leondyr's lungs as the appendage connected and dented her chestplate, and she thanked the gods for her fine Evermist armor and steel breast cups. Although she hated the damned cups—they were always cold when she first put them on and later heated up when she exerted herself—they had saved her from a stunned reaction more than once in her fighting career, and now they saved her life.

But it didn't help her from being knocked back. Leondyr landed ten feet away from the Yashan-monster, *Shaselingas* in hand, and began to roll to her feet. With startling speed, Yashan sprang at her, mouth open and fangs dripping something appalling. Before she could move, he had her pinned.

"Shall I consummate our marriage before we've sworn our vows?" he cooed foully in her ear.

Leondyr ground her jaw down hard, and decided it was time to test out Arolyn's theory on whether Yashan was an "it."

She kneed him.

Yashan shrieked, buggy eyes wide, and Leondyr scrambled away as the creature clutched himself in a vaguely groinlike area.

Well, so much for my advisor's advice.

But the pot-shot didn't take Yashan out for long, and Leondyr knew it wouldn't. He swung wildly with all his strength, and the Commander-General watched as his sword went for her neck in a freak stroke of blind luck.

She brought *Shaselingas* up to guard—

And her mother's sword *shattered* as it connected with the raw pressure and strength that backed his.

The tinkling scream of steel breaking into a thousand shards filled Leondyr's hearing, and she stared, wide-mouthed, at the remains of the fabled sword of Kalyra. Her body went numb and the only coherent thing she could do was back away as Yashan slowly pulled himself up to his full height, and took a step toward her.

The Commander-General brought the broken sword up slowly as she fell into stance, her last futile stand against the creature. She could not leave the circle. Once she stepped in, Chacar had told her, she was enclosed by a barrier of mystic origin that kept her in and intruders out. Her or her opponent's death was the only thing that could take it down. And just as Yashan's magics couldn't work in here, so couldn't she leave. It had been the only way that Arolyn could convince Yashan to fight in a mage-formed circle of the enemy's make. And the duel had required she carry only two weapons—her sword and her body—which was exactly what she had brought. Before, the odds were even, but now, as when her army had been cut down by Yashan's foul magic, she was outnumbered.

It's hopeless! her mind shrieked. *There's nothing I can do! Nothing—!*

And then, even as Yashan's dragging gait touched her path of hasty footsteps in the sand, something caught Leondyr's eye.

She brought the sword up closer, and peered over its top.

She frowned, puzzled at what she saw.

It was *hollow*. The sword was *hollow*.

And with a click and a hum, the remainder of *Shaselingas* dropped into the sand.

Leaving behind a hilt, broad crossguards, and a dagger-sized blade.

A blade inside the sword? she thought. *How . . . ?*

From above her, Leondyr heard a roar and saw Yashan springing toward her, madness on his face, claw clicking, sword lifted high.

She would later be surprised how easy her next action was. One moment she was standing still, and the next minute she was twisting in a motion her mother had beat into her since she was a child. Her arm extended as the claw raked through her armor and tore her side, and the dagger flowed up like steel poison into Yashan's eye, finding a space that a bulky *sword* would have never fit into. The domed insectoid orb collapsed in a rain of ichor and black fluid, and Yashan screamed horribly as the dagger found a new sheath.

Leondyr released the hilt of the weapon, and it seemed, of its own accord, to burrow farther into the creature's skull. With one last howl of mingled anger and hate, Yashan spasmed and died, his body landing on Leondyr's as she began to roll away.

Dead weight made her yelp and the Commander-General thought she heard something crunch in her rib cage. Horror consumed her, the crawling sensation of something unbelievably vile touching her skin, and she scrabbled uselessly in the black sands underneath Yashan's massive corpse.

There was a spark of light around her, and part of Leondyr realized the circle had been banished while the other part of her screamed incoherently. Voices swarmed around her in excitement and congratulations, but all she wanted now was to *get the horrible creature that was on her OFF.*

After a moment, Yashan was removed and Leondyr pushed her way, shakily, to her feet. Arolyn was standing nearby, old eyes wide, and Shayrn was walking toward her, face set.

"Majes—"

She shoved him aside in a daze, and knelt beside the body of Yashan. Carefully, despite her revulsion, she removed the blade from the stiffening corpse's eye, and wiped it on one of Yashan's wings.

Then she shoved it into her belt. A sheath would come later.

Made of Queen Kalyra, she thought, staring at it, *sword of Queen Ysanne. Grandmother, you didn't* forge *this weapon, you took an already-made sword and turned it into a vessel for the knife. You must have been a wise old lady to tell my mother what was hidden inside* Shaselingas, *and my mother was wise for guessing that such a blade could never handle much stress on its length and making sure I knew the dagger better than any weapon.* She smiled.

My grandmother's design, my mother's sword—

Queen Leondyr rubbed the hilt.

—and my *dagger.*

THE SORCERESS' APPRENTICE

by Deborah Wheeler

Deborah Wheeler has been writing for these anthologies almost as long as I've been editing them—maybe, for all I can remember offhand, as long. By now her biographical details must be almost as familiar to you readers as they are to me. She probably feels the same way, for when our mutual agent forwarded her story to me, she didn't bother to update her autobiography.

She has two delightful children whom I regard as honorary granddaughters, both very intelligent and articulate. She has now stopped practicing chiropractic to become a full-time writer, and has sold her first novel, *Jaydium*, to DAW Books. She lives in Southern California, and it is always a treat when she and her family can come up for a visit.

Her most exciting news is that she recently spent six months in Lyons, France. Both children attended school there, and came back chattering French as though they had been speaking it all their lives. Deborah says she found living in France incredibly stimulating, intellectually and creatively, and she is still working on stories and ideas concocted there.

In this story, she addresses the question of when a young woman ceases to be an apprentice, and becomes a full-fledged sorceress.

With every tug and shove of the scrubbing brush across the mosaic floor, Tahanna cursed softly under her breath. She'd spent all afternoon preparing Vashkiri's audience chamber for the petitions which the old sorceress received on the first day of every month. Her knees ached, her back ached, her hands were chapped and raw. She could have gotten the job done in half the time with a simple spell, but Vashkiri had forbidden it.

She was tired of cleaning—there was still the great carved chair to polish—tired of wearing apprentice's drab and, most of all, tired of studying magic every minute she wasn't cleaning this or carrying that—and then never being allowed to use a scrap of it.

Tahanna sat back on her heels and pushed a wisp of sweat-dampened hair back from her forehead. She longed to sit in the great chair and try out a spell, any spell, just to hear how it sounded in her own voice. There would be no harm done, and she'd revoke it right away. But no, she repeated to herself for the thousandth time that day, *Vashkiri had forbidden it.*

Fire and Darkness! It was so unfair.

Savagely, Tahanna attacked the rich dark wood of the chair with citron oil. Then she paused, the polishing cloth hanging limp in her fingers. A seductive thought snaked through her mind. What was she studying all this magic for, if not to use it? How would she know she was good enough if she never got to try? Would there ever be a better time than now?

Clinging to her new determination, Tahanna strode off towards Vashkiri's private tower. She raced up the stairs, taking them two at a time. Her heart pounded as she reached the top. Her mouth went dry, but she kept on going.

Vashkiri the sorceress stood just outside her door, leaning on her ebony cane and looking for all the world as if she'd been waiting for Tahanna's arrival. Her robe of gold-stitched silk brushed the floor. Her black eyes snapped as they fixed on Tahanna's.

"Vashkiri—*magistera*—" Tahanna panted. A spasm of doubt curled around her tongue. She'd forgotten the faint smell of burning copper that always clung to the sorceress, forgotten how small and frail and terrifying she was.

Tahanna took a deep breath and silently recited a charm for fortitude. Her tongue unfroze. "The time has come for me to begin exercising the art you've taught me." Her voice rang out in the hallway, more powerful and resonant than she'd ever heard it. "I've worked hard for you for all these years. I've memorized every spell you've taught me. I know all the precautions and counter-indications, all the possible cancellations, nullifications and synergies. But you—you never let me try out the tiniest bit of it! Well, that's got to change. You've prepared me to work the true magic—now let me do it!"

For a long moment, Vashkiri did not move. Her face, as usual, looked frozen into a permanent expression of disapproval.

Tahanna's stomach tightened in dread. She'd gone too far, she knew it. Vashkiri would surely kick her out now, if she didn't turn her into a gerbil first. But whatever happened, she'd been right to stand up for herself.

"You think you're ready to work the true magic, my girl?"

Tahanna raised her chin defiantly. "Yes. I *am* ready."

The pleated leather of Vashkiri's face folded into a smile. "Perhaps you are right. Perhaps it is time."

Tahanna stared in open-mouthed astonishment as the old sorceress went on, "You think you have earned the chance to prove yourself. Then you must take my place in the great chair tomorrow and I will take yours in the scullery." She turned her back on Tahanna and made her way down the passageway, her cane tapping. "Oh, yes, it will be a welcome change to be scrubbing floors again."

Fire and Darkness! Tahanna murmured reverently. *A miracle!*

Tahanna awoke before dawn. Vashkiri's big bed, heaped with plushy sheepskins, was almost too comfortable to sleep in. With a twinge, she thought of the cot in her own garret, the thin blanket, the chipped bowl. The next moment, she noticed the curl of jasmine-scented steam arising from the porcelain ewer on the marble wash stand.

It was true, it was all true! sang through her mind as she bathed and dressed. No more endless lessons without the ghost of a chance to use them. No more scrubbing that any farm brat could do better. No more rough canvas next to her skin, but finest silk. Vashkiri's wardrobe bulged with a dozen ceremonial robes, each more gorgeous than the last. She was still debating between the peacock-patterned gold and the rose-petals-on-snow when a soft tap sounded at her door.

"Who—who is it?"

"Breakfast, magistera." The door swung open and Vashkiri hobbled in. She wore a shapeless smock over peasant-style pantaloons and carried a breakfast tray in both hands. Tahanna's mouth watered at the sight of dewberries in clotted cream, buttery crescent rolls, and cinnamon tea. She stammered her thanks as Vashkiri left, and only when she was sipping the last fragrant drops of tea did she realize that the old woman hadn't used her cane.

She had too much to do to wonder about that, dressing her hair and figuring out how to put on the traditional regalia—tiara and veils, pectoral, arm bands, wide-collared cape. She had arranged everything securely enough so it wouldn't fall off when Vashkiri returned to tell her that the petitioners had arrived and were waiting in the antechamber. Picking up the heavy, elaborately ornamented Wand of Office, she went to take her new place.

Tahanna settled herself in the great chair and surveyed the audience chamber with satisfaction. The mosaic floor she'd worked so hard over yesterday now shone as if she'd coated it with glass. Not even Vashkiri could have found fault with it. The petitioners had better be impressed. And they would be, Tahanna reflected. Vashkiri's audience chamber was the jewel of her entire castle—spacious and elegant with its carved ivory-and-sandalwood screens and, best of all, its superb acoustics. Any incantation spoken under its arching roof would sound awe-inspiring.

Tahanna drew a deep breath and motioned to Vashkiri to let the first petitioner approach. She studied him as he strode across the expanse of gleaming tiles. His turban was of cloth-of-gold, as were the sash around his ample belly and his curl-toed slippers. Rich men made generous gifts, Tahanna thought. She determined to do her very best for him. She would not take any shortcuts, she would carefully consider all the implications of whatever spell she used. She would show Vashkiri she could work the true magic as well as any seasoned sorceress.

The rich man sweated as he recited the ritual greeting. Tahanna made him wait a suitable time before she asked what he wished. His request sounded simple enough. He had a hoard of gold which he valued above anything else and he'd been terrified that someone might steal it. He'd hired extra guards and bought new and bigger locks, but still he couldn't sleep at night.

Tahanna kept her face stern as she considered the problem. She could cast an invisible wall around the treasure, one which would keep out even the most determined thief, but then the owner wouldn't be able to get in, either. An obvious pitfall. She deliberated and rejected several spells before selecting one. As she recited it, her words resounded through the chamber. Was that truly her voice, so rich and vibrant? She hoped Vashkiri was eavesdropping.

Feeling pleased with her solution, she received the next petitioner. They came in together, a group of elders from a farming district five hundred leagues away. Tahanna was gratified they'd come so far to seek her help. Their problem, they told her, was the flocks of dragonets which had taken to ravishing the entire asparagus crop. Tahanna personally could live without asparagus but, *Each to his own.* A simple repulsion spell ought to keep the fields free. She was careful to shape the spell to be specific to dragonets and not to farmers or honeybees or anything else which rightfully belonged there.

The tiara and pectoral had become unmistakably heavier as Tahanna watched the elders leave. Her arm ached from holding up the Wand of Office and she wished it had fewer focusing gems and glitter-byes. Unconsciously, her mouth curved down at the corners into an expression of disapproval. She recited the charm for calming the nerves, but couldn't tell if it worked or not. She was so tired, all she wanted to do was crawl away somewhere and sleep. Why hadn't Vashkiri told her she'd feel like this?

Struggling to regain her poise, Tahanna stiffened her spine and signaled for the final petitioner.

As the tall young man approached, her heart beat faster. His short, simple tunic and sandals revealed muscles shapely enough to make a sculptor swoon. True, his legs were a little hairy and he could use a shave, but his eyes were huge and dark-lashed and brooding. She wondered if there were some way she could keep him at the castle while she solved his problems, but Vashkiri would undoubtedly forbid that, too.

Slowly he raised one hand to her. On his palm, she saw a glowing pentagram.

"By my magic, I have already divined your problem," she said grandly. "You are a werewolf."

"Aye, such is my curse." Tahanna found his outland accent as charming as his figure.

"Each passage of the moon's fullness, like to a woman's ripe belly, then must I suffer the most dreadful transformation," he went on. "A wolf I become, aye! a furred beast—huge and slavering, belling my sins to the naked sky. And—" with a wink that turned Tahanna's knees to water, "—keeping the neighbors awake all night."

Although her head was spinning from the intoxicating presence of the young werewolf, Tahanna applied herself to solving his problems. She couldn't remember any references in the texts to an un-werewolfing spell—it was probably too specific—so she blended together several elements, for size, hairlessness, bloodthirstiness, everything else she could think of that might pertain to wolfhood. She checked it twice before pronouncing it.

When the werewolf had departed, with a breathtaking grin, Tahanna sat in the great chair for a long time before she could summon the strength to stand. Her skin exuded the faint odor of burning copper. Despite her weariness, her spirits soared. She'd done it—worked the true magic. Now, where was old Vashkiri to see it?

Vashkiri stood waiting, arms folded and face bland, in the servant's entrance. As she helped Tahanna up the stairs to the bedroom tower, she said nothing at all about her performance.

Over the next week, Tahanna did little but eat ravenously and sleep. She kept expecting Vashkiri to send her back to her own garret, but night after night she slept in the sumptuous bed, bathed in the scented water, ate the delectable food. After a few days, her hopes began to rise. Perhaps the old woman had meant the change to be permanent.

Tahanna realized she had passed the crucial test and was now a full-fledged sorceress. A true professional. She began taking exercise daily, as well as applying herself once more to her studies. There was so much more to learn, now that she'd proved herself worthy.

A month later, Tahanna sat alone in the great carved chair after the last petitioner had departed. Her bones ached with weariness, but her senses were still clear. The endurance exercises she'd been practicing since the last audience day had helped greatly. Her skin and hair reeked of the smell of burning copper.

But there was no denying what she had to do next and no graceful way out of it. What could she say to Vashkiri, "You were right and I was wrong and can I please have my garret back"? She'd been so sure she was ready, so pleased with her command of magic. And what a mess she'd made of it!

Slowly, as if all her joints hurt, Tahanna took off the ceremonial regalia and placed them on the chair. She had no right to wear them now. She searched the audience chamber. After a few moments, Vashkiri appeared at the servant's entrance and asked, "You wished to see me, magistera?"

As Tahanna approached the old sorceress, she found she couldn't look Vashkiri in the face. Her shame was too painful to bear.

"I'm not ready to do magic after all," she said. "Everything I thought I did so well has turned into disaster. They're all back, all the people I tried to help last month. I couldn't think what to do, so I told them all to come back tomorrow. And all the new petitions, the ones I granted today, *they'll* be back next month."

"If that's all it is, you don't need me—but supper does. It won't make itself, you know." Vashkiri started off down the rush-floored corridor toward the scullery. There was a new spring in her step, a new roundness to her cheeks. Without glancing back at Tahanna, she added, "You'd better get right to work. You'll have a bit of research to do, figuring out what to do before tomorrow morning."

"You don't understand!" Half in tears, Tahanna ran after her. "You don't know what I've done!" She blurted out how she'd protected the rich merchant's gold from thieves—thanks to her, it now smelled like a combination of wet dogs and rotten cauliflower. No one, not even the rich man, could stand to be in the same room with it for more than a few seconds at a time.

The old sorceress picked up an empty bucket in each hand and started toward the courtyard well at a surprisingly brisk pace. "I daresay he'll find a way to live with it," she said. "Either that, or live a little poorer."

"But he came to me for help!" Tahanna wailed. "And what about those poor asparagus farmers? How was I to know the dragonets also ate cabbage grubs? Without them, the grubs have multiplied like crazy—every cabbage patch in the district is infested with them now! The farmers will be ruined because of me!"

"Did you revoke the dragonet repulsion spell?" Vashkiri asked as she put down the buckets in front of the water pump and began working the handle vigorously.

Tahanna shook her head. "I wasn't sure whether to do that or set a new one for the grubs. I thought you would—"

"*I* have enough on my hands, just keeping this place running, thank you," Vashkiri replied tartly.

Tahanna followed her back to the castle kitchen, where Vashkiri dipped out a panful of water and began scrubbing potatoes. Tahanna sat down at the table and absently began peeling one.

It took her three tries to summon enough courage to admit her last failure. The werewolf no longer assumed a lupine form with each full moon. No fur, no slavering, no huge monstrous beast. He now turned into a tiny hairless lapdog. And he still kept the neighbors awake all night.

At this confession, Vashkiri put down the potato she was scrubbing and covered her face with both hands. Slowly her shoulders began to shake and a strange sound bubbled up from her throat. But her expression was perfectly serious when she lowered her hands.

"Surely you must agree," Tahanna said, "I'm not ready yet. Maybe I'll *never* be ready."

"My old teacher said exactly the same thing to me forty years ago when I wanted her to take the job back. As I remember, what I'd done was a spell to make hidden things visible. A wealthy merchant had died and his son couldn't find the will. The poor lad thought he was coming to me for help."

Tahanna blinked in surprise. "What happened?"

"The lawyers discovered papers proving him illegitimate." Vashkiri's black eyes twinkled. "Now listen to me, my dear. You'll be just fine. Trust me. Besides, I've been waiting for years to retire. I'm certainly not going to give it up now."

"But—but—it's criminal negligence to turn me loose on these people! I haven't the faintest idea what I'm doing."

Vashkiri shook her head. "My dear, neither does anyone else at your stage. You are no less competent than I was when I demanded my chance. There is nothing I can tell you which will teach you better than having to mend your own mistakes. You'll make more of them, never fear. Some worse, some better. Probably none less memorable. But remember this—the most terrible thing that can happen is that people will learn better than to seek magical remedies for problems they ought to be solving for themselves."

The old sorceress reached out and patted the young sorceress affectionately on the cheek. For a long moment neither said anything. Then both of them shrugged and got back to work.

MAGE-SIGHT

by Lynne Alisse Witten

Lynne Witten starts off her autobiography by telling me she's forty; well, it happens to us all; and considering the unpleasantness of the alternative, I think I'd rather be forty than never get there. Actually, I'd not mind being forty again; it's surprising how young forty feels when one looks back from sixty-two.

She begins her letter by saying she is an "orientation and mobility instructor." Before I could ask what the heck that was, she explained it, saying she teaches blind people to get around by themselves.

Many of our writers are special education instructors—which usually means they love to teach but have no stomach for being—as most public school teachers today must be—a policeman. Me, too; I'm a dropout from three teachers' colleges—nothing on earth would induce me to treat kids that way. If I have to spend all my time just keeping order, I'd rather be a policewoman.

When I started reading this story, I almost rejected it out of hand, thinking it a "generic fantasy" with too many familiar elements. I was delighted to find it quite original—and very much worth sticking with.

The woman on the road was so ordinary-looking no one would ever have taken her for a mage. Hair the color of dull, black ash, fading gray at the hairline; nondescript features, with a few more lines than the year before; a body more sturdy than one would generally suppose a mage would have. (After all; what sort of mage would wear the body of a peasant? Weren't mages supposed to be thin and delicate? Be so caught up in their magic that they forgot to eat? Now, an *evil* mage might be round and fat, in token of the good eating that surely came with the ill-gotten gain and power obtained through the effort and sacrifice of others rather than the self. But surely even an evil mage would not appear so . . . plain.) The only feature to connect the woman with the popular image of a mage were her eyes. . . . She always seemed to be looking at something *else;* not at the physical reality immediately before her, but at something deeper, beyond the surface physicality of ordinary life.

Her name was Kerel and she walked down the road with an easy grace that belied her years, walking stick in one hand, thin roll of bedding with most of her other possessions rolled inside over her other shoulder. No, no one would have taken her for anything magical at all. An ex-soldier, perhaps, by her bearing. True, she had no sword and no visible scars, but she wore a leather jerkin with rings of metal sewn on it. Not much in the way of armor, but more than civilians generally wore.

Overhead, a falcon called. Kerel turned her face toward the sound and smiled. A fine bird; a kestrel. The falcon cried, "Kee, kee, kee," again, then soared off over the tree tops.

The woman returned her odd gaze to the road ahead just as a small gray lynx bounded out of the forest. She had little time to prepare as the cat leapt straight for her shoulder. It landed a little short of the mark, more on her back, and slipped a little. Its claws found purchase in the leather and metal as it climbed up to perch on her shoulder.

The woman grunted and staggered a little as the cat settled himself. She turned to glare at the animal.

"Really, Tinean. If you insist on behaving like the kitten you *aren't* anymore, you've got to lose some weight!" she said severely.

The cat was singularly unimpressed. He whiskered her in the nose, making her turn her face away, licked her cheek with his rough tongue, and started purring loudly, directly in her ear.

"All right, *all right*!" she said, laughing and trying not

to sneeze. "You win! I'll never mention your weight again!"

Tinean, recognizing the lie for what it was, yowled softly and allowed her to rub his head, deftly maintaining his precarious balance and twitching his ears with pleasure. Of course this action brought his long ear tufts dangerously close to her nose and eyes, forcing her to keep moving her head to avoid them. It was an old game and both the players knew just how long to keep it up before it wore too thin to be any fun anymore.

A few hours later, near dusk, Kerel, with Tinean still on her shoulder, arrived at the town of Maporl. The guard at the gate looked suspiciously at Tinean.

"Names," he said.

"Kerel and Whiskers."

Tinean snorted and swatted the back of Kerel's head with his short tail. He made no secret of his dislike of the "public" name Kerel used for him when one was required.

The guard looked back at Kerel and noticed her eyes. He sighed and shook his head. "Mages and their name games," he said under his breath as he waved them through.

Kerel smiled and walked on. She walked through Maporl's dusty streets, hardly looking at either side, but warily alert for anything. She had not lived so long by ignoring necessities, but she saw no need to advertise her alertness to others. Especially to anyone who might be as wary as herself.

Tinean, however, was always eager to see what he could see. His bright eyes missed absolutely nothing visible. His tufted ears caught sounds Kerel would never hear and his nose quivered in eager curiosity and anticipation of delicacies to come. He knew better than to try and help himself, though. He just fidgeted on Kerel's shoulder, seeing no reason to walk when he could ride.

Kerel paused at an open door on the left side of the street. The inn was not the best Maporl had to offer, but certainly not the worst. It was, however, what Kerel was looking for. She entered and looked toward the landlord behind the trestles and planks that served as a counter.

He looked at Tinean, who looked right back. The landlord nodded to Kerel, who went to a table in the back, Tinean still on her shoulder. She sat and Tinean leapt down, stretched, and curled up on her feet. She leaned back against the wall and closed her eyes, allowing herself to relax, if only briefly.

The barmaid looked to the landlord, to see if he had anything to say about the furry, but he only shrugged and gestured her over to his newest customers.

"What'll you have, lady," asked the serving girl in her flattest voice. There'd be no extra to be had *here*.

Kerel raised her head and opened her eyes. Tinean, sensing an imminent meal, jumped up to the bench beside her and waited patiently for Kerel to order. He stared into the serving girl's eyes with his yellow, unblinking gaze. She took a step back, drawing in her breath sharply.

The corners of Kerel's mouth quirked slightly and she reached a hand down to scratch the cat's ears. "Where are your manners, boy? Haven't I told you it isn't polite to stare?" Tinean closed his eyes in contentment and leaned his head into the blunt fingers. He obviously didn't care about being polite, but he did enjoy a good head rub.

"You'll have to excuse him; he really doesn't know any better," said Kerel, facing the girl again. "I'll have a bowl of that stew I smell, a slice of bread, and a cup of mead. My friend will have a bowl of stew as well, but he'll pass on the bread and mead."

Tinean responded with a soft cat-whine. Kerel laughed, scratched the other ear and said, "Absolutely not. You know what happened *last* time I let you have mead!" Tinean shook his head and snorted. As if to show that he did not care at all about his loss, he started grooming his right front paw.

The serving girl watched the exchange with growing certainty and shrugged. "Magikers and their familiars!" she snorted and stalked off to fill the order.

The corners of Kerel's mouth twitched again as she turned her face toward the receding back. Her gaze went far beyond the girl, though; already focusing on other scenes.

The few other patrons in the common room of the inn observed the exchange and then went back to their own business. This was not a *regular* gathering place for those of a sorcerous bent, but they were not that uncommon. As long as there were not too many of them in any one place at one time, and as long as they did not let their disagreements get out of hand, all was well, and their coin spent as well as any other. Familiars were generally welcome, too. Often these "animals" behaved better than some of the two-legged patrons.

Kerel was just mopping up the last of the gravy with the last bit of bread when Tinean let out a low rumble in his throat. By now, it was full dark and the common room was over half full and much noisier.

Tinean sat next to Kerel, ears back, the hair on the back of his neck standing up, and his eyes focused on the door. Kerel raised her head, face toward the door as well. She nodded and said, "I see him."

The "him" was a tall, blond man standing just inside the door. *He* looked the part of a mage. Slender, aristocratic bearing, pale skin made even paler by his black clothing and the equally black cloak that swirled around him. He looked about the room, his eyes lighting on Kerel. He smiled quickly and strode purposefully to her table in a suddenly silent room.

"So. You've come to see me," he said as he sat, without asking. Tinean growled again, and curled his lips to show, subtly, his fangs.

Kerel quieted him with a touch, but he still kept staring at the newcomer, obviously inattentive to Kerel's earlier admonitions against staring.

"As you see," she replied softly. "I couldn't let our . . . *business* remain unfinished any longer, Delayhey. I must say, though, I didn't expect to see you quite so soon."

"I, too, am eager to have this out of the way. Formal challenge given, and not answered at *first* opportunity. . . . Well, my reputation would never stand for it. And I don't like to leave unfinished business, either" He smiled nastily and leaned back in a casual stretch. "I *really* thought you were dead. No one should have survived that attack. . . ." His own eyes took on a more distant appearance. "No one ever has. No one but you." He frowned slightly.

Kerel leaned back against the wall again, casting her strange gaze on the sorcerer. She smiled.

"Ah, but you underestimated me," she said.

"Oh, I don't think so," he replied, coming back to himself. "And no one's luck holds forever."

"As you say," she said, inclining her head a little. "When?" she asked. As the challenged party, he had the choice of time. The place was wherever the combatants chanced, or chose, to meet.

"Oh, I think *dawn* would be appropriate, don't you?" He leaned forward and fingered her mead cup. "Still, why be hard on ourselves. I think I'd rather sleep late." He leaned back again, hands on the table, arms held out straight. "How about mid-morning. Time enough for breakfast. . . . A last meal. . . ?"

"As you please," she responded, inclining her head a little in a mock bow and smiling.

Delayhey stiffened slightly, but made no response. He just said "At dawn, then; the South Gate. We wouldn't want to raze the town, would we?"

"*I* wouldn't. I'm sure I can't speak for you. Not that I would ever want to, you understand."

Delayhey smiled, showing perfect white teeth. "Until tomorrow, then." He rose suddenly, nearly knocking over his stool. Swirling his cape, he was gone before anyone quite realized it.

Kerel sighed. "Flamboyant as always, eh, Tinean?"

The lynx twitched his ears, then rubbed his head against her wrist. He purred loudly enough for everyone in the unnaturally silent common room to hear. Conversation gradually resumed, but never quite regained the relaxed tone it had had before Delayhey's entrance.

Kerel sighed again. She took a coin out of her pouch and laid it on the table beside her empty bowl. "Come on, Fluffy. Let's get some sleep."

* * *

Neither Kerel nor Tinean got much sleep, however. They prepared for the coming battle. Kerel knew she had the ability, she knew Tinean would supply all the backup and connections to additional power that she would need, she knew that her *real* backup was there and available. Still, it didn't do to take anything for granted. Defeat in the coming battle would mean death for herself, her familiars, and her remaining friends, when the victor found them. And he would find them.

Dawn came not long after she finally fell asleep. The sun was lighting the horizon not long after the "Kee, kee, kee" cry of a bird began to stir her from sleep. She tried to go back to sleep, if only for a few minutes, but Tinean put a stop to that when he butted against her. She came awake immediately, resigned but ready for the coming conflict.

As the appointed hour approached, Kerel and Tinean made their way through the streets to the South gate. Many people were already at the designated spot, including most of the city guard.

Kerel took her place and waited, ready. Tinean sat by her side, fastidiously licking a paw.

At the last moment, Delayhey *appeared* in his spot.

Kerel sighed. "Flamboyant to the end, I see," she said under her breath. Aloud she said, "Challenge has been given and accepted. You can still avoid this, if you agree to accompany me to the High Ones for trial."

Delayhey laughed aloud. It was not a pleasant sound at all and held no mirth. "I think not, my friend. I am quite guilty and there is only one way *that* trial can come out. Here, I am equally sure of the outcome and much happier about it."

Even as he spoke, he raised his hands to cast his first spell, completely against the rules. But, then, Delayhey had never gone by the rules, nor did Kerel expect him to. She raised her own hands for the counterspell, deflecting his bolt into a clear space, away from the city's walls. Tinean stood beside her, total attention on their adversary. Every hair on his body stood on end and his eyes held a faraway look very like Kerel's.

When the first mage bolt exploded in the open, the crowd dispersed, back into the city walls. The people were curious, but wanted to be able to talk about it over mead and ale that night. They joined the more cautious watchers on top of the walls.

Kerel focused all her attention on her adversary, dropping into easy rapport with Tinean. Overhead, a bird cried out in the lightning sky. She raised her hands and drew a pattern in the air, trapping Delayhey's hands in a paralysis spell.

Delayhey, already in rapport with his own familiar, ignored his hands and used the tongue of his snake to draw the pattern of the counterspell. His next spell was more elaborate and deadly. Kerel and Tinean were suddenly surrounded by fire, engulfed by fire, all but consumed by fire.

Although Kerel felt the heat of Delayhey's spell, she carried too many protections on herself and Tinean for it to destroy them immediately, as it was intended to do. Still, she had to counter it quickly, before she had to breathe the flames.

Tinean, too, knew to hold his breathe and wait. He trusted Kerel and knew she would soon dissipate the fire. He also caught the glimmer of what she intended to do in the back of her mind. He focused his attention where he had last seen Delayhey, in preparation.

As soon as the flames vanished, Kerel threw a light lance spell at Delayhey. The evil mage recognized what was coming, but he could not stop it. His only hope was to stop the caster, but he lacked the power to do any real damage. He could only hope to distract her enough to lessen or negate the effects of the magic.

Delayhey drew all the power he could from his familiar and created a cloud of blackness around his opponent's head.

This should have stopped her, or at least changed the course of the spell as the target had to be seen for it to work. It did not, however. Her hands and voice completed the work they had begun. Delayhey had only a moment to realize his failure, then he was gone with a blast of power that shook the very walls of the city. The observers standing there were knocked down, and some fell off of the wall on both sides. An acrid smell hung in the air and dust settled into a large indentation in the ground where the sorcerer had stood.

Kerel staggered and nearly fell. Tinean had already collapsed on the ground, all but unconscious with exhaustion.

As those watchers who were able regained their feet, they began to notice who the victor was. There was uniform jubilation over the outcome of the sorcerous battle, for Delayhey had terrorized the area for several months. A few of the braver ones ran out to clap the victor on the back, all but knocking her off her feet. They quickly caught her up and half carried her through the gate. Tinean staggered up and let out a yowl that was heard even over the sounds of anticipated celebration. Kerel scooped him up to her shoulder.

"What did I tell you about losing weight?" she asked. Tinean didn't even bother to reply. He only had energy enough to hold onto the leather with his claws.

After a celebration that went on long into the night, Kerel and Tinean at last were able to return to their room. Kerel wanted nothing more than to lie down and sleep forever, but she had one more task to accomplish.

Kerel sat cross-legged in the middle of the hard wood floor. She could still hear carousers below, but they wouldn't affect her concentration. She called Tinean and he came and sat in her lap, dropping into rapport as he settled. They both began the deep breathing, preliminary to the contact she planned to make. Soon, their breathing was synchronized and Kerel began to invoke the proper mental images, in their proper order, in order to make contact.

The dark room grew light before her eyes, but only to the inner sight of herself and Tinean.

"So, it is done?" came the voice in her head.

"Yes," she replied. "He reacted just as you thought he would. When I began the spell, he countered with the darkness. I knew I had him then."

"Yes, Daughter. As I hoped. Did any of the observers guess?"

"That that foul creature stole my sight when he destroyed the rest of my mage group? I doubt it. They are somewhat accustomed to mages here, but not on an everyday basis. Certainly not enough to know that I can see through the eyes of fur and feathers, though I didn't have to use Miaca's eyes this time. Fortunately, Delayhey never knew, either, though I was afraid he'd guessed last night. He was just surprised and annoyed I wasn't dead along with Bearil and the others." She sighed mentally. "The power he stole was focused in the wrong direction."

"True. And you must take care that none ever learn *that* particular focus of power. You know better than I the danger of that secret being revealed."

"Truly. I'll start back tomorrow, before anyone with a little more knowledge can start to add things up."

"I'll look forward to your arrival, then."

Contact faded and the room was dark again, figuratively and literally. For Kerel, though, the physical darkness was permanent.

The next morning, as soon as the gate opened, a rather nondescript woman with a lynx trotting beside her left the city by the north gate. Her gaze was fixed on something only she could see and a falcon called, "Kee, kee, kee," overhead.

ETHER AND THE SKEPTIC

by Katy Huth Jones

Katy Huth Jones—any relation to Davy—he of the famous locker?—says that she began writing when she was very young—she says her mother still has one of her early stories—illustrated, of course. (Of course. Would you believe I received a comic book manuscript—in illustrated form—among my manuscripts last week? Honest Indian—though what's so honest, I wonder, about an Indian? They are proverbially honest—just as a doornail serves as the expression for deadness; as for me, I'd join Scrooge as thinking a coffin-nail fitter to proclaim that particular stage of deadness.)

As I was saying before I got sidetracked by my own attempts to be funny, Katy's been a lifelong writer; she "laid aside writing in college to major in music; but realized I didn't want music to exclude the rest of life as it must in order to become the BEST."

I think it was Georges Bizet, composer of Carmen, who authored a quote a former voice teacher of mine had posted in his studio; "Ah, music; what a wonderful hobby; what a miserable profession." I, too; I suspect music is the only profession harder than writing in which to make a living.

Thirteen years ago she married a Texan who is a safety consultant. They were foster parents for two years and now have two sons, David, nine, and Robert, two.

She teaches her kids at home, and edits a small newsletter for a countywide home schooling group. "Ether and the Skeptic" is her first published fiction. She says she's "been privileged to teach the creative process to children and instill a little of my enthusiasm for writing . . . I feel that all those thousands and thousands of words written and rewritten have been worth it."

Ether hated being an ordinary peasant. She thought perhaps there'd been a mixup at her birth; surely she was not really supposed to have been born into a peasant family. Her mother always called her Ethie, but Ether knew her real name must be Ethereal, and her mother simply forgot to tell her. By the time Ether thought to ask, it was too late; her mother died giving birth to Ether's fifth brother. Her father remarried shortly thereafter, and Ether's stepmother had already borne him four more sons. No sisters! Five full brothers and four half ones. There was no one else to share her load of endless cleaning, cooking, mending, tending, washing, hoeing, gathering, cleaning. Since her mother and then her stepmother had been always pregnant, or just given birth, it fell to Ether to run the household from the earliest age. Never mind that her brothers and half-brothers could divide their chores and have lots of free time in between. Her father would not allow them to help with women's work; it was demeaning.

At sixteen, Ether still dreamed that someday a handsome, gray-templed noble would ride up to her one-room, wattle-and-daub cottage on his prancing black stallion and announce to her peasant father that he was looking for his long-lost daughter. Then she would come out of the house, and the nobleman would jump down from his horse and gather her in his powerful arms.

"Ethereal," he would say. "I've been searching for you all these years."

And then he would carry her off to a grand manor house, where she would have silk dresses to wear, and learn to read and write.

As things now stood, Ether had not much chance of marrying out of her situation into a better one. Though her mother had been a lovely woman, for a peasant, only her brothers had her dark eyes and long eyelashes, her rosy cheeks and full lips. Ether had pale skin and hair, eyes too large, nose too small. Even had she the chance to go with her father to the nearby village, no man would look at her twice. Ether knew she was doomed to live in the same house with the same brothers and half-brothers for the rest of her life.

Then one day, her stepmother had the misfortune of dying in childbirth, too. This time the babe did not live, but this time it had been a girl.

Ether could not bear it. It was not fair that her only sister die, that she be left to mother nine boys by herself when she was only sixteen years old.

So Ether ran away.

She did not take a thing except her mother's old, tattered cloak and a crust of hard bread. She followed the path that led to the dirt road beyond the village. She'd heard her father say that all roads led to the castle. There, she believed, her life would change.

It was morning when Ether left, and by noon she felt hot and tired, hungry and thirsty, so she sat down on a stump under a gnarled oak tree and ate half the bread. She hadn't thought to bring any water, but she knew there was a river nearby, the same river where she had washed clothes and pots, and from where she had always carried drinking water to the house. She would look for it later.

As she stood up to continue walking, Ether saw a strange stick in the middle of the road. She hadn't noticed it there before she sat down. Not knowing what to expect, she bent down to pick it up. It was a worn, smoothly carved length of oak, not quite long enough for a walking stick. The designs were not familiar to her. Ether felt funny holding it, as if she had stolen it.

She looked around, almost expecting the owner to appear out of the forest and claim the stick, but there was no one else as far as she could see. Ether decided to keep it. If nothing else, she could sell it.

She continued along the road, twirling the stick and humming a tune her stepmother used to sing. As she walked, she looked up at the treetops almost covering the road and watched the afternoon sun's rays struggle through the branches.

Because she was looking up, Ether didn't notice the man until she was almost beside him.

She stopped, frozen in her place.

The young man had shoulder-length brown curls and eyes as green as his tunic and hosen. His long sleeves were embroidered with three bold black stripes. He sat on a tree stump with his legs crossed, resting his chin against one hand. He wore no weapons that Ether could see.

"Hello," she said.

The stranger nodded his head, but only glanced, bored, in her direction.

"I'm going to the castle," Ether announced, hoping that would impress him.

"Everyone goes there eventually," he said with a sigh. "There's nothing there to see."

"Maybe not for you, but I'm going to a wizard's convention. You see, this is my magic wand." Ether had no idea if there was such a thing as a wizard's convention, but she was determined to get the man's attention.

He shook his head. "I don't believe in magic, and I don't believe you do, either." He stood up, and Ether pointed the stick at him, just in case.

"If you try anything, I'll—I'll turn you into a lizard." She waved the stick and tried to look menacing.

He laughed then. "Do you know how ridiculous you look, wench? Go on home, now, where you belong."

That did it. Ether had been pushed around by males long enough.

"I don't look as ridiculous as you! You are a lizard!"

To Ether's complete surprise, a tingling sensation went from her arm, through the stick, and flashed as a blue flame to the man and—

—he disappeared.

Well, not quite vanished. Where he had been standing, a smooth green lizard with three black stripes down its back stood motionless in the dirt.

Ether gasped and dropped the stick. The lizard stared at her with unblinking emerald eyes. Ether looked from the stick to the lizard and back again at the stick. Gingerly she picked it up.

"A real magic wand," she whispered. "What do you think about magic now, lizard?" It served him right for doubting like he did. But Ether decided she had better be careful what she said out loud as long as the wand was in her hand.

Not really knowing what to do about the lizard, Ether continued down the road. She glanced back after a little while and saw that the lizard was following her, scampering down the middle of the road.

And when Ether stopped for the night, venturing into the forest to find the river, the lizard followed her there, too. After washing her face, she ate the rest of her bread and lay down on a pile of leaves, pulling the old cloak over her shoulders.

In the morning, Ether found the lizard asleep on a nearby rock. She felt sorry for him then, in a way. Perhaps he still thought as a man inside the lizard's body. Perhaps he hoped she might turn him back into a man. Though she figured she probably could reverse the magic, she decided to leave him as he was. It served him right for being rude.

But later that morning, after Ether had covered a good distance and noticed that the lizard was lagging behind, she stopped and waited for him to catch up, then held out her hand.

"Come, and I'll carry you," she said. The lizard ran into her hand, and Ether let him climb to her shoulder.

That was one good thing about having nine brothers; since they were always bringing home lizards and snakes and spiders and other crawly things, she had learned at an early age not to be frightened of them.

Late in the afternoon, Ether crested a hill and gasped at the sight of the round stone castle sitting on the opposite hill. In the valley between, the wide river flowed lazily on. Not far from where Ether stood, a wooden raft ferried men and horses to the opposite shore. She watched them head toward the open castle gate as the raft was poled back across the river.

Since she wanted to reach the castle before night fell, Ether hurried down the hill to meet the ferryman.

"Two coppers for one passenger," the gnarled old man said. He took off his cap and scratched his head.

"I have no money," Ether explained. She felt the lizard try to hide under her hair.

"No coppers, no ferry." The old man scratched his chest through his threadbare, stained tunic.

For a moment, Ether considered turning him into a lizard too, but since it wouldn't help her get across the river, she decided to try something else.

Ether walked to the bank not far down from the raft and touched the tip of her stick to the water. She said the first thing that came into her mind.

"River, stop."

Suddenly, the water stopped flowing, as if a dam had been lowered into it. The rest of the river continued to flow downstream, but where Ether's stick held it back was a smooth wall of water.

The ferryman stood on the floating raft, his eyes wide and his mouth hanging open.

Ether walked across the slippery rocks of the river bottom. When she reached the other side, she touched the damned water with her stick and said, "River, flow." Immediately the water crashed down into the empty bed and rushed downstream. The ferryman yelped as he clung to the raft riding the crest of the water. Ether watched him until he disappeared among the trees.

The lizard moved along Ether's shoulder to get a better look. She smiled and walked toward the castle gate. As she came closer, she saw how big the castle really was, and fear began to eat away at the confidence she'd found in crossing the river. There was an armed guard on either side of the tall wooden doors. An iron portcullis was partially closed just inside the gateway.

Ether met the eyes of one of the helmeted guards. He had his sword resting against one mailed shoulder. A scar across his cheek added to his ferocity, but his angry glare alone was almost enough to make Ether turn back.

Then she remembered her stick and felt a little better.

As she started toward the open gate, the guard with the scar thrust his sword out, blocking her way.

"State your business, wench."

Ether cleared her throat. "I'm here for the wizard's convention."

The other guard spoke. "There is no wizard convention here."

"Are you a wizard yourself?" Ether asked.

"Of course not," he answered.

"What about you, sir?" Ether asked the guard with the scar.

"I do not need sorcery," he growled. "And if you do not leave, I will show you my own kind of magic." He twirled his sword and pointed it at Ether's heart.

Ether wanted very much to turn him into a lizard, but she realized that the other guard could kill her before she could defend herself, and that would not get her into the castle.

"If neither of you are wizards," she countered, "then how do you know there is not a wizard's convention?"

The guard with the scarred cheek opened his mouth to speak, then closed it again. He scowled at her. "Even if there was a wizard's convention, you are certainly no wizard, wench."

"If you don't believe I am one, I can prove it to you." Either pointed her stick at the guard. "You will let me pass."

He lowered his sword.

"That will not be necessary." He inclined his head. "You may pass."

Ether felt herself trembling as she walked under the portcullis, but she held her head high and pretended not to be afraid.

She entered the vast courtyard filled with people. There were guards such as the two she'd met, noblemen and women in the finest clothing Ether had ever seen, and peasants like herself rushing from place to place, some with arms laden with sacks and baskets, others carrying or leading chickens or goats. The walls of the castle were actually buildings three stories high, on the top of which ran a walkway where many soldiers stood. She saw some of them pointing at her, and she wondered if any of them had seen what she'd done to the river.

In the middle of the courtyard a round stone tower rose above the milling people and animals. Wooden buildings with thatched roofs nestled against this tower as well as the castle walls.

Ether slowly walked through the crowd toward the

tower, though she had no idea what to look for or what she would find. When she reached the wooden building facing her, the lizard scampered up and down her arm. She held out her hand so it could sit there.

"What is it? Is this someplace important?"

The lizard shook its head from side to side, then turned and pointed with its snout toward the castle wall on Ether's right.

"Over there?" she said, pointing in the same direction.

The lizard nodded and slowly blinked its eyes.

Ether held on to the lizard with one hand and the stick with the other as she pushed her way to the building beneath the stone wall. It was only a shack even smaller than her own house. The rough wooden door was ajar.

When the lizard pushed against her hand, Ether pushed open the door.

"Hello?" Her voice trembled.

The light from a fat candle in a wall sconce bathed the room with its soft glow. The only furnishings were a rush-filled mattress and a rude wooden table and bench. Seated on the bench was an old man, older than the ferryman, but dressed in a homespun robe. His long white beard flowed in wisps down his chest. The sparse hair on his head was also white.

"Come in," he said in a quavering voice.

Ether stepped inside. The lizard jumped down from her hand and ran to the old man, climbing up his robe and settling in his lap.

"I told you not to be such a skeptic," the man told the lizard.

"Do you know him?" Ether asked, realizing as she asked the question how stupid it sounded.

"Yes, I know him." The old man smiled at Ether, and she saw the tiredness in his face. "Jymn has worked for me since he was a boy."

"His name is Jymn?"

"I call him the Skeptic, for always he doubts what I see. Perhaps now he will trust me, though I only grow older and more feeble."

"Who are you?" Ether watched the lizard and tried to remember what the man named Jymn had looked like.

"I am Chandar, the last of the wizards."

"The last?" Ether felt a great sadness as she looked into his pale, tired eyes.

"For four hundred years I have looked for someone to carry on my work, for someone with heart for magic."

Ether held up the stick. "This is yours, isn't it?"

Chandar nodded, but when Ether tried to give it back to him, he held up a trembling hand.

"No. I no longer have the strength to wield it. It belongs to you now."

"But—" Ether stopped herself before saying what she'd heard all her life—that she was only a girl. After all, hadn't she used the wand? True, she wasn't sure about what she was doing, but magic had been done.

Ether looked down at the lizard in Chandar's lap. It stared up at her with bright green eyes.

"What about Jymn? Should I turn him back?"

Chandar smiled. "That is your choice. But remember, the magic does not come from the wand. It comes from within you."

"Within me?"

"All that was needed was the opportunity to unlock your potential. I sent the Skeptic to provide you with that opportunity."

"Do you mean that he left the stick for me to find?"

"Of course. You have always had the power, but it could not be channeled without the wand. I brought you here to teach you how to use your power."

Ether looked back at the lizard. If he was going to be like her father and brothers, she would rather leave him as he was. But she supposed that Chandar needed Jymn's help. "I guess I had better change him back."

Chandar nodded and placed the lizard on the dirt floor. "Just do the first thing that comes into your heart."

Ether stared at Chandar, then she closed her eyes and pictured Jymn as she had seen him on the road. She pointed the wand at him.

"You are a man," she said.

Jymn stood beside the old wizard, the same long curly hair, the same green tunic with three black stripes on the sleeves, the same intense green eyes.

"Now do you believe?" asked the wizard.

"Yes," Ether and Jymn said in unison, then both laughed together.

"How did you know I had the power?" Ether asked Chandar. "You don't even know my name."

"The more you grow, the more you will understand," said the wizard.

"What is your name, lady?" Jymn asked her, his eyes sparkling.

Ether clutched the rune-carved wand at her side, stood up straight, and threw her shoulders back.

"Call me Ethereal."

THE LIMWITCH

by Rebekah Jensen

After accepting each of these stories I try to summarize the plot in one sentence. I feel very strongly that a story—all the way from *Mutiny on the Bounty* to *To Kill a Mockingbird*—if it's to be readable at all, should be capable of being summarized in one line; otherwise it won't be focused enough to read. I have checked this by summing up every story I write—and any I read—in one line.

Every workable story I buy can be summarized that simply; one of the things I stress when I'm teaching writing is "What's your story about?" If the writer doesn't know, the story usually isn't worth reading—and probably not worth writing. The stories I reject usually can't be summed up; and that's the lesson for today.

This is another "first sale." Rebekah Jensen says she "writes because she loves words and their ability to get her persistent mind pictures on paper." She wishes to dedicate this story to her high school English teacher, Mr. Shafer.

Having just graduated her husband from Harvey Mudd College—where's that? Here I thought Harvey Mudd was a character in Star Trek—she now plans to go back to school to study linguistics. Her dream in life is to have a rambling house full of books—some of which she hopes will be her own.

An admirable—and, judging by this, an attainable dream.

So what's this story about? I wrote down on it, in my customary simplistic way, "A young witch gets a familiar." Like all stories, of course, there's more to it than that; but that's a good place to start.

Mellisa threw down her ash pencil in disgust. "I'll never make a good witch," she declared angrily to the empty room, "I never could rhyme!" She kicked the leg of her desk and glared at the papyrus spellsheet in front of her. Despite her wishes, the awkward sentences remained.

"There once was a man from Algonkar . . ." she mumbled. Word upon word a small green mist grew in the center of a spellcircle on the floor in front of her. "Whose shoes were known to leak water . . ." The mist suddenly developed pink spots and began to writhe violently.

"Oh, don't do that!" she pleaded to the green entity, "I know it doesn't *quite* rhyme, but . . ." She trailed off as the mist disappeared in a final fit of agony.

All she was doing was trying to summon a familiar, every second year magic student had one. Her instructor had made her stay after class, to try spellcasting again for the millionth time. Her classmates had filed out past her, smirking, each followed by their personal bundle of fur or fangs or both.

She sighed and tried afresh. "There was a boy who loved berries . . ." This time the mist was a bluish shade of red. "uh . . . who also liked small . . . little . . ." the mist began to fade, "Cherries!" The mist solidified suddenly. Mellisa was so surprised she almost forgot to continue.

"Oh! But he once ate an orange," the mist grew a couple of feet and one eye, Mellisa looked at it in hope. "And it gave him a . . ." The eye blinked at her expectantly.

"It gave him a . . . uh . . . cornge, um bornge, surunge . . . Oh, no, don't, please, oh, oh . . . crud." The cute blue mist full of promise vanished abruptly.

Mellisa sighed tragically. Her life was ruined, she would be the laughing stock of the second grade, her instructor would beat her. . . . She sagged against her chair dramatically. Then the thought of her teacher reminded her of something he had told her earlier that day in class.

"Don't make it so complicated, Mellissandra," he had finally said in exasperation, "Write about something you know!"

She pulled out a new spellsheet and began again slowly. "There once was a witch sans familiar . . ." A pale yellow mist grew feebly, "But her rhyming was very peculiar." The mist swayed perilously but somehow survived.

"She . . . umm . . . needed a verse!" The mist turned into fur and two legs and two arms appeared. She was on a roll, she could feel it, "Um . . . but . . . uh . . ." two *more* arms appeared, "she couldn't rehearse!" The fuzz developed eyes and a mouth.

Suddenly she was stuck. "Um! Er!," she began frantically, the fur acquired a sickly greenish tinge. "And she . . . and she . . ." The creature was beginning to fade around the edges.

Desperately she blurted, "And she promised it'd be very dear to her!" The entity solidified and with a thump collapsed on the floor.

"Yes!" She shouted and leapt out of her seat. She did a little dance around her desk then went slowly toward the little creature she had created. It was whimpering in a scrawny heap inside her spellcircle. She approached it slowly, hand outstretched.

It wasn't much to look at, one leg was longer than the other so it sort of leaned to the left. It had four arms, placed at random locations around its yellow-green body and one eye was red and one eye purple and the other one black. It looked up at her pitifully. She gently reached to touch it on the head. Lashing out, it sank its tiny sharp teeth into her finger. Humming softly, Mellisa roughly grabbed it by the scruff of its neck and bound it up unmercifully in her sweater.

It struggled frantically in her arms. She nonchalantly whacked it upside the head, then spoke to it sweetly. The creature looked up at her in confusion and pain.

"Come on, you poor teeny thing," she crooned, "Mommy Witch will find you a blanket and you can have some chicken broth." She smiled at the sickly creature in her arms and ignored its steadily weaker struggles. She was rocking it and talking to it amiably as she walked out of the room.

Mellisa almost skipped up the school hallway carrying her hard-won bundle. She thought gleefully of those taunts of her classmates turning into jealous mutters. They won't make fun of her anymore, that's for sure.

"There once was a fuzzball named Martid," she murmured to the helpless creature, "who got me all that I wanted. . . ."

And so this is the story of Melissa who, in the depth of her seven-year-old despair had been about to give up and become a horse trainer or perhaps a potter's wife, discovered magic. Through her well-meaning tutor and a natural talent for painful rhyming, Mellisa the failure eventually became Mellissandra the Magnificent or Mellissandra the Maleficent, depending on whether you were addressing her highness herself, or her highness's badly-abused subjects. It is unknown, however, by what name her poor malformed creature thought of her. She kept it locked away in a room, you see, for they say that a familiar reflects the true soul of a Limwitch.

SMILE OF THE GODDESS

by Lorina J. Stephens

Lorina J. Stephens lives in Canada and lists a number of small-press credits. She attended Clarion Writer's Workshop, but says she does not feel it was a landmark moment in her writing. Writing, she says, "like life, is a journey, not a destination."

Does that imply the old adage applies—that to travel hopefully is more important than to arrive? She has written a travel book, about Niagara Escarpment, which she describes as a coffee-table book. I didn't think those things were written, just manufactured. She also has won a literary prize.

The note I scribbled on this story describes it as "Very positive" dealing with "a Goddess and a conqueror who needs love." Well, don't we all?

She watched him ride under the dark of the moon, his generals beside him, an army at his back. He paused at the crest of the hill. Before him lay a pan of dried salt—the remnant of a sea she remembered retreating millennia ago—beyond that a dark rise that was the city of Nahrain of the kingdom of Oduman. Barad's kingdom.

A desert wind chilled his face. The roan under him snorted.

Consider, Barad, she said to him.

He touched his ear, his dark eyes raising to a river of stars. The beard he'd taken to did nothing to soften his face. Such a hard face, a fierce face. She heard him form her name, *Seditha*? wondering, hoping he had indeed received the blessing of the goddess.

I can give you what you asked.

An image of his supplication in her temple filled his mind—the goat he'd sacrificed, the golden platters of dates, nuts, and oranges, the way he'd prostrated himself before her priestess. King Barad on his belly. King Barad who had conquered a desert, who had liberated a people, who had forged peace when it seemed none could be achieved, tenuous though that peace might be.

King Barad had once again come to the goddess Seditha to ask her blessing upon a political mission.

Again she questioned his need: *Are you sure you want to raid Nahrain?*

Yes! he thought.

Are you sure this mission is entirely political?

Yes!

There isn't anything of wounded pride?

No!

Then be it on your head. I warned you.

There was hesitation in him at that moment. She almost pitied him. Barad feared nothing. Except Seditha. What would it be like to live in fear of the goddess?

His hesitation lasted momentarily. Indecision hadn't won him a kingdom. And it wouldn't resolve this problem before him. An alliance between Oduman's two noble houses would be forged, he thought, whether Andulyn in Nahrain wanted to wed him or not.

There *would* be peace.

He signaled his generals. No quarter was to be given.

She watched him ride down off the hill onto the hard salt.

Seditha's attention shifted to the city of Nahrain, to the palace, to a suite of rooms where the noblewoman Andulyn slept under down coverlets.

All these past days Andulyn, too, had visited a temple of Seditha, brought sacrifices, offered herself before the priestesses. Prayers of deliverance had been made. Prayers of supplication. Prayers of tears.

What Barad didn't know was that Nahrain was already in seige. And that Andulyn's prayers had been for the city. It was for this simple reason no response to overtures of marriage had been made. Barad's entourage had not been allowed to return.

But Seditha had warned Barad. All he could see was the smile of the goddess.

And so he rode. Peace out of war. This is what he told himself. This is what she saw.

They came upon the white walls of Nahrain in a planned formation. Twenty of his best had gone on before, scaled the walls. It had been so simple. Few guards. Little fuss. The gates now swung open.

Seditha listened to Barad thinking, knew he suspected something amiss when this first stage had gone so easily.

Thought of ambush appeared in his mind.

She felt him tense.

He signaled the second team.

Little more than dark shapes, they slipped through the gates. She watched them move as one unit through the streets, divide into two, then three, one group to the main stables, another to the markets, others to break up yet again and raid villagers' homes and disrupt movement in Nahrain. Behind them, at the appointed time, Barad led four teams toward the palace—to take out the guards, to hold the palace gates, to secure the way into Andulyn's rooms.

The others, the lesser captains and regular footmen, scythed through the narrow streets. The team intent on the stables went quickly, carefully, their faces lined with strain when not one guard was encountered. Within sight of the stables the captain paused, raising his hand to halt his men. Across the street, at the corner, an archer stood on point. Seditha saw where two others watched the team's back. The captain signaled two men to go. They fell into a crouched lope, circling the stables. What should have been an easy victory sat ill with the captain when his men returned. There were no guards. The stables were unattended.

Seditha watched his apprehension swell.

He nodded to his archers. Flame burst at arrow points, arced through the darkness, and burst upon the stables.

He achieved his goal. The stables were secured. Horses ran shrieking from flaming stalls.

It was one of the archers who pointed to what else scurried from fire.

"Rats," the captain hissed. Hundreds of them.

Seditha watched his horror and kept her promise to give Barad victory in this mission.

Now she watched where another team took and held the market square. Should dawn arrive and Barad still not have his quarry, they would be sure to prevent any amassing of people.

But it was here, in the square, this captain held his men, gorge in his throat. Where only hours from now should have been a babel of color and wares, now stood a laden wagon, even in the moonless night grim in its cargo. Rats scurried over the shapes. It was then the captain realized there were rats aplenty in the square—dead, alive—hundreds of them there with the corpses. Beyond this, in a walled enclosure, was the glow of fire, the stink of burning flesh.

One of the men retched.

When his men bolted, the captain did nothing to stop them. Fighting was one thing. To die in this way was another.

He turned on his heel, kicked a rat out of the way, and fled.

In yet other districts of Nahrain soldiers ran in the grip of bloodlust. One group broke into a tavern that should have been open, that should have been raucous with revelry. There were people within, hollow eyed, sullenly drunk. A soldier yelled out, "Nahrainian pigs!"

Not one person moved. They all just stared at Barad's men as if they were fools. A girl, for she was no more than a girl, swaggered up to the handsomest of the soldiers, grinned from a shrunken face like bleached linen, her teeth seemingly too large. She tossed her hair from her shoulders, exposing her neck. He froze, horror stricken. His gaze shot round the room, marking now the coughing, the rats that were everywhere.

Seditha watched it all dissolve into terror when Barad's men realized why there had been little resistance.

Within the palace itself, Barad also met minimal opposition. They had made it up to the east wing, on the second floor. His success sat heavily with him.

Worried, Barad? she asked.

He flinched, eyes darting. Light from wall braziers lit his face, his elaborate armor glinting. She might have thought to take him as a consort had he not been so in awe of her. She could have blessed him with gods for children.

But she let none of this touch him, only her concern.

This is too easy, he thought.

She smiled and he felt the bitterness of it, her warnings replaying in his mind.

Do you need to marry Andulyn that badly? she asked him now.

Yes!

Will a marriage without love be the foundation for peace?

Love has nothing to do with this.

Doesn't it? Perhaps you've been too long from the battlefield.

What's that supposed to mean?

That you long for conquest.

Again his glance darted. No guards. No opposition. This was too easy.

What trickery is this? he asked.

No trickery, Barad.

Then where are the guards?

Sick, dead, tending their loved ones.

She felt a shudder run through him.

One of his men brought word Andulyn's rooms were secured.

He closed his eyes. *Seditha, please.*

I'm giving you what you asked.

Yes. And I should be careful of what I ask.

You're learning, Barad.

He turned then and strode into Andulyn's rooms. Braziers burned brightly, the air hazy with incense, although underneath that heavy aroma lay another smell—sour, sickly. His gaze flashed to the windows where tapestries had been pulled. Everywhere there were remnants of medicaments, simples. He passed by scribes, councillors, leeches—all of them weary and beyond fear of him.

She watched him go into the main chamber where he found Andulyn on her knees, weeping over the body of her father, Dorain. Death was familiar to Barad. This Seditha knew. He recognized it quickly in Dorain. But what she knew he wasn't prepared for was the manner of Dorain's death.

She felt his panic stir, heard his conclusions.

Plague. It was there in the swellings under Dorain's arms.

Heat shot through him. She could feel him balance between fight or flight. But how to fight plague? And how to flee from it?

You warned me, Seditha.

She longed to embrace him, to return his arrogance and strength to him, but did nothing. It would have served nothing. If Barad were to forge peace in his kingdom, he would have need of this.

But it would have soothed her to have given him peace.

And I chose not to listen, he thought.

Such self-recrimination in him. It would be so easy to reach out, to touch him, to ease his pain. This would not make a strong king.

She watched his resolve sharpen, focus. Fight. This was another enemy to him, she knew.

He inhaled sharply, bent, set his hands under Andulyn's shoulders and pulled her up, up, looked at her red-rimmed eyes so glazed, her mouth pale and trembling, aware of the swellings under her arms. And suddenly Seditha felt his pain when he thought of this gentle maid dying.

Seditha wanted to cry out for his pain. So long she'd waited for some one person to touch him in the way no campaign could touch him. She only hoped Andulyn would.

"I could not answer you, my lord Barad," Andulyn said.

"I can see that." He touched her cheek to take the edge off his statement.

"I would have honored you, my lord."

He could see the tears brim again in her eyes, as could Seditha. He lifted Andulyn into his arms and carried her to her bed, ordering his men to make preparations for an honorable burial for Dorain, to bring him the leeches.

While he watched the leeches prepare an infusion of yellow powder and water, he questioned the councillors about what action was being taken in the city. This was fascinating to Seditha. Even now, when the man within him screamed out for Andulyn to heal, he knew his responsibility. The city needed him. Personal matters could wait. But for the first time, Seditha could see him battle with himself.

Barad's reaction when the councillors informed him they were following Lady Andulyn's orders gave Seditha further hope that at last Barad was ready for peace.

He knelt by Andulyn then and asked her why she was having refuse collected from the streets, why it was necessary to burn the dead, why she was opening royal coffers to build every household a bath.

She touched his cheek, trembling, smiling at the way he worried. "I asked the goddess Seditha to show me how to save the people of Nahrain."

And she asked nothing for herself, Seditha said to him. *And because of that you'll let her die?*

Accusation there. Now he feared this woman would die and leave him ignorant of her strength.

Afraid you'll lose your political alliance?

He studied Andulyn's face, amazed this small woman could bear herself so nobly in the face of so much death. Her first statement to him had been a veiled apology, her second a reassurance she would have honored him.

No, Seditha—afraid I'll lose a cherished companion. And a teacher. There is so much I could learn from her, and share with her.

This sounds like love, Barad.

He touched Andulyn's fevered cheek, smiled. "I'll have your orders carried out, my lady."

Seditha smiled and this time Barad felt the warmth of the goddess, not the bitterness.

She won't die, Barad.

Am I such a stubborn man that you had to give me such hard lessons?

You already know the answer to that.

He laughed, drawing glances from his men. And laughed again. *Seditha, thank you. I am unworthy of the attention you give me.*

Don't insult me, Barad.

But she was laughing also when he bent and kissed Andulyn's lips—a liberty, a small token of affection, a sign of his faith in the goddess.

"You cannot return to the capital, my lord," Andulyn said.

"I have no intention of returning to the capital until you are well and Nahrain is whole. Seditha has smiled upon us. With that I am content."

Seditha watched as he rose from Andulyn's side, unbuckled his armor, and asked of the councillors where he could begin to work.

JUST REWARD

by Karen Luk

Karen Luk is another of our very young writers: she's fifteen, and "Just Reward" is her first fiction sale.

Which, of course, makes me think of a famous story told of every young creative person from Mozart to the late Randall Garrett; a young person approached him saying he wanted to write a symphony (novel, song cycle, movie script, or what have you). Randall—or Mozart or whomever—answered "Oh, you're too young."

"But—but—didn't you write your first (novel, symphony, whatever) when you were fifteen (or whatever?)"

"Yes; but I didn't have to ask anybody how to do it."

I'm not quite sure what the point of this little tale may be, but most of the singularly young writers I've published don't tell me how young they are, either; I seldom find out how young they are till their contract comes back countersigned by parents.

And I guess that the moral of this is, don't write me a long chatty letter telling me how young you are; let me be pleasantly surprised when I've bought your first story.

". . . So after I rid the silver dragon of its huge wings, I charged in for the killing blow. But the silver scales were harder to hack through than I thought. Then, I noticed there were a few scales missing from the beast's neck." Noxen the Nefarious paused as he took a long pull of ale.

He was surrounded by young women who were intently listening to his latest story of yet to be proven bravery. Many youthful men were hoping to follow in footsteps. Yet, on the other hand, there was an older man waiting for his chance to spoil his tale.

"The beast didn't even use its fiery breath on me," continued Noxen. "But it did get me more than once with its razor-sharp talons on each limb. Despite my wounds, I cried out my battle-cry and lunged for the dragon's neck.

"My sword lodged itself in the unscaled area of the neck. Black blood spattered on me like rain all over my armor. Shortly after, I went over to examine the carcass of the silver dragon. It shuddered once, then lay still. And that's how I saved a village from the dragon's reign of terror."

There were scattered cheers and applause from Noxen's audience. The young women draped themselves onto Noxen the Nefarious' muscle-toned body. A handful of questions were asked about the story:

"Did you find the dragon's hoard of treasure?"

"Was a beauteous maiden waiting for you?"

"Where is the dragon's body?"

"Where's your proof?"

The last question came from the older man in the audience. Noxen the Nefarious slyly grinned. He had been hoping for someone to ask him that particular question. He ripped open his shirt, to reveal three claw marks across his broad chest. Some of the women gingerly touched the livid scars. Noxen the Nefarious grunted as if the marks still pained him somewhat. The older man left the tavern, scowling about how some men flaunt themselves for a bedding.

Just as the older man left, a woman stepped through the doorway of the tavern. She wore close-fitting leathers and a blood-hued mantle. A few of the men made rude remarks about the woman's figure. Her silvery-blonde hair framed her sharp visage. Verdant eyes seemed to bore their way to Noxen the Nefarious. The crowd of gathered people made a pathway amongst themselves for the woman.

"You are Noxen the Nefarious," stated the woman; it was definitely not a question.

"Aye, I be Noxen the Nefarious," returned he.

"I have a task for you to do for me," said the woman. "I can pay you handsomely, if you care to give your service to me."

"What is this so-called task?"

"I have need of someone to dispose of the man who has murdered my . . . husband." The woman then took the time to withdraw a heavy pouch of gold. She let the small sack drop onto the table with a very audible thunk. "I think I have found the man to do this task for me."

"Aye, you have. Tell you what though, give me half of that sack, and let me. . . ." He let his voice trail off. The woman arched an eyebrow in apprehension.

"So be it," she finally said. "You can collect all of your payment after the task is done—or nothing, agreed?"

Noxen the Nefarious nodded. The woman put the pouch of gold back into her cloak.

"Good," she went on, "meet me on the morrow's noon, at the silver dragon's lair. Be prompt, if you wish for all of your reward." He opened his mouth to pose an inquiry about the job. She raised a hand to stop Noxen's queries about it.

"No questions, or else you will forfeit everything."

The woman then spun on her heel and left the tavern. The audience eventually dispersed. The young women gathered around Noxen the Nefarious to fondle his new scars. He let the women have their way with him for now.

Why work up a sweat? When I can have better company the next night, thought Noxen the Nefarious.

The next day at noon, Noxen the Nefarious impatiently stood at the cave entrance of the dead dragon. The woman suddenly appeared next to him. Her green eyes seemed to glare at Noxen's soul. In her hand, she held a blazing torch. The woman beckoned Noxen the Nefarious to follow her into the lair.

He took haste in following her into the murkiness and darkness of the cave. When he had defeated the silver dragon, Noxen had not searched the cave for treasure because of his wounds. He wanted to ask why the woman wanted him to venture within the cavern with her, but thought better of it.

The torch flickered as it illuminated the cavern's walls. Noxen saw shades of reds, tans, and browns. The colors blended into one other as they met. There were layers of the rock as the woman and Noxen ventured deeper into the cave. It took a while for Noxen the Nefarious to notice that the woman had stopped.

She was kneeling next to a circle of jagged rocks. The rocks surrounded some gray-splotched, smooth stones. The woman tenderly caressed the egg-shaped stones. Noxen the Nefarious sucked in air noisily to draw her attention. She looked up to him with her piercing emerald eyes.

"Don't you know what these are?" queried the woman, letting the control on her anger go. "They are eggs!"

"So what?" snapped Noxen the Nefarious.

"Did you ever think that the dragon might have kin?" asked the woman.

"A dragon?" he retorted. "A dragon is just a huge beast who terrorizes people. It's a good thing that there are men like me to kill them.

"Now, where's the man I'm supposed to kill? If he isn't here, I think I will partake of some of my reward now." The woman let the torch drop from her empty hands. The cave was plunged into darkness.

Noxen the Nefarious stepped forward to claim the reward the woman had subtly promised. But he couldn't even twitch a muscle. The air in the cave seemed to glow and ripple around the woman, as if disturbed by some unseen force. Noxen's eyes were locked with the woman's verdant gaze. It was extremely hot in the cavern, but he felt a cold prickling at his skin. Noxen the Nefarious sensed true fear traveling up his spine and its unfeeling hands around his throat.

The woman's skin puffed out as the silver scales came forth. In a molten silver transformation, wings sprouted from the back of the scale-covered woman. A serpentlike tail grew out of the end of her buttocks. Her finger- and toenails stretched and hardened to form talons. The once woman's body expanded to reveal the magnificent shape of a middle-aged dragon.

The woman's neck elongated as her arms and legs did. The nose of the dragon formed with its nostrils enlarging, as the mouth and snout was pulled forward. Noxen the Nefarious stood still as if he were chiseled out of stone. His gaze never wavered from the dragon's brilliant green eyes, as the woman had changed into a dragon.

"You killed my mate," boomed the silver dragon finally. "For no apparent reason, except for your own pitiful human greed. My mate had been with me for nearly two whole centuries! He meant you no harm, but you *assumed* that he did. Now my unborn children shall never know their father.

"Your reward is not for you but for my dead mate and for my unborn children!"

The silver dragon lifted its gaze from the man below her. The dragon reared its head back, then opened up her massive jaws. . . .

That was the last thing Noxen the Nefarious ever saw in his life.

BOYS WILL BE GIRLS

by Vicki Kirchhoff

This is another first story; remarkably good, which reminds me of some of the other excellent "first stories" I've read, such as that of Jennifer Roberson.

Any honest editor will tell you that this is the reward which makes up for all the—to put it politely, dreck, we find in the slush pile.

Since the letter in which Vicki Kirchhoff sent her autobiography is handwritten—and, as I've said before, I don't know what they teach nowadays in schools, but it certainly isn't legible penmanship, I suppose for want of anything else to say, the secrets of her past will remain a great, deep, dark secret, except that on a line near the bottom of a closely scribbled page of faint ball-point ink, she mentions that she wishes to dedicate this story to Curt, "without whom it would probably still be sitting in a pile . . ."

Sorry, Vicki. I seem to make out also something to the effect that she's five feet eleven and that she's never—underlined—played basketball. As my late father used to say when he was baffled or frustrated, "What's that got to do with the price of cheese?" Or with anything else?

Search me!

"How much for the woman?"

Dain felt a beefy hand clamp down on his shoulder as he contemplated the mug of ale in front of him. He also felt his partner Kenna's booted toe kick him in the shin. He glanced up at her, ignoring the man behind him.

The hand squeezed and he winced as pain shot down his arm. "I'm talking to you, little man."

"She's not for sale," Dain replied and his partner smiled.

Not that he'd have been able to sell her anyway. They had been together for years and theirs was a partnership that had survived more wars and blood than either would have liked. It was something that, as mercenaries and outlaws, they had come to accept . . . that and dealing with men like the one currently cutting off all feeling in Dain's left arm.

A pouch of coins landed on the table in front of him and the pressure on his shoulder decreased. He picked up the pouch. It was heavier than he'd have expected. He flashed Kenna a grin. "I dunno, I'd hate to part with her."

She grinned back, having the advantage of being able to see the brute behind him. She shifted in her chair so she could free her sword from the scabbard beneath her skirts. If it did come to a fight, she wanted to be prepared.

The man behind Dain was taller than he by almost a foot and had the muscles of someone who did heavy work. He reeked of smoke and sweat and his fingers left soot stains on Dain's jerkin. Very likely a smith, she decided. The only real problem he might pose was if he was as skilled with the use of weapons as he must be with making them.

Dain emptied the pouch onto the table and gold coins spilled among the remnants of their meal. Kenna's eyes lit up. They hadn't come into that amount of money in a long time. She met Dain's gaze and a plan was sealed.

He dropped the coins back into the pouch and shrugged, not an easy thing to do with the weight on his left shoulder. He slipped his right hand down onto the well worn grip of the mace that rested against his leg. "Sure," he said. "For this kind of gold, I think I can part with her. I'm warning you, though, she's a lot of trouble to keep."

The weight left his shoulder and Kenna rose, hands behind her back. "I'm sure I'm more than man enough to handle her," boasted the smith.

Dain finally got a good look at the man and was glad

that it was Kenna facing him. He disliked even odds, especially when he didn't know anything about his opponent.

As the man moved by him, he slipped the leather strap of his mace around his wrist. It was his own personal precaution. No plan worked all the time.

Kenna beamed as she awaited the smith's approach and danced back from his first attempt to grab her. "Not so quickly," she said batting his hand away.

His eyes ran up and down her body. "I paid for you. I can do what I please."

He stopped his next lunge short as he discovered three feet of sharpened steel resting between his legs. "You were saying?" she crooned.

As a smith, she was sure that he would have appreciated how finely her blade had been crafted. At the moment, she was pretty sure its artistic merit was not foremost on his mind. He tried to step away and felt Dain's mace in the small of his back, pinning him against the tip of Kenna's blade.

She smiled as she watched tiny beads of sweat break the surface of his skin. "What's the matter? Not getting what you expected?"

"I told you she was a lot of trouble to keep," Dain said, sliding his mace away to give the man a clear path to the door.

A nudge from Kenna's blade was all he needed to turn tail and run. Dain sighed and took a long draw on his ale. "Come on, I think we should go before he finds some friends and gets brave again."

She nodded, sliding her sword back into its scabbard and grabbing a piece of bread and some cheese. "I suppose he does have just cause for wanting his money back."

Dain tucked the pouch in his belt and they headed out the door. "You're right. I'd have let him have you for about half the price."

He dodged her kick and smiled. "I honestly don't know why I keep company with you. We've had to leave more taverns in a hurry because you can't resist teasing men."

She stopped and glared at him. "Teasing men? Do you think I want every drunken slob in a bar pawing at me?"

He blinked in the setting sun as they emerged. "You must be doing something. I can't imagine that they do it without being encouraged."

He gathered his horse's reins and hauled himself into the saddle. Kenna snorted. "Perhaps members of your sex believe that anything in skirts is fair game."

"Nonsense," Dain scoffed. "Admit it, my friend. You're a tease."

She sat hard in her saddle. "Don't be silly. If I put you in skirts, you'd have the same trouble."

He laughed. "If you put me in skirts, the only trouble I'd have is walking without tripping myself. Honestly, Kenna, I don't know what you're thinking."

He kicked his horse into a trot. "It would take more than skirts to make a woman out of me."

She cast him a sideways glance. "So, if a man were to show interest in you, it couldn't possibly be because you were leading him on . . . right?"

He chuckled. "I can see what you're getting at and I'm not putting on skirts for any reason."

She smirked. "Not even for my share of the gold?"

He looked at her as if he thought she'd had too much to drink. "Do you know how much gold is in this pouch?"

She shrugged in silence, her grin never fading. He toyed with the pouch until he couldn't stand it any longer. "Okay, okay, what's your plan?"

She urged her horse forward so they were even. "Well, if we dress you as a woman and me as a man, we can settle our differences about whether I'm a tease or men are lechers. If you're right, I'll let you have all the gold. If I'm right, it's mine."

He snorted. "All I have to do is wear a skirt and if nobody wants me, I win?"

"Right."

He smiled. "My dear partner, that's a bet I can't possibly lose."

"Is it a deal, then?" she asked offering him her hand."

He took it. "It's a deal."

* * *

Kenna was hard put to keep the smirk off her lips as she glanced sideways at Dain squirming in his saddle. The long blonde hair he wore seemed to have a life of its own and slipped constantly into his face. It had taken him several tries to mount his horse in Kenna's borrowed skirts and he'd been infuriated by her laughter. Even if she lost the bet, it was worth it to watch him suffer.

Farm hands stopped to watch them as they reached the outskirts of the city. Dain pulled his floppy hat farther down over his face, an action which seemed to encourage his admirers. Kenna smiled, the money would be hers in no time.

She urged her horse closer and leaned forward. "You may concede any time, you know."

He set his jaw. "They're only staring because I look ridiculous. The bet still stands."

"As you wish, my sweet," she teased leaning back.

Eyes continued to follow him as they entered the town. He kept his head down, an action that she knew from experience would only make him more enticing. Men tended to prefer the shy, withdrawn type. She had always found meeting a man's gaze to be a good way to make him lose interest. The only reason she wore skirts in towns at all was because women with swords were few and far between and the price on their heads was enough in some places to turn honest folk against them.

She halted her horse outside the nearest tavern and dismounted. "Need help down?" she inquired.

He grumbled something but accepted the hand she offered. "Come, my dear," she said taking his arm. "A long day on the road makes a man thirsty."

Her eyes swept over the place quickly. The clientele looked to be mostly farmers and local tradesmen. There was no one who appeared to be a serious threat in case things got messy.

Beneath the brim of his hat, Dain also surveyed the tavern. Many of the patrons' eyes lingered on him. He must be quite a sight, blonde hair in his face, hat pulled nearly to his eyes. Only the fact that he wore his mace beneath his skirts allowed him enough confidence to enter the inn at all. He prayed that no one they knew would be stopping in town.

Kenna chose a table near the center of the room, a deviation from their normal routine, but then this was hardly a normal situation. Still, he'd have felt better with a wall against his back.

"An ale for myself and my lady," Kenna cried to the serving wench.

Dain winced and brushed the hair out of his face again. His partner seemed to be enjoying his discomfort. Still, he told himself, once he won the bet, she would think differently.

He smiled. Certainly he was getting many stares, but these farm hands were not likely to try anything while Kenna wore her sword so openly.

A man who reminded them of the smith from the last town approached them. "Quite a lady ye have there, lad," he said.

"Good as gold," she assured him. "My truest love."

He smiled and motioned to the serving wench who set ales in front of both of them. "How long have ye been married?"

Kenna beamed. "We're not yet wed, sir. We're traveling to my father's lands and will be married in less than a fortnight."

The man slapped her between the shoulders. "Ah, soon to be wed." He raised his mug. "Men! A drink to them. Health and good cheer!"

A rousing cheer erupted from the bar and, as Kenna downed her ale, she caught the gleam in her partner's eye. Her story about them being engaged to be married may have cost her the bet.

"Another ale for the lad," the man said. "We're celebratin'."

Dain chuckled. The kindly patrons were about to get his partner blind drunk in celebration. Not only would she lose the bet, she'd be ill in the morning. Things were looking brighter.

Kenna regarded the cup in her hands. "But I can't."

"Come now, lad," the man said resting a hand on her shoulder.

"When Oldren pays, everyone drinks."

She chewed on her lower lip, trying to find a way to empty her mug without drinking it. "I can't. I have to keep my lady and her virtue safe."

Oldren smiled. "Lad, not a man in this room would compromise the virtue of such a lovely lass. You've no fear of that. Drink up!"

He set another cup in front of her. "What's yer name?"

"Joseph," she replied.

She was tempted to toss her ale in Dain's smirking face.

"Send the boy over here!" cried someone from across the tavern. "Let him drink with us."

Oldren glanced over and Kenna used the distraction to empty both tankards onto the inn floor. By the time he looked back at her, she was wiping her mouth on her sleeve. "Come, Joseph, let's drink."

Dain grinned as his partner was all but dragged over to another table. He felt smug in the fact that this proved that she was the one always getting them into trouble.

He felt a draft as the inn door opened. Four men stood in the doorway just for a moment and then made their way quickly to a dark corner table. Dain's grip on his mug tightened as he recognized them. They were bounty hunters; and bounty hunters he and Kenna knew well.

He watched them from beneath his hat. Kenna was busy telling some wild tale about their long courtship and there was a good chance she hadn't noticed them. He had to get her attention. The game was over.

He wondered that there were only four of them. They were a team of six and he could hardly hope that the other two had been killed. It was much more likely that they were out seeing to the horses. He wondered if they'd recognized his and his partner's mounts outside.

One of them glanced in his direction and he turned his eyes away. He could not risk them recognizing him. He hitched up his skirt so he could loosen the strap of his mace and let it rest against the leg of his chair.

Kenna was getting frustrated. Every time she emptied a mug, another was pressed in her hand. She was trying hard to play drunk in the hope that they'd stop, and her faked staggering was helpful in spilling most of the contents of her tankard but she was tiring of the game and nearly ready to concede defeat rather than suffer any more of Oldren's generosity. "My lady," she protested, a nice stumble sending her mug skittering across the floor.

"Don't worry, lad," Oldren assured her giving her another ale. "She's perfectly safe."

That was when she noticed the four bounty hunters in the corner. Two of them were staring at Dain who had good enough sense to keep his head down. It was time to go.

"Gotta leave," she said.

"One more round!" Oldren shouted clamping a beefy hand on her arm. "Your lady's not going anywhere."

The others cheered and Oldren handed her another tankard as two of the men in the corner approached Dain. She pulled hard against Oldren's grip and broke free only to slip on the pool of ale at her feet. She landed hard, knowing there was no way to reach her partner before the bounty hunters.

Dain kept his eyes on his ale. He didn't dare watch the men across the room. His every instinct demanded that he leave, but he couldn't desert his partner. Besides, at the moment, his disguise was his best protection.

He heard a crash from where Kenna was and glanced up to see bounty hunters on either side of him. "My, aren't you a pretty thing," one of them said.

Dain was relieved to note that neither one had a weapon drawn, but their leers made him twitchy. They couldn't possibly believe he was a woman, much less an attractive one. He lowered his eyes and said nothing, waiting for the laughter.

"Quiet, too," said the other. "I like quiet women."

One of them began to stroke his hair, He moved away, but that only brought him closer to the other. "I doubt anyone would mind if we borrowed you for a while."

Dain's one hand gripped the handle of his mace. These men were not common brigands. As far as he knew, he and Kenna were the only prey they'd failed to catch. If he did anything to reveal his true identity, he would stand no chance against them. Sure, it wouldn't be a fair fight, but he'd be on the losing side.

"Get your handsh off my lady!" Kenna shouted from across the tavern.

Her heart and mind were racing as she took a couple of unsteady steps. The more drunk they thought her, the less of a threat she would pose and they would need any advantage they could get. She prayed that Dain would keep to his role and cursed herself for thinking of the silly wager in the first place.

She made three attempts before she finally drew her sword. The bounty hunters beside Dain were laughing and she felt men move on either side of her. "Come on, boy, they're only interested in educating the wench."

"I'll kill the neksht man who lays handsh on her!" she cried stumbling forward.

One of them grabbed her right arm and yanked her back. She let herself fall into the bounty hunter's arms, nearly knocking him over as well. "Not so fast, boy. You're gonna have to prove yourself man enough to keep her."

He set her on her feet. "I'll fight you all!" she cried teetering.

She flailed her sword in front of her and let it slip from her grasp. She bent down to retrieve it and a shove sent her sprawling. The laughter of the men around her cheered her slightly. At least they had no idea who they were taunting.

She rose, using the nearest chair for support. "I'll shee you gentlemen outshide."

She nearly collided with Dain on the way out. "Don't worry, my darling, it won't take long."

Dain watched her stumble out of the tavern with the two snickering bounty hunters following her. He wished her luck, but he had his own problems.

He was hauled from his chair and crushed in an enthusiastic embrace. "Don't fret, wench, they'll just tire him out."

Dain managed to hook the toe of his boot into the wrist strap of his mace to keep it concealed beneath his skirts. "You aren't going to hurt me, are you?"

The two men beside him each took an arm and dragged him back into their corner, their icy glares stopping any protest from other patrons. One man drew a knife as they pressed their captive up against a wall, the other eyed the prize from top to bottom. "Not if you're a good girl, we won't."

"But . . ." Dain stammered fumbling to get his mace within reach. I don't know what you want me to do."

The bounty hunters exchanged amused glances. "Don't worry, we'll show you all you need to know."

Dain smiled as his hand found the familiar worn leather of his weapon. "I'm sure you will."

With one hand, he ripped free of the skirts, entangling them around the knife of his armed opponent. His other swung the mace hard between the unarmed man's legs. He crumpled with a scream as his companion struggled to free his weapon.

Dain grinned, pinning fabric and blade to the wall with his left hand. "So, whatcha gonna show me?"

Kenna groaned and pushed herself to her knees. Once outside the inn, she'd been pushed face first into the ground. The dust clung to her ale-soaked clothing and her own horse nearly stepped on her hand as she reached for her sword. She was not having a good day.

She reached up to her saddle and used it to haul herself to her feet. She also slid free one of the knives concealed there and slipped it into her sleeve.

"Come on, boy," taunted one of the men. "We're waiting."

She took a deep breath and listened carefully to the shuffling of feet behind her. If this ploy failed, it would be two on one and they'd know they weren't dealing with a drunken, love-sick boy. She said a quick prayer and spun releasing the knife as she did so. It struck one of the amused bounty hunters in the chest and sank in up to the hilt. His mirth changed to horror and he fell.

It took some time for his companion to realize what had happened. He drew his sword and charged. Kenna sidestepped and deflected the blow, but it sliced through one of her saddlebags. Her attacker halted, eyes drawn to the green shafted arrows that spilled onto the ground . . . arrows that were well known to be a sign of her handiwork. His gaze moved to her face and then to the body of her companion.

She smiled and beckoned him on. One to one she felt she could best him, but he must have felt the same way for he turned and bolted down the street.

She swore. She wanted to chase him down. He would certainly alert the remaining two of his group and she had no idea how Dain was faring. She decided to help her partner in the hope that they would be gone before help showed up.

As she turned back toward the inn, someone crashed through the door and impaled himself on her sword before he even realized she was there. Dain emerged right behind him. "Coward!" he spat.

She tried hard not to smirk at him and the way the blonde wig sat askew on his head. She wiped the blood from her blade to keep from looking at him. "One of them got away and I'll just bet he'll be back with his two friends."

He glared at her as he helped her gather up her fallen arrows. "No more bets."

As soon as they were mounted, Dain tossed the bag of coins at her. "Not a word to anyone about this."

She chuckled. "I doubt that last man is likely to tell. I doubt anyone would believe him if he did."

He pulled off the wig. "I'm still not convinced that you don't do it on purpose."

She smiled. "I'll take blacksmiths over bounty hunters any day. You just attract the wrong kind of men."

She kicked her horse into a gallop and laughed all the way down the trail.

TAKING SHAPE

by Lisa Deason

Lisa Deason says that on receiving the letter telling of the acceptance of this story, she jumped up and down like a rabbit—"something my character Dirya could probably appreciate." This is not her first sale; she reminded me that she had appeared in *Sword and Sorceress IX*.

She is currently between jobs and using the time to write; she has the first draft of a science fiction novel with a fantasy one hot on its heels. She is about to turn twenty and doesn't plan to marry "until I find someone who can at least tie writing as my number one love."

Jeilun was fighting like a demon, doling death left and right as though she were an unstoppable force of nature and the dozen warriors attacking her were mere nuisances. Her sword flashed in fatal arcs, each blow landing precisely where she directed it. Her opponents were armored, but she was taking them apart as though they were wearing paper. Without fail, her blade found the lesser-protected areas: the shoulder joints, the elbows, the groins, the knees, even the eyes. They were defeated but just didn't know it yet.

The siege had been a complete surprise. Even though there had been trouble with invaders for the past few weeks, so much so that Lord Seville had had to hire freelance soldiers like Jeilun to supplement his own army, they had thought that the fighting was over. Then, moments ago, the main door of the castle had been rammed and warriors had flooded inside, scattering in all directions. Jeilun had literally run into Dirya, one of the kitchen helpers, as she fled from a veritable hoard of warriors.

Dirya watched the soldier play her opponents like a master musician would play a symphony. To be able to fight like that. . .!

Battle-response sang abruptly in her blood and her shape blurred. In panic, she reined the shift in, looking quickly about to see if anyone had saw. The hallway was empty save for the soldier and the warriors.

Jeilun finished off the last of the warriors, then turned to Dirya. "We'd better find Lord Seville's people and see how bad the damage is." Her voice was dark and harsh, fitting her appearance. She was clothed entirely in black, from her tunic, vest and breeches to the patch that covered her missing right eye. Her hair was brown in color, her face a mass of scars.

Dirya fell in behind the soldier as she started slowly, alertly, down the hallway. She instinctively yielded to the sense of control that radiated from the tall woman. Her long dead parents would chide her for not taking charge of her own situation, but . . . she had never been what her parents wanted, had she?

Jeilun was covertly studying the girl. The soldier was extremely observant—she had to be in her line of work with only one eye—and even though she had been fighting, she had caught Dirya's momentary lapse. *That proves what I've always suspected. She's a shifter as sure as I'm standing here,* she thought, hyperaware of her surroundings even as she mused to herself. The young, blonde woman seemed human enough but Jeilun had caught a hint of . . . something . . . in her, as she had served dinner to herself and the other soldiers. There was a wildness of sorts in the girl's blue eyes along with an almost circular swirl to the iris pattern. Taken all together, it spelled *shifter*.

Yet the girl was unlike any of the nonhuman shapechangers Jeilun had ever met. Shifters were usually proud to a fault and eager to show off their battle skills. Dirya was different. The soldier usually ascribed to the live and let live philosophy but the faint look of desperate loneliness lurking in the girl's strange eyes called to Jeilun. She decided to ask.

"So," she said quietly as they walked, her remaining eye constantly scanning the passage ahead of them. "Why are you pretending to be human?"

Dirya started badly. "Wh-what do you. . . ?"

"Peace, girl. I know a shifter when I see one. I was just wondering why you're hiding out here. Are you in some sort of trouble?"

Caught! There was no use in lying. "No. I'm not an outlaw, merely a freak," she admitted softly, uncomfortable with the subject. She had worked as a kitchen helper for eight years with Lord Seville's staff and had successfully kept anyone from discovering her secret. She nervously fingered the collar of the beige apron that marked her menial position, feeling as though it was choking her.

The soldier was puzzled but remained silent. If Dirya wanted to tell her, she would. Jeilun wasn't the sort to push.

Dirya tried. "It's just that . . ." she trailed off, floundering. "You know that shifters are born with an animal shape, typically that of a predator, and a human one, correct?"

Jeilun silenced her with a quick gesture as they came to a corridor and they crossed carefully. "Yes," she answered. "What form do you have?"

Dirya's face colored in embarrassment. "A . . . rabbit."

To her relief, Jeilun didn't laugh. *So that's it,* the soldier thought. Shifters were infamous fighters in either form but Dirya was small as well as having a docile animal shape.

The shifter continued, "Mother was a lioness, Father a hawk, and they could both take on opponents twice their sizes and rip their throats out. They were only killed when they were severely outnumbered." The memory should have made her enormously sad, but all it stirred was a faint echo of regret. Her parents had finally turned her out, unable to do any more for her since she couldn't go to battle with them as all the other children did. Under pressure from the shifter community, she had left.

She had been informed of her parents' death shortly after she had joined Lord Seville's staff. "They were terribly disappointed that I couldn't even fight in human form."

Jeilun regarded her with a brief but knowing look. "You couldn't use something heavy like a broadsword or a staff but you do have some muscle. If you have the eye for it, you could be an excellent archer. How did you do with shortswords or throwing weapons?"

"I've never tried them."

Jeilun's eye went wide as she spared another glance back at her. "What did they do, prop you up with a full-sized sword and shield and watch you fall over?" Her words were meant to be sarcastic, but when Dirya nodded, she gasped. "Lord and Lady! What did they think they were doing? You're not a giant, you can't be expected to fight like one. Going at it that way, you were bound to fail.

"I'll tell you this, my friend," she went on. "I'd rather fight a big man than a small one. I got the worst beating of my life when I underestimated a woman half my size." Jeilun shook her head, a rueful smile tugging at her harsh mouth. Abruptly, she stopped, going into a defensive stance. "Someone's coming."

Three men appeared around the next corner. Two of them carried swords, the third had a pair of throwing knives in his hand, a dozen or so more at his waist. The swordsmen advanced on them.

Dirya backed away so to give the soldier room to work. For a moment, there was a stand-off, then one of the men took a swipe at the tall, scarred woman. While their weapons tangled, the other sought to attack from her blind side.

"To the right!" Dirya cried in warning but Jeilun, with her hyperawareness, had already sensed his movement and sidestepped the blow.

Jeilun's sword carved a great circle in the air and sliced the first man across the neck, coming up under the point of his helmet's visor and finding the soft flesh beneath. The man dropped without a sound. She rushed the other swordsman, knocking his weapon aside then driving her blade clean through the small eye-slit of his helmet. Then she turned to the third who was standing frozen, one knife poised to throw, but looking stunned at the swift slaughter he had just witnessed.

Then he suddenly went into motion, the knife becoming a blur as it left his hand. Jeilun jerked aside and the knife missed but only by a fraction. She tried to close the distance between them, to bring him within reach of her sword, but he backed away and another knife streaked out of his hand.

This one connected, taking Jeilun in the shoulder of her sword arm. She merely transferred her weapon to the other hand, a grim set to her eye and mouth, and strode forward. Another knife split the air. She dove but too slowly and was caught in the thigh. This one downed her.

With greater confidence, he took careful and precise aim at her heart. Out of nowhere, something struck him and the throw went wild.

He yelped, startled, frantically searching the hallway for his attacker. There . . . at his feet! But it flashed away, changing directions in a heartbeat and standing between himself and the soldier.

It was a rabbit.

The man laughed and stamped his boot at the impudent creature. "Shoo! Yah, get away!"

But it sat perfectly still, unfazed. If a rabbit could be said to smile, this one was.

He let another knife fly, but the rabbit was long gone. It darted like lightning around him, through his feet and setting him off-balance as he instinctively tried to avoid the rush. He twirled, arms flailing, as the small animal raced circles around him. The man was panicking, backing up and throwing another knife at the creature, missing badly. He tripped over his own feet in his haste and fell. The rabbit kicked him in the head with its powerful hind legs, stunning him even though his helmet.

A sword suddenly sprouted from his throat. He shuddered violently, then went limp. Jeilun was wavering on her feet, the knives still protruding from her shoulder and thigh. Yet the gleam in her eye was fierce as she pulled the sword free of its grisly sheath, then thrust it into its scabbard before collapsing.

The rabbit blurred into Dirya's human form and she hurried to the soldier's side.

Jeilun's scarred face had gone white with pain, but her voice was calm and normal. "You're going to have to pull these knives out for me," she told Dirya, "and when you do, the bleeding's going to get worse."

Dirya paused in brief thought and bent, struggling with the dead knife thrower's armor. She used one of the throwing knives to cut what looked to be enough cloth from the tunic underneath, then returned to the soldier.

"Ready?" she asked and Jeilun nodded. Dirya bit her lip, taking hold of the knife in the woman's bloody shoulder.

"Quickly," the soldier urged.

She yanked it free, trying to do so cleanly and swiftly. Jeilun made a guttural sound but didn't scream. True to her word, the wound began spouting thick red blood. Dirya bound the injury, strapping her as tightly as she could, then repeated the process with the other knife.

By the time she was finished, Jeilun was barely conscious.

"Sitting ducks," the soldier murmured. "Got to move."

"Don't you worry," Dirya said firmly, helping the woman up. The soldier was too heavy for her but, after a moment of sagging under her weight, the shifter took a deep breath and firmed the grips she had around the woman's waist and on the arm slung over her thin shoulders. She *would not* fail. She *would not*.

They staggered along, each step a new mountain to climb. Blood stained the entire front of Jeilun's tunic and down her injured leg, both wounds continuing to bleed despite Dirya's best efforts.

Footsteps. Dirya looked up to find a lone warrior in their path.

"Well," he said, tapping the flat of his sword against his palm. "What have we here?"

Jeilun's lips moved next to Dirya's ear. "Run. Leave me."

Dirya considered her options. Taking up Jeilun's sword would be foolish since she didn't know how to use it. In rabbit form she could distract the man as she had the knife thrower; this time, however, Jeilun couldn't finish him off. Abandoning the soldier never entered her mind.

But if neither her human nor animal form could avail her, perhaps there was a third thing she could try. . . .

Dirya carefully lowered the soldier to the ground, then faced the man. Anger boiled inside her like a hurricane on the rise and she let it, encouraged it. It would give her the strength she needed. She concentrated on the questions that had plagued her her whole life, letting them ring in her mind like war bells. Why was she different? Why was she cursed so?

The shift swept through her like wildfire. Halfway through the transformation, she *strained* in desperation and brought it to a halt, freezing between forms. She took a step toward the man on a foot that was paw-shaped but still human-sized.

Her gamble would be for nothing if the man decided to attack. "Come . . . here. . . ." she breathed, beckoning slowly as she snarled, showing teeth that were elongated and razor sharp in a face that was both human and animal. The shift lurched, trying to complete one form or the other. *Come on. . . .*

It worked. The man screamed bloody murder and ran back the way he came. Dirya returned to human form and, as gently as possible, helped Jeilun to her feet and managed to get her into the hands of the healers without further incidents. While waiting as Jeilun's wounds were cleaned and bandaged, she met Lord Seville himself.

"Have you got the invaders out?" Dirya asked as though she had the perfect right to know.

He looked at her without the faintest idea of who she was but answered, "I think so. The soldiers are clearing up the stragglers."

"Good."

Lord Seville, still looking quizzically at her, started to turn away. She stopped him.

"My lord, I hear one of your kitchen helpers is leaving."

"Helpers come and go," he replied, baffled.

"This one's going. I'll make sure to collect the rest of my pay." With that, she shrugged out of her blood-stained beige apron and handed it to him. Then she walked away, head high, leaving him staring in astonishment.

After Jeilun was suitably cared for, Dirya was allowed to sit by her.

"I'd like to leave with you," she said, "if you'll have me."

"It's not a pretty life, you know."

"Neither is helping in the kitchen," she retorted, a light in her eyes that had never been there before. "But I'd be *free*." Then, a little shyly, she added, "And I won't be alone anymore."

The soldier smiled at last. "Nor I. I'd like a partner to travel with. And a friend."

"A friend," Dirya repeated, smiling back.

A companionable silence settled, broken when Jeilun asked, "So how did you take care of that last warrior we came across? I blacked out after I told you to run."

Dirya's smile widened. "I just let him know that rabbits have teeth, too."

JUSTICE IS MINE

by Carolee J. Edwards

This is a nice little story with a twister in the tail. You readers, especially those of you who have been with me for the last ten years, would never make the mistake of thinking that just because I don't really see what's funny about the average TV sitcom, I have no sense of humor. My sense of humor exists; it's just a little better buried than most.

I also tend to prefer, for this spot in my anthologies, a story with a wry twister in the tail—and of that sort, this little gem is a perfect example.

Carolee J. Edwards says she is in her "mid-thirties"—not very specific that—and is "a journeyman in a number of arts: embroidery, cooking, music." But only in the last year has she begun to write. I'd say this was a pretty good start—if not a masterpiece, it will do to be going on with till a masterpiece comes along. She adds another to our list of unusual occupations; she's a police dispatcher. She calls this "not a surprising career, since my father spent over twenty years as a cop." She adds "I'm not giving up my day job yet, but it is good to get a toe wet in the writing business."

For such a short story, maybe it is only a toe—and a little toe at that—but it's a good start.

Sku Olalfila stomped upon the pile of dirty laundry, then began ripping the covers off her bunk. The pillows flew across her room, followed by other, more breakable objects. Curses flew along with the debris as her anger was vented like an erupting volcano. The door to her room opened and some of her messmates ducked in and took her arms, before the damage became serious.

"Just what is setting off this explosion, Sku?" asked Eoador. "I've seen less damage from a tavern brawl."

"Tinian!" Sku got past her gritted teeth. "Did you hear the news from the assize? That turd bribed the judge, and the girl's father, and walked out a free, 'innocent' man!"

"Not so innocent," said Arkin, "but not proven guilty. Damn, I thought we finally had the bastard."

"I still have the bruises I got keeping the mob from lynching him," Sku cried. "Lowen is still on light duty, with a cast on his arm. It took all we had not to let the crowd take him from us. I joined the guard to enforce the law, even to keep it for worms like him. Now my belly burns me, thinking of him laughing at us."

"We did our duty," said Mara, Arkin's shieldmate. "That Judge Danhut was ready to take a bribe to gild his pension is not something we could control. Though I'll admit I am surprised to hear that the father took the money, too."

"Undoubtedly Tinian pointed out to him that the judge was already getting a fee, and that his daughter was ruined anyway—the man probably felt he at least got a bride price that way. All he had to do was say that he couldn't identify the man he saw in his daughter's room that night."

"Maybe so", said Arkin. "Though money's a lousy reason to deny your kin, many a man looks the other way for it."

It took a lot of wine to cool the guards that night. The one they believed responsible for attacks on a dozen young women was free to seek another victim. Sku burned the deepest of all, and her anger did not leave her the next day, or the day after that. She traded shifts with the others, staying in Tinian's area, waiting for a chance to truly give him justice.

The girl's scream was close by when Sku heard it rise in the night air. She bolted down the street and into the house where everyone was stirring. The cries had not stopped when the figure in black bowled past Sku, into the alleyways. By the light of the banked fire, she saw his profile and knew him. Sku leapt to the backways, hot on Tinian's trail.

He tried to lose her in the twisted alleys, but she knew them better than he did. This time, Sku muttered to herself, you won't evade justice. Her dagger was still in its sheath, but in her mind she already had it in her hand, the steel drawn, like a lodestone to the north, to sink in his vile flesh. She could make certain that he hurt no one else.

He miscalculated the turns and found himself against a high wall. She could take him now, she knew it as certain as her name. He looked back at her, and she stared in his eyes. There was hate, and fear: and also she saw herself there. Not as the sheepdog guarding the flock, bringing back the wandering lamb. In his eyes she saw herself shown as the sharp-fanged wolf, gutting the unarmed sheep. Inside Sku the need for revenge fought with oath taken, that the right to punish was not hers. She decided.

Sku yanked out her blade and charged at him. "Tinian!" she called. "You may lean against the Temple wall, but you cannot claim sanctuary there. Surrender or die!"

He looked back, and then scurried up the rough stones like a long-toed rat, going over the top. She heard him in the temple grove, yelling for sanctuary. Sku slid her dagger into its sheath and went back the way she came, to the duties awaiting her.

Sku was drinking at her favorite inn when Mara stopped in a few days later. "Sku", said Mara, "I don't understand why you aren't tearing your quarters apart again. Tinian got away from you, though at least he won't be allowed outside the temple of Hanat for a long while. Why aren't you still mad?"

"To take sanctuary, he had to become an acolyte of the temple. They'll keep him busy with very lowly tasks for years," said Sku. "He might not have been hanged, but you could call it imprisonment at hard labor. And the priests of Hanat know what he's been up to in town. I think they didn't tell him everything before he swore himself to the temple's service."

"What didn't they tell him?" asked Mara.

"That all of Hanat's servants," Sku smiled, "are eunuchs."

MARION ZIMMER BRADLEY, Editor

THE DARKOVER ANTHOLOGIES